THE HOUSE TIBET

Georgia Savage was born in Tasmania but has spent most of her life in Victoria. She moved to Queensland in 1980 and lived on the Gold Coast, where she began to write full time. After four years, she returned to Melbourne, where she now lives. She has had a number of short stories published, as well as three novels: *The Tournament* (1983), *Slate and Me and Blanche McBride* (1983), and *The Estuary* (1987). *The House Tibet* is her first work to be published in America.

The
HOUSE
TIBET

Georgia Savage

PENGUIN BOOKS

*To the memory of my
grandmother, Ann, and
my mother, Iris*

PENGUIN BOOKS
Published by the Penguin Group
Viking Penguin, a division of Penguin Books USA Inc.,
375 Hudson Street, New York, New York 10014, U.S.A.
Penguin Books Ltd, 27 Wrights Lane, London W8 5TZ, England
Penguin Books Australia Ltd, Ringwood, Victoria, Australia
Penguin Books Canada Ltd, 10 Alcorn Avenue, Suite 300,
Toronto, Ontario, Canada M4V 3B2
Penguin Books (N.Z.) Ltd, 182–190 Wairau Road,
Auckland 10, New Zealand

Penguin Books Ltd, Registered Offices: Harmondsworth, Middlesex, England

First published in Australia by McPhee Gribble Publishers 1989
First published in the United States of America by Graywolf Press 1991

Published in Penguin Books 1992

1 3 5 7 9 10 8 6 4 2

PUBLISHER'S NOTE
This is a work of fiction. Names, characters, places, and incidents either are the product of
the author's imagination or are used fictitiously, and any resemblance to actual persons,
living or dead, events, or locales is entirely coincidental.

THE LIBRARY OF CONGRESS HAS CATALOGUED THE HARDCOVER AS FOLLOWS:
Savage, Georgia.
The house tibet / Georgia Savage.
p.   cm.
ISBN 1-55597-144-X (hc.)
ISBN 0 14 01.6813 3 (pbk.)
I. Title.
PR9619.3.S274H6   1991
823–dc20   90–21203

Printed in the United States of America

Acknowledgements

I wish to thank the Literature Board of the Australia Council for the generous support given to me during part of the period when I was writing this book.

The first chapter of *The House Tibet* was originally published in *Overland*, December 1987.

The epigraph to *The House Tibet* is Emily Dickinson's poem No. 508 from *Emily Dickinson: The Complete Poems*, Faber and Faber, 1970.

I also wish to thank the following friends who each contributed in some way while I was working on the manuscript: Gary Banks, Matthew Condon, Brett Errey, Lily Hu, Merna McRae, Rosie Smith, Gary and Sally Temczuk and Laurann Yen.

Special thanks to Ron Savage.

I'm ceded – I've stopped being Theirs –
The name They dropped upon my face
With water, in the country church
Is finished using, now,
And they can put it with my Dolls,
My childhood, and the string of spools,
I've finished threading – too –

Emily Dickinson

Part One

THE BLUE
PLAID DRESS

———————————

Chapter One

WHILE IT WAS happening I watched the moon. It was in a piece of sky behind his shoulder. With the upright of the window on one side, the curve of his shoulder on the other and the white-faced moon in between it was like looking into one of the Japanese drawings my mother's so keen about. At the same time there was a part of my mind noticing that the piece of him prodding between my legs was warm. (No. Not between my legs, higher than that. Prodding into my body. Into ME.) For some funny reason I'd imagined that when it happened to you, that part of a man would be cold. Being skin and blood and stuff how could it? But I hadn't thought of that. I'd just imagined it would be cold and slippery. Like a snake, I suppose.

I went on staring at the moon even when the pain split me and I called out. I kept staring until it was over and his face was in my hair. Then in an awful mixture of sobbing and breathy laughter he was saying over and over, 'Vicky, Vicky, I'm sorry.'

Because there was nothing else to do, I said, 'It's all right, Dad. It doesn't matter,' and I remember being surprised at how funny and faraway my voice sounded.

I'd been in my room trying on the dress my mother had bought me for Caroline Teasdale's birthday party. Usually, my mother who's very creative made my clothes but she'd been having trouble with an impacted wisdom tooth and hadn't felt like sewing so she took me to David Jones which she still calls Buckleys and there we saw a dress in layers of scalloped pink and red. I fell in love with that dress. It was like the petals of a poppy and I could see myself dancing in it while Christopher, Caroline's brother watched in admiration. But my mother said the dress wasn't elegant and she bought instead a taffeta one of lilac and blue plaid with a prissy little collar.

For a week I mourned the poppy dress. My friend Samantha mourned it with me. *Her* mother's a gynaecologist too busy to shop so Samantha buys her own clothes and gets the most wonderful things. She told me on the bus that the poppy dress would have illuminated my dark eyes and moth-wing eyebrows. (Sam's very poetic.) But at home the mirror told me the only thing the plaid dress illuminated was the fact that my chest was still skating-rink flat while Samantha, who's only four months older than I, already had two distinct volcano peaks rising from hers.

I was thinking about Sam's volcanoes and leaning forward at the same time to check out my teeth in the mirror when I heard my parents quarrelling.

My mother had been working in her studio which is beside my bedroom. (I'd been hearing the hiss of the wheel and the clack of the pedal for some time.) Mum's a potter and quite a good one. When she was younger she had a few shows of her own work and was even asked to send some pieces for exhibition in Japan. But Dad, who's an architect and knows about most things, told her that if she did, she'd make a fool of herself. After that she gave up having exhibitions of her work and just made pieces for members of the family for Christmas and stuff like that.

As usual they were arguing about money and I knew it

was bad because I heard the wheel stop and then a piece of furniture, probably the stool Mum sits on, fall over. Knocking things over is most unlike my mother who's quite a careful person.

'Yes, it is in my name,' I heard her say. 'But it's still *ours*.'

Sounding really angry, my father cut her off, '*My* share bonus – in *your* name!'

'I didn't want to put it in the cheque account. I thought we should put it towards our winter holiday.'

'How much other money have you got in there?'

'Very little.'

'How much is very little?'

'Just the two thousand Mum gave me when she sold her car.'

My father exploded then and I heard him call her a liar and a cheat. That wasn't fair. Mum's a funny person but she's awfully honest. If she finds money in a shop or anything she always hands it in.

I didn't want to hear anymore so I left the mirror and turned my transistor onto some heavy rock. If it comes to that, I didn't *need* to hear anymore. I knew exactly the way the argument would go. Dad would start using what my mother called gutter language and he'd keep doing it until she went to find her car keys. When she did, she'd leave the house and drive to her mother's place two suburbs away. After that Dad would slam around the house for a while then sit in his study drinking claret. He'd go on drinking until he fell asleep in his chair. Sometime during the night he'd ring my Nanna's house where Mum was. She'd come home then and in the morning they'd both act as if none of it had happened.

Aunt Penelope, my mother's sister who's a feminist, says my parents' quarrels aren't about money at all, that they're about power. I'm not sure what she means by that and I don't see how she'd know anyway. She probably hasn't ever heard one of them.

In a little while, just as I'd thought, my mother left the house. I saw her go across the patio. Her face was set and she slapped her feet down angrily. Mum has big feet and gets her shoes custom made, a fact which launches a lot of jokes in our family.

On her way to the garage she didn't even look in the direction the music blasting from my room, though normally she'd come to the window to tell me to turn it off – IMMEDIATELY. I turned it off myself in the end because I found I wasn't in the mood for Jimmy Barnes.

It must have been nine-thirty when my father came into the room. For once I hadn't finished my homework. Instead I'd been doing what my mother calls paddling around. Sorting my tapes and re-reading some old letters from a penfriend in Switzerland. I was still wearing the plaid dress, or rather I was just taking it off. I'd pulled it over my head but it still covered my arms and chest when Dad opened the door. He was carrying a glass of wine and he said, 'What're you doing, sweetie?'

Here I think I should stop my narrative flow for a moment to describe my father. He's tall and slim and very nice looking with thick curly brown hair cut shortish and eyes of hare-bell blue. At least that's what my mother calls them. And she says his mouth would be considered beautiful even on a woman. His clothes are nice too. He wears blue shirts and tweed suits. The suits are expensive ones but looking sort of lived-in. His shoes are always dark brown imported brogues.

'Nothing much,' I told him and hauled the dress off and flung it onto the bed. 'Can I have a drink?'

He said, 'You know you shouldn't,' but he came across to me and handed me the glass.

I took a gulp though I didn't like it much. Then I held the glass out to him. Before he took it, he reached out an index finger and lifted a piece of hair away from my eyes. At that moment a sudden wind rattled the rose bushes outside the window.

'I'm cold,' I said and folded my arms across the bra I didn't really need.

'Come here – I'll warm you,' said Dad. He put the glass of claret beside my transistor and folded me inside his arms. His clothes were warm and a bit rough, making me feel comforted and special and I stayed there leaning against him while he stroked the skin just below the small of my back.

Suddenly he slipped his hand into my pants and moved it slowly backwards and forwards across my bottom. Then, not taking his hand away he sort of juggled me down onto my bed and just before my body touched it he moved his hand and pulled my underpants down, grabbed my ankle and lifted it, so that before I knew it one of my legs was free.

What happened next was horrible. I was crushed and half suffocated, then prodded and split by the warm part of him. All I could do was stare at the moon and try to pretend it wasn't happening. In the end, after he'd collapsed in that awful half-laughing, half-sobbing, he left me, going out and shutting the door quietly behind him.

For a long time I lay on my bed not moving. My cheeks were wet, which is funny because I don't remember crying. The room around me and even the inside of my head it seemed, had become a swamp. A dreadful, dark, hot, stinging swamp where now and then cruel little thoughts darted like fishes. I kept them away some of the time by counting up the places where I was hurting. My knee, one wrist, the side of my face and the other place.

The worst part of it was knowing my father had gone. I don't mean just out of the room. I mean for good. The person smelling of birthday aftershave who'd taught me to swim and ride a bike and tended every little cut and scratch for me was gone and in his place was a stranger who didn't give a solitary little second of his thoughts for anything that happened to me. Not only that, the stranger was still somewhere in the house and might come back some other time and force himself into the most private, private part of me.

Later on, when my eyes were hot and gritty and past tears altogether, other thoughts came. I saw myself as I'd been that morning getting on the bus, my hair shining and my eyes wanting to look for Christopher Teasdale sitting at the back. And I knew I'd never be able to get on the bus again because if I did, everyone would look at me and know as if they'd been there watching, what had happened in my room. No one would sit with me or even speak and if I somehow managed to last through the shame of the trip to school, I knew that when Miss Wilmot asked me to run and play tennis and things like that, what I'd done would show and she'd know too.

They'll blame me, I thought. The lot of them and they'll be right because I stood around with almost nothing on. Then I asked for a drink of wine from his glass like someone in the television show Maree Simmons and her mother watch all the time.

There'd always been something bad in me. I'd proved that when I borrowed Mum's watch and lost it and lied and lied, never owning up. In fact there were plenty of things my mother didn't like about me, like my going wild over some of the musicians on 'MTV' and wanting to be seen in sleazy clothes. Carmen Jones, she sometimes called me. And it was that side of me my father had recognized. Then remembering the funny shivery feeling which shot through me when he touched my bottom, my face grew hot. I tried to think of something else, but the only thoughts that came were of the people who said my father was a fine man. *Everyone* said it and although he made little jokes about the girls in his TAFE class who got crushes on him and rang him up at home, he always put them off kindly, so I knew he didn't want to do to them what he'd done to me.

But in spite of all those things whirling around inside my head, in spite of the fact that I was frightened by the thought of the man-shape somewhere in the house, I kept waiting for my *real* father to come back and say something to me that would put everything back in its right place again. I truly believed that all I had to do was wait and my door would open again and he'd be there to say, 'What happened didn't happen at all. It's gone – been wiped away and in the morning I'll look at you and you'll be my shining girl again.' But he didn't come near me and if I hadn't heard James drop something in his room, I might have gone on waiting for the rest of the night.

James is eight and it's my job to see he gets to bed. If I don't he's capable of finding things to do in his room until four a.m. As it was, when I turned my head and saw the clock, it was 11.47 so I got up and crept silently along the hall to the bathroom to clean myself. I didn't have a shower. I didn't want to make a noise and have someone find me with nothing on. I simply filled the washbasin and bathed myself with water as hot as I could bear. I put some Dettol in it and I swabbed and swabbed trying to get inside as well where it stung. I began blubbing a bit then, hanging onto the washbasin with both my hands and whispering, 'Don't let this be happening to me. Make it stop. *Please* make it stop.' I don't know if I was talking to the washbasin or the taps or the moon outside or what. It didn't matter anyway because nothing changed. I was still there with the stinging inside me and my feet growing cold on the floor. In the end I rinsed myself and the washcloth too in clean water and tiptoed across the dining room to the kitchen to hide the cloth at the bottom of the plastic thing we put the rubbish in.

There was no sign of my mother and although lights were on in almost every room, no sign of my father either. I put most of the lights out and crept back along the hall. In my room, I found this long satin nightie my grandmother gave me and put it on. Then I went to James's room.

He was lying on his bed the wrong way with his feet where his head should have been. While I was in the bathroom he must have given up the struggle to stay awake because his eyes were closed and he was breathing peacefully. Golly knows what he'd been doing earlier. His hair was plastered to his forehead as if he'd been perspiring and the earplug of his radio was still in his ear. When I pulled it out he opened his eyes, looked at me, gave a long sleep-sigh and closed them again. So although he was still wearing shorts and a grubby T-shirt I covered him up and left him. At the door, just before I switched off the light, I turned to look at him. His hand was clenched under his cheek and he was frowning.

In my room again I stayed awake for a long time while the moon which sees everything, still watched me. In the end I must have slept because suddenly my room was full of daylight and when I turned my head to look out the window there in the sky, as high it seemed as the moon had been, was my brother, James. He was whizzing between two gumtrees on a flimsy flying-fox thing that he'd rigged up. I was at the window in time to see him hit the second gum with a terrible thwack and fall to the ground where he lay without moving – a coathanger gadget of wood and wire still in his hand.

I don't remember getting out the window but I know that on the way to James my foot came down heavily on a pricky seedpod and hurt like fury. Then I was beside him. His eyes were closed and his face was white, the circular scar on the side of his chin showing up like a tattoo. He was dead. I could see that and such a wave of love for my sad little brother rushed over me that I wanted to put my mouth against his, to breath my living *person* into him so that he'd sit up and give me one of his strange smiles. And if I couldn't do that, then I wanted to die too. To stop being anything at all the way my father says we do when our life is over.

But James wasn't dead because the corners of his mouth moved, his eyes opened and his face lit up, blazed in fact, with pleasure at the memory of his flight. Then, although he must have been hurting everywhere, he got to his feet and carrying the coathanger thing marched towards the house.

As he went his back and his birdie-little-legs were as tense, as *defiant* as a bundle of gelignite. Watching him I had the feeling that if someone could find a way to untense that back of his, there'd be nothing wrong with James at all and he'd start speaking. The trouble was that no one seemed to know how.

He reached the door and went inside without collapsing so I crossed the lawn and climbed back into my room. It seems a funny thing to say but I'd forgotten the night before and when I saw the plaid dress lying crushed on the bed with a watery looking bloodstain on it, I took a little while to work out what the mark was. When I did I grabbed the dress and raced with it to the bathroom where I ran water from the hot tap onto the stain. I thought I'd see it disappear. Instead it turned brown, in places almost black, and although I scrubbed it like mad between my knuckles it didn't move. I was holding it up and staring at it when behind me, my mother's voice said, 'Victoria, what *are* you doing?'

She'd come into the bathroom and was standing close to me so I tried to hide the dress. But it was no use, she'd seen it and she snatched it from me, sending a little shower of water over both of us.

Then she saw the stain. She couldn't miss it. It was so dark it seemed to leap from the material.

'You filthy girl,' was what she said to me. 'You've started a period and got it on the dress.'

'I don't have periods.' The sunlight coming through the window was bouncing off one of the taps. It struck into my eyes so I moved my head. It followed me. I moved my head again and said, 'Last night Dad . . .' then my voice drained away into silence.

My mother was silent too. Keeping my face away from the light I looked at her. She'd stopped staring at the dress and was staring at me. She went on staring for a long time. And then she *knew*. I saw it in her face. In some spooky way her mind had made the jump from the stained dress to what happened in my bedroom the night before. I still don't know how she did it. Whether she read my thoughts or whether the facts were so terrible that she's *felt* them or something. Perhaps she knew because it was *me*. Perhaps that was enough but suddenly frightened of her I shrank against the towel rack as she flung the dress into the bath. 'Get dressed,' she said and her voice was cold and quick. 'Then go to school. I don't want to see you.'

Suddenly I was no longer frightened, just angry and I stood upright and glared back at my mother. Her face loomed big and white. 'Where's my father?' I shouted.

I saw her eyes widen until there was a rim of white around the pupil. 'He's gone to work,' she said. 'Into the city. He went at seven. *He* didn't want to see you either.'

I turned after that and blundered from the bathroom. There seemed to be a sort of humming around my head like bees and I don't know how I found my room because that humming made it impossible for me to think or even see properly.

Chapter Two

I STAYED ON the school bus just long enough to make sure James had followed me. He's small for his age and always climbs the steps head down like someone tackling Everest. At the top he lifted his eyes, pinpointed my position and went to sit beside his friend, Trout. I raced for the door then, flinging, 'Go without me,' at the driver.

The bus left and I watched it go with my brother's face staring from the back window. To get there he must have climbed over Christopher Teasdale – even *trodden* on him. The day before I'd have been mortified. That morning the thought of James scrambling over Christopher's feet actually pleased me.

The bus went down the hill and turned at the Tower Hotel with James still watching from the back. When it was out of sight I crossed the road and hurried to the railway station. I was on my way to my grandmother Barbie's place to ask if I could come and live with her. I'd have to tell her what my father had done to me the night before but I knew that when I got it out she'd offer me a home straightaway.

There was a crowd on the train, mostly students. I managed to squeeze into a seat only to find myself opposite an Italian with a chocolate-coloured suit and hooded eyes.

He kept those eyes on me until I hated him. It wasn't hard to work out what he'd learned by staring at me and I sat not looking at him, my face stiff and my breath almost stopped. When the train pulled up at the next station I left my seat and went to stand with a bunch of noisy kids at the end of the compartment. They were too busy making jokes and stuff about someone called Sligo to notice me.

At Clifton Hill where I got out, I had to use the underpass to reach the tram stop. I *hate* that underpass with its pissy smell and rotten messages on the walls so I stayed close to some students who'd left the train with me. At the halfway mark they wheeled to the left and disappeared up the ramp to the other platform. Suddenly I was alone. I looked behind me. The way back seemed dark and hostile. That made me hurry on.

Near the outlet two people, a boy and a girl, stood talking. I didn't like the look of them and edged to the opposite wall as I got closer. The girl was wearing layers of black op-shop clothes and funny little granny boots. Her hair was dyed a red-grape colour and jelled up into an *impossible* shape. The boy had on a tram conductor's coat over summer baggies. I could tell by their spooky white faces that they were drug freaks and I was certain one would lunge any minute and grab me while the other sliced through the strap of my bag with a knife. Likely as not they'd stick me with a syringe as well.

I heard my footsteps echoing along the tunnel and again I thought of turning back but I didn't because I thought their drug-crazed legs would easily overtake me. What a guinea I was. They didn't even look at me. As I passed I heard the girl say, 'No. My idea is to bring the guitars in for twelve bars, then you do your bit.'

Her friend mumbled something but I didn't wait to listen. They were talking *music* for heaven's sake and the next moment I ran from the tunnel, up the ramp and into the sunshine.

In Queens Parade I caught a tram full of girls and women on their way to work. I was glad of that, thinking there'd be no one to stare at me but as I moved along the aisle I noticed the younger ones each gave me the quick up-and-down as if we were lining up against each other at the start of a race or something. Those looks made me angry enough to push my way through the pack until I found a middle-aged woman knitting furiously at some large lacy thing and I planted myself facing her with my back to everyone else.

With flickery sunshine reaching me I swayed and jerked on my strap and thought about James and the frantic face he'd shown me from the bus. Leaving him for good was going to be terrible for both of us but it wasn't likely Barbie would take him in too. I suppose I might as well come out and say it – James has caused a lot of trouble in our family and looks set to cause a lot more. He doesn't speak you see, and my father as well as the dozens of people who've examined him both under and out of anaesthetic believe he could if he wanted to. No one knows for sure though.

When James was born my father, who was frantic to have a son, went around carolling, '*James James Morrison Morrison Weatherby George Dupree,*' for days on end. I can remember him singing it all over the house. He even sang it on the way home from the hospital with Mum and the baby. And he talked about the things he and James would do together like going to the cricket at the MCG, and taking canoe trips down the Murray. I was five then, not old enough to realize that even in a blind fit Dad wouldn't go canoeing anywhere let alone up in the country. But I *was* old enough to hear something false, sort of too-hearty in his voice when he'd turn to me and say, 'Of course Miss *Victoria* Ferguson will always be special to me.'

Anyway, Dad's delight in James lasted until it became obvious the new baby wasn't likely to grow into the kind of boy he'd hoped for. James was pale and fretful, crying almost all the time. It turned out that he had what's known as a trigger nerve in his stomach and he'd indulge in vomiting attacks which had to be seen to be believed. One evening when Dad was holding James in his study he let go with a stream of sickly-smelling milk which shot a metre and a half through the air and landed on a set of Dad's drawings. After that I don't remember my father ever picking James up again and the awful part of it was that when he was still a baby, my brother's head always turned towards the sound of Dad's voice and his eyes followed him all the time when he was in the room.

When James started walking it seemed to me he spent half his time trying to please Dad but his overtures usually had the opposite effect, like the time he opened a can of blue enamel and tried to paint Dad's golf clubs. You wouldn't believe the mess he made and when Dad saw it he bellowed at Mum, 'For God's sake remove this bloody insect before I kill it.'

For my father the last straw came when it turned out that James wasn't going to talk and at the end of the medical and psychological examinations I mentioned before (they went on for two years) Dad began to invest in me the hopes he'd had for his son. He asked Mr Kenny the builder to come and fix a blackboard, over two metres long, onto one wall of his study and every evening after dinner he took me in there for tutoring. When I was quite a little kid we did three quarters of an hour maths and three quarters of an hour English every night.

My father had a mania for what he called the correct use of language. For instance I was never allowed to say I'd entered our suburban block by the little gate. Instead I had to say the *pedestrian* gate. One day I pointed out that as I often came in on my bicycle the word pedestrian wasn't strictly correct. Dad told me not to split hairs and began to talk of something else.

By the time I was eight I was doing year seven maths and knew what a conjunctive pronoun was.

It didn't take James long to find us at those lessons. He'd come into the study, grab the side of my chair with both hands and watch and listen. At first Dad sent him out but he kept coming back and what with pleas from me and everything, in the end he was often allowed to stay. He had to keep still though and that was never easy for him.

When James was six a spooky thing happened during one of my maths lessons. Dad had told me to take 1,173 to the power of four. It was a trick question of course to see if I'd *multiply* by four and while I was working on it James grabbed one of Dad's pencils and wrote the answer on the bottom of the page. He wrote it in awful figures two centimetres high with the strokes not joining properly. But the answer was the right one.

Of course Dad said it was an accident. Then he said I'd whispered the answer to James but as I hadn't even *finished* the sum he knew that wasn't true. Egged on by me he gave James a whole series of problems to do and he did them all *in his head*. The result of that performance was that my brother had to suffer a further round of examinations by doctors and psychologists who came to the conclusion that James was a child with an extraordinarily high IQ and that for some reason they couldn't define, he'd chosen not to use it.

I wish I could say that from then on my father persevered with James, encouraging him to learn. But he didn't. If anything the light thrown on my brother's intelligence made Dad more bitter and as far as I can remember he didn't ever speak to him again. The result of that was that James went on doing things like diving off the roof of the tennis club pavilion in order, so my Aunt Penelope said, to make Dad notice him.

As for Mum, she persevered with James up to the time he was expelled from the Durbridge school. Then she more or less wiped her hands of him too. (That's how he became *my* responsibility.)

At four, James had been sent to a play school for autistic

17

children. The second week he became violent when Mum took him there. He refused to leave the car, banging his head repeatedly against the dashboard until Mum became frightened and took him home. Next, he was taken to the Gordon Education Centre, another place for autistic children. It was out at Box Hill and had only nine pupils but it turned out to be little more than a child-minding centre where the staff turned the cassette-music up full blast and left the children alone to beat each other up and do things like using the space behind the piano as a loo. James went to the school without a fuss but he also went on a hunger strike and when it became obvious that he was prepared to starve himself to death rather than remain at the Gordon Education Centre, he was taken away.

When the Durbridge School opened a couple of kilometres from our place it seemed a miracle to my parents. (The founders of Durbridge believed that to learn successfully, children needed to be happy. The pupils baked their own bread for lunch and made their own pottery counters for maths. They spent whole days building tree houses and were even allowed to help construct the *swimming* pool.)

James started there in the first term. His teacher, Mrs Golding, was a tall serene-looking woman who wore her dark hair swept to one side and plaited. She had dimples, big shiny eyes and a low voice. In those days she laughed a lot. James took one look at her and handed over his heart. He still didn't speak but that didn't worry Mrs Golding. Soon he was her favourite pupil and I'm sure his little life story would have been a different one if she'd stayed at the school. As it was she went off her head when her son, Garth, was killed one Saturday on his Harley Davidson.

Instead of staying away to grieve as everyone expected her to do, Mrs Golding turned up to teach on the Monday after Garth's death. She had charcoal-dark rings under her eyes and her plait had been cut off raggedly as if she'd done it with a knife. Not only that but she faced the class wearing a full set of bikie leathers and when Melanie Sutton asked why she was dressed that way Mrs Golding beamed at her and said, 'I'm Garth.'

The next day another woman turned up to teach in her place. She was young and brisk with streaky blonde curls and bib-and-brace overalls. Melanie Sutton asked her where Mrs Golding was.

'Gone on holidays,' said the new teacher.

A few minutes later James marched to her desk and put a note on it. In big untidy letters it said, 'Yor a fuken lire.' They were the first words he wrote and because of them he was expelled from Durbridge.

After that he stayed at home until the next February when my parents did what Aunt Penelope said they should have done in the first place. They sent him to Grammar with me. From then on, at school anyway, James was little trouble. He sat at the front of his class and although he still made no attempt to speak he took part in most of the activities.

There's not much more to tell about my little brother except that he has thick fair hair so fine it sort of floats when he walks and he has eyes of the same hare-bell blue as Dad.

Chapter Three

In Canterbury when I opened the gate in the wall of my grandmother's garden everything inside seemed cold and green and eerie because of all the ivy. Then I saw Barbie and the eeriness vanished. She was standing by a clump of chrysanthemums zapping weeds with a miniature flame-thrower while her cat, Germaine, watched. Also watching was the smirking little Polynesian statue which had been sitting by the pond so long its eyebrows and its lower lip were covered with bright green moss.

Barbie's not at all what you picture when you think of grandmothers. She wears designer-denim, plays a lot of tennis and writes book reviews for a women's magazine. Although she's *old* – over fifty I think, she's still quite pretty with what they call chestnut hair and almost three-cornered eyes of brilliant blue. (My mother says the hair is tinted but if it is you can't tell. It's cut short and there is a little tuft at the crown which sticks up and bothers Barbie. Every so often she puts up a hand that's surprisingly big and strong to flatten it.)

When she was young Barbie saved up and went overseas, working in England for a few years as a typist in some hush-hush government department and playing cricket at County level in the women's competition. Returning here in the 1950s she kept on with her cricket. She even played once for a team of men in a little town near Bendigo where she was holidaying. Apparently the locals were one short and Barbie, wearing a floppy shirt and with her hair pinned up beneath a cap, took his place.

She made a score of eighteen but towards the end of the afternoon when she was fielding, her cap came off and her hair fell down. The shock of it all caused the batsmen to walk off the field. The umpires followed them.

That night at an emergency meeting the men in charge of the local competition disqualified Barbie's team for five years but the next morning, for fear of making country cricket a laughing stock, they reversed the decision and hushed the whole thing up.

For Barbie the matter didn't finish there. At the end of her holiday, as she was boarding the train at Bendigo, one of the batsmen who'd abandoned the crease rushed onto the platform and gave her eleven roses picked from the park. A year later they were married and a year after that my father was born.

I don't know a lot about the next part of Barbie's life. It's not talked about in our family but from the bits and pieces I *have* heard I've learned that things went along well until my father was nine or ten and then Grandpa scooted off to America because of some sort of trouble at the bank where he worked. He didn't come back but stayed in the USA to make a fortune from *cosmetics*. In time Barbie divorced him and he married again but when he did he settled quite a lot of money on my grandmother so that she was able to buy the house in Canterbury and educate my father properly. And even though Grandpa didn't ever visit them or anything, each Christmas until the year he caught pneumonia on a skiing holiday and died he sent Barbie a box of expensive nourishing creams and things.

In her forties Barbie married again. That marriage only

lasted two weeks and isn't talked about in our family either. (I've asked my mother several times how a marriage could last such a short time. She's always told me there are things little girls don't need to know so I'm still in the dark.)

Zapping the weeds, Barbie had her back to me but as I pushed the gate shut it made a noise and she turned and saw me.

'Victoria,' she said as the flame-thrower moved off-target and shrivelled the side of a little berry bush. 'What a nice surprise but why aren't you at school?'

I'd planned to start by saying something really sensible. Instead I blurted, 'I've come to live with you.'

Barbie studied my face then turned her attention to the garden but after tut-tutting over the burnt bush, she leant the flame-thrower against the trunk of the magnolia and turned back to me.

'There's been a row at home, has there?'

I nodded.

'About James?'

'No.'

She studied me again. 'Let's go inside. I'm ready for coffee anyway,' and she pulled off her gloves and threw them down beside Germaine, who jumped, making Barbie laugh.

I laughed too, a high silly sound which didn't want to stop but I shut it off by saying to myself, 'It's all right. It's over. All you have to do is *tell* her.'

Inside Barbie left me in the kitchen and went to the dining room to put on some music. (My grandmother's a person who can't bear silence in the house.) I watched her through the arch as she put on a tape of syrupy guitar pieces. Back in the kitchen she slid a cloth over one end of the table and put a plate of date slice on it.

Everything in the room from the starchy little table-cloth to the pot of herbs on the window sill was so normal, so perfect I wanted to smash it all up by shouting, 'Look at me. Just look at me! I'm hurting here between my legs and need to tell someone.' But instead of doing that I stood with my tongue *dead* while Barbie crossed to the bench and after setting out mugs with echidnas painted on them began to make what my mother calls plastic coffee.

Her back was to me and watching her as she filled the jug and everything I realized that I couldn't tell her what had happened to me. That I'd *never* be able to tell her. Apart from anything else there were no words to use. I thought of the ones I'd learned in sex-education classes at school. They seemed as far removed from the hot, hurting thing my father had done to me as a Zulu's language would be. As for the ones I heard on the school bus, at least they were blunt enough to tell people what they meant but I knew there was no way I could blurt even one of them out in that smart little kitchen. So I stayed dumb and felt my throat go dry.

Finally Barbie turned back to me and smiled showing the wire clips on her big cream teeth. 'Come on,' she said. 'It can't be as bad as that. Did you fight with your mother?'

I shook my head.

'Your father?'

I didn't say anything, just tried to swallow and couldn't.

'So it was Dad.' She put her head on one side. 'What was it about? A new dress? An outing – something you wanted badly?'

The word dress made it impossible for me to look at her trying-to-be-sympathetic face and I lowered my eyes and stared at the pattern of the tiles on the floor. Keeping my eyes there I said, 'He came into my room last night. Late. Mum had gone out.' I stopped, then in a whisper added, 'He'd been drinking and he hurt me.'

I heard Barbie switch off the jug though it hadn't boiled.

'You mean he beat you?'

I lifted my eyes and because her face had changed, had

23

become well, sort of *wary*, I looked back at the floor again.

'Victoria,' her voice was louder, 'what exactly are you trying to say?'

The last chords of one of the guitar pieces floated into the room and stopped, leaving a sort of vibration in the air.

I looked up again and holding Barbie's eyes with mine shouted, 'Don't you know? He . . .' Again I found there were no words to use.

More music rushed into the room as we stared at each other then I saw my grandmother's face sort of shut inside itself like a shop with its lights being turned out at the end of the day.

This time it was Barbie who didn't speak. Instead she turned again to the bench where she moved a carton of milk from one place to another then back again.

'It hurt me,' I said. 'It still hurts.'

Her hands grew still and as I watched I saw a flush come up into her neck and stain it. After a while, in a voice that was high and quick, she said, 'You don't take sugar, do you?'

I didn't answer because I knew by then that like my mother Barbie knew what had happened in my room and like my mother she hated me for it. I'm sure I was right about that but Barbie had been to England and played cricket and everything and I think she was just naturally more cunning than my mother because she picked up the electric jug and filled first one, then the other mug and as she did she said, 'Victoria I know that in some ways life hasn't been easy for you. For the first five years you were an only child and although I know you've always been ex-tremely fond of James, no doubt your nose was put a little out of joint by his arrival.' She stood stirring the coffees in turn then picked them up and took them to the table. She didn't look at me as she went past. I looked at her though and saw that her face was the same hot colour as her neck.

Still not looking at me she sat and said, 'Come, my dear, let's have our coffee and talk this thing through.'

I didn't move and Barbie lifted her coffee to her mouth and put it down again untasted. 'Come and sit,' she said leaning over to pat the seat of the chair nearest her. Then she waited.

There was nothing for me to do but slide into the chair. I didn't touch my coffee though and I kept my eyes down. (My grandmother's manner was *full* of friendship but I could see her big hands. They were flat on the table, one each side of her coffee mug as if she was ready all the time for some sort of action.)

We both waited, then Barbie began to speak again. 'In the years when James had all those visits to doctors and so on you must have felt left out – I'm sure you did and I'm angry with myself for not realizing it. But darling, since then your Daddy's more than made it up to you. Heavens, when I think of everything you've had – music lessons, tennis lessons. In fact every little thing your heart desired.' She stopped speaking long enough to pick up the plate of date slice and offer it to me. When I shook my head she put it down and said, 'And what about all the lessons he's given you himself? Though in my opinion they were a mistake. It doesn't seem right to me for a little girl to be closeted with her Daddy night after night studying when she should be outside playing on the lawn.

'On top of that he's encouraged you to read the wrong sort of books. Greek myths and things were not meant for children and I can see you've got things all mixed up inside your head so that you're not quite sure what's real and what's just make-believe. Are you listening to me, darling?'

I nodded my head but I didn't look at her.

'And this business about what you *think* happened last night. No doubt some silly little thing *did* happen. Perhaps Daddy came in and kissed you goodnight just as you were slipping off to sleep and perhaps afterwards you had some funny little dream but dearest girl you mustn't mix up what's inside your head with your own daddy who's worked so hard to give you all a good life, though God knows he's had his disappointments.'

There was a moment while Barbie was speaking when I almost believed what she was saying but I could feel the sore part of myself squashed on the chair and then I realized that even if I'd shouted at Barbie, 'It *did* happen – my mother knows it happened,' she'd have smothered the sound with another lot of words. And if I'd asked to see a doctor or someone she'd say I was simply seeking attention. She'd have to say that because it was obvious that as long as she lived she was never going to believe anything as bad as what I was trying to tell her about my father who was also her son though I'd never really thought of him as being that before.

When I'd worked all that out I stopped listening to her. But I stayed there, I even drank my coffee because although she'd made me feel small and messy and ashamed the way James was when he had blue paint from the golf clubs in his hair, I wanted her to like me. And that's something I still don't understand about myself.

In the end I let her kiss me. I even promised to go to school for the rest of the day and I listened while she told me to be a sweet clever girl who'd make everyone proud of me. Then I left, going through the garden past the burnt berry bush and the statue with its silly green eyebrows and smirking lip.

Chapter Four

FROM THE CITY I took a number eighteen tram out to the Carlton football ground then I walked across the park to my Aunt Penelope's place. (Earlier I'd called at her office only to find she was at home for the day.) Aunt Penelope's a psychologist who works for the Premier's Department in an office high above Spring Street. To reach it I went up in a lift then trod about a kilometre of silent carpet until I reached a woman at a desk. Behind her was a painting of a lot of rectangles in different shades of blue. The woman stared at me across a copy of *Follow Me* and asked why I wanted to see Penelope.

Another woman, carrying a carton of fruit yoghurt, came out of a nearby door and stopped to listen.

'I'm her niece,' I said and asked if Penelope was sick.

The women exchanged a glance and the one at the desk said, 'She phoned in to say she's gone down with a twenty-four hour virus.'

'It seems an almost permanent condition with Pen,' said the other. Then she walked past us so that I received a little furnace blast from her perfume.

After that I left and as I went I asked myself why my aunt

chose to work in such a creepy place with such creepy people.

In Carlton the door to Penelope's terrace house was ajar so I knocked and went in. I found my aunt in the room she calls the conversation pit. (It has big windows facing the sun, millions of books and a bright rug on the floor.) Aunt Penelope was lolling in her favourite chair. Another woman was in the window seat, her back propped against the end and her feet, in sandals and white cotton sox, up on the cushions.

On the coffee table between the two of them lay the remains of lunch – ribbon sandwiches, a bowl of strawberries and two wine bottles, one empty, the other nearly empty. Also lying there was a bunch of dahlias. They were blood red and still wrapped in paper with a pattern of poodles on it.

Aunt Penelope didn't ask me what I was doing there. That's not what she calls her style. (My aunt is very concerned with style.) Instead she waved a hand with a glass in it and said, 'My niece Victoria – Liz Latimer.'

Liz *Latimer*! I couldn't believe it. I was actually in the same room as the woman who'd been sued for libel and everything; whose last novel was being studied by the class ahead of me at school. (Amanda Reece showed me a bunch of dirty words in it one morning on the bus.) I stared at her, Liz Latimer, I mean. Stared rudely, I suppose, while she turned her head and gave me a smile which was gone long before it reached full stretch. She was about Aunt Penelope's age – thirty-eight – and she had on a little-girl dress of printed cotton over a chest which was as flat as mine. Her haircut was a little girl's too and so was her mouth but her eyes were old eyes like the eyes of the monkey that once held its hand out to me from a cage at the zoo. (My mother said it was asking me for something to eat but for days after I kept remembering its eyes and thinking it wanted me to take it home with me or something.)

Aunt Penelope told me to get myself some orange juice from the kitchen and then to help myself to what was left of the sandwiches. Although I wasn't hungry I did as she said then took the things to a chair opposite Liz Latimer. I was thinking how silly I'd been not to come there in the first place because my aunt was the one person on earth guaranteed to help me. For years she'd spent most of her energy in combatting what she calls the colonization of women so I knew she'd be on the far-side-of-furious when she found out what had happened to me. But she'd be cool about it too. I could see her reaching for the telephone and in a calm, brisk voice setting out to make my mother and father, my grandmother too, die with shame over the way they'd treated me. And when that was done, still in a brisk way she'd almost certainly turn her little study into a room for me and say that she'd enroll me in the local High. (Aunt Penelope doesn't approve of private schools. She says they turn out batches of T'rak Road Rangers who don't know which way up is and what's more, don't care.)

The trouble though was that for the time being my aunt was concentrating on Liz Latimer and seemed to have forgotten I was there. Sitting back a bit in my chair I told myself to be patient for a while and did my best to concentrate on what was being said.

Aunt Penelope was talking, waving her free hand and rolling her eyes. (My aunt's very dramatic. *Volatile* is the word she uses for herself.) She's a short person with a deep throaty voice, big-round breasts and fattish thighs. In describing her I need to say that in spite of what my mother calls her iniquitously high salary she likes to get around in old jeans and joggers.

'Daniel and I were living in North Adelaide at the time,' she said. 'We had this wonderful apartment – four huge rooms behind a chiropractic clinic. The view was stunning.'

(Liz Latimer's eyes were locked onto Aunt Penelope's face.)

'It was in that bloody place our relationship fell apart.' My aunt put her glass on the table and fiddled around getting a cigarette alight. When it was, she sat watching the smoke for a while, then went on, 'Daniel had given up his job at the university to do research and play part-time with the orchestra. The trouble was though, there was nothing part-time about his drinking and he began missing rehearsals. I might tell you he was also working on a book about Peter Sculthorpe. He'd read bits of it out and ask me to criticize and when I did there'd be a row.' She lay back in her chair, drew heavily on her cigarette then let the smoke come slowly from her nostrils. 'He was like all the others. He couldn't cope with my being smarter than he.' She sat up again. 'He kept asking me to have a child. Did you know that?'

Liz Latimer said, 'No, I didn't.'

'It became his favourite theme. Have a child, he'd say and then we'll be a family. Shit! Can you picture it? Daniel wiped out by lunchtime, me doing a postgraduate course, and baby makes three.'

My aunt poured the last of the wine into her glass then lay back again and closed her eyes. 'But it wasn't that that drove me out. It was his bloody women.'

'Karen and Joyce, you mean?'

'And the others. Do you know they'd ring and ask to speak to me. *Me!*' Aunt Penelope's eyes flew open. 'They rang at all hours. Once Karen rang when Dan and I were fucking.'

I looked at Liz Latimer. She'd folded her lips inside her mouth and was scarcely breathing as my aunt went on. 'In time, of course, I learned to deal with the calls. I'd hand the phone to Dan and say, "This is your problem. You solve it."'

Liz Latimer relaxed her mouth and said, 'You did leave though.'

'In the end, yes.' Aunt Penelope stared into her glass.

'I suppose I thought it'd bring him to his senses and in a way it did. He followed me over here, you know, and asked me to go back, but by then Karen was pregnant so there was no point.'

Liz Latimer folded her lips in that funny way again, then let them go and said, 'Tell me, Pen, is that what men want? A Karen, who hangs round like a golliwog in striped overalls and a wild perm?'

'They want the bloody lot – everything! But most of all they want a mother who'll make them endless cups of coffee and be there to fuck when no one more interesting is available. Then they use that relationship as a base to launch their plans for fucking other women.' My aunt had got out another cigarette and was stabbing the air with it. 'But while all this is going on, the bastards are pursuing the real business of their lives.'

Without moving her feet, Liz Latimer leaned her body towards Penelope. 'Which is?' she said.

'Their friendships with other men. To put it another way, they find their image, their reflection only in the eyes of other men. And that reflection is the thing that matters most to them.'

'What you're really saying is that you don't believe it's possible for a woman to achieve a good and lasting relationship with a man.'

'Not for women like us, it isn't.' My aunt lay back in her chair again and closed her eyes.

For at least a minute Liz Latimer sat watching her then without looking at her watch, she said, 'Heavens, the time! I must go,' and she swung her feet to the floor and stood.

Aunt Penelope didn't move. 'It can't be late,' she said from a throat that needed clearing. 'We've just finished lunch.'

'It's late for me,' Liz Latimer told her. 'I haven't done my day's stint yet.' She took her bag from beneath the bunch of dahlias on the table. 'Don't get up, Pen. You look so comfortable there. I can see myself out.' Already on her way to the door, she said, 'Goodbye Victoria. I hope we meet again,' and after giving me a lightning-quick smile she was gone.

Frowning, Aunt Penelope got out of her chair and followed her. She was away for some time and when she came back she was carrying a fresh bottle of wine. As she put it on the table she lurched a little and it was then I realized she was drunk.

'Well,' she said turning to me. 'What did you think of her?'

'For someone famous, she didn't say much.'

'No, the bitch never does.' She paused and leaned forward a little to stare at me with rounded eyes. 'You know what she'll do, don't you?'

'No.'

'She'll get into her little beige utility, run it around the first corner, then park and write down every bloody word I said.'

I found nothing to say but Aunt Penelope who'd stopped looking at me and was opening the wine didn't notice. As she filled her glass she said, 'You know what makes me *really* mad?'

I wasn't meant to answer because she rushed on. 'Everything I said will be in her next novel.' She whacked the palm of her hand against the base of her throat and kept it there. '*My* lines! That little lady will pass them off as hers and the point is that not in her wildest dreams would she have the intelligence to think of them herself.'

She sat, then looked at me and blinked as if suddenly seeing me. 'Do you want something to eat?'

To my surprise both my plate and glass were empty but when I tried to tell my aunt I'd already eaten she didn't hear me because she was speaking again herself.

'Intelligence has always been my problem – my handicap,' she said. 'All the way through university I was *punished* for it. The separatists hate me for it and now people like Liz Latimer use me for it.' She took a drink then looked at me again. 'Anyway, what are you doing here?'

This time I knew the school-bus words would do. 'Last night my father fucked me.' (I was so relieved to get it out at last I think I said the sentence as a single word.)

Aunt Penelope stared at me until I felt my own eyes begin to waver, then when I thought she'd never look away again she put her head back and let go with peal after peal of laughter. Finally she controlled herself enough to say, 'That's all I needed in my life.'

'It's true,' I said.

'Oh, I believe you, Victoria. I'm just the one who would.' She gave another laugh, a shuddery sort of one and said, 'You see I'm another of your charming father's victims. You and I will have to form a club – the Tony Ferguson Fucked Me Club.'

'I don't know what you mean.' My voice was a whisper.

'Then, my dear, I'll tell you.' She finished the wine in her glass and reached again for the bottle. 'The night you were born, my little Victoria, your father and I slept together and we fucked all night. Not that he's much good at it if you want to know.' She stopped talking to peer across at me. 'The joke is, of course, that I've always been in love with the bastard. I met him first you know, and I'm the one he should have married, not my pallid sister who spends her life bent over a bloody potter's wheel so she won't have to face what goes on around her.' Taking a shuddery sort of *breath*, Aunt Penelope began to cry.

There was a lot more of it. I sat with the empty plate on my lap and listened as her voice, rising and falling, went on and on. She said she was the one whose intelligence and warmth would have made my father happy. Then still crying most of the time she told me about two other failed love affairs she'd had. In the end she seemed to fall asleep but just before she did, she turned her wet face to me and wailed, 'All I wanted, Victoria, was to be *accepted*.'

Not moving a muscle I stayed where I was for ten, perhaps fifteen minutes, then I stood and tiptoed towards the door. Just before I reached it Aunt Penelope's voice said, 'That creep didn't even say thanks for lunch.'

I turned. Her eyes were closed, her head sideways against the chair. Without waiting to hear more I hurried out, closing the door behind me.

Chapter Five

I DON'T REMEMBER walking back to Clifton Hill. All I
know is that I wanted to die. The things Aunt Penelope
had wailed at me kept rushing through my head, mix-
ing themselves up with the knowledge that I had nowhere
to go and no one to go *to*; that the best I could hope for was
to find some place where I could kill myself. As I went
along the underpass towards the station, I felt that if someone flew at me and stabbed me into a bloodstained little
heap by the wall, I'd welcome it. Three big boys wearing
combat boots and studded wrist bands *did* come towards
me. They looked at me as they drew level and one of them
said something and the others laughed. Then they were
gone.

That laughter made me so ashamed, so *desperate*, I was
ready to throw myself under the first train like the Russian
woman I saw on television. The thing that stopped me was
the sight of James sunning himself on the opposite platform.
He was sitting on a freight trolley with his bag beside him
on the ground. Head down, he was pushing something
small, a coin perhaps, backwards and forwards along the
surface of the trolley. One of his feet beat time to some
little rhythm of his own.

Without giving myself time to think, I wheeled to the right and was inside the waiting room before he had time to see me.

James was waiting for *me*. That was obvious. He must've got off the school bus the first time it stopped and guessing I'd gone to the station, he'd followed me there. And knowing him, he'd go on waiting for me till the day's last train had gone. It's an awful thing to have to say but I didn't care. On top of everything else, the problem of my little brother was one I no longer wanted to know about.

The waiting room at Clifton Hill station is *revolting*. It's cold and dark with pee-green walls done over with a design of black which looks as if someone has swirled it on with a rag. You've no idea how awful it is. Scraped into the paint are dozens of silly messages like 'Acka and Monk and Rambo were here'. Shivering at the *chaddiness* of it, I turned to look at a poster on the end wall. Whoever put it there must've been trying to be funny because it showed a stretch of pale clean sand with green waves breaking at its edge. Girls in bikinis were playing leap-frog in the shallows. I went closer and saw palm trees and tall buildings so white they seemed to sparkle. 'Winter in Queensland – the Sunshine State' said the caption.

Behind me a train rushed into the opposite platform. It stopped, made a heavy humming sound and rushed out again. I went on staring at the poster. *I'll bet it's Surfers Paradise*, I thought. *I could go there and no one would find me. I could go by train – they wouldn't think of that. I could go* TODAY. *Leave this rotten place where fathers turn into monsters and women into witches. Up there no one will know what I am and what I've done. I can get a job and find a little flat. Caroline Teasdale says it's even warm enough to sleep on the beach. And later, when I've saved some money, I'll get a dog, a big grey one like a wolf. Every night and morning we'll walk by the sea. People will look at us and wonder who we are, but no one will come near and no one will bother us.*

A train was coming in on the Ivanhoe line. I heard it and ran to the doorway. Flattening myself against the wall, I waited until it'd pulled right along the platform, hiding me from James, then I ran from the waiting room and the moment it stopped, scrambled aboard.

When I reached home I checked out the garage before going into the house. It was empty. I thought it would be. On Thursdays Mum takes a pottery class in a room behind a craft shop in Heidelberg. (One of her pupils, Mrs Gilblast, is only 133 centimetres tall.)

For the next half hour I had a crazy conversation on the phone with some woman at Spencer Street railway station. It started off when I rang to find out how much a single half-fare was to Surfers Paradise. The woman, thinking I knew none of the trains ran all the way to Surfers, began asking me if I was making a hoax call. She even told me what the *penalty* was for making one. I kept her on the line by telling her a lot of lies about how my mother was going into hospital for an operation and how I was going up to stay with my gran until she came out again. After that she told me I'd have to take the train to a place called Murwillumbah in New South Wales. I said that Murwillumbah – I had some trouble pronouncing it – had an interesting name but that I wanted to go to Queensland, not New South Wales. She accused me again of making a hoax call and by the time we'd sorted that out, I'd begun to wonder how *Turks* and everyone get on in this country.

In the end the woman became quite friendly with me, telling me how her mother, who had arthritis in her hands and feet, liked to go up to the Gold Coast every winter because there the swelling in her extremities went down and she was able to get out of her woolly slippers. I didn't want to know all that stuff but didn't like to say so because I still didn't know how much the train fare was as far as Murwillumbah. By the time her conversation about her mother dried up, I'd had an inspiration and asked her would it be better if my gran called her from Surfers. She said, 'No, no, not at all,' and promptly told me that the first class fare was $70.65, economy $50.30 and a sleeper $130.65. She even told me the train left Spencer Street at 6.56 in the evening and that when I reached Murwillumbah I'd be able to catch a bus to Surfers. Before she could get onto the subject of her mother's feet again, I thanked her and hung up.

The next thing I did was find my bank book and check on the balance. It was $387.83, which I'd saved towards a trip to Switzerland I'd intended taking when I'd done my VCE. (Once $300 had seemed like a million. Suddenly it wasn't much at all because I knew I'd need a sleeper on the train so I could lock myself in at night. *It'll be worth it, though,* I told myself, *because this way no one will see me and remember later on when my picture's in the paper and everything.*)

Still thinking about the stuff they'd put in the paper, I checked my watch. The time was 3.07 which meant I had less than an hour and a half to get to the bank, come home, pack and leave before my mother returned. Minutes later, wearing jeans and some of Mum's makeup to make me look older than I was, I was cycling towards the local branch of our bank.

I hadn't withdrawn money there before and was extremely nervous about it because I thought I'd be asked what I was going to do with it. I became even more nervous when I had to turn and go another way because water from a burst main had blocked off part of Heidelberg Road. That took me *eleven* extra minutes and by the time I'd parked my bike and was going through the bank door, my stomach was churning like a low-speed vitamizer.

I'd expected to have to wait inside the bank. I always did after school when I put the money *in*. This time though, the place was almost empty and I went straight to the counter. When the teller there had finished fiddling with her drawer of money, I pushed my book through that ravine thing underneath the bullet-proof glass and said to her, 'I'd like to take my money out, please.'

I hate the way they have those glass panels in banks because it means you have to shout at the teller so everyone within two kilometres hears all your business. That's what happened to me when I asked for my money. I mean I felt everything in the place *stop*. Looking back after all this time, I'd say that was just my imagination because it turned out the teller wasn't interested in me at all. What she was interested in was whether I was going to close the account or not.

At first I didn't know what she meant, let alone why she was saying it. So we had this dumb conversation which seemed to me to be off the point, but in the end, realizing she wanted me to keep my account open, I agreed to leave two dollars there. After that she filled out a withdrawal form for me and almost before I knew it, I was outside getting on my bike again. (It was 3.43 by my watch.)

Getting my money had been so easy I couldn't believe it, and as I went towards home I remember saying to myself, *Banks should be different somehow. They should be* INTEREST-ED *in you. At least in kids. I mean, I don't think they should take you down into the vault and show you your money or something but they should come down halfway between and ask what you plan to do with it. As it is, they're practically* INVITING *you to leave home.*

James found me when I'd almost finished packing. A little while before I'd taken a suitcase from the cupboard in the hall and put it on the chair beside my bed. I was busily stuffing summer clothes into it when he came in behind me. At first I didn't know he was there. It wasn't until I lifted my head and reached for my favourite shirt that I saw his reflection in the mirror on the dressing table. I froze then, one hand stretched towards the shirt. (The two faces in the mirror were so alike – both of them sad and white, James's mouth stained with raspberry cordial or something, mine with Mum's lipstick.)

Slowly my brother moved his eyes from my face to the case on the chair and back again. Then he went to the dressing table and touched the bank book lying there with money sticking out of it.

'I'm going on a holiday,' I said. The words came out thin and false and when our eyes met in the mirror, I dropped mine.

'I *have* to go.' My voice was quick now and firmer. 'I don't want to but I have no choice.'

Head tilted to one side, he watched me for a few more moments. I held my breath and waited for tears and a tantrum, but all he did was turn and go out of the room. I grabbed the shirt, shoved it in on top of my other clothes and shut the suitcase. Then I ran along the hall to my parents' bedroom and chose a handbag of my mother's, taking care to take one she wouldn't miss immediately. As I flew back, I noticed the door of the hall cupboard had swung open again. I shut it and hurried on. Back in my bedroom, I put my money, some tissues and a comb in the handbag. It was 4.16 and I was ready to leave. I looked around the room, at the INXS poster on the wall and the string of little Ming-blue horses marching along my desk. I saw my books and the curtains my mother had let me choose. Suddenly they blurred and all I wanted to do was go back to the time – just a day away – when the room had been my favourite place in the world.

A noise in the hall made me turn. As I did I saw James coming through the doorway. He'd pulled up his fallen sox but his mouth was still raspberry coloured. At his side he lugged a bulging airways bag.

'You can't come with me.' Panic made my voice a shout.

'You *can't*. It's impossible.'

His answer was to put the bag down and fold his arms across his scrawny little chest.

I went to him, leaned down and put my face close to his. 'Listen, later on when I'm settled, maybe I can send for you.'

He didn't move.

'I'd take you with me if I could,' I said and began to cry. 'I've only enough money for myself. I thought I had a lot but it turns out it isn't much at all.'

James uncrossed his arms, turned and beckoned for me to follow him. Then he went out into the hall and headed for his bedroom. I shot a glance at the bedside clock and hurried after him. He was in his room. He'd pulled a chair over to the open wardrobe and as I watched, he put both his pillows and some books onto the seat of it. After scrambling up onto this pre*carious* perch, he reached to the back of the shelf at the top of the wardrobe and pulled out one of those tartan tins you put shortbread in at Christmas. Turning to show me the tin, he fell. I'd seen that coming and was in time to sort of catch him. We landed with the chair and pillows on top of us. James was still clutching the tin. He scrambled to his feet, took the lid off and beaming, showed me the contents – a bundle of banknotes.

I reached out, took the money and counted it. '*Forty-four dollars*,' I said, then, 'where did you get it? You stole it, didn't you?'

He shook his head.

'You must have,' I said and that was the moment I heard our mother's car turn into the drive.

I froze again but only for a moment. Then, after stuffing the money into the waistband of my jeans, I tidied the room, shutting the wardrobe and putting the other things back in place. That done, I stood close to the wall near the door and waited. James came to stand beside me. I heard the front door open and my mother walk through the house to the kitchen. There was a silence – then she filled the electric kettle.

She'll stay there, I thought, *until she's had a cigarette and two cups of Lapsang Soochong*.

'Here.' I thrust the money back at James and ran to my bedroom where I opened one of the side windows. Next I took the suitcase to the window and hoisted it up onto the sill. When it was balanced there, I pushed it and watched it topple out. It landed with a little crash on the daphne bush, flattening it. I grabbed Mum's handbag from the bed and scrambled out the window too. While I was turning the case around so I could reach the handle, James and his bag landed beside me.

As we'd done earlier in the dressing table mirror, we stared at each other. Then, solemnly, he handed the bank-notes back to me. Wanting to bawl again, I took them and put them in the handbag. After that I picked up the case and with James in tow, headed across the lawn towards the gate.

Chapter Six

JAMES AND I took a roundabout route to Spencer Street Station, going out to Camberwell by bus, then catching a train. Altogether it took us an hour and a half but was worth it because we didn't see a soul we knew.

We reached Spencer Street at 5.20 – rush hour. Trains came and went every *minute* as swarms of people hurried up and down the ramps. Now and then a message you couldn't understand came over the public address system and when it did, some of the younger commuters leapt the fences beside the ramps and ran, pushing people. I stood with my case in the middle of it and looked for James who'd vanished the minute we got off the train. At last, in a thinning of the crowd, I saw him coming towards me pushing a V-Line trolley.

Delighted with himself, James pushed our luggage all the way to the interstate ticket office, allowing me to help him only on the last and steepest bit.

There was hardly anyone at the ticket counter, hardly any staff either. I planted myself behind a garlicky woman with black wool stockings and clogs and prayed I'd find answers to awkward questions when my turn came. The woman was arguing with the Asian counter clerk about money.

That made *me* think of money and I realized that when I'd paid for two sleeping berths there'd be little left for us to live on while I scouted for a job and everything. There was a moment then when I wished I could put my brother in a taxi and send him home. Thinking of how he'd fight against it gave me my first smile that day. Turning to share it with him, I found nothing behind me but the trolley and our luggage. James had gone again.

There was no time to rush out and look for him because the garlicky woman was leaving and the clerk was already looking at me.

'Two single half-fare sleepers to Murwillumbah,' I said trying to make it sound the sort of thing I asked for every day.

In his quacking Asian voice he told me there was no chance of us getting sleepers on the train that night.

'Can you check please.' (This time my voice was about as assertive as *tissue* paper.)

The clerk shrugged but went to the nearest computer and clicked the keys for what seemed a ridiculously long time, coming back finally to tell me that we could have sleeping berths but not in the same compartment.

'We *have* to be in the same compartment. My little brother's deaf and dumb.'

The term deaf and dumb meant nothing to the clerk who stood regarding me with unreadable Hong Kong eyes.

At a loss, I looked wildly around for James. He was still missing.

'I'm travelling with my little brother,' I told the clerk. 'He can't speak or hear.' I pointed to my mouth, then my ear and shook my head.

The clerk, who looked about seven*teen*, said, 'You and boy go alone?'

Yes, our mother's sick. She's in hospital and we're going to our grandmother's.'

'Where is father?'

'No father.'

At that moment James, out of breath, crashed into the counter beside me. Pulling himself upright he gave the Asian the angel-smile he pulls out of the cupboard about twice a year. Then he offered him a Smartie.

The clerk smiled too, his eyes lightening, cheeks stretching. 'You come back later.' He helped himself to a Smartie with a hand as *elegant* as a girl's. 'You come six-fifteen. Perhaps I find some luck for you.'

I thanked him and we went out. I was feeling very strange. Sort of let-down, I suppose, because in the bottom of my heart I'd expected to be stopped at the ticket office. I thought that someone there would insist on knowing my age and that when they did they'd ring the police and in the end my mother would come for us. I think all along I'd believed that we'd go home that evening to a world which had become normal again. When none of that happened, I was left with a feeling in my chest which was heavy and empty all at the same time, though I know that doesn't sound possible.

'I didn't know it was so easy for kids to run away,' I said to James as we parked our luggage next to someone else's in the main waiting room. 'But if no one even cares about us, we might as well keep going.'

James nodded and crammed some Smarties into his mouth.

'Have you had any proper food today?' I asked.

He shook his head.

'Then we'll go and get a meal. Give me the Smarties.'

For a few seconds James defied me with his eyes, then he handed the packet over. (Sugary things and some food colourings affect James, making him unmanageable. One of the doctors who examined him, warned my parents that children like James should be kept on a diet which was free of such things. Dad said ideas like that merely give kids a licence for bad behaviour and he and Mum let James go on eating whatever he wished. I believed what the doctor said though. I'd noticed that my brother was often at his worst the day after he'd binged at someone's birthday party. It was because of this that I'd decided to be a paediatrician when I grew up.)

At six-fifteen we were back at the ticket office where the clerk greeted us as if we were the only friends he had in Australia. (Perhaps we *were*.) Anyway, with smiles and quacks, he told us he'd managed to rearrange the bookings so that James and I could travel together all the way to Murwillumbah. He also told us that to make the Queensland connection we had to put in a day in Sydney, arriving there at 8.45 a.m. and leaving at six-thirty in the evening.

During the conversation James, who'd been warned that he was supposed to be deaf and dumb, played the part of an idiot, wrinkling his brow and letting his head droop to one side. When I punched him below the level of the counter, he gave me an injured look and went back to being an idiot.

Finally we had our tickets and left to a flutter of smiles, nods and waves from our Asian friend.

Our train left from platform one and as we pushed our way through the crowd, I saw the girl I'd seen that morning in the Clifton Hill underpass. (I recognized her cyclamen hair and little granny boots as she leant from the door of one of the economy class carriages.) She was being seen off by a group of young people in op-shop clothes. They were laughing and I heard one of them call the girl *Delia*.

'People vanish in the mangroves at Byron Bay and are never heard of again,' someone said.

The girl said, 'I can't wait.' Then we were past.

The conductor met us at the door of the sleeping compartment. He checked our tickets and finding we were travelling alone asked if we were the Babes in the Wood. He had grey hair and false teeth which moved a bit when he spoke so I didn't think it likely that he'd do us any harm. Just the same I made sure my voice wasn't friendly or anything when I repeated the piece about our mother being in hospital.

'Never mind,' he said, 'we'll look after you. You're number thirteen and fourteen. Go on in and I'll be along later to make up your beds.'

I turned and looked back the way we'd come. I told myself I was saying goodbye to Melbourne but the truth is that I was still hoping I'd see someone we knew hurrying towards us who'd say, 'Come on, sillybillies, let's go home.' On the next track a very old engine, all polished up, was going past. It blew out a cloud of steam which rose in the air and formed a fluffy tree-shape. I thought of the blossom tree just inside our gate. In spring when the flowers were out it looked as if a cloud of white stars had fallen on it. I loved that tree, waited through each winter for it to bloom and when it did I told myself it sort of represented me. (I know that's a dumb way to go on and I've never told anyone before, but it's how I felt.)

I won't see it again, I thought and wanting to bawl again, I turned and climbed onto the train.

James had already found our compartment and was grinning at me from the doorway. I cheered up a bit when I got inside. It was narrow but nice, like a tiny house for two. I was about to shut the door behind me when the conductor turned up.

'The Babes left their luggage on the platform,' he said, pushing in our bags.

When he'd gone, I did shut the door, locking it. Then I watched while James checked out the compartment. He was like a cat in a new home, looking at everything, touching everything. He found the collapsible table beneath the window and was delighted by the way the shower curtain ran on a circular track. The loo under the washbasin sent him into fits of laughter. When there was nothing left for him to look at he sat by the window making faces at anyone who passed.

To stop him, I asked where he'd got the forty-four dollars he'd given me. He swung around and built a little tower with his hands by flattening them and putting them one on top of the other in quick succession.

'You didn't save it,' I said. 'You couldn't have.'

He nodded and made his eyes innocent.

Going to stand in front of him, I said again, 'Where did you get it?'

This time he did the actions of someone dealing cards.

'You mean you played cards for *money*?'

He nodded.

'Where?'

Bending his head he did imaginary writing.

'At school?'

Still all innocence, he smiled and nodded again.

I stood thinking that if he did play cards, he'd probably win because he'd remember all the ones other people put down. Before I could say anything though there were quick steps in the corridor, a whistle blew and slowly the train began to move. James turned back to the window then and I sort of gave up about the money but not before I'd said, 'If I find out . . .' and made a fist and thumped it into his shoulder.

Our compartment was airconditioned and cold. I was wearing a jumper but James had on only a shirt and shorts. When I looked in his bag to get him something warmer, I found he'd packed the dumbest things. On top, there was a cream pleated coat Mum bought him when he was *four*. It'd never been worn and I don't know why she got it in the first place, let alone why James had brought it with him. He'd put in as well his football boots, a pile of Phantom comics, his scrabble set, his swim shorts, one grubby T-shirt and a six inch hunting knife I know he'd been forbidden to buy.

After looking at that collection, I gave him one of my jumpers to wear. Naturally it was too big for him with the sleeves hanging well below his hands. That amused James who started his Basil Fawlty walks and kept on with them until I said, 'You'd better learn to speak soon, Jamie, because you're never going to be happy till you're on television or something.' (It was a funny thing that I called him Jamie because we always got into trouble at home if we used the diminutive of someone's name.)

In the hour before moontime when the world outside the window was dark and sort of spooky, the conductor came to show us how the bunks pulled down from the wall. (He seemed to be in a hurry and didn't *look* at us or anything.) You can imagine how James loved the little wooden ladder which hooked onto the top bunk. I didn't want him to sleep up there. He's a restless sleeper who throws himself around a lot but I'd decided to save the argument till later.

About eleven, when he was almost asleep at the window, we rushed through a little station sitting alone in the middle of the moonlit paddocks. On the platform was a woman. Her shoes lay on the ground beside her and there was no one else in sight. She looked thirty, even *forty*, and as we rushed by she turned her back, pulled down the waistband of her pants, and bending, showed her bare bottom to the train. While she did it she looked over her shoulder with the expression on her face of a little kid cheeking someone. Then the station and the woman's bare white bottom had vanished as if they'd never been. After the first shock, James and I looked at each other and began to laugh. We laughed until we were *limp*. With me, it was as if someone had pulled a plug and let everything inside me out. And when the laughter was finally over, the sort of tightness in my chest had gone. As for James, he closed his eyes on a final giggle, opened them, closed them again and was asleep. I settled him in a comfortable position and covered him with a blanket. Then I climbed onto the other end of the same bunk. I'd meant to stay awake in case someone tried to get into our compartment but the next thing I knew it was daylight and the conductor was banging on the door to tell us we'd be having breakfast in half an hour.

The day in Sydney was the longest of my life. It started badly when I tried to change our ticket for economy ones at Central Station. (I knew it was a risky thing to do but with less than sixty dollars of our money left, some sort of refund was essential.) I'd taken the pre*caution* of buying the tickets in the names of Christine and David Teasdale, but thinking our photographs were probably in all the morning papers, I kept my head down as much as possible when I went to the booking office.

The man who took the tickets from me, examined them as if he expected them to be forgeries. After that he put them on the counter and keeping his hand on them, said, 'I reckon we can change them.' (The person working next to him had stopped to listen in.) 'But before we do, we'd better check with your folks.'

'Don't bother. They wouldn't agree.' I heard my voice come out as a guilty little whisper.

'I'll bet they wouldn't.'

I waited, my face hot, for the questions to start but all the man did was shake his head and hand the tickets back to me. With James behind me, I hurried out not looking back but feeling the eyes of both men following me.

After checking our luggage into the cloakroom we caught a bus up to the centre of the city. There, the first thing I did was find a newsagent's and nick inside to look at the newspaper headlines. I meant all along to buy a paper but the minute I turned one over to see the bottom of the front page, the owner who had one mad eye and one green plastic *patch*, leaned over the counter and bawled at me for touching it.

With my face fiery again I paid for the paper and got out of the shop before he could call the pest exterminator or something. As I went I was thinking, *They hate kids. Everyone does. They just want them off the face of the* EARTH.

Not far from the newsagent's was a mall where I sat to

scan the paper. (James who was in a sulk because I'd refused to let him spend money on a video game he'd seen, sat beside me and banged the sides of his shoes together.) I went through the paper from beginning to end, then back the other way. When I reached the racing page, I still thought I was going to see a photo of my brother and me, probably my mother too with her eyes puffed and everything saying how much she wanted us back. But I was wrong. There was nothing about James and me, let alone my mother. And even when I knew that, I kept looking. I looked long enough for a crowd to gather in the mall and a police band concert to begin.

When I finally put the paper on the seat beside me and raised my head, I guess I wasn't focussing properly because for at least a minute I sat watching my brother down at the front of the crowd mimicking every move made by the conductor of the band. In the end that moved *me*. If it hadn't, I think I'd have gone on sitting and being sorry for myself forever.

When I'd dragged James from the mall, we walked and looked in shops and sat and walked some more. Early in the afternoon, thank Jeepers, we found this min*ute* cinema where James's favourite film was playing. *Blue Thunder* it's called and we sat through it twice. James wanted to and I let him because it was such a good place for us to hide. Early in the film there's a part when the hero and his friend hover their helicopter outside an apartment where an extremely shapely woman is doing Yoga with nothing on. The two men watch her as she sort of puts one leg behind her head while she's sitting, then the other and stands up. (That's the only way I can describe what she does. You'd have to see it to understand.) Anyway, the men hover there in mid-air and watch her. They are both policemen – I forgot to mention that – and they're in a police helicopter. You can see they're getting a big kick out of seeing her tie herself into knots while she's naked and the first time I ever saw the film

I thought it was quite funny but there in Sydney with a stale-ish ham and salad roll in my hand, I worked out that the woman knew all along they were watching and from that moment none of it seemed funny to me at all. I mean she didn't pull down the blind or go and put some clothes on or anything, so in a way she was just as bad as they were. Maybe worse.

Seeing all that made me feel uncomfortable even in the dark cinema and the second time the scene came around I went to the loo so I'd miss it. In there I tried to work out what it all *meant*. The police officers watching her, I mean, and it being on film for kids to see and worry about and no one turning up to say the two men shouldn't have been there in the first place. It was enough to put people off films forever. (If you're wondering why I didn't take my brother out of the cinema, I couldn't have *got* him out before the helicopter duel at the end, and I knew it.)

At half past five we were back at Central Station where we bought chicken and baked potatoes in the restaurant and took them to a corner table to eat.

We'd been there about two minutes when a girl my age came in. Stopping just inside the glass doors, she swept the room with her eyes, then after buying a can of Coke at the counter, brought it to our table although there was a free one right next to us.

'I'm Sandra,' she said, smiling at me. 'Do you mind if I sit here?' And without waiting for an answer she pulled out a chair and sat.

She was fairly fat and dressed in a fluffy jumper and mini-skirt. She had freckles and small, surprisingly pretty grey eyes. (Her eyelids were the same aqua as her jumper.) On one wrist she wore a watch with a row of silver hearts on the band, on the other, a collection of coloured bracelets. Mixed up with the bracelets was the strap of a little draw-string bag.

The first thing she did when she'd sat was disengage the

strap from the bracelets and plonk the bag on the corner of the table. Then, without speaking again she put a straw into the can of Coke and bent to drink. While she did, she studied me.

Both James and I had stopped eating and were watching her.

Finally she lifted her head and said, 'You two travelling?'

I nodded.

'Alone?'

Another nod.

'Where d'y'live?'

'Adelaide.'

'Where're y'going?'

'Surfers.'

'Lucky you.' She looked around the restaurant as if for inspiration. Then turning back to me, she said, 'I live in Surry Hills but I work in the city.'

'What do you do?'

'This and that.'

There was a silence. James had started eating again but was still watching Sandra.

She took another drink, then said, 'You want some daisies or somethin'? I got some.'

'Daisies?'

'Yeah, daisies.' She shrugged. 'You know, lift-offs, dream-beans.'

She was talking about pills – drugs. She was *selling* them. That's what she meant by 'this and that'. I knew kids as young as I took them, *sold* them too, but not that way. Not coming up to you in front of everyone and asking two seconds after you'd met.

'I don't want any. I don't take them,' I said and heard my voice sounding all high and prissy.

She shrugged again and reaching for the Coke knocked her bag from the table.

'Shit,' she said and bent to pick it up. While she was

fumbling for it, James and I exchanged a look. He grimaced, which could have meant anything at all.

Sandra was upright again and putting the strap of her bag back on her wrist. 'I better be going,' she said. 'I gotta deliver this letter for an advertising office.' She stood, clamped the arm with the bag on it across her middle and after saying, 'See y',' turned, and not hurrying or anything, walked from the restaurant.

I went back to my food which was getting cold. I knew Sandra had given me a good opportunity to lecture my brother on the subject of kids who come out of nowhere and offer you things like lift-offs and dream-beans. I was trying to work out a way to do it without making the entire scene sound irre*sist*ible when James reached out and shook Sandra's drink can. Liquid swished around in it and when it did, something, I don't know what, made me look for my own bag. When we sat I'd put it by my feet. It wasn't there anymore.

I bobbed up to tell James, then bent to look again. I even felt around for it with my hand but the only things I found were chair legs and empty air.

The next moment I was on my feet, saying to James, 'Don't leave the table.' Then I ran.

The interstate terminal at Central Station is really this huge hall about three kilometres long with one of those skeleton ceilings with the see-through bit in the middle. The restaurant is at the very end so that from outside the doorway I was able to stand and look along the entire length of the waiting room. Close to me on the left was this neat group of tables and chairs with coloured umbrellas over them. Further down were kiosks and some of those daggy old coach lights on posts. On the right hand side was a series of tough-looking lounges where people sat with their cases and kids and things. Other people were moving about and groups of them stood here and there but there was no sign of Sandra.

Knowing that she'd got away with our train tickets as well as the last of our money, *wrecked* me and instead of racing to the street in the hope that I'd see her as she hurried away, I stayed where I was and told myself I might as well give up because on top of everything else, fate was now punishing me for the things I'd done. Then a knot of people halfway along the waiting room moved and I saw the splash of Sandra's jumper as it disappeared through a doorway between the lounges on the right.

I flew to the door, jumping suitcases on the way and knocking into a man who swore at me as I ran on. The door led to the women's toilets – a place of harsh light and that bleachy smell public loos always have. Rushing into a room on the right I saw a fat white-faced woman feeding a baby from a fat white breast. She rolled patient eyes at me as I hesitated then backed out. A bunch of girls was coming from another door. They were laughing and as I pushed past and in through the door, one shrieked, 'So we did it right there, with the venetian blind rattling.'

I was in the room where the cubicles were. Again there was no sign of Sandra but I knew all I had to do was wait. A toilet flushed. I was panting. One of the doors opened and a middle-aged woman came out. She straightened her skirt, moved to a basin, rinsed one hand, dried it a bit and went out. I went closer to the cubicles, was about to stoop and look beneath each orange door in turn when the one in front of me flew open and Sandra and I were face to face.

Her eyes widened to full and she took a step backwards but she was cool enough to say, 'What do *you* want?'

'My bag! I want my bag!'

She gave a tough little toss of her head. 'Don't look at me. I haven't got it.'

'Yes you have. You took it.' My eyes swept the cubicle behind her. My bag wasn't in sight but it took me *no* time to work out that she'd taken my things from it and stuffed it down the loo.

'Don't talk piss,' she said and went to go past me but instead of letting her, I shoved her back into the cubicle, shouting, 'Give me my money, you bitch. Give it back.'

'I haven't got it.' She sounded so sure of herself that I lost control and hit her across the face with the side of my fist. The pain of it, perhaps the shock, brought tears to her eyes and again she tried to push past me. But I'd gone mad. I was as strong as a man and I grabbed her shoulders, pushing her so that she stumbled against the loo. Before she had time to right herself, I'd grabbed her again and pushed her face down onto the pedestal. The seat was up and I heard the crack her cheekbone made as it met the china. I know I was out of my mind because I cracked her face against the pedestal again, then dragged her back up and tore the silly little bag from her wrist. When I opened it, I smelt cheap perfume. I was crying and among the rubbish inside it was the red purse I kept my money in. Snatching it out, I threw Sandra's bag on the floor. Then I looked at her.

She was crouching and trying to lean away from me all at the same time. Her hair was mucked up and one side of her face was mottled red and white. I hated that fat mottled face so much, I smashed into it again with the fist holding the purse. I wanted to go on hitting it but suddenly I was exhausted and all I did was push her so that she fell onto the floor. Seeing her lying there crying wasn't enough for me and I took a handful of her hair and tugged it before I left. As I turned away I saw my bag, the contents spilling out, behind the door. In one movement I knelt, scooped the things back in and picked it up.

I didn't stop to wash my face. I saw it though in the watching mirror. My hair had fallen forward and beneath it my eyes were big and dark and mad.

In the outer room the woman feeding the baby hadn't moved. God knows if she'd heard the fight or not. Not caring if she had, I went past her and out the door.

James had left the restaurant in spite of being told not to.

He was standing, ghost-faced, outside the door with his eyes scanning the crowd. We didn't go back to our food. It wouldn't have been there anyway, so what we did was buy chips and things at a kiosk. Then we went towards the luggage room with me stuffing food into my mouth and flinging back over my shoulder to James my opinion of that scab Sandra and her *mottled* face.

Chapter Seven

THE TRAIN TRIP that night was pretty much the same as the previous one except that this time no retard showed us her bottom from a railway platform. James wanted the top bunk so badly I let him have it. It didn't matter anyway because he flaked ten seconds after he climbed into it and didn't stir till morning. I know I slept because I dreamt I was trying to shove someone, I don't know who, into a giant Coke can while someone else watched from a helicopter. I probably dreamt a lot of other stuff as well but that's all I remember.

We were having breakfast – the cheapest on the menu – when the train pulled into Byron Bay. The girl in granny boots got out there. I saw her on the platform with a big wicker basket instead of a suitcase. (Some of her gear was hanging out of it.) She was met by a pregnant girl in a sarong and after a bit of a fight over who'd carry the basket, they went off arm in arm and laughing.

The name Byron Bay seemed extremely romantic to me. The sort of place where poets would die young and tragically. Because of that I checked out the view from each side of the dining car. On the east, there seemed to be a hotel and railway station all in one. On the west, the usual old water

tower, a few rows of houses then paddocks and trees of a
dynamic green. Behind all that was a peaked little mountain
range like the ones you see in Hawaii on 'Magnum P.I.'
(My parents argued quite bitterly about our watching Magnum, with my mother saying she approved of it because it
portrayed essentially moral values such as loyalty to one's
friends. My father told her she was talking drivel but
occasionally we watched it just the same.)

The rest of the trip to Murwillumbah was through
countryside in shades of blue, purple-ish through to smoky
– and green, green, green. With the mountain range sort of
defining everything, we rushed past cane fields, banana
plantations and forests of soaring trees.

At Murwillumbah we changed to a bus which took us
through more of that blue-green Hawaiian landscape then
across the Tweed River and into Queensland. From then on
we went past houses. I suppose about thirty kilometres of
them. Many looked like holiday homes, plain little places
on stilts, with a car underneath or perhaps the washing.
Here and there were new-looking apartment blocks. They
were coloured like icy-poles and each one had a swimming
pool. I bet they belonged to television stars and film direc-
tors and things.

On a bend of the road, James nudged me and there in the
front of us was the sea – a thousand glittering hectares of it.
James was pressed against the window. I was almost as bad,
wanting like mad for the bus to stop so we could *really* look.
It didn't of course and in a moment or two the road had
turned again and the sea was gone.

Soon the traffic increased, and so did the number of tall
buildings. They became a forest, throwing forest-shadows
across the bus. Then suddenly we swung to the left, slowed
and stopped. We'd reached the terminal at Surfers Paradise.
An awful loneliness came over me then. I saw other passen-
gers met with hugs and everything. For us there was
nothing. I suppose I should stop for a minute to explain that

since leaving Melbourne I hadn't once let myself think about the moment of our arrival. I certainly hadn't faced the fact that there'd be no one to take charge of us when we left the bus depot. As for Surfers Paradise itself, I'd had some dopey idea it would be a beautiful but sleepy tropical village where people in shorts and those unfinished straw hats walked around with fishing rods and things. I thought they'd be friendly too and come up and offer strangers like us somewhere to stay. At least I thought they'd be *approachable*. Instead they rushed past city-style with nobody sparing a glance for two crumpled kids with a suitcase and travel bag.

Even the people's clothes were city ones. Women wore fifteen centimetre heels and loads of shine and stuff on their faces. We saw a girl go past leading a poodle with a jewelled collar. Behind her were two men hand in hand. One of them had lavender bib-and-brace overalls on with his hair coloured to match. That made James nudge me again but the next moment, spotting a sun-bleached surfie with his board, he grabbed my hand and was ready to drag me in the same direction.

The loneliness I felt seemed to set me apart from everyone, even my brother, and wanting to be somewhere quiet where I'd have the chance to work out if I should stay in such a mixed-up place, I disengaged my hand and with James following, went to the office of the bus depot to ask the way to the beach.

'Turn right at the next corner, love,' said the attendant, so leaving our bags with him, we went to find the sea again. At the corner, the crowd thinned a little and when it did, James began to run. Reaching the Esplanade ahead of me, he plunged across it, looking neither right nor left. A chorus of car horns erupted around him but James, his eyes on the ocean, probably didn't hear them.

On *my* way across the road I passed a woman wearing a hat with two big eyes worked on the front in raffia. Those eyes reminded me of the breakfast egg my mother brought into my bedroom when I had the measles. She'd drawn a face on it and when I saw it I said it looked like Mrs King. (Mrs King's Dad's secretary, a blond lady of about thirty with smooth skin and extremely surprised eyebrows.)

My mother got the giggles when I said that and couldn't stop. She went on giggling in little bursts out in the kitchen until my father told her she was making a fool of herself. I didn't think she was. I really liked the way my mother was that day and used to wish she'd giggle and things more often.

At the top of the beach walkway I stopped to look at the sea. Glass-green waves were bouncing in to boil and foam on the sand and zoom out again. All I wanted then was to be in that water, to be tossed around by it and sort of *cleaned*.

I shouldn't have stood around though thinking all that stuff because while I was doing it, my brother was stripping to his underpants and marching into the ocean. I began to run then, kicking off my shoes as I went and shrieking at him. I remember thinking how frail he looked with his milk-skin and sharp little shoulder blades. Then a wave hit him and he disappeared. I think my brain stopped working, perhaps even my *lungs*, because I have no memory of running on. All I know is that suddenly I was standing at the edge of the water as the sea deposited my brother like a gift or something at my feet.

I suppose I should have shrieked at him then about the danger of surf beaches. What I did instead was kneel in the shallows and hold him while he coughed up half the South Pacific.

The minute he'd stopped spluttering water, James was ready for the sea again. This time, telling him I was coming too, I made him wait while I found someone to mind my bag and shoes. In the end I gave them to a woman sitting on the sand with two little kids. She wore glasses and was bending over doing tiny coloured stitches on a piece of material the size of a bookmark. She didn't *look* like a thief, but in case she was, I put the twelve dollars we had left in the pocket of my shirt before handing her my things.

I think the wave that dumped my brother gave him the monster fright of his life because when he got back into the water he behaved in a practically *normal* manner, staying in the shallows and fairly close to me. I stood in the water too and didn't take my eyes from him, in fact I scarcely blinked because I'm blowed if I could see how even the group of lifesavers up behind us would find someone the size of James once he'd been swept out into that mysterious rocking ocean.

By the time I got James out of the water, his fingers were wrinkled and his teeth chattering. (He didn't want to leave even then but followed when I said I was going anyway.) He stood glaring at me when I stretched out on the sand to dry. That didn't last long though and soon he was into moat construction with the kids of the woman who'd minded my bag and things. I was free then to look at the people on the beach. There were family groups of pale southerners and here and there other bodies as oiled and lifeless as sardines. Spunky young guys, singly and in pairs, walked up and down in pink or lemon tops and dinky little white shorts. I saw a baby drop a banana in the sand and begin to bawl and up near the fence a row of teenage girls took off the bras of their swimsuits and sat topless. I wanted to look at those girls, to work out what sort of people they were to do such a thing, but for some reason couldn't make myself. Instead I concentrated on the surfies battling with their boards to the right of the flagged area.

The husband of the bag-minding woman came jogging towards us in swimming briefs clinging like a *skin*. Seeing him, his daughter squealed and ran to meet him. He lifted her up and she threw her arms and legs around him. The mother looked up briefly and went back to her embroidery. The man put the girl down. She stood with her lips sort of bunched up until he'd stretched out face-down on the sand, then she ran to him, sat astride his back and bouncing up and down, shouted, 'You're my horsey,' over and over. The mother took no notice, just went on stitching her bit of linen or whatever it was. I looked away, my face heating up, and after a while, because I couldn't bear to be near *any* of them, I got up and went to find my brother's clothes. As I did I thought, *One day that woman will put her dumb needlework down and when she does, without giving any warning, she'll decide she doesn't* WANT *a daughter in her life. And I'll bet from then on she won't even want to remember the time when she* HAD *one.*

Chapter Eight

WE WERE ON a bus called the Surfside and watching for the blue roof of a place called Sundale. That's what the attendant at the bus depot told us to do when I asked him the way to the nearest CES office.

'It's up in Southport, love,' he said. 'That's the next suburb north. Take the Surfside and get off at Sundale. The employment office's in Short Street, just an easy walk from there.' With a laugh, he added, 'A short walk to Short Street,' and was so pleased with it, he repeated it as he swung James's bag across the counter.

(On the way back to the depot, I'd seen a man drop a folded newspaper into a council rubbish bin as he walked past. By then I was pretty certain there'd be nothing in it about James and me. Just the same, I couldn't stop myself snitching it out of the bin when he'd gone. In the bus I opened it and whizzed my eyes up and down each page. I was right. There were articles about someone's pet python, and a man who'd attacked a police officer with his wooden leg, but not a word about our mother looking for us. And in spite of knowing all along there wouldn't be, when I put the paper down I had a sort of ache in my chest as if something inside there had been bruised.)

We saw the blue roof the man told us to watch for. We saw it as we crossed a bridge at a place where the Nerang River opened out into a large expanse of water. To the right of the bridge was a fleet of yachts, each one sitting on its own reflection like a piece of giant origami. As we watched, a paddle steamer covered in beer advertisements moved out from under the bridge and as the wash from it reached the yachts, their reflections shattered and then the yachts themselves began to rock.

James pointed to a speedboat towing a man hanging from a pink and red parachute. I lost sight of him almost immediately because the bus turned sharply to the left, turned again and beside us was the Sundale shopping centre.

We climbed from the bus into a place of glarey sun and a few miserable palm trees. On the bus stop seat was a row of old ladies. They had masses of shopping bags and must have been on some sort of organized outing because they all wore beads and hats with flowers and things on them.

'Look at the Mormons!' one of them said. She didn't need to say it because the entire row was already looking as two tall young men in business suits fought each other at the edge of the driveway. I don't think they had much exper*tise* but they were going at it like maniacs. One of them had a briefcase in his left hand and he was sort of holding off his opponent with it while trying to punch him with the right. You've no idea how funny they looked fighting there in suits and ties and everything.

When the fight was over I was extremely depressed because after the first laugh it gave me, it'd made me think of the fight I'd had with Sandra at the station in Sydney and that wasn't something I'd been planning to *dwell* on. James, though, was splitting himself which was a bit of luck because being tired and hungry, he'd been sliding closer to obstreperous every minute. As it was I was able to leave him with our luggage while I rushed into the shopping centre to buy food and a carton of orange juice at the Big W there. After that we struggled around to the back of Sundale then across the road to a vacant block between a football ground and a piece of land where some earthmoving equipment and a few old cars stood.

The block itself had a low wire fence on the street side and on the other, a ricketty jetty running out into the river. In the middle of the block was a little forest of scraggy trees – she-oaks, I think they were.

When James and I reached the trees, we saw a girl standing among them. She had on wide cottony kind of pants with red and green apples on them and she was bending over from the waist drying a mop of dark curly hair on a piece of towel. A small black cat was playing around her bare feet. The girl hadn't heard us coming but as we drew level with her, James trod on a piece of tin which crackled, making her throw back her hair and look at us.

I quickened my step, at the same time giving James a nudge with the case so he'd do the same.

The girl came to the edge of the trees, peered at us and said, 'Polly – that's not you, is it?'

Thinking of Sandra again, I kept walking and didn't answer.

At a smooth piece of ground by the river we squatted down and with the case for a table and James's hunting knife for cutlery, began to eat.

I had my mouth crammed with bread and peanut butter when a voice behind me said, 'I've got a cup if you need one for the orange juice.'

I turned. The girl in the cotton pants was standing a couple of metres away holding the cat. (It had a funny face, mostly black with a white stroke above one side of its mouth like a half moustache.)

My mouth was too full for me to answer the girl even if I'd wanted to and after lowering her head a little, she said, 'I'm not after the orange juice, but if you try to drink it from the carton you'll lose half of it.'

Still chewing, I studied her. In the sunlight her eyes were big and pale like the cat's. Her skin was tanned and sort of *clean* looking and where the cat had its funny little moustache she had two black moles. It was hard to tell her age but she was about my height and I guessed not much older. Certainly she was nothing like that low pig Sandra and thinking, *Perhaps her father owns this block.* I swallowed as quickly as I could and said, 'Thanks. We'd like that.'

'I'll go to the colonial cabinet then.' As she spoke, the girl smiled, showing teeth which were very white but a bit uneven. (Beside each of the two top front ones there was a baby tooth which hadn't grown down properly.)

James and I watched while she went back into the trees. After kneeling and pushing aside a piece of roofing iron which lay on the ground, she fished around in a hole and finally came back to us carrying a plastic cup.

When he'd had a drink, James scooped up the cat. It lay contentedly across his legs and licked his salty arm with a tongue as pink as a flower petal.

'It's name's Bobby Deerfield,' the girl told James. 'You know . . . after the film.'

Not taking his eyes from the cat, James nodded. All his life he'd wanted to own an animal. He had pictures of everything from Clydesdales to Siamese kittens Blu-Tacked up in his room and was forever bringing home stray dogs which always vanished the same night. 'Just as well,' my father used to say. 'We don't have a lifestyle geared to hosting animals.'

The girl turned back to me. 'Have you seen it? The film I mean.'

I shook my head and offered her a drink which she accepted but not in a *pushy* way. (I must stop here to say I was finding it hard not to like her. I mean, apart from anything else, it was great to be having a proper conver*sation*.)

The girl finished the drink and sat down next to me. As she did she wrapped her arms around her knees like someone settling in for a long stay.

'Shall I tell you about it?' she said and when I'd nodded, went on, 'You'd love it. We had it on tape and I watched it over and over till Mum swapped it. It's about this racing driver, Bobby Deerfield – *that's* Al Pacino. I think he's gorgeous, don't you?' She waited for another nod. 'Anyway he goes to this sanitorium place to visit a friend and he meets this girl who's got leukaemia or something and can't stop eating. Lillian's her name and I hated her. Of course they fall in love and she runs away with him, only Lillian's not really in love with him at first. She only falls in love with him when he does this daggy take-off of Mae West.'

The girl leant across and put the empty cup on the case, nearly missing it. 'The first time they go to bed together Al Pacino touches her hair and a hunk of it comes out in his hand but he still doesn't realize she's sick or anything. They travel all around these places in Europe and Lillian goes up in a balloon. In the end she asks Bobby Deerfield to take her back to the sanatorium because her hair's fallen right out and she knows she's dying.'

When she'd finished speaking the girl sat looking out at the river. Her eyes were narrowed and I knew she was seeing bits of the film. After a while she turned to me and said, 'I'm going to be an actress, you know. I think about it all the time. The first thing I did when I left home was have my hair permed and throw m'glasses away.' She laughed. 'I threw them out of the bus as we crossed the border.'

'Can you see without them?'

'Things get a bit blurry. That's how I came to mistake you for Polly, but I get by and when I'm rich and everything I'll get contact lenses. My name's Marcelle, by the way, what's yours?'

I wasn't ready for the question and when I tried to think of a name for myself, nothing came to me. Not even Caroline *Teasdale*.

The girl was watching me carefully. 'You could be Lillian if you wanted to.'

'I don't feel like Lillian.'

'Kate then.'

'That's okay, but half the girls in my *class* were called that.'

We went through a few more names and finally Marcelle said, '*You* choose.'

I sat looking across the river as Marcelle had done and after about an *hour*, I turned to her and said, 'I'm going to be Morgan.'

'Morgan? What sort of name's that?'

When I didn't answer, she said, 'I think it's a man's name.'

'No, it's not. There used to be this woman called Morgan le Fay. She was King Arthur's sister or something and when I heard it, I thought it was the most fatally romantic name in history.'

After giving me another long look, Marcelle said, 'Okay then. You could be Morgan Kristofferson. That's cool and it'd look great in lights.'

'I think it's a bit much.'

'Then you could be Morgan Christie. If you wanted, you could be Morgan l.F. Christie.'

I tried the name out a couple of times myself. 'It's perfect,' I said and we grinned our satisfaction at each other.

'What about one for your brother? It is y'brother, I suppose.'

I nodded and turned to look at James who'd taken off his shoes and socks and was fiddling around at the river edge. 'He'd like to be Max, I'm sure. His big hero is *Mad* Max.'

Hearing what I'd said, James made a fist and gave an overdone victory salute.

'He doesn't say much,' said Marcelle.

'He doesn't speak at all.'

'You mean he's dumb.'

'Well, in that way he is, but in other ways he's well above average.'

Marcelle hurried to say, 'I'm sure he is,' and after that we sat in a friendly sort of silence until she said, 'I thought I'd shimmy over the Main Beach this afternoon. You feel like coming?'

'I'd like to but I've got to find Short Street and go to the CES.'

She bugged her eyes at me as if I'd said I was going to visit death row.

'I've got to go,' I said. 'I've got to get a job.'

'Well you won't get one there, Morgan Christie. That's the last thing you'll get.'

'What do you mean?'

'I mean, in the first place, there's no jobs on the Gold Coast but there's about two million people looking for them. In the second, the creeps at the CES work in with Community Health and everyone so a kid like you'd be picked up straight away. That's what happened to Polly.'

'Who was this Polly?'

'A kid who came through here a few months ago. She had her little brother with her too.'

'What happened to her?'

'She went to the CES like you want to, and was picked up by this youth worker. He was dressed all spunky in a Sweathog T-shirt and jeans and stuff. Polly thought he was cool and told him all about herself. I only saw her once after that so I suppose they sent her home.'

'Is that what they do? Send you home?'

'It all depends. Violent kids, you know, real wild ones that damage property and stuff are given to the cops but if a kid comes from a posh sort of home they try to send 'em back. You can see why. It saves them trouble. That's all they think about.'

'What about kids, well, in the middle? I mean from

decent homes who *can't* go back. What happens to them?'

'Nothing much. If they pick you up they give you a lot of dumb counselling and crap and they try to make you call in at a halfway house or something. Then they let you go. What else can they do? I reckon there's fifty, maybe *sixty* thousand kids like us living out and they can't put us all in homes and places, so they don't try.'

It's no exaggeration for me to say that I was stunned by what Marcelle had said and I was still trying to make sense out of it all when she touched me on the arm and said, 'Just keep out of sight. You'll be okay.'

'But you don't understand. I've got to get a job. Our money's nearly gone.'

'You don't need much. Look, you can stay with us. We get fruit – over-ripe stuff – nearly every day along at the market and we get an odd day's work there as well, packing. We get by.'

'Who's we?'

'Me and Allie and Angel. The other two's down at Surfers. They'll be back later. And there's Joss. He turns up most nights.'

'Where do you live?'

Throwing out her arms, Marcelle said, 'Here of course.'

I must have been boggling at her because she laughed and said, 'It's great. In good weather we sleep over in the trees. When it rains we get in the cars next door. I'm not kidding when I say we manage. Joss usually brings a bit of hot food at night and there's ways of getting other stuff.'

'Who's Joss?'

'A Chinese kid who does all this Karate. He's a bit older than me. Sixteen he is, nearly seventeen. I'm fifteen – almost.'

'How old are the other two?'

'Allie and Angel? Allie's fifteen but God knows how old Angel is. Could be anything from sixteen to nineteen. Y'can't tell. Anyway, how old are you?'

Not dropping my eyes, I said, 'Nearly fifteen too.'

'You don't look it. Never mind, I was telling you about Joss. I know he looks different from us and everything, but he's a doll. He works most nights at the restaurant up the road and he's got a room at this house they call Tibet. He sleeps there sometimes but mostly he comes down here with us.'

'What does he do at the restaurant?'

'Washes dishes and stuff in the kitchen.'

'Is he your . . .' I said and stopped.

'My bloke? No, we're just mates. I've fucked him a couple of times but only in a friendly sort of way.'

The easy way she said a thing like that rocked me. As if it was *nothing*! And the funny part is that instead of feeling I should grab our gear and go, I wanted to stay right where I was and find out more about her.

We sat through another silence. During it I sneaked a few glances at Marcelle. In spite of the way she lived and the things she *said*, she seemed to be well, sort of comfortable with herself.

She was looking across the river to where a line of two and three-storeyed houses stood. They had terraced gardens and nearly every one had a king-sized cabin cruiser tied up in front as well.

'What about the people over there?' I said. 'Don't they dob you in?'

Marcelle shook her head. 'No, it's really weird but they don't seem to see us.' She began to speak in her idea of an educated accent. 'We have our parties on the lawn, darling, and come and go in our white jeans and big white boats, but we take care never to look sideways at the new kind of abos on the river bank.' She dropped back to her own voice. 'It's true. The bastards go right past and don't see us. Mind you, we don't show ourselves *off*. I mean we keep quiet and we don't light fires or anything. But there's times, you know, when you feel like doing something mad like standing on the bank with nothing on and a feather in your navel so that just for once they'd know you were alive.'

In a little while, a wind blowing in from the sea began to ruffle the surface of the river. Then clouds went across the sun and when they did, Marcelle rubbed the tops of her arms. 'The wind comes in about this time every day. It drops again in the evenings but the nights are pretty cold. In about a month we'll have to move into a house. I've got one sussed out up in Leopard Tree Lane. I'll show it to you later.' She stood, 'Come on. let's shift this stuff.'

Between us we carried James' and my things to a spot in the trees where Marcelle began rigging up a windbreak by spiking two corners of a ratty old blanket onto twiggy bits of a branch. (I had to help her because although she had a good idea where the twigs were, she couldn't see them properly.) Then, after using the toilet at the football ground next door, we settled ourselves on the dry tree-sheddings behind the blanket.

It was great sitting there with a friend while traffic hummed away over on the bridge and now and then the rainbow sail of a surf-ski flitted past the trees. Marcelle and I went on talking while James, who'd followed us, stretched out and in spite of himself I'm sure, fell asleep. The cat, purring madly, got onto his chest and fell asleep too.

Marcelle looked at them and laughed. 'Cop Bobby,' she said. 'I think he's given me the flick. I've had him since he was four weeks old, y'know. Mrs Cassidy in the flat next to us gave him to me and when I left, I put him in my old lady's sewing basket and he left with me.' Stretching out on her back, she said, 'Do you want to hear about my old lady?'

'Of course I do.'

'Well, Mum and Dad broke up because of his betting and Mum went to work at a photographer's. This was in Sydney, by the way. She was developing photos and stuff in a little shop in the city. The next thing I know she's had her hair streaked and is having it off with this young bloke of twenty. *Twenty!* Then she moved him into our flat and from then on the happy home fell apart because all the silly bitch wanted to do was sit in his lap and fiddle with his hair. She even squeezed his bloody blackheads for him. Can you believe it?' Marcelle sat up again to look at me. 'Before long she'd stopped cooking and everything. Just came home each night with kebabs and coleslaw and stuff. That's when I counted up m'savings and moved out.'

'With Bobby in a basket?'

'Right.'

'Marcelle?'

'Yes.'

'Can I ask you something?'

'Sure.'

'I don't know how to.'

She sighed and moved, leaning over to prop herself on one elbow. 'I know. You want five bucks. Right?'

The cheesed-off way she said it made me laugh. 'No, it's nothing like that. If you want to know, it's about sex, I suppose.'

'Sex-I-suppose.' Marcelle laughed too. 'Are you asking me what it's like?'

'No, of course not. I'm trying to ask how you can talk about it so *easily*. As if it's nothing. Yet other people make such a big thing out of it. I mean, at our place it was supposed to be so awful or sacred or something that no one even mentioned it.'

'Like the Pope going to the toilet.'

'That's it exactly. And yet everyone knows he does.'

'Often probably.' After giggling a bit, Marcelle was quiet, then she said, 'I think what's gone wrong with everybody is that they've made such a big hushed-up secret out of sex and all that stuff that it's driving them all mad. It's like having a nuclear bomb in the rubbish bin at the back door with the lid on it and some people are trying to take their bombs out and look at them and other people are tying the lids down tighter.'

There was a long silence between us while we both thought about it. I heard boys' voices start up over on the football field and the little thud of them kicking a ball around. Finally I said, 'My father fucked me and then went out of the room as if it hadn't happened.'

Marcelle didn't answer and I said, 'That's why I left.'

'Nothing else to do, is there?'

'Did it happen to you too?'

'No, I was lucky there. My old man was too busy with the racing papers to know I was in the flat. I don't think he knew Mum was there either because I once heard her tell Aunt Bet that the only thing he wanted to fuck was the TAB.'

Marcelle had been looking towards the river but suddenly she rolled over so that she could see my face. 'If it's worrying you,' she said, 'forget it. It happens to everybody, or almost.'

'But it can't. I mean, if it did, everyone would know.'

'I reckon they do. That's the bomb they keep the lid on. Everyone *knows* about fathers getting at their daughters but no one talks about it.'

'But *why* don't they?'

Marcelle wrinkled up her forehead. 'Because I suppose if it was brought right out into the open, then everything would just fall apart. I mean, how could judges and people like that send you to gaol if everyone ad*mitted* that they were taking off their wigs and rushing home to get into their daughters?'

I thought about that, then I said, 'So what can we *do*?'

'I don't know. Honest I don't. Just live out here like this, I guess, where we can have our own rules.'

There was another silence which I broke by saying, 'What about men? Don't they come here and hassle you?'

'Yes, sometimes, but mostly they're old winos and it's

easy enough to dodge them. When one of them *moves* in, we shift camp for a few days. There was a night though about three months back when a gang of bikies pulled in here. It was just on dusk and Allie was here alone. The bikies came cruising round the road then one of them saw her and turned back and came in here still on his bike. The others followed him. They started out being friendly but smart-arse. You know. Then they said they were going to fuck her and was she going to be nice about it or did they need to quieten her down first.'

'What did she *do*?'

'She was standing over there by the river so she backed slowly down the bank and as soon as she felt the water on her feet, she turned and thrashed out into it, clothes and all. When she was a fair way out she invited them to come and get her before the sharks did.'

'What happened?'

'They stood on the bank bitching at her for a while, then they turned away and got back on their bikes and rode off.'

'Wasn't she scared?'

'She was *shitting*. It was cold and getting dark but she said she'd made up her mind she'd drown before she'd let them touch her. As it was she nearly did drown. The tide was going out and she got carried down past the bridge. In the end a bloke fishing helped her out.'

'Are there *really* sharks in there?'

'The locals say there aren't but Allie says that night she could feel them all around her whether they were there or *not*. She shook for hours afterwards, I can tell you that. When the rest of us got back we took the risk and lit a fire because she couldn't stop. I guess it's because of those blokes really that Joss comes down here at night.'

I sat thinking about Allie and the bikies. Then I looked at Marcelle. With her hair dry at last and making this mass of curls around her face she was well, pretty but gutsy too and with a little shock I thought, *I like her more than I've ever liked anyone bar James, and that's different.* I went on looking at her, then I told her about the fight I'd had with the girl in Sydney.

Marcelle loved the story. 'I can just see you pulling the bitch's hair,' she said and laughed. 'Look out any bikie who fools with you.'

Her words made *me* feel gutsy and I settled back on the tree-sheddings and feeling good about myself for the first time since who-knows-when, dozed off.

Chapter Nine

A VOICE WOKE me. I'd been having a dream and
thought I'd heard a police siren. For a moment I
thought I was still on the train, then I saw the sky
and remembering everything, sat up to see a boy standing at
the edge of the trees. His head was against the sun and all I
could see of him was the round shape of his head with the
sun sort of radiating out from it.

From behind me, Marcelle's voice said, 'Morgan meet
Joss,' and the boy, not speaking, gave me a funny little
bow.

It was an extremely theatrical moment. I mean with the
sun making a kind of halo around the boy's head and the
bow and everything. I squinted my eyes and tried to see his
face but it was impossible and all I got was the impression of
someone so foreign beside the drab old Australian trees that
he could have come from outer space.

He turned from me to Marcelle and it was then that I
remembered my brother. Looking wildly round the clearing, I said, 'Where's James?'

'Max, you mean.' Marcelle moved so that I could see her.
'He's over by the river floating boats he made out of paper

and stuff.' She grinned down at me. 'Don't worry. I've been watching him.'

I nodded and looked again at Joss. His back was to me and I saw his coarse blacker-than-black hair with every thread sort of separate. I noticed too how thin he was and the fact that he was taller than most Chinese kids I knew.

'I'll see you tomorrow,' he said to Marcelle. His voice was a surprise. Instead of being a quacky sing-song, it was flat and Australian and decidedly unexotic. His walk was an Asian one though because after he'd given me another of his funny little bows, he left and as he went I saw that he was looser in the hips than Australian boys as if the bones there had been connected with a different *fitting* or something.

Outside the fence he stopped for a moment and spoke to these two girls, then he left them as well and went off in the direction of the highway.

'I think it's Allie and Angel,' said Marcelle as the girls turned in at the gateway and came towards us.

Her eyesight had let her down again. I knew that because there was nothing of a bikie-baiter about either of the girls. One of them was tall and so thin you wouldn't believe. She had long fair hair and wore one of those floaty long-sleeved dresses they sell in Indian shops. The other was no more than a hundred and sixty centimetres with light brown hair shorn off to about fifteen *milli*metres. Her dress was a short striped one hitched up in front by a stomach that looked about three years pregnant. Both of them wore thongs and the pregnant one carried a canvas shoulder bag.

When they were close to us the tall girl did this funny thing. Without speaking or anything she veered off and sank to the ground with her back against a tree and her eyes closed.

Watching her, I thought, *God, I bet it* IS *Angel because she looks like one with her floaty dress and hair and long fragile eyelashes. That means the* RETARD *is Marcelle's friend Allie.*

The shock of it made me look at the short girl again and because I had no intention of examining her swollen stomach, I concentrated on her eyes. They were grey and sort of shiny with a lot of little flecks in them of the colour that Miss Kingsmill our English teacher used to call *russet*.

The funny thing is that I'd seen a pair of eyes like that before and although I realize this isn't the place to interrupt my story, I think that what I have to say about the other pair is quite interesting. They belonged to Elli Johannesen's mother, who sometimes came to serve in the tuckshop at school. Mrs Johannesen had grown up in Holland where her father was a leader in the Resistance movement during World War II. Because of this she didn't see very much of him during those years but there were times when he'd turn up unexpectedly and stay with his family for a day or two. When that happened he used to hide in a secret room they'd made behind the coal in the cellar. (To make the wall he hid behind look genuine, they had a tap sticking out of it connected to a bucket of water at the back.) Anyway, one day the German Gestapo came to search the place when he was hiding there and they lined up his wife and children while one of them held a revolver at the mother's head. They said that unless the children told them where their father was hiding, they'd shoot her. The children remained as dumb as my brother James and in the end, after trying the fake tap and everything, the Germans went away.

Mrs Johannesen's father survived the war and when it was over was decorated for bravery by the Dutch Queen and later by the King of England as well.

That story really impressed me when I heard it and I used to look at Mrs Johannesen in the tuck shop and wonder if I'd be as de*fiant* as she was in such circumstances.

I can't tell you how funny it was to see the same eyes on the girl in Queensland with her shorn-off hair and everything. (I forgot to tell you that in her left ear she had three silver stud earrings. The bottom one had a sparkley stone in it which might have been a diamond. In fact, I decided it was because it was so small.)

Beaming as if she expected us to *love* each other, Marcelle said, 'Morgan meet Allie. Allie meet Morgan le Fay Christie.'

The name made Allie raise an eyebrow and while she was doing it, Marcelle pointed to James and said he was my brother Max. Then she added, 'He's a good little kid, but dumb.'

Allie looked from Marcelle to me and back again. 'What kind of dumb? Can't talk or just plain dumb?'

'He can't speak,' I told her.

Allie gave me a bit of a going over then with her Resistance eyes. She was about to say something but Marcelle got in first by asking why she and Angel were so late getting back.

'We've been back a good while,' said Allie. 'We've been over by the bridge watching all the drama.'

'What drama?'

Allie laughed then, making her eyes spark and showing teeth that were absolutely perfect. I can tell you that if it hadn't been for her daggy hair and Great Dividing Range stomach, she could have gone on television and advertised someone's toothpaste for them.

'This big hot-shot poser was sailing across the Broadwater underneath the parachute. You know how they do,' she said. 'Every so often he'd zoom down and bang his bum on the water, then fly up again. Only he misjudged one trip down and banged his bum on someone's launch instead.'

'Shit!' said Marcelle. 'Was he hurt?'

'It didn't do him any good, right? For one thing the speedboat towing him kept going for a bit and he was dragged off into the water.'

'So what happened?'

'It took them a long time to get him out and in the end that yellow launch from Air Sea Rescue turned up. They brought him back and by then an ambulance was waiting.' She stopped there and frowned. 'If you want to know I was sorry for the poor bastard but must admit that when he hit the boat I laughed m'self legless.'

Marcelle said, 'We heard the ambulance, didn't we Morgan?'

I nodded, but by then Allie had turned away and was looking for a place to sit. When she had, she plonked her bag between her feet and said, 'We had our own bit of drama down at Surfers. Angel here put on a turn in Orchid Avenue. Didn't you, mate?'

Without opening her eyes, Angel made a sound, half-sigh, half-grunt. After that Marcelle and I waited and when Allie had run her hand over her mouse-fur hair, she said, 'We were sloping along past those pricey shops up the northern end, when Angel began to shake and stuff. The next thing I was walking alone because she'd decided to sit on the kerb and there she stayed.'

'God, man, what did you do?'

'Tried a bit of blackmail but that didn't budge her. By then I was shitting because I thought that any moment she'd start to chuck and when she did, I knew some old tart in one of the shops would ring the cops.'

'So?'

'So I left her and raced, or rather waddled, to the nearest caff and got her a milkshake with double the dose of flavouring in it. She got most of it down, thank Christ and held it, so I hauled her up and got her as far as those tables in Cavill Avenue where people sit to play chess.' Allie stopped for breath, and again Marcelle and I waited.

'I parked her there and went as fast as I could round to the shop where that kid Darryl works and after a bit of hassle got a couple of TCs from him.'

'You mean he *gave* them to you?'

'Darryl? Like hell. The bastard knew he had me hanging and I had to give him the last of the dough I got from m'bracelet. But at least Angel came good and I've still got one TC left. That'll see her through because her dole cheque comes tomorrow.'

'I thought you were cutting her down,' said Marcelle.

Before answering, Allie looked at Angel and gave this big sigh. 'I am,' she said. 'You know that. It takes time, that's all.' The next moment, she'd turned again to tap me on the ankle and say, 'Hey, are you the two kids the Victorian cops are looking for?'

It seemed to take my mind half an hour to get from the subject of Angel and TCs – whatever *they* were – to Allie's question. And when it did, about as long again to realize that people in our family were trying to find us. Having got that far I knew my mother had gone on television to ask us to come home, just as I'd imagined. My heart moved then. I felt it. Felt it move inside me like a pe*ony* or something responding to sun. Altogether it was about the best moment of my life and while I was still glowing from it, Angel opened her big sort of empty blue eyes and said, 'Take no notice of her. She's having you on.'

I stood staring at her and she said, 'She's crapping. She doesn't know anything about you.'

'Yes, she does,' I was almost shouting. 'She even knows where we come from.'

Marcelle said, 'She guessed, that's all. Anyone would.'

'*How* would they?'

'By your clothes. The way you talk. Lots of things. Sydney-siders can always pick Vickies.'

I told her I didn't believe her but inside me my heart had shut up shop again.

'It's true,' said Angel. 'Ask her.'

I looked at Allie who spread her hands and shrugged. 'Okay. So I made a joke and it fell flat.'

'So it should've,' said Angel, leaning back and closing her eyes again.

I turned from them, looked across the river and clamped

my teeth down onto my bottom lip. More than anything I wanted to bawl, but I was damned if I was going to let a pig like Allie see me doing it.

I heard Marcelle say, 'She didn't mean it, Morgan.' Instead of answering, I left them and went to the river where I sat on a rock and stared across at a house with dark blue shutters.

I stayed there a long time and no one came near me. Once Marcelle called me to come and have a slice of rockmelon but I didn't answer. I suppose I was in the same state I'd been in when I left my Aunt Penelope's house a couple of days before. I even thought of killing myself again – of swimming out into the rippley water and sinking under until nothing but my hair was left to float and then in a little while that would be gone too. Even the fact that James had left his boats and gone out onto the rotting little jetty and was bouncing up and down on the end of it in this really dumb way didn't bother me. He kept looking at me when he did it and that didn't bother me either.

In the end it was Allie who stopped him. Going to stand at the start of the jetty, she called to him, 'Hey, sport, come here. I've got something for you.'

James stopped bouncing and stood looking at her in the way kids do when they're not certain if they're being conned or not.

'I must've known you were coming,' said Allie, 'because I got these down at Surfers today,' and she produced a pair of red rubber thongs from behind her back and dangled them.

Still wearing the suspicious look, James left the end of the jetty and walked towards her. She went a few steps towards *him* and they met a couple of metres from the shore. James looked at the thongs, then grinned at Allie and took them. He spent a moment or two undoing the tie that held them, before bending and putting them on. From where I was I could see they were at least two sizes too big but that didn't seem to worry my brother who flicked his feet around in a sort of dance. When he stopped, he positively *beamed* at Allie.

'Not too big?' she said and when James shook his head, went on, 'I grabbed them and shoved them in m'bag but when we got outside the shop I found they were too small for my feet.'

I stood then, and in this loud voice said, 'If that means they're stolen, my brother doesn't want them.'

Allie turned around to face me, not quickly or anything but by the time she did she had two patches of temper showing on her cheeks.

I hated her, and I met her eyes bang-on and said, 'Giving a kid stuff that's stolen only teaches them to do it too.'

I saw her sort of puff her breath out, then she dropped her eyes and walked off the jetty. I thought she was going back to where Marcelle was but she didn't. She came to me instead, stood in front of me and looking at me again said, 'Morgan, there's something you need to learn *instantly*. If you want t'stay here and hang around with us, you'd better be prepared to help y'self to things you really need because no one in this shit of a world is going t'give them to you. And if you haven't got the guts f'that, then you'd better go back where you came from.'

Meeting her eyes again, I said, 'I don't call a pair of thongs something I really need.'

'No, but your brother does, dickbrain.'

'Oh, yes?' I could feel some temper patches showing on my cheeks too.

'Oh, yes! In case you don't know it, people exercise their dirty bloody greyhounds all round here. They shit everywhere so the ground's crawling with bloody hookworm. Which means bare feet are out. Right out.'

'That's a lie,' I said. 'Marcelle doesn't wear anything on her feet.'

'Yeah, well Marcelle's just the one f'him to copy, isn't

she? I mean we should all have glasses so we could chuck them away and go around knocking into everything and tripping over everything until our legs are black and blue like hers.'

'If it's true about the hookworm, then James's got his school shoes. He can wear them.'

'Max, y'mean,' said Allie and she said it sort of automatically as if she'd spent a lot of time correcting people when they called someone by the wrong name. 'If you want him to clomp all over the Gold Coast advertising the fact that he's from the south, go ahead and do it, but in the meantime, the thing I'm trying t'tell you is that either you nick things or you go under.' Her voice had sort of run out of steam as she spread her hands the way she'd done before. 'It's up to you.'

I guess I'd run out of steam too because I said, 'I don't want my brother learning to steal, that's all.'

'Then take him home.'

'I can't.' The words came out as if I had a mouthful of *flannel* or something and then an awful thing happened because I stood there on the river bank with that girl I didn't like watching me, and began to cry. I didn't make a noise or anything, just stood with my eyes feeling sort of cooked, and a stream of tears running down and dripping off my chin. I'm not sure how long that went on but suddenly Marcelle was there too, putting her arms around me and saying, 'That's good, man, let it out and in a little while you'll feel better and we'll all be mates again.'

I did as she said. I mean I pushed my face into her hair until I could feel her bone against mine, and I bawled and bawled while Marcelle held me and patted me. Then Allie was holding me as well. I could feel her arms, and her stomach too, against my hip. I think we all stood there bawling until Allie backed off a bit and said, 'Jesus Christ, all this over a pair of thongs. How'll we be when we do a bank?' And after that we were laughing as well as crying and in the end we wiped our faces on bits of tissue and didn't quite look at each other but I, for one, felt a *lot* better. I mean I didn't exactly *like* Allie, but I knew I could put up with her if I had to, and when she said, 'I'll take the kid over to the shop for a carton of milk. That's something he does need,' I didn't object. She must've expected me to because she was walking away but turned back to grin a bit and say, 'I'll pay for it. This time anyway.'

I grinned a bit too and she went to where James was and said, 'Okay, Maximillian, let's go,' and without even looking back at me, my brother went off with her with his big thongs making this slapping sound against his feet.

Chapter Ten

I**N QUEENSLAND THERE** isn't any evening – the dark comes down, whoosh, about six o'clock, so in our squat among the trees, we used to go to bed extremely early. With no television or even a fire to stare at, Marcelle and Allie would stretch out beneath their ratty blankets and pass the hours between seven-thirty and eleven by pretending they were writing a film. They'd invented all these characters and each night wrote a few more scenes. As they went along they designed the sets and costumes as well and when they were doing *that* part, Angel would sometimes come out of her fog and join in.

You'll probably die when I tell you the stuff they were writing but when I got to Tibet and I told Xam about it, he said it almost certainly had socio*logical* significance because no doubt it was made up of their unconscious needs and desires, so I'll go ahead and tell you anyway.

That first night, we went to bed with my brother wedged between Marcelle and me. (The girls had told me this revolting stuff about how gangs of men on the Gold Coast con young boys with promises of trips in racing cars and helicopters and things, then imprison them in special houses where they use them for sex and finally overdose them on drugs. I wasn't sure whether to believe these stories or not but agreed it was best to have J-Max where we could *defend* him if we had to.)

When I first heard the outline of the film, I thought Allie had found a really sneaky way of getting at me because – would you believe – it was about this girl, Gemma, who wanted to play cricket. I lay and listened with my cheeks getting hottish again but as the story progressed I worked out there was no possible way anyone in Queensland could know about my grandmother's cricketing days, let alone connect her with me. Besides it soon became obvious even to a lame-brain like me that neither Allie nor Marcelle knew that girls do play cricket and have their own Tests and everything.

The film started with this really smashing scene in Coonabarabran, the country town where Gemma lived. She was alone at the cricket ground with the setting sun slanting down through trees, and she'd bowl down the pitch, then run after the ball, pick it up, walk behind the stumps and bowl back the other way. (She had to do all this stuff alone because the boys in the town wouldn't let her play against them. That bit really reminded me of Barb and for a while I considered telling my new friends about her. In the end I didn't because in the first place, I didn't think they'd believe me, and in the second, if they did, I thought they'd think I was some big smartarse or something.)

Anyway, in the film Gemma sticks at the bowling practice until she wins a competition and gets to meet this gorgeous fast bowler, Dennis Hampton, who is visiting Australia with the English Test team. Gemma, who's been totally *rapt* in him for about five years, goes off the planet because he seems to be just as rapt in her.

After all these romantic shots of them walking round the town hand in hand, and others of Dennis showing her how to improve her run-up, there's one where they have sex among fallen jacaranda flowers behind the cricket pavilion.

Apparently there were big arguments about this scene because Allie wanted it to be tough and sweaty, with the camera concentrating all through on Gemma's face in order to show that what Allie called the first full fuck in a girl's life isn't necessarily a su*blime* experience.

Marcelle didn't agree, saying her first fuck had been delicious from the word go. So things were deadlocked until Angel said, 'The way to shoot the scene is start out tough and end up delicious.' (When they told all this stuff to me, I didn't say a word, just listened and listened.)

Instead of staying with Gemma, Dennis goes back to England with the rest of the team. And the only time she hears from him again is when she gets a postcard saying what a great time he had in Coonabarabran.

Too wrecked after that to concentrate on cricket, Gemma takes a job with her brother the local vet. In the surgery there she meets this Russian ballet dancer, Sergei, who has high cheekbones and slanting Tartar eyes. (He's in Australia making a film and his poodle has been hit by the producer's Mercedes.)

Bored out of his brain with the outback, Sergei is attracted to Gemma because she's beautiful and sad and practically the first woman he's met who doesn't fall all over him. When *he* leaves the country, Gemma goes with him. (The poodle, Natasha, stays in Coonabarabran with Gemma's brother.)

The trouble is, though, that Sergei's as gay as a guitar, and when they get to Paris, takes Gemma to his hairdresser and has her hair cut and styled like a boy's. Then he takes her to his tailor where he orders dozens of suits and pastel shirts and things for her.

Together they travel through Europe, always being photographed and written up in glossy magazines. Sergei tells everyone that Gemma is a boy who's had a sex operation and because of that, all his gay friends want to have sex with her. She always refuses and in time becomes the toast of the international set.

That's as far as the film had got because Allie and Marcelle were arguing about what should happen next. Marcelle wanted the couple to run into Dennis Hampton somewhere, but Allie said, 'We've done that bit. What we need is a new direction. Something tougher. Something that *matters*.'

The argument went on until their voices petered out and I knew they were asleep. J-Max had been asleep for hours and Angel, who'd spoken a few times during the argument was quiet and probably asleep too. *This is my chance*, I thought, *to go through everything I've seen and heard since getting here. To sort it all out.* But there must have been too much to sort out because all I did was lie listening to the hum of traffic over on the bridge and now and then, the panic-bleat of a siren.

In the end, the thing I thought about was my mother, and when I did I remembered all these really dumb things, like the way she'd bring the washing in from the line in a big Fijian basket, and how she loved raspberry jam on toast for breakfast. I lay awake for a long time then, trying to work out why I wanted to see her so much when she'd hate me if I *did*.

Some time in the night I saw Angel roll from underneath the blankets and sneak away. I even sat up a bit to watch. At first I thought she was going over to the loo but instead she went to the gateway and turned right. It was still wondering if I should wake Marcelle and tell her when I fell asleep, and in the morning, finding Angel where she was when we went to bed, I told myself that seeing her nick off must have been part of some dumb dream.

'What happened to the Chinese kid last night?' I said. 'I thought he was coming back.'

'He went to Brisbane to see this exhibition of kick-boxing. I guess he stayed the night up there with his mate.' Marcelle paused before saying, 'Were you disappointed when he didn't show?' She was grinning at me and watching my face so I rolled over in the water and looked the other way.

We were at Main Beach, lying in the shallows beneath a clean and windless sky while J-Max constructed this elaborate bunker nearby. Every so often a wave would move our bodies sort of *languidly* and then drain away from us again.

Because I could feel Marcelle still grinning at my back, I said, 'Tell me about Allie and Angel. Have you been with them long?'

'About four months, I s'pose. We met at the fruit market just after I got here.'

'Angel does drugs, doesn't she?'

Marcelle waited while a wave washed over us, then said, 'Angel? She's hooked like a barramundi.'

'And Allie wants to get her off?'

'She tries but I don't see her doing it.'

'Why doesn't she take her to one of those places where they de*tox*ify you?'

Taking off Angel's slow voice, Marcelle said, 'Because Angel doesn't want to go.'

'Have they been together long?'

'About six months, I think. Angel was studying music down in Sydney at the place she calls the Con. She got kicked out for never turning up and went to Casino with some bloke who shot through with her bits of jewellery and stuff. Allie found her in a bad way down there and she's been trying to hold her up ever since.'

'How did she get hooked?'

'Christ knows – I've never bothered to ask. I mean, how does *any*body?'

'Does Allie do drugs?'

'No. Allie's pretty straight.' Rolling onto her back and squinting up at the sun, Marcelle said, 'Things'll be better for the pair of them soon because when the baby's born, Allie'll be on welfare too.'

I said, 'The *baby*?' in this silly squeaky voice and Marcelle spun her head to look at me.

'Don't tell me you didn't notice?'

'Of course I did. It's just that I didn't think of it being *born*. I mean I didn't . . . '

Marcelle interrupted me. 'It can't stay where it is, can it?'

We both shrieked after that and finally I said, 'I suppose it's going to be adopted.'

'Not on y'life. That's why Allie split from home. Y'see, she had this boyfriend, Mike, who was apprenticed and everything. They'd been going together for about three years. That's where she got the diamond earring. Anyway, he was killed on his motorbike and a fortnight later, Allie realised she was in the club. When her Mum and Dad found out, they told her she had to get rid of it.'

'So she left?'

'Right – because Allie means to keep that kid no matter what.'

'But how can she when she lives out in the open? I mean, where will it *sleep*?'

'Allie's got all that worked out. With the welfare cheque, she'll have enough for a room like the one Joss's got. In fact he said she can have that till she gets fixed up.'

'What about its clothes and a pram and all that stuff?'

'She won't need a pram straight off, will she? As for the clothes, one day next week we're going round the op-shops to get a proper layette. And although Allie doesn't know it, I've still got the money from m'last day's packing and I'm going to buy nappies and things with it as a surprise.'

'What if it gets sick? Babies do.'

'Allie says it won't, because she'll be looking after it

twenty-four hours a day. And anyway, don't forget the hospital here's free, so if it gets a wog or something she can take it there.'

We stopped talking then to watch this really old couple walk out into the water. They were wrinkled and brown like the nuts you see in health shop windows, lying there with a bunch of wheat and a couple of pumpkins. Both of them had on funny old swimsuits but you could see they didn't care. His was a baggy pair of shorts gone greyish and hers was an old-fashioned black suit which showed a band of crepey white skin at the top of her legs. As they went past they gave us big false-tooth smiles and when the water was up to their knees, they each scooped up handfuls and splashed it onto their chest. Then they lunged into the surf and swam out past the breakers to where the sea was fairly calm. They had to dive under waves and everything to do it and when they had, Marcelle said, 'I hope when I'm old and a mess and everything, I'll have the guts to go swimming and stuff like that.'

I said, 'You don't think you'll ever get *that* old, do you?' And we both shrieked again but afterwards we were quiet for a long time as we watched the old pair out in the sea with just their heads showing like two seals.

In the end I asked Marcelle why Allie's parents hadn't wanted her to have the baby.

'Worried what the neighbours'd say, I suppose, but her old lady said it was because there wasn't room for a kid. She works at home, Allie's Mum. Does sewing for this old fart from Vaucluse with a lot of dress shops. So the house is always full of half-made dresses and stuff. Allie said she gets paid peanuts and works about a hundred hours a day, and she's always tired and hard t'get on with.'

'What about her father?'

'He's as weird as a washing machine. He teaches wood-work at a tech school and he and Allie's Mum haven't spoken to each other for about thirteen years.'

At that stage, J-Max abandoned his earthworks and came to stand close to us so that he could listen. Marcelle shot out a hand and grabbed his ankle. They fooled around splashing each other for a while, and when they were sick of it, J-Max sat in the water facing us while Marcelle went back to her story.

'It's true what I said. Allie's olds don't speak. What they used t'do, was pass messages through her. She told me her old man doesn't really live in the house. I mean he eats there and has his shower and everything but he sleeps out in the shed in the back yard on this camp stretcher beside the motor mower. She said he's got a tranny out there and some pigeons and a bit of lino on the floor. Every payday he puts fifty bucks for his board on the kitchen table and that's it.'

Marcelle stopped talking then to watch the pair of old seals who'd finally come back to shore. After flashing their false teeth at us again, they went up onto the sand, towelled themselves down and took off on a run along the beach.

'What *groovers*,' said Marcelle and we laughed again with J-Max joining in.

When we were laughed out, I asked Marcelle to go on with Allie's story.

'There's nothing else t'tell. She just left like I said.'

That's all I got out of her but I did learn one other thing that first morning down at Main Beach. Marcelle's legs *were* covered with bruises. They were in a range of colours, the older ones pale and lemony, more recent ones still dark and angry looking.

Chapter Eleven

AFTER LUNCH THAT day Allie made me go shop-lifting with her. (She called it foraging.) I know I'm a piker and everything, but I tried to get out of it by using my brother's morals as an excuse.

Fixing me with her Johannesen eyes, Allie said, 'He eats, doesn't he?' And I had no answer for that.

Allie had several foraging systems, all of them simple. When briefing me, she said that only simple ones worked. Her favourite was known as the bottomless-bag stooge. By that I mean that in her shopping bag she had this false bottom resting on two fifteen-centimetre strips of wood. Going through the checkout, she'd pay for some fiddling item, flash the empty bag at the girl and leave with a hidden cargo of cheese and things.

She told me about kids who empty out the contents of a Cornflake packet behind stuff on the shelves and fill it with dearer things, and of others who'd follow some granny around the supermarket putting in their trolley exactly what she put in hers. Then, while she was dithering in front of the cat food or something, they'd switch trolleys and sail off with her handbag. (Allie looked down on that particular stooge, saying, 'We don't scav on pensioners, only on companies.')

On the day I'm telling you about, Allie draped a beach towel around my neck, then we crossed the road to Sundale and after leaving J-Max with Marcelle and Angel, rode the escalator up to the Big W. I'm not joking when I say I felt like someone mounting to the scaffold. I kept thinking something would inter*vene*. But nothing did and then I was in the store and following Allie on legs which no longer had any connection with the rest of me. I can't tell you how cool *she* was, giving me a tub of Nuttelex margarine and telling me to hold it in the crook of my arm under the towel. After that she grabbed some milk and led me towards the line of checkouts.

The tub of margarine felt the size of a suitcase and I knew nothing on earth would stop the checkout girl seeing it. But I was wrong about that because as Allie plonked the carton of milk on the counter, she leaned in towards the girl – a gum-chewing blond about her own age. 'Hey, your ear-rings are just *fab*,' she said. 'Where did you get them?' And after that the girl was too busy telling her how much they cost and everything to even notice me.

Going down on the escalator, my eyes were still sort of out of focus with fright and at the bottom I grabbed Allie by the arm and said, 'Don't make me do it again. Honestly, I *died*.'

She was staring at me and I said, 'Can't you see? If I get caught, Max and I'll be separated. He'd have no one then.'

'Yes, he would. He'd have me, for one. But it won't come to that because you can forget the foraging.' She surprised me by putting her head back and laughing so that I saw her excellent teeth. 'If you want to know, you were a dis*aster*. You had *guilty* written all over you and if I hadn't started that dumb conversation, the girl would've pressed the panic button for sure.' Still laughing she set off to find the others.

After that humiliation we caught the Surfside bus as far as Leopard Tree Lane so Marcelle could show me the winter quarters she'd picked out for us. (On the bus I sat by myself and stared out the window at the tourists and things in the shopping centre. From where I was I could hear Allie and Marcelle giggling and guessed they were talking about what I looked like with *guilty* written on my face.)

Leopard Tree Lane turned out to be a steep little street running off the highway, and the safe-house, as Marcelle called it, was a deserted white weatherboard built up on stilts, Queensland style. It stood in a madly overgrown garden, facing the Broadwater with another little house in front and a high-rise office block at the back. Marcelle told us she'd already sussed it out, the safe-house I mean, and that someone as small as J-Max could easily shimmy through the bathroom window at the back and open the door for the rest of us.

Taking care not to *look* at the house, we drifted up the lane which led us into Scarborough Street and from there we went to the market. That was my second surprise for the afternoon. I'd expected something like an extra-large fruit shop. Instead it was a sort of bazaar, housed in this big tent. Perhaps tent isn't the right word because it was about a hundred metres long and had three gigantic steel posts supporting the roof section. Because of the sun beating down on all that canvas, the air inside was hot and smelt of people's sweat and rotting fruit. You also got a whiff of incense now and then from the dress shop run by girls wearing saris and all this Indian jewellery.

Jammed between fast food stalls was a place where they sold revolting ornaments like baby-shoes made from sea-shells. At another, some woman read the Tarot cards, but according to Marcelle she was hardly ever there.

'She belongs to this spooky church where they talk to dead people,' she told me, 'And I've heard that when things are slack she'll read the cards for five bucks.'

'A rip-off at five *cents*,' said Allie and marched us on.

The fruit stall turned out to be about ten times the size of an ordinary fruit shop and had every kind of fruit you've ever heard of – all of it cheap. Little pineapples, the ones they call 'roughs' were twenty cents each, and bags of passionfruit, a dollar. The place was run by a Basque family, and Pablo, the one Marcelle and Allie always tried to see, wore a black beret and smoked daggy little cigars. He was a short roly-poly bloke with snapping black eyes and he kept trotting out the same lame jokes. For instance, he'd tell some old dag with shorts and scaly legs that the figs were as sweet as a virgin's kiss. I didn't like him much but the other girls used to laugh at his jokes and kid him along and in the end he'd load them up with bananas and a paw-paw that wouldn't see another day out.

That first time we went there I was watching this Japanese couple picking mangoes out of a box and *sniffing* them, when Pablo shouted, 'Catch this, sweet'art,' and landed a watermelon in my arms.

I said, 'Oh,' in this silly way and was ready to thank him but before I could he'd bobbed behind me and the next moment his fingers shot between my legs and hooked up into my vagina. For a second or two I was sort of paralysed, then I dropped the watermelon on the floor, and dodging and bumping my way through the crowd got outside and into the street.

I was *flying* and was at the post office corner before the others caught me. They wouldn't have caught me at all if Gerry, the cook from the Chinese restaurant where Joss worked, hadn't picked them up, but anyway while I was waiting for the lights, this blue utility pulled up beside me with J-Max and everyone grinning from it.

'Hop in,' called Marcelle.

I shook my head and just before the lights changed, Angel, who was in the front, opened the door and scrambled out and joined me on the footpath.

That was another surprise. Angel hadn't made any other friendly gestures towards me. Not that she'd been unfriendly. It's just that I'd been mostly invisible to her. Anyway, I went slowly after that with Angel's stick arm sometimes brushing mine and when we'd turned at Short Street and were heading into the seaweedy wind, she said, 'You shouldn't take any notice of Pablo.'

'Not take any notice!' I yelled. 'He shot his rotten hand right between my legs.'

An Australia Post guy straddling his little motorbike in front of a shop heard me and gave this leery whistle. Ignoring him, Angel said, 'Pablo didn't mean anything by it.'

'Not much, he didn't.'

'No, listen Morgan, I'm serious. He does that sort of thing because it's an *agony* to be alive – if you know what I mean.'

'No, I don't!'

'Then I can't explain. But it's not the Pablos you have to watch. What he does, he does in the open. The whole world can see for all he cares.' Angel stopped walking to get her breath, and feeling I owed her something for getting out of the ute, I stopped too.

When she had her breath, she said, 'Poor old Pablo sees you as the top banana in the young and sexy league and by touching you the way he did with half his family looking on, he's . . . well, acknowledging the fact that he can never have you.'

'He's dead right about that.'

'But Morgan, he probably doesn't even want to. If you pulled your underpants down and said, "Okay, Spunky, help y'self", I'll bet he'd be gone like smoke.'

'You'd be joking.'

'No, honest. Look – what I'm trying to tell you is that the ones y'have to watch are the blokes who never let on they see you, let alone want to fuck you. The ones you pass in the street with their wife on their arm and never looking sideways. They're the ones to dodge because they're ready to go like a *geyser*.'

There was something in what Angel said, and I knew it, but instead of saying so, I kept quiet and when she'd looked at me a while with her made-in-heaven eyes, she said, 'Come on, we'd better get home while there's still some watermelon left.'

'Don't tell me they've still got it?'

'Yes, Allie picked it up.'

'She would!'

We started walking again and when we'd turned the next corner and were heading for Sundale, I said, 'If I'd taken that melon after letting that bloke feel me up, I'd think I was the same as a *prostitute*.'

'Not much of a feel-up, and anyway, if your vaj's all you've got to use, what else can you do?'

'I'd rather starve.'

'You won't always feel that way because feeling that way's a luxury. Whether you like it or not, men run the world and to every single one of them, the old vaj is just another kind of folding money.' She did a bit of a gasp for breath and went on, 'I reckon as long as you've got a *choice*, you're okay. I mean, if you do something for money and you've made the choice to do it and no one else, then you're still in front. So hang onto that choice, Morgan. I wish t'Christ *I* had.' After saying that, Angel fastened her teeth on her bottom lip and didn't speak again until we got home.

I thought Allie would blitz me for chucking the melon away but she was too busy fiddling round making a plate of fruit salad for J-Max. They were pretty thick, Allie and my brother, and hung around a lot together. Their friendship deepened that afternoon when J-Max found a seagull which'd had its feet fastened together by a rubber band. (How could *anyone* be such a bastard?) The poor thing couldn't stand properly, let alone get a grip on the ground for a take-off. All it did was flop around in this pathetic way with one wing flapping. God knows how long it's been doing that because when J-Max spotted it by the jetty, it was close to exhaustion.

Allie was the one who caught the seagull and got the rubber band off its legs. It took her a long time, with both her hands being badly pecked and although she swore a bit she kept on being gentle with the bird. The trouble was though, that when the band came off we found its feet were useless and it still couldn't stand. What Allie did then was put it in Bobby Deerfield's basket and march it off to the vet's place up near the Southport School. Needless to say, all through the rubber-band-removing operation, Bobby was frothing to get at the seagull and I don't suppose that exactly helped it. Anyway by the time Allie and J-Max got it to the vet's, it was dead. Allie then stooged my brother into believing the damn thing died happy because it'd known someone was trying to help it. I thought the help had probably finished it off, but Allie's sermon went down well with J-Max and for the rest of our time at the river he was always finding tailess gekhos and things to show her. I've got to admit though that when it came to getting him past things like video games, she had the touch. He'd spot one in an arcade and if tired or hungry or something, would put on a full-blown temper-turn when I tried to move him on. That's where Allie came in. She'd tell him she wanted to show him a house where twenty-year-old Siamese twins lived and he'd believe her. Of course she'd show him some ordinary house with the paint all washed off in Queensland storms and nothing more spectacular inside than a fat fox terrier, but by the time my brother found that out, Allie's description of what twenty-year-old Siamese twins looked like would have shot the video game right out of his head.

The other person J-Max got along with was the Chinese boy, Joss. To tell you the truth I've been putting off talking about Joss because I wasn't exactly rapt in having him around. For one thing he wore these flat black Kung Fu shoes you buy at the market and if he wanted to, he could move without making a noise. I found that spooky but J-Max thought it was brilliant and spent a lot of time trying to do the same. The other thing I found spooky about Joss was that I still hadn't *seen* him properly. I mean he only turned up after dark and anyway I didn't feel disposed to stare at him in case he thought I wanted him to stare at me. So what I had to do was try to grab a look at him when he was looking somewhere else.

I think I said earlier that the shape of his head and his bowing and everything made him seem as foreign as someone from another planet. Well, the first night he brought food to us, I found the most foreign thing about him was his *nose*. It didn't stick out the way ours do. Instead it sat there, small and rounded on the end as if someone with not bad taste had popped it in place when the rest of him was finished. His hair was different too – thick and straight and black enough to be a wig. More than once I thought I'd like to touch that wiggy hair to see if it felt the same as, say, J-Max's, but of course I didn't do it.

Something else I watched was the way Joss treated Marcelle. I still hadn't got over the casual way she'd mentioned having sex with him and I wanted to find out if he despised her the way my mother said boys do if you let them take smaller liberties than *that*. Well, all I can say is he didn't seem to despise her. It's true he called her silly names like Marzipan and Marsupial, but each time he did, he gave her this smashing smile and it seemed to me that he liked her in an easy-going, distinctly unsneaky way. I mean he must have, to bother making *up* the names. So in the end I decided that the Chinese have a different attitude to sex. Either that or my mother was lying in the first place.

At the restaurant where Joss worked, they had two 'sittings' at dinner and between them, he'd come down the hill with hot food for us in takeaway cartons. Later in the night, he'd come back again and if we were still awake would squat beside us for a while to talk. Then, wrapping himself in this old duffel coat, he'd doss down nearby.

After a diet of sandwiches and fruit and stuff, I can't tell you how good that Chinese food tasted. The first time we had it, though, I was about to dive my fork into something Joss called *hong shao zhu*, when Allie looked across at me and said, 'Not bad, is it, for scrapings off the plates?'

Fork in mid-air, I stared at her, and J-Max copying me, did the same.

'She's stooging you again,' said Marcelle. 'It's supposed to be off the plates but Gerry gives us fresh stuff instead.'

'Why would he do that?'

I didn't look at Joss when I spoke but he was the one who answered. 'I take it as part of my wages.'

'Joss doesn't believe in having money,' said Marcelle. 'He says all he ever wants to own is a bed, a chair and a book he can change for another as soon as he's read it.' She waited for him to comment, but all he did was put another dollop of food on J-Max's plate, then he straightened up, gave us one of his funny spaceman bows and left.

Another thing I should tell you about Joss is that although he was born in Australia and everything he can speak Chinese. Sometimes the girls got him to say a few words so they could laugh at the flutey sounds he made. He used Chinese too when showing J-Max bits of Kung Fu, which he called *Goong Fu*. (Marcelle told him he was a dickbrain to be teaching foreign words to someone who couldn't speak but Joss told her that if my brother grew up to be a master spy or something, being able to understand Chinese could be a great advantage to him and after thinking it over the rest of us agreed.)

At night, very late, when everything had stopped except the traffic on the bridge and the groaning old dredge in the Broadwater, I'd lie awake looking through the branches at the kingsize Queensland stars and wait for Joss and Marcelle to get together. I thought he'd come and wake her or perhaps give a soft whistle so she'd sneak out of bed the way I'd seen, or thought I'd seen Angel do on the first night.

I'm not sure even now how I felt about Marcelle and Joss having sex because although I was dreading it happening, I also *wanted* it to happen, even if it was only to get it over.

As things turned out, there was no reason for me to be so concerned about it because I'm certain on those nights Marcelle stayed where she was. And if it comes to that so did Joss.

Chapter Twelve

ALTOGETHER WE STAYED by the Nerang for three days and a bit. On the day that was to be our last, I thought I'd made this big breakthrough with Allie. To start at the beginning, there was some sort of regatta that day and because of it, a lot of locals got up at five and started zooming their boats all over the Broadwater reminding me of those half-spider, half-fly things that zip around on the surface of ponds. With throttles wide open, the boats zipped up and down the river as well, and with no hope of getting back to sleep, we lay where we were and bitched about them.

'I think we should move,' said Allie. 'Go to the safe-house earlier than we'd planned.'

When no one answered, she went on, 'Last night the Bette Midler type inside me got me up fourteen times to pee. I did a teaspoonful each trip and ended up with frozen feet so I reckon I'm ready for the pleasures of an indoor toilet.'

'We could move tonight,' Marcelle said.

'Too many people about,' Allie told her. 'Let's leave it till the town's simmered down a bit.'

We got up soon after that and were having breakfast

when this tiny red plane appeared and began doing all these fancy rolls and things above us. It looked as if it was made of *paper* or something and its engine gave out this awful high-pitched buzzing sound.

'Jesus, all I needed was the bloody Red Baron.'

When Allie said that, J-Max raised an imaginary rifle and after following the plane's flight for a while pretended to shoot it down.

'That's what you need in the film,' I said.

Allie swung her eyes to me. 'The Red Baron? Don't be such a nugget.'

'Not the Red *Baron*, a Palestinian freedom fighter with a gun.' I waited to be put down again and when I wasn't, said, 'You know – one of those spunks who used to be on the news every night hanging out of a jeep and firing his gun in the air. He could kidnap Gemma and hold her for ransom in this old farmhouse in Normandy or somewhere. Sergei tries to rescue her and blows it but by then she's in love with the Palestinian anyway.'

'What happens in the end?' Allie's voice told me she was at least interested, so I said, 'There's a big battle scene where the freedom fighter gets shot and dies, and Gemma goes to his village back in Palestine to wait for the birth of his child and learn to make bombs and stuff.'

'Did you think this stuff up just now?'

'I started last night. The rest came when I saw J. . . ., I mean Max, raising the rifle.'

Allie turned to the others. 'She's got to be some sort of genius, right? So we make her top script writer and a partner in Nerang Films as well. And we get going this *minute* on the freedom fighter and the snatch scene.' Patting the ground beside her, she said, 'Move over here, Morgan le Fay Christie and let's get into it.'

It was a great moment for me because I knew I'd managed to click at last with Allie the way my brother did on day one. And that wasn't all because when we started work on my scenario I found I could see the sets as if I'd *been* there. I mean I could see the stone floor of the farmhouse in Normandy and stuff like that. And I could see the characters and their clothes and everything. When the others found this out, they said I had some sort of gift. I don't know about that. All I know is that you go on this high when you're being creative. I did anyway, and I knew then that I didn't want to spend my life being a paediatrician in some poxy office thirty floors above the ground in Collins Street. Instead I wanted to be a film writer and make up things about people, even make the *people* up and later watch them come to life as the actors and the person with the camera took over.

I was still on the high when Marcelle and J-Max and I took off for Main Beach. On the way we brought two Chiko Rolls and shared them as we walked. (I can still remember the taste of those rolls and the way I felt with the traffic jazzing past and the boom of the surf over on our left.)

The beach was practically deserted, with the red danger flag snapping on its pole and big angry-looking breakers crashing in on the sand. The only people in the water were the wet-suited surfies who probably didn't care if they lived or died as long as they went out on a Big One. After watching till we were goosebumpy, we voted to leave the surfies to it, and splurge on hot showers at the dressing sheds.

Up on the Esplanade, we met Allie and Angel who'd travelled down by bus. Allie then proceeded to spoil *everything* by blasting me for sending J-Max off to the men's shed.

After calling me a cretin, she gave me the story again about little kids being snatched by blokes with Ferraris and things. And when I said I wasn't sure I believed it, she turned and with her gross beachball stomach stuck out in front of her, marched into the men's shed herself. I still can't believe she did that. I know there was no one *there* that day, but you could tell by the way she went, that if it had been thirty in the shade and the place swarming, she'd have done it anyway.

With Allie taking over my brother's life like that, there was nothing for me to do but go around the corner to the women's shed where I undressed and got under the shower and stood bawling like a little kid myself. I don't know what I was bawling about. I just knew I wanted to be home again looking at the flamingoes on the shower curtain and knowing there was a family outside to work things out for me.

I was still crying when Marcelle bobbed into my shower stall to offer me her cake of Pears soap. Being her, she dropped it and when I bent to pick it up, I saw her skinny legs with all the bruises on them. I did this crazy thing then. I put my arm around her legs and sort of pressed my face against her knees. Then I stood up and thanked her for the soap as if I hadn't done it at all.

Instead of asking if I was out of my tree or something, Marcelle smiled, showing her baby teeth, and said wasn't a hot shower heaven.

'Fabulous,' I said, 'and when we're famous film people we'll have six every day.'

In the afternoon we went to the food market as usual. It was Saturday – did I mention that – and in Southport most of the shops and things were open. It's on Saturdays that the locals come out of the gingerbread houses which line the off-peak streets. A lot of them are old, the locals, I mean, and they wear plastic raincoats and daggy cotton dresses. I must say that they're much friendlier than the business people and tourist types who crowd the streets on weekdays. (One thing I really liked about the locals was the way you'd see them sitting in a row on the bus stop seat cackling away like a lot of water-birds.)

At the market, as we were going past the Indian shop, Marcelle grabbed both Allie and me by the arm. 'Look,' she said, 'the Tarot lady.'

'Save your money,' Allie told her. 'She's a crooked old cow who keeps files on everyone.'

But Marcelle didn't hear. She'd let go of us and was already on her way to the woman's stall. In her haste she tripped on this narrow wooden *plinth* thing across the doorway and stumbling, crashed into the card table inside.

'Enjoy your trip?' said the woman seated there. (Later Angel said she looked like someone called Papa Doc who used to run Haiti. I don't know about that – all I know is that she was as spooky as hell with this teaky skin, little round glasses worn halfway down her nose and a squashed old Akubra hat. Beside her was a baby asleep in a pusher. It must have been her grandchild because she was at least as old as my mother's Mum, who's sixty. On top of every-thing else, she was enormous, with thighs overflowing her chair and a sleeveless blouse showing off arms which had an extra rolling-pin shape of flesh hanging from the elbow to the armpit.

Marcelle who'd got herself together, blurted, 'How much?'

'Got fifteen dollars, love?'

'Ten,' said Marcelle quickly and the woman, giving the tiniest smile, nodded her to the chair opposite. While the rest of us crowded the doorway, Marcelle was handed a pack of cards which she cut five times and passed back.

Slowly, stopping more than once to tap one with her forefinger, the woman laid the cards in a complicated pattern on the table. Then she sat for ages looking at them. (The baby in the pusher must have dirtied its nappy and in the hot little room the smell was practically *nuclear*. I must say I felt really weird waiting to hear someone's fortune with that smell filling my nose and mouth.)

Finally, sweeping the cards back into a pack, the Tarot Lady looked up at Marcelle and with absolutely no expression on her face said, 'Come back next week, love. I'll read for you then.'

It took Marcelle a moment or two to realize she was being given the flick. 'You said you'd read now. You said you'd do it for ten dollars.'

'Make it next week and I'll read for nothing.'

Marcelle sat staring at the woman but she'd already moved her eyes and with her head tipped back was looking at me. 'Come here.' She lifted a fat forefinger and beckoned with it.

I didn't move and someone, Allie probably, pushed me forward.

'Show me your hand.'

Feeling stupid, I help out my left hand, palm up.

'The other one, love.'

When I'd switched hands, the woman said, 'Yes, I thought so. Tears everywhere. All around you. Torrents of them and not all yours.' She paused and pointed to a line running from the middle of the palm to the base of the third finger. 'See this? The sun line. And strongly marked. You, my girl, will end up with everything you want.' She leaned back in her chair then and flapped her hand towards the door. 'Now shoo off, the lot of you. I want to clean up my grandson's bum.'

Away from the smell, Marcelle said, 'The chaddy old bitch. Why did she do that to me?'

'To get you in, of course,' said Angel. 'She knows you'll be back next week handing over your fifteen bucks without a murmur.'

'She said she'd read for me for nothing.'

'You didn't swallow that, did you?'

'What about Morgan? She told her all that stuff about tears and everything.'

'She told her precisely fuck-all like she always does.'

'*You* went to her once.'

'Yes and she told me I was going to get a sum of money with a nine in it.'

'So?'

'That was the week someone hooked m'dole money.'

Allie broke the argument up by saying, 'Let's slope along to the fruit stall and ask Pablo to read the passionfruit pips for us.'

Everyone laughed then except Marcelle and even she laughed a few minutes later when J-Max spotted one of the girls at the Indian shop putting up a sign which read, 'Cumma Bums – $4.00'.

Chapter Thirteen

IT WAS A dramatically moonlit night and so cold we decided to risk lighting a little fire. Instead of sitting around to enjoy it though, we were hiding in a bunch in the trees listening to the sound of this boat coming in towards our jetty.

I heard Marcelle whisper, 'They never come this side,' then, 'it's coming right in,' and all through that and the sound of the boat and everything I could hear Allie saying the word Jesus over and over.

We heard the boat's engine slow until it was just ticking over. There was this burst of loud laughter and I found I couldn't bear it. Couldn't bear just standing there like that, and shaking off Allie's hand which must've grabbed me earlier, I sneaked to the edge of the trees and looked out. J-Max followed me. I didn't hear him and didn't look to check. I just felt him there.

I had to squint to see what was happening down by the jetty because the house behind it on the other shore was lit up like crazy. Every room was lit and its terrace, the garden, even the mooring strip at the water's edge had burst out in this bloom of coloured lights. In spite of that I made out three man-shapes in something that looked like an army duck.

It was like watching a scene on television. I saw one of the shapes bend down then straighten up and slide over the side to land in the water with a splash. Turning, he reached his arms back while one of the others handed him something. There was more laughter and someone said, 'Push us out a bit, will y'mate.'

The next moment J-Max blew *his* breath out in a laugh and I heard Joss's voice say, 'Hang on. I'll dump m'parcels first.'

I called Marcelle and the others then and we watched as Joss went back into the water to push the front of the duck around. When it had turned and moved out into the river, this burst of 'Up There Cazaly' floated back from it. (The word *fuck* had been added to the lyric.)

We met Joss back at the fire. Allie, who had her cool back in place, said, 'You frightened shit out of us. Anyway, what's this *hello sailor* bit?'

Instead of answering he leaned down and plonked his parcels on my case which was still being used as a table. Then he looked down at his wet Kung Fu shoes. Still looking at them, he said, 'My grandmother's feet were only eight centimetres long.'

'You're *pissed*,' said Allie.

Again he didn't answer, just sat on the ground in a movement that for *him* was a clumsy one and began pulling his shoes off.

While he was doing that Marcelle leaned over and opened one of the parcels – a cardboard box about twenty-five centimetres square. 'Wow,' she said, and looking too, I saw a cake with creamy icing on top and these triangles of toffee sitting up like weather vanes.

'Where did this come from?' said Marce.

'A raffle at the Surf Club.'

'No, it didn't. It's the kind Gerry makes.' Levelling a finger at him, Marcelle said, 'It's your birthday, isn't it?' And without waiting for an answer she rummaged in the other parcel and pulled out a can of tomato juice. 'What are we supposed to do with this?'

Joss produced a bottle of vodka from inside his duffel coat. 'Mix this with it.'

'It *is* your birthday,' said Allie. 'That's why you're not at work. You went to the Surf Club and got pissed instead.'

While they were still arguing, Marcelle went to find things to drink out of. *I* scavved around for wood and built the fire up a bit. When I had, I sat on the ground opposite Joss and took my first really good look at him. He was staring into the fire and with the light from it flickering on his face, looked as if he was made of gold or something like a statue in one of those ruined temples they have in Asian jungles.

He must've felt my stare because suddenly he raised his eyes and said, 'It's true about my grandmother's feet.'

'Being eight centimetres long?'

'Yes.'

I didn't know what to say to that. I don't think the others did either and we waited while he poured some vodka then tomato juice into the cups and glasses on the case. Leaving the drinks where they were, he said, 'They'd been de*formed* by binding. That's something they used to do to girls in China.'

'What do y'mean?' said Allie, reaching for a drink.

'They bound them to make them small,' said Angel. 'I've read about it.'

'Don't be mad. They wouldn't be able to walk.'

'They couldn't. Not properly. They sort of swayed about and it was supposed to be a turn-on. So were the bunged-up feet. Their lilies they called them.'

'That's disgusting,' Allie said. 'And anyway, how would they do the housework?'

'They didn't have to. They had slaves and servants for that. *Their* feet were okay.'

'I still don't believe it.' Allie passed me her drink. 'How

could you stop anyone's feet growing?'

Joss said, 'I told you. They bound them up. They started when the kids were about two and the bones still soft. They bound them up as tight as hell with strips of cloth.'

'But *why*?'

'I told you that too. It was supposed to be a turn-on.'

'Like bondage?' Allie, who'd been sitting, got up and tottered around the fire as if she had crippled feet. 'Hey Joss, is this a turn-on?'

The solemn way he said, 'Not at the moment,' made us shriek. Even Angel did.

I tried the drink then. There was no taste of alcohol, only tomato juice so I took a few big mouthfuls. Almost straightaway I got this glow-y feeling inside me. It felt so good I took another drink and let J-Max have a sip.

Angel, who'd been scrabbling in her tatty bag, produced a tin of makings and began to roll a cigarette. When she had it alight, I smelt marihuana in the mixture. (I'd smelt it before. On the school bus at home the big kids used to pass a cigarette around the back rows and in a little while fall off the seats laughing.)

'You *scab*,' said Allie. 'You've had dope all along and never let on.'

'Only as much as a midge could shit. Besides I was keeping it for an occasion.'

'And this is it!' Marcelle reached out and took the cigarette from Angel. After a couple of puffs, she passed it to me.

I put my hand out to take it and was suddenly back in my room at home reaching for my father's glass of wine. I was soiled and worthless again – the girl my mother despised. I stayed frozen like that with all my pleasure in our party gone until Marcelle said, 'Morgan le Fay, are you paralytic already?' She was sitting cross-legged with the cat lying in the hammock of her skirt and she grinned at me in a way that made this surge of feeling for her spread out in my chest. *I don't care what I am,* I thought, *as long as I'm like her.* And I took the cigarette and smoked some of it. (After all that, it was a disappointment to me – just a tobacco taste. I'd expected something else but I'm not sure what.)

The cake made up for the dope though. It was smashing. Thin little layers of biscuit stuck together with fluffy stuff flavoured with rum. We cut it into six chunks and ate the lot. While we were hoe-ing into it, Allie asked Joss to tell us about his father's escape from the communists in China.

'You've heard it before,' he said.

'Yes, and I want to hear it again. One day I'm going to turn it into a film.'

'The commos won't let you in to do it.'

'They will when I'm famous,' said Allie and although we all laughed, *I* believed her. (I don't know why I did. Probably because of those Resistance eyes of hers.)

'Morgan hasn't heard it. Neither has Max.'

Joss gave me an inquiring look and after getting all these Harpo Marx nods from J-Max, poured himself a vodka which he drank without adding any tomato juice. Then, after frowning into the fire for a bit, he said, 'The Old Man's family lived at a place called Ruijin or Tiger Ridge. It's in Jiangxi Province, not far from the spot where the Long March began.'

Not being sure what the Long March was, I giggled because I had this vision of a row of *tigers* lying on their stomachs in the moonlight to look down on an ant-line of people in straw hats and frogged jackets, creeping round the side of a mountain.

Joss gave me this surprised look, then stared back into the fire. 'The family had a lot of land and servants and things, and in 1949 when they heard the communists were close, the blokes there thought it'd be a good idea to smoke-off for a while. They thought the panic was only temp'ry; that old Chiang Kai-Shek would crunch the commos quick-smart and things'd go back to being normal.'

Joss settled himself back on his heels and it seemed to me that as he talked his voice became less Australian. Well, not his voice so much as the way these ups and downs crept into it. 'My grandfather was a scholarly old guy who put his inks and brushes away and took off to the west. He didn't think the commos would go that way but they did and as time went on he was caught and shot. Dad went south. My grandmother who had to stay behind because of her feet, gave him these pieces of gold to see him on his way. He did his own Long March then through countryside he said was really something with all these little villages and mountains and valleys and stuff. In the end, he reached the port of Shantou. He was as broke as a dog when he got there though. I reckon somewhere along the way he'd been stooged for his gold – not that he ever admitted it.'

Joss felt around on the ground for his glass and with it empty in his hand, said, 'Dad spent a couple of days hanging round the streets of Shantou, then he ran into this young bloke who used to be at school with him. Their meeting was the biggest fluke on earth and gave the Old Man this big belief in good luck and everything because it turned out his old schoolmate worked for this government department that was flat-out helping students skip the country.'

Joss was staring into the fire again and I don't think he'd have gone on if Allie hadn't prompted him. 'This friend gave your Dad twenty dollars, didn't he, and he used it to get across to Taiwan.'

'Right. He meant to join the army but when he got there he was ill with fever and landed in hospital instead.'

Before Joss could go on there was this loud static-y crackle from across the river and a voice said, 'Testing. One, two, three – Mary had a little . . . ' then it cut off in another burst of static.

We all laughed and Allie, jabbing the opener into a fresh can of tomato juice, said, 'Parties everywhere.'

Joss went to hand Allie the bottle of vodka, knocking it sideways but catching it before any spilt. That made us laugh like mad and when we'd stopped, Allie said, 'Joss's old man didn't join the army at all because the Americans who were advising the military by then, said, "Less men – more machines", and they wouldn't take him. So what he did was go up into the hills where they grow the tea and get a job picking.'

'That's where he met Joss's mother,' said Marcelle. 'She belonged to this rich family who owned all the tea and everything.'

'More good luck,' I said.

Sort of *fo*cussing on me, Joss said, 'They've made it sound like Chinese soap, but it wasn't that easy. Mum came from the poor side of the family and she and Dad had to work for a long time before they had enough to marry on.' He paused and in a softer voice said, 'Lihuan. That was my mother's name.'

'Lee-wahn,' I said imitating him. 'It's pretty. Like a bird's call.' And Joss gave me this smashing smile across the fire.

Still looking at me, he said, 'My Dad was pretty educated and by the time they got married he was working in the head office of the tea company. So was Mum, and by saving like crazy for another five years they had enough to leave China altogether.'

'And they came to Australia,' I said but before anyone could answer me, the heavy metal sound of 'Bon Jovi' rocketed across the river as the party opposite took off.

We laughed again and jiggled our arms and things in time to the music while Joss took advantage of the interruption to pour another drink. This time he added a splash of tomato juice and when he had he reached across the dying fire and gave it to me.

'To the Nerang Gang,' I said and tossed some down.

J-Max, who'd been jiggling with the rest of us, nudged me to remind me he was still there. I was about to give him a mouthful of drink when Allie, reaching past Angel, took it away from me. 'He's had enough,' she said and passed it back to Joss.

I thought that was pretty un*necessary* if you want to know, but because Joss was speaking again, I didn't say anything.

'Mum and Dad didn't come to Oz then,' he said. 'They went to Vietnam – Saigon – and set up business importing tea.' He swilled what was left of the drink around in the glass then tossed it down the way I'd done. 'They stayed there for just on seven years and made a pile but Dad couldn't settle. There was war there too, always had been, I think, and he'd made up his mind that no one, least of all the *Yanks*, would stop the communists. So they sold up, 1967 it was, and that's when they came here.'

'With the Boat People?'

'No the Boat People were later. Dad and Mum came by plane like anyone else.'

He picked a few twigs up from the ground and fed them to the fire. They made a little blaze and watching it, he said, 'They liked it here. They said they felt safe.' He was about to say something else but changed his mind.

Again Allie prompted, 'They settled in Melbourne, didn't they and started importing tea.'

'Right,' said Joss. 'The Old Man's luck was still holding and because of that they decided to have a child. They'd always put it off but anyway I was born and Dad called me Jitung.' He looked up at me again. 'Lau Jitung – that's my name.'

'Where's the Joss come from?'

'Kids at school.'

'Jitung means *follow me* or something, doesn't it?' said Marcelle.

'More like *follow the tradition*. Dad called me that because he wanted me to go to uni then into the business with him but none of that happened because when I was fourteen this bloke turned up. He was a . . .' Joss stopped again, stuck this time for the right word.

Allie supplied it. 'An en*forcer*.'

'Right – this enforcer came from one of the Triads, the Chinese Mafia, that is. He told my old man that unless he paid fifteen per cent of his income to them, they'd burn the warehouse down. Dad laughed at him. He didn't believe something like that could happen here. He was wrong as hell though because it did, only they didn't burn the warehouse. They planted a heap of smack there instead and tipped off the cops.' Holding my eyes, Joss said, 'My Dad was sent to Pentridge for six years because no one believed him when he told them what'd happened. Not the cops or the solicitors or anybody.'

Joss looked down again then but not before I'd seen these two fat tears squeeze their way out of his eyes. Those tears really shocked me. I know it's a dumb thing to say, but I'd never thought of Chinese people *crying*, certainly not Joss because he'd seemed to be so walled off inside himself.

There was a lull in the music from across the river and during it, Allie said, 'By the time all this happened there was only Joss and his Dad. His Mum'd died two years earlier. He was with neighbours when he heard the verdict and he lit out and ran. He got to the Hume Highway and ran until he dropped. The next day he started off again and kept going, scavving for food and sometimes doing a bit of work until he reached Queensland, and he's never been back.' Allie leaned forward to peer into my face. 'Now you know why Joss doesn't want to own anything. He says that if you've got a dollar some bastard thinks it should be theirs but when you've got stuff-all, no one even *looks* at you.'

'But what about later on?' said Marcelle. 'What about when he wants to get married and everything?'

Allie let out a laugh. 'Don't be mad. Who'd have him?'

I suppose it was the vodka because I went silly the way I did down at Main Beach when I embraced Marcelle's knees because I stood, leaned over the remains of the fire and grabbed a handful of Joss's wiggy hair. Using it to pull his head up, I said, 'I would. *I'd* have you.'

The other exploded then. Even Joss laughed, and feeling a real retard I let go of his hair as Allie said, 'If she wants to marry you, Joss, you're done for. The old chook who reads the Tarot cards told her she'll end up with everything she wants.' Turning to me, she said, 'Sit down, Mrs Lau, and I'll tell you . . .'

We never found out what it was she meant to say because instead of getting it out, she bent forward, clutched at her back down low and said, 'Shit! Oh, Jesus!' and drew her breath in with a sort of whistling sound. After a moment she straightened up. 'God! I had this pain. Like a knife. Must've eaten too much cake.' She picked up her cup. 'Better have another drink.' Then, changing her mind she put the cup down again and said, 'I'll go over to the toilet first. You coming, Mrs Lau?'

'Might as well.'

With some help from Marcelle, Allie struggled up from the ground but instead of turning from the fire she stayed where she was with this funny look on her face. 'I'm all wet,' she said. 'It's running down my legs.' And she put her hand between her legs and held it here while she stared around our little circle of faces. 'What's *happening* to me?'

Angel who hadn't spoken for about a *year*, said, 'It's the baby. It's coming.'

Still holding herself, Allie said, 'It can't be. It's too early.'

'That's what happened to my sister,' Angel told her. 'She was buying this brass antelope in the Fijian shop at home when the water broke.'

Allie boggled at Angel. I suppose we all did. Then suddenly Allie was doubled up again. This time making little moaning noises.

By the time she'd stopped, Joss was there holding her

arm. 'You'll have to get to hospital. It isn't far. Can you walk it?'

Allie didn't answer – just looked at him and her face was like Mrs Paisley's was back in Ivanhoe the day she came in from next door to tell us that she'd found her white Chinchilla, Dumfries, dead in the drive.

Joss took time out to study that face, then turning to Marcelle, said, 'I'll call an ambulance,' and after jamming his feet into his still-wet shoes, he took off.

We sat again. There was nothing else to do. No one spoke. I don't think Joss was away long but it was long enough for Allie to double up again and for me to imagine her baby being born there beside the river in the dirt and twigs and stuff.

Joss came back running flat-out. Between gasps, he said, 'The ambulance wouldn't come so I rang the cops. They'll be here soon. I'll take Allie out to the road. The rest of you put sand where the fire was and get the case and stuff out of sight. Then go into the trees and lie down. When the cops come, keep y'faces down.'

We did what he said, bumping into each other and making a hash of things. When the remains of the fire had been covered and everything moved, we ran into the trees and lay where we could watch Allie and Joss out by the fence.

'P'raps they won't come,' said Marcelle and as she did this police car with its blue light on top came around the bend near Sundale and drove slowly along the street.

'Faces down,' I said, shoving J-Max's head towards the ground. 'Don't look up or they'll see us.'

I looked up though. I couldn't help myself. I saw the cop car stop and one get out. There was another lull in the party music and I heard him say to Allie, 'You the kid in labour?' Then he said, 'Don't drop it here, mate,' and opened the back door of the car.

Allie got in and as she did, the cop said to Joss, 'You too, sport.'

Joss backed away. '*I'm* not having any baby.'

'Shut it.' The cop hauled Joss away from the fence and slammed him against the car. There was a noise as his head hit it. I began to giggle then. I giggled fit to burst. Then Marcelle shoved *my* face down into the dirt and when I looked up again the car was flying back along the road and the street outside our camping place was empty.

Chapter Fourteen

W E WERE BOWLING along the highway in the ute belonging to Gerry the Chinese cook. I don't know what time it was but it must've been late because the moon had moved across the sky and anyway the traffic had thinned a lot. I was in the back with Angel. Our gear was there too resting on lettuce leaves and a few withered spring onions. J-Max, clutching Bobby Deerfield, was in the front with Marcelle and Gerry.

After Joss and Allie disappeared in the police car, Marcelle had insisted that we pack and move. 'They'll get out of Allie that we live here,' she said. 'It'll be easy because she'll be shitting herself.'

Thinking of Allie's Johanessen eyes, I said I didn't think she'd give much away.

'Maybe not,' said Marcelle, 'But we're still moving.'

I thought she was planning to go to the house in Leopard Tree Lane but when I mentioned it, she said, 'Not straight-away. We'll spend a few days first down at the Labrador marina, then come back.'

At that point Angel said she couldn't be bothered going anywhere and did Marce think there'd be someone from

Community Health sitting in the labour ward with a notebook taking down everything Allie said.

Giggling again, I said Liz Latimer might be there. Marcelle ignored that and said to Angel, 'I'm not that dumb but by tomorrow Allie'll have a kid and you can bet that some creepy bastard'll be there wanting to know where she's gonna take it and stuff like that.' She knelt to move the cover from the hole she called the colonial cabinet and with her voice muffled, said, 'It won't have any *clothes*, for Christ's sake.' After that she began hauling things out of the hole and when Angel saw that she meant to move anyway, she stood and stretched and said she might as well come too.

It was weird I can tell you packing there in the patchy dark with the music still going full-belt across the river. As it turned out, I didn't have much to do. J-Max's bag and mine hadn't ever been properly unpacked. Just as well because I was at a stage where everything seemed hil*arious*, such as when I tried to open my case at the back and couldn't work out where the catches had gone. J-Max, who'd wrapped himself in a piece of blanket with a bit of it pulled up over his head like an Arab or something, threw himself into the operation. He found missing shoes and things and was the one who finally got our bags closed. That done, he set about helping Marcelle. (If Angel did any packing, I didn't see her but I suppose she must have because when I *did* notice her she was sitting against a tree at the edge of the forest. Her now-bulging velvet bag was next to her feet and she was smoking dope again although she'd told us earlier she had none left.)

When all of Marcelle's stuff was spread out on the ground, she looked at it and said, 'There's no way we can take all this shit with us. Anyway, we won't need plates and things where we're going,' and she began putting a lot of it back in the cabinet.

'What if someone finds it?' I said.

'Tough tits.'

When Marcelle had finally covered the hole up again, she and J-Max began jamming the balance of her stuff into an old suitcase and a collection of plastic bags. They worked fast and when they'd finished, Marcelle stepped back to say, 'What we need now is transport.' She pushed up her sleeve and stood scratching her elbow. 'I don't fancy our chances at hitching so what I'll do is nick up the hill and see if I can con Gerry into picking us up when he finishes.'

She pulled down her sleeve, fiddled a bit with her hair and headed for the gate, stopping on the way to call back, 'Don't panic if I'm a while.'

A while? She was *years*. In fact it began to look as if she wasn't coming back. During the wait I sat with Angel, but when J-Max, who couldn't keep still, went in the direction of the river, I moved so that I could see him. Still in his blanket he climbed onto the jetty, went out a little way and lay down to watch the water through the slats. After a while he stood up and dropping the blanket began to dance this weird little dance in time to the music. He stayed there with his dance becoming more and more spastic until the tape ended. Then, bundled in his blanket again he came back to shore. Going fast, he went past me and out to the gateway to stand staring down the road – not in the direction Marcelle had gone – the other way, the way the police took Allie and Joss. And he kept that up all the time Marcelle was away – out to the jetty, back to the road, stopping sometimes to poke a stick at the place where the fire had been or to pick up an empty can and chuck it into the trees. At one stage he found the vodka bottle and brought it to me. There was still a bit in it, but instead of waiting to see what I'd do, he took off again on his river-road-and-back-again patrol.

Angel and I finished the vodka between us. We drank it slowly, passing the bottle backwards and forwards. We didn't put anything in it, just swallowed it as it was. I thought it'd be *gross* but there was really no taste, just a sort of breathless bite at the back of the throat as it went down.

Not long after we'd finished it, Gerry's utility rolled down the hill and stopped at the gate.

I don't know how to tell you what it felt like to be whizzing along beside the Broadwater in the ute. I don't know how to put it in words because I was sitting there taking everything in but I was sort of *watching* myself doing it. For instance I could see this pot-bellied moon with all the craters and things showing and I could hear the surf over on the other side of the Spit but I was conscious of *seeing* the moon and *hearing* the surf. It made me feel extremely *cool* and I remember thinking, *This's probably how adults feel all the time*.

We were travelling north and at the first big intersection the traffic lights were on the zonk. It took us a long time to get across. I didn't mind. I sat there taking everything in and not caring if it took us the rest of the night.

The next lights were working but the traffic was still held up and for a while we sat parked beside this funny little timber house with fancy shutters and stuff. It was built up on stilts and there was a Moke parked underneath. Seeing it, I wondered if it belonged to the youth worker Marcelle and Allie knew. It looked purple, the Moke I mean, but the lights on the highway were turning just about everything purple so it was impossible to be sure.

Every window in the house was open and the shutters folded back without regard for the cold sea air. The lights were on too and just outside one of the windows I could see this strange Queensland tree with no leaves, just bare branches moving like bunches of fat fingers near the sill. Inside someone was playing a daggy old song on a harmon-ica. Normally I'd have hated it but that night the funny wailing sound seemed so good to me that I closed my eyes for a while to take it in.

We were held up again at the next intersection and this time a van, with a sunset scene on the side and surf boards and spare tyres on top, pulled up beside us. (The two blokes in it were level with the part of the ute where Angel sat.)

The surfie on the *passenger* side had a shaved head and he wound his window down and made a grab at a piece of Angel's floaty hair. Missing it, he said, 'Why don't you get your arse in here, chick. Bang it on some upholstery for a change?'

And do you know what Angel did? She picked up her bag and stood. Then with a flash of her long white legs she climbed over the side of the utility and onto the road. The door of the van opened, Angel got in and the door closed again. At that moment the traffic lights changed and when they did, almost before in fact, the van took off, going fast up the highway with a piece of Angel's Indian dress hanging out the bottom of the door. I went on watching their tail-lights until they'd disappeared in the stream of north-bound traffic.

One saw a surfie and then there were three, I thought and sitting among the suitcases and lettuce leaves, had another giggling fit. It didn't last long though because it wasn't much fun being in the back of the ute by myself and I was glad when Gerry turned in towards the Broadwater at this big neon sign with 'Blue Waters' written on it. (Most things on the Gold Coast have these lame names like Blue Waters and Golden Sands. There's even a Florida Gardens and an Isle of *Capri*. The few names that are halfway cool were pinched from the Aborigines. Tallebudgera Creek, for instance.)

Gerry drove across a carpark with a couple of speed traps on it and stopped at this row of dry-looking trees on the far side. As a matter of fact, the carpark had trees on *three* sides. Put there as windbreaks, I suppose.

Except for a couple of cars on the other side of the park, the place was empty. Empty and sad. I didn't move, just stayed where I was, looking at the dark dry trees and the stretch of concrete until Marcelle came to the back of the ute to say, 'Where the *fuck's* Angel?'

'Gone,' I said, turning to her.

'What do you mean – gone?'

I shrugged. 'Gone. She took off in that van with the surfies.'

'*What* van?'

'The one with the boards and stuff on top. You must've seen it. It had this . . .'

She didn't let me finish. 'Morgan what are you *on* about?'

I got up on my knees and swivelled to face her properly. 'At the lights – the third set, this van pulled up with surfies in it. One had a shaved head.'

'And?'

'Angel got out and climbed in with them.'

'What did she say, for God's sake?'

'Nothing. She didn't say . . .'

'Did she know them or something?'

'I don't think so. She just *went*. A bit of her dress was . . .'

Grabbing the edge of the truck, Marcelle yelled at me, 'Why didn't you tell us. Bang on the window or something?'

I was flabbered. I hadn't seen Marcelle angry before, I didn't know she *could* be angry and in this little-kid voice, I said, 'I thought you'd seen them.'

'Seen them? How could I see them? I can't see *anything*.' And there, right in the middle of her anger, we met each other's eyes and both spurted into laughter.

'Shut up, you two,' said Gerry who'd come to the back of the ute too. 'We're not supposed to be here.' He turned and walked in an impatient little circle. Completing it, he said, 'I saw the van. I even saw Angel, only I didn't know it was her. I remember thinking, that girl's got hair like Angel. Then they were gone.'

I suppose I should stop here for a minute and say something about Gerry. He was a Chinese-Malay of about twenty-six with a big moon face and moony eyes as well. I'm making him sound the pits, I know, but really in a funny way, he wasn't bad looking. He always spoke softly and had very little accent. Except for the way his voice went up at the end of sentences, you'd have thought he'd been born in Australia. He was *married* to an Australian girl and his father owned all these restaurants in Malaysia. When Gerry left school his father put him into the family business but by the time he was twenty-three, he'd run up gambling debts of almost twenty thousand dollars and instead of paying them, his Dad shipped him out of the country. (I knew all this stuff because Joss'd told Marcelle and she told me.) Gerry still gambled a lot. At cards mainly. And the other thing he did was wait all the time for his father to ring him and invite him home.

Marcelle, who'd stopped laughing, called Angel a sneaky bitch. Then more slowly, she said, 'I don't know what Allie's going to say.'

'Allie's better off without her,' said Gerry.

'She'll worry though,' said Marcelle. 'She tried all the time to look out for her.'

'I know that,' Gerry told her. 'So does Angel. That's why she's gone. She's a mighty cool lady. Allie's not available so she's found someone who is.' He lifted his hands. 'Simple as that.'

For a while Marcelle stood looking at the ground, then she said, 'I reckon you're right. I reckon if she hadn't gone tonight, she'd have gone tomorrow. I still don't know what Allie'll say though.'

'Maybe she'll come back,' I said. 'Angel, I mean.'

'No chance. *Angel* will end up shark bait.' Without another word Marcelle went to the back of the truck, let the flap down and began unloading our stuff.

I helped her. So did Gerry. (J-Max had gone after Bobby Deerfield who'd jumped out of the ute and headed for the trees the minute the door opened.) When all our gear was on the ground, Gerry looked at his watch and said, 'Jesus, I'd better go. I told Karen I'd be home early. She'll *kill* me.' He shook his head. 'I must be off m'face to get mixed up with kids.'

Marce was bending over her suitcase and she said something that sounded like, 'Don't bitch. You've been paid.' I'm not *certain* that's what she said. I think it was though.

Gerry said, 'Any time, sweetheart,' and gave her bottom a bit of a slap. Then he got in his ute, started the engine up, turned and with a wave drove back across the carpark.

As he swung into the road, Marcelle muttered, 'One more bastard.' Then, picking up her case and things, she nudged me with one of her parcels. 'Okay man – let's go and suss the place out.'

So we shoved our gear under one of the trees and after that, finding this gap between two others, pushed our way through into the grounds of the marina.

Part Two

THE YACHT

DESTRY

Chapter Fifteen

I STARTED WRITING that stuff about leaving home when I was working at this place called The Rose Club down at Mermaid Beach. I stopped though after a while because I knew I wasn't going to be able to get down the part about what happened to Marcelle. Later, at Tibet, when Mrs Werther who owns it, told Xam she'd heard me crying in my sleep and stuff like that, he said I should try, because in his opinion it was the best possible way to get the grief and everything out of myself. He said if more people did that half the psychiatrists in business could shut up shop.

The day we talked about it I showed him some of the earlier bits. Being such a *scholar* he said he thought it'd be a good idea if I started putting commas where they belonged instead of popping them anywhere that took my fancy. He also said I should try to make the chapters a uniform length. As I didn't intend showing the uncensored version to anyone but Allie, I didn't think any of that mattered, and anyway, how can you make the things that happen to you a uniform length? It'd be like getting up in the morning and announcing that each of the day's events was going to get eight and a half minutes of your time *exactly*.

Xam also suggested that I take out ninety per cent of the brackets. I decided not to do that either but at least I started writing again. I started in the room that used to be Joss's and when I was stuck, I'd look out the window and see the little mountain range that always reminded me of 'Magnum P.I.'.

I suppose what I'm doing at the moment is leading up to saying that although I know it's the pits to come out with the line that sneaking through the trees into Blue Waters was like a dream, I'm putting it down anyway. Apart from anything else, it's true because all the time it was happening I had this feeling that I was about two steps away from myself.

When Marce and I got through the trees we met J-Max who still hadn't found the cat. Marcelle told him not to worry, that Bobby Deerfield was used to travelling and would be somewhere close by watching us. And there in the shadow of the wind-dried trees, she gave us this funny little lecture about cats being just as faithful as dogs if only people had the brains to realize it.

While she was saying all this I stood staring at the forest of masts in front of us. I'd seen pictures of marinas in magazines and places, and the boats there always looked like sardines tied up in pairs. I can tell you sardines were the last thing the yachts at Blue Waters looked like. Sitting on the water just being themselves, they were spooky but sort of *noble* too. There were about fifty of them – big ones and as I said before their masts soared up to make this forest.

The main mooring jetty was on our left and ran some distance out into the Broadwater. Meeting it at right angles was a series of shorter ones which more or less filled the water-space in front of us. The main jetty came back almost to where we were standing and I realize now that the lawns and buildings and things were all sitting on reclaimed land.

Over on our right was the clubhouse. It was made of shiny tiles like someone's bathroom and had a dim light burning inside. On the other side of it was this three-storey apartment block in a sort of Moorish style with wrought iron balconies everywhere and a lot of dark-flowered creeper hanging from it.

The jetties were fenced off from the lawn by cyclone wire with these skinny little doors in it. I was staring at all that wire when Marcelle touched my arm. 'Come on,' she said. 'Let's find a yacht-squat,' and instead of going to one of the cyclone doors, she went to the carpark end of the fence which was hidden from the clubhouse by a palm with un*dressed*-looking roots bulging out from halfway down its trunk. There, she grabbed the wire with both hands and pulled it away from its post.

Going to her, I said, 'Have you been here before?'

Instead of answering she pulled the wire out further and told me to shimmy through. After that I held the wire for her and then the two of us walked along the jetty.

That walk was the *spookiest* thing! I could hear our footfalls following us, could hear the lapping sound of the water and each time we passed a yacht, a sort of humming as the wind touched its rigging.

Marcelle stopped behind another of the undressed-looking palms. I stopped too. I think that by then I really was in a dream state because when she went to the edge of the jetty and began fumbling with a rope tied around this post thing standing there, I thought, *She's going to let that yacht in front of us go*, but I didn't ask her why or anything. Not that it mattered because the post wasn't a post at all – it was a gangplank and when the rope finally fell away, the middle section came down with a rattle of chains and things to form a really cool little bridge over to the yacht.

While I was still gaping at it, Marcelle touched my arm and said, 'Time to get our gear and move in.'

It was then I remembered J-Max. It seemed hours since I'd seen him. In a panic I swung around to find him behind me, pulling faces through the wire. He was wearing Bobby Deerfield over one shoulder like one of those daggy old furs with feet and everything.

I guess the dream state I've been talking about was helped along by the vodka I'd had because I laughed like mad when one of our cases stuck as we pushed it through the gap in the wire and laughed the same way when Marcelle tripped and fell as she led us down into the dark salt-and-diesel smelling cabin of the yacht.

Destry, the boat she'd chosen was about fifteen metres long and was fitted out with a lot of fancy wood panelling and stuff. Altogether you could say it had everything you'd find in a house — a stove, a loo, even a wardrobe just forward of the main living area. There were two bunks in this main area, one along each wall and just before the next doorway, a dining table and seats.

My brother chose that first night on *Destry* to go off his face. While Marcelle was bumping around by matchlight as she searched for a lamp and got it going, he was whirlwinding his way through the cabin, opening cupboards and slamming them shut. He pulled the door right *off* one of them, and days later, when he and I left the yacht for the last time, it was standing propped against the stove. He whirled his way through the forward part too, flushing the loo though Marcelle had told him this was only ever done at sea. (Excited by all the activity, Bobby Deerfield flew round with him.)

In a locker above one of the forward bunks, J-Max found a spear gun and a bundle of spears. After loading the gun he came to stand in the doorway with it levelled in my direction. His eyes were slitted and he looked absolutely *bonkers*. Having seen him like that a couple of times before, I knew I had to do something to calm him down but that night not only my brain but my arms and legs were sort of cotton-y and what I did was lean against one of the bunks and boggle at him.

In the end it was Marcelle who talked him down. She did it by saying in this extremely *casual* way, 'Tomorrow, I'll go to the hospital to see Allie. I guess I'll see the baby too.'

J-Max switched his eyes to her, and when she said, 'Maybe the next day they'll let Max in too,' he lowered the gun until the point of the spear was resting on the floor.

'You'd like that, wouldn't you, Maxie boy?' I said going to him and taking the gun. There were tears in the poor little bugger's eyes so I let the gun fall and held him and rocked him and told him that both Allie and Joss were okay and that he'd be seeing them soon. Then I took off his shirt and pants and when Marcelle had put some blankets onto one of the bunks, we put him to bed. He went to sleep finally with his stick-legs splayed to make room for the cat.

With J-Max flaked, Marcelle made her own tour of the cupboards. She used the lamp for this, explaining that the boat probably had its own electricity; that big yachts have some way of charging the supply up when they're out at sea. 'We don't want to light the place up like Christmas though, do we?' she said, 'And anyway, this old diver's-helmet lamp makes everything really *intimate*.'

She seemed so familiar with things on the *Destry* that I asked her again if she'd been there before. This time she answered, but only briefly, saying, 'Yes, I was once.'

When I asked if Allie and Angel had been there too, she said it was before she met them and then changed the subject by telling me to come and look at the store of tinned food.

There was everything there – tins of vegetables, crab, lamb's tongue, squab, even pheasant. And in a cupboard lined with zinc or something there was enough gin and stuff to last a year.

Using wafer biscuits and tinned lychees we made ourselves a supper then sat cross-legged on the empty bunk to eat it. Marcelle made drinks too – long pink ones tasting of aniseed. Jellybeans, she called them and wouldn't say what was in them.

During supper I asked her if the owners of the yacht were likely to turn up for the rest of the regatta.

'No way,' she said. 'This is an ocean-going yacht. People with boats like this don't take part in piddling little regattas.' She broke into her phoney upperclass accent, 'That's strictly for nerds, my deah,' then using her natural voice again, added, 'The owners of this thing probably only take it out once a year, and go on a trip around the islands when they do.'

'Does anyone live here? On the yachts, I mean.'

'They probably don't even live in Queensland and when they do come, they stay in that posh place over there.' Marcelle gestured in the direction of the apartment block.

'What if someone sees us?'

'It won't matter. Not so long as we're tidy and everything. They'll just think we're here for the day with our olds. Of course we can't run about the place *screaming* but if we keep quiet, it'll be okay.'

'Are the apartments just holiday places?'

'I guess so.'

'Someone must live there – I saw this light in the club-house place.'

When I said that Marcelle was at the table topping up her drink. Without turning she said, 'I think there's a manager or something.'

'*He'll* know we don't belong.'

'Then we don't let him see us.' She turned, the drink in her hand. 'The gates are all locked. So no one's coming in. *Right*.'

'Right,' I said and after a bit of a silence asked what she thought the police would do to Joss.

'It all depends.'

'On what?'

'How he handles cop-shop aggro.'

'What's that supposed to mean?'

Marcelle climbed back onto the bunk, settled herself and said, 'When they took Tiny Timms in down at Broadbeach, they made him strip then they started flipping his wanga with this rubber band and telling him how small it was. The poor little sod's only thirteen and he began to howl. After that they held a revolver at this head – a cocked one – and said that if he told anyone what they'd done, they'd waste him. She leaned forward a bit and peered at me. '*Waste* him. That's the word they used. Anyway he passed out.'

'And what happened?'

'When he came round, they let him go. They had to. He hadn't *done* anything. They pulled him in when he was walking along the street minding his business. But the bastards told him that they'd be watching for him so he went home. Back to Wagga. He said he reckoned it was better to be bashed once a week by his old man than be offside with the cops up here.'

After a while I said, 'And what about Joss? Will they do all that stuff to him?'

Marcelle took a drink then wiped her mouth with the side of her hand. 'I sort of doubt it. Joss's different to Tiny – tougher. I mean it's hard to stir him. Even when he's steaming he doesn't show it. I reckon he'll just take what they hang on him and turn his head away. Of course that might add to the aggro but when you look at it, they can't *do* him for much. He's got a room and a job and everything.'

I was remembering Joss with the fat Chinese tears squeezing out of his eyes. *He didn't look so tough then*, I thought but I didn't say anything. To tell you the truth I was finding it a bit hard to concentrate on the conversation. I'd been sipping at my jellybean off and on while we talked and suddenly it seemed as if the air around me had become *oily* or something because I couldn't even focus my eyes properly.

Marcelle said, 'He was pretty pissed and if they do him on anything, they'll do him on that.'

I made this big effort to see her properly and said, 'What will that mean?'

Waving her free hand, she said, 'Maybe a warning.

Maybe a bond. Maybe three months inside.'

We went to bed soon after that with Marcelle taking one
of the forward bunks and me stretching out on the one
opposite J-Max. By then I wasn't feeling so good. I don't
just mean that I was worried about Joss and everything,
though I was. I didn't feel too good *physically*. Apart from
anything else I didn't like the way the wind was whistling
and clicking somewhere above my head and I hated the way
the boat seemed to be moving. Not just rocking, but
travelling along when I knew it wasn't. The feeling was so
strong I sat up once to peer out the nearest porthole. The
sight of the ghostly rocking yacht next door reassured me
but didn't do my squeamy stomach any good.

I think I slept, then I was awake with just time to get my
face over the side of the bunk before I bucketed. It was a
geyser job – the kind J-Max did when he was a baby.
Afterwards I lay telling myself I had to get off the bunk and
clean it up but I couldn't because I knew that if I so much as
moved I'd be sick again. So I stayed where I was, smelling
the mess on the floor, until I went to sleep again.

I woke some time before daylight and vomited again.
This time Marcelle heard me and came to hold my head.
When I'd finished she cleaned my face with something and
brought me a drink of orange juice. I turned my head away
from it and she said, 'Just get a bit down. It always works
with my old lady. She gets the chucks when she starts on
Tia Maria and stuff.'

I don't know if it was because of the orange juice, but I
did stop vomiting. I was left with pains in the head though
so bad that I felt as if my skull was an eggshell with
something live inside banging to get out. I wanted to ask
Marcelle for Disprin or something but she was cleaning the
floor and before she'd finished it, I'd fallen asleep again.

I woke in daylight to find myself alone. I didn't realize I
was at first. In fact when I saw the light from the porthole

slanting past my eyes, I had this crazy idea for a minute that I was lying on one of the pews in the chapel at school. Then the boat rocked wildly in the wash of something zooming up the Broadwater and I remembered that we'd come aboard the *Destry* and slept there. I sat up then, hitting my already hurting head on the locker above me.

Rubbing the spot and swearing, I looked around for the others and saw instead this note propped at the bottom of the bunk. It was next to snoozing Bobby Deerfield and written in big round letters which said:

> *Didn't want to wake you*
> *but had to go to the hospital*
> *so took Max. Back at 4.*
>   *Love you*
>   *Marcelle Farnham.*
> *S.P. If you feel sick have some more juice.*

I looked at my watch. It said 7.36 but it said the same thing when I looked at it later so I had no idea how far off four o'clock was. The wind, stronger then ever, was making things on the boat creak and groan and instead of getting up for juice, I lay listening to it all. Then I slid into this fit of homesickness. I don't want to go into detail about it except to say that it was pretty bad. I kept remembering this smell in our house at Ivanhoe. Not sultana loaf cooking or stuff like that but the way my mother's wardrobe smelt when you opened it. A mixture of shut-up clothes and herbal hair conditioner.

Lying there alone I howled for a long time. Then I heard this scary sound – a flapping of big wings which came over the yacht and stopped as if some bird had brought bad news or something. I felt then like the ancient mariner in the poem we did with Miss Shadboldt in year six. (I *hated* that poem and still do.)

Of course it was only some sea-bird resting on the

rigging because the next time a boat went by it flew off but its visit was the pits for me and it was then that I decided to go home.

I knew no one in my family would want to see me but I worked out that if I got a room somewhere near to them and a job and sent J-Max to school and everything, in time they'd decide I was okay and want to be friends with me again.

I was imagining myself meeting my mother in the supermarket, imagining how she'd be surprised then really glad to see me, when Marcelle and J-Max came down from the cockpit of the yacht. They came down quickly, one after the other with their elbows stuck out like a pair of birds tumbling from the sky and when I saw them I forgot the other spooky bird and forgot the Ivanhoe supermarket too. In fact it was quite a weird experience to have. One minute I was crying about my mother, the next I was looking at Marcelle with a carton of vanilla custard in her hand, and knowing I'd only go back home again if *she* could go with me.

Chapter Sixteen

WHILE J-MAX rushed to greet Bobby, Marcelle, talking all the time, rummaged in the cupboard for something to put the custard in. 'I've been shitting', she said. 'I thought I'd find you *dead* or something.' Turning for a moment to hold up the carton, she went on, 'I got this stuff because I thought it'd be easy for you to get down. I got it as soon as we got off the bus and I've been carrying it all day.' She'd found a bowl by then and after filling it with custard brought it across to me. 'And what a day it's been! We saw Allie and if you want to know, Max's been an *angel*. I took him because I was scared to leave him here with you asleep and everything. And would you believe, when we got to the hospital the sister let him in. So he saw Allie too.'

I'd tried the custard and was spooning into it like mad. Through a mouthful I said, 'Is she okay?'

'No, she's not. That's what I've got t'tell you. She's off her face with worry.'

'*Why?*'

'Well, she had the baby. She had a boy. They told her that much but they wouldn't let her see it.'

I'd stopped eating to stare at her and she said, 'They took it away from her. They took it away as soon as it was born.'

'You mean they *killed* it?'

'Of course not, dickbrain, they took it to give to someone else.'

'I don't understand.'

'Neither does Allie. Like I said, she's off her face. They told her she signed adoption papers in what they called the prep room or something, and they said it would be better for her if she didn't see the baby. She says she didn't. Sign – I mean. She says all she signed was some form saying it was okay to give her an anaesthetic and she said that if it came to the crunch that's no good anyway because she's under age.'

After a while, I said, 'That's the worst thing I ever heard.'

'I know. And imagine how Allie feels. She's sitting there with her boobs all bound up and everything, and someone else is going to get her kid.'

I *was* imagining how Allie felt and when I did, I had another weird moment because it was then for the first time that I realized I'd be a woman too; that I'd have kids to carry and look after, and sitting on the messy bunk with my head still hurting, I saw this sort of *mother*-path stretching in front of me. And you know what – looking along it I felt good. I think I could say I even felt a bit im*port*ant and when Marcelle said, 'Allie says she's going to fight for the baby, that she'll keep on fighting. She says she'll fight forever,' I said, 'That's what I'd do. I'd go to the *Queen* if I had to.'

In a little while I asked Marcelle if she'd told Allie about Angel going off with the surfies.

'Not exactly. But when she asked where she was and I started spinning, she guessed. She said she'd always known Angel would piss off when the baby came.'

'Did she mind?'

'She said she didn't but I reckon she did.'

After that we looked at each other and found nothing to say.

That evening there was this fireworks display over the Broadwater. It started soon after Marcelle went to get some Disprin at the little shopping centre along the road. We'd looked for headache tablets on the *Destry* and although we'd found about six kinds of *mouth*wash and something called Lubafax, we couldn't see any painkillers. Marcelle said then that yachties are a lot of pisspots, and probably used up the Disprins each time they came aboard. To tell you the truth, my headache had gone but Marcelle went to the shops anyway.

By then I knew a lot more about her visit to the hospital. For instance she'd told me that when she got to the Gold Coast one, she'd been sent away because the police hadn't taken Allie there. Instead they'd taken her to this place in the next street called the Manhattan Maternity Home.

'It's known round here as the Hattan,' said Marcelle. 'And it's real posh. Allie wouldn't have gone there in a fit but it turns out they've got this one public ward.'

She went on to say that about a dozen times Allie asked the nurses there to ring the youth worker, Ingrid Frew, and although they kept saying they would, she could tell they didn't mean it. In the end she stopped asking and made up her mind to go to Legal Aid for help when she left the place.

I'd also learned that no one had seen Joss. Allie hadn't anyway. She told Marcelle the last she saw of him was when the police left her at the Hattan. Her guess was that he'd be shoved before the court on Monday and bucketed with whatever the cops thought would stick.

When the first of the fireworks went off, J-Max and I were sitting up on the deck in the dark. Bobby Deerfield was there too along with a carton of sand Marcelle had fixed for him to shit in. Anyway, I heard this gunshot and spun my head to see showers of colour in the sky. What followed was just great – rockets sunbursting above the black Broadwater, then as the wind caught the *particles* we'd see them zip across the sky like tiny swarms of fighter planes. Often a flower-shape would start to form but the wind always got it before it finished. I suppose in one way that spoilt the display but in another it was good because it made it seem as if the fireworks had a sort of mind of their own.

We stayed there watching for at least an hour. No one bothered us although lights were on over in the clubhouse and we could see people moving round in there. Now and then a lit-up boat slid past out in the channel and once a single green glow, shooting across the water like a star gone mad, veered towards us then away again.

Marcelle didn't reappear until the fireworks were over. If you want to know, she was away so long I though she'd gone back to the hospital. When she did turn up and I asked where she'd been, all she said was, 'I ran into someone I know,' and began to talk about the fireworks. But later that night when J-Max was asleep, she said, 'Morgan, I want to ask you this big favour.'

I was at the sink at the time cleaning my teeth and made a 'Yes' kind of sound around my toothbrush.

'I want you to visit Allie tomorrow instead of me.'

Without turning, I took the toothbrush out of my mouth. 'Why can't you go?'

I felt her step towards me. 'Because there's something I've got to do.' Her voice changed, became faster, 'Morgan I've got this chance. To *be* someone. But I can't pike on Allie. If you won't go for me, I'll have to turn it up.'

I faced her then and said, 'What sort of chance?'

She watched me for a moment then switched her eyes to the nearest porthole. 'There's this guy – he's about thirty or something. I know him a bit and he's got a friend who works on *Vogue*. He wants to take all these photos of me – what he calls a portfolio and send it to his friend.'

'Tomorrow?'

Marcelle clasped her hands together and hunched her shoulders up the way Mia Farrow does. 'Morgan, I couldn't *argue*, could I?'

'I guess not.'

'He wants me to go out with him on this cabin cruiser called *French Mustard*. He said he'll take some *fantastic* photos of me.'

I didn't say anything and Marcelle who was watching me again, said, 'There's no need to look like that, it's on the level. I know because he does stuff for one of the Brisbane papers. And he did an article on the Gold Coast for *Playboy*. I've seen it.'

She started to say something else, but I cut in to ask where she'd met him.

'He was buying cigarettes up at the shop. But I've met him before. He once gave me a lift all the way from Burleigh East to Surfers. He's real nice. He's got two kids of his own. He told me. They're away at school because his marriage is bust up.'

I was quiet a little while and then I said, 'Allie will expect to see you. She'll be watching for you. Specially with the baby gone and everything.'

'I know that. That's why I'm asking you to go. Look Morgan . . .' She reached out and put her hands on my shoulders. 'It's only one day. You can tell Allie what's happened. She'll understand. She means to make something of herself too.'

'What if nothing comes of the photos? I mean, I know it will but just for argument, what if no one wants them?'

Ignoring that, Marcelle let go of my shoulders and put her face even closer to mine. 'Listen. You know as well as me that everyone gets one big chance. This's mine. If I don't grab it, I'll never get another. And before you tell me I've got plenty of time, let me tell you that all those skinny models you see in *Vogue* and places are about twelve years old. That's the big con and all these dumbfucks buy the stuff because it looks good on kids like us with no boobs or bums or anything.'

I guess I didn't look convinced, because still eyeballing

me, she said, 'In the modelling game, you're *old* at nineteen.'

'If that's true, why bother?'

'Because it'll *lead* to things. Films and stuff. Once I've been in *Vogue*, I'm made.'

I thought it over and could see she was right, but I didn't say anything, just stepped around her and went to sit on my bunk. There, leaning forward to avoid the locker on the wall, I began to undress. As I unbuttoned my shirt, I said, 'What's this guy's name, anyway?'

'Jim – Jim Donally.'

'And he's a journalist?'

Marcelle who was fiddling at the sink, kept her back to me when she said, 'I don't know that you'd call him *that* because he does all sorts of things. He's spent years down near Sydney farming oysters and at one stage he had his own bistro place. It was called Oysters Galore.'

'So what's he doing now?'

She turned then, grinned at me and said, 'He's *here*. At Blue Waters.'

'Y'mean on a yacht?'

'No, he's the manager. He's filling in for a month for his mate who's the *real* manager and he's got the use of his boat and everything.'

'Does he know we're squatting here?'

'Of course he doesn't. I told him I was in a flat with friends up behind the highway.'

After that I took my time folding my shirt and when I'd put it down beside me I said, 'He'll want to fuck you. You know that, don't you?'

Marcelle's answer was a shrug.

'Will you let him?'

She shrugged again and as she did a man's voice, coming from nowhere, said, 'Shit! I've done my knee.'

Another voice, a girl's said, 'What's noo?' She sounded American and when she'd spoken she laughed.

We waited – with staring eyes – for them to come trooping down into the cabin of the *Destry* but nothing happened. They didn't speak again and in a little while Marcelle picked up the lamp and put it on the floor. Then she crept to the steps, went up them and out of sight. She wasn't away long and when she reappeared she leaned against the side of the doorway, gave this exaggerated sigh and said, 'Just a guy and his bird. Been bonking on a boat, I guess. I watched them go across the lawn towards the carpark.'

'But we didn't hear their steps or anything.'

'Probably had bare feet or thongs.'

Almost immediately there was the sound of a car starting up. We heard it go out to the highway then turn and zip away to the south. When it'd gone, I stood to take my jeans off and as I did, not looking at Marcelle, I said, 'You fucked Gerry last night, didn't you?'

'How else were we going to get here?'

Pulling my jeans off over my feet, I said, 'We could've thought of *something*.'

Marcelle didn't answer and I said, 'You don't really mind, do you – fucking people just to get things?'

I was looking at her then and she shrugged the way she'd done before and said, 'It's no big deal.'

I got in between the blankets and before I turned my face towards the wall, I said, 'I wish you didn't do it, that's all. I really wish you didn't.'

Again she didn't say anything. In fact for a while I didn't hear any sound at all, then the light from the lamp moved and I heard her go through to the bunk in the forward cabin.

Getting ready for her date on *French Mustard*, Marcelle was full of jokes and conversation. I helped her with this getting ready, doing stuff like rinsing her hair with a bottle of mineral water. (We had to do that because the water in the shower was salty.) Our quarrel of the night before, if you could call it that, wasn't mentioned. I was conscious of it though. All the time she was painting out the bruises on her legs with Starlet cover-up, I was thinking of this man, three *times* the size of her with hair on his back and everything, swarming all over her and shoving himself inside her while she lay there telling herself it was no big deal.

In the end I said to her, 'What's this Jim Donally look like anyway?'

She was working on her eyelashes by then and she turned and squinted at me in a funny way so the mascara wouldn't smudge. 'He's not bad, specially for an old guy. He's real brown and got this nice smooth skin. His teeth are okay too.' She blinked then and her lashes flew back leaving a tiny row of dots above each of her eyes. 'I always look at their teeth, like people do with horses.' Giggling, she turned back to the mirror. 'His legs aren't bad either. He's only short but his legs are okay. *Bloody hell!*' She'd seen the smudges on her face and there was a pause while she cleaned them off with a tissue. Then she said, 'You can quit worrying. He's real respectable. He's in the Liberal Party and everything. He told me he's got to be careful what he does because he's up for something called pre-section.'

'You mean pre-se*lection*.'

'Yeah, that's it.' Marcelle turned to me again. 'Hey, what's it mean?'

'I'm not sure but I know that if you get it, it means that you're right *in* with them.'

'*There*, y'see.'

When her face was finished you wouldn't have known her. Honestly. It was perfect. She made me think of those dolls like my grandmother had that smashed to pieces if you dropped them. I suppose I'm trying to say that she didn't look *real* and I wondered if she shouldn't have just breezed off to meet this Donally guy with nothing on her face at all.

She took ages choosing the gear to wear, deciding in the end on a T-shirt with a hibiscus painted on it and a pair of baggy white shorts. The shorts were pretty crumpled but Marcelle said she thought the creases would drop out in the sea air. Anyway they looked fantastic on.

Getting dressed, she pulled the T-shirt on over her head and said, 'My Aunt Bet says that women don't dress up to please men. She says they do it to frighten off other women.'

'What do you mean, frighten off?'

'She says women put on make-up and jewellery and all that junk for the same reason cats stand the hair up on their backs. She says they do it to show other women what hotshots they are. It's like they're saying, 'Don't eye off my bloke. I've got all this ammu*nition* and you couldn't get him if you tried because you've got none.'

I thought about it and said, 'Do you believe her?'

'I dunno. Do you?'

'I don't know either.'

Marcelle said, 'Well, I hope I don't frighten the tarts on bloody *Vogue* when I get in it,' and we both doubled-up.

At eleven by the clock over on the front of the clubhouse (Marcelle had checked about a hundred times) she picked up Bobby Deerfield and kissed his nose. Then she made for J-Max who was hoe-ing into crackers and some fancy spread. I think she meant to kiss him too but changed her mind and gave him a little punch on the arm instead.

'Wish me luck,' she said and ran towards the steps. At the bottom she turned and said, 'I wish Aunt Bet could see me – going out on a boat with a photographer and everything.' She paused and her face sort of softened. 'I loved it when Aunt Bet visited. She came every Sunday and she used to make me laugh but her and Mum had this big row and she stopped. She used to have a job in a health-food shop and she met this bloke in there who'd made a pile out of gambling. He started taking her out and though Mum said nothing would come of it, the next thing we knew they were married and he'd given up the gambling and gone into building flats and things. Then he got into some sort of weird religion and used to sit in the garden meditating under this tree shaped like an umbrella. He had his head shaved and used to sit there with oil on his chest and his big fat belly, and when Aunt Bet's baby was born, he grabbed the afterbirth and ate it.'

Marcelle stood looking at me with her big pale eyes and when I didn't say anything, she said, 'Isn't that re*volting*.'

After a while I said, 'I don't believe you,' and she said, 'It's true. Everyone knows. It was after that her and Mum had the row.'

I said again, 'I don't believe you.'

'It doesn't matter if you don't,' said Marcelle, 'because he did. He ate the afterbirth.' Then she laughed and turned and ran up the steps without tripping once and was gone.

That's the last thing Marcelle said to me. 'He ate the afterbirth.' That's the last thing she said.

Chapter Seventeen

J-MAX AND I watched Marcelle go out on *French Mustard*. We'd raced from the marina and along the shoreline until we came to this patch of sand covered with sweet-potato vine. With the wind smacking into our faces, we watched the cruiser go out into the Broadwater, turn and begin to bash its way through white-caps toward the rock-walled channel leading out to sea. It was a big, fast-looking boat with these two tall *wand* things curving back from the sides of the cabin. We could see Marcelle in the cockpit with a man not much taller than she was. Just before they turned she seemed to be looking right at us and we waved, but I don't suppose she saw us because she didn't wave back or anything.

On the way back to Blue Waters my brother was hit with diarrhoea. It came on him so suddenly he had to rush and squat beside a thorn bush at the back of the bait shop. And he had to squat again in the trees at the marina carpark.

It turned out there were diarrhoea tablets aboard *Destry* – burnt orange ones done up in foil. I gave J-Max the child-dose and repeated it two hours later. In spite of that the squitters didn't stop till mid-afternoon and by the time I'd washed his shorts and got a pair dry enough for him to put on it was almost four o'clock. I was pretty sure that visiting hour at the Hattan would be over when we got there but we caught the bus and went anyway, arriving as everyone else was trooping out.

The sister in charge of Allie's ward wouldn't let us in. We'd ridden up in the lift and met her in the corridor as she stepped from her office. There were streaks of grey in her hair and she had these washed-out blue eyes which looked as if they'd just come from seeing about two hundred years of terrible things. (They looked as if they could see all the terrible things in *your* life too.)

Slowly those eyes inspected me then turned to J-Max, taking in his wild hair and the shorts still damp between the legs. 'You can't visit here,' she said. 'You're too late.' She didn't sound cross or anything, just *tired* so I told her we were late because my brother had diarrhoea.

'Then you *certainly* can't visit.'

You could tell she meant it and already J-Max was stomping off towards the stairs but suddenly he stopped and stood looking into one of the wards. When I reached him I looked in too and there was Allie. She was sitting up in one of the beds, staring straight ahead and crying without making a sound.

I guess she felt our eyes on her because after a moment she turned her head and saw us. I don't think I'd ever seen anyone's face light up the way they're always doing in books, but Allie's did. It lit up like *sun*flowers and she sang out, 'Hey, Mrs Lau.'

I called back, 'We can't come in. Max's got the shits.'

The next thing the sister was behind me grabbing my elbow. 'Out!' she said and tried to grab J-Max too. He dodged her and tore into the ward, running on this slightly curved track. He didn't stop when he reached Allie's bed but she put out her hand and they smacked their palms together in the groovy way West Indian cricketers do when they get the wicket of someone they really want. Then J-

Max was back with me and we were being hustled towards the lift. I didn't mind. I mean I know a one-minute glimpse of us wasn't going to make up to anyone for having their baby stolen, but at least it was *something*.

Just before we reached the lift, the sister let us stop long enough to look out a window at the Broadwater. It was quite a shock to see it from that height because I'd imagined it to be like a sort of sea canyon, with dark and scary depths. Instead it was so shallow that from where we were you could see almost all the bottom.

'You could *walk* across it,' I said.

In this dry voice the sister said, 'I wouldn't try it.' Then she took us to the lift and pressed the button and waited till the doors opened for us.

We were back on *Destry* having tea when *French Mustard* came rocketing in. J-Max was eating with one hand and drawing with the other. Perhaps I should stop here to say that since finding some felt-tipped pens and a pile of scribblers in one of the lockers, he'd spent most of his time aboard the yacht drawing pictures of a creature Marcelle nicknamed Mr Mecho-Muscleman, a half-robot, half-human with steely muscles and a tiny oblong head. He'd drawn him storming castles, flying spaceships, fighting sea-monsters and even driving in drag races.

We both knew it was *French Mustard* coming in. Nothing else around Blue Waters made that space-race sound. J-Max gave me an *It's her* look and went back to Mr Mecho-Muscleman but I left my tea and rushed up to the cockpit to share the last few minutes of Marcelle's trip.

I was in time to see *French Mustard* do a sweep in front of the marina, then throttled back a lot, go in a clockwise circle and come to a neat stop by this dinghy tied to a buoy in the stretch of water opposite the place where *Destry* was moored.

I had a good view of Jim Donally as he hopped about turning off the engine then moving to the bow to fish for the buoy rope. There was no sign of Marcelle and I thought she was still down in the cabin doing her hair or something.

The wind had dropped a bit but there were these heavy clouds over the Broadwater with a few shafts of light coming through them at a slant the way they come from the back wall of a cinema.

Donally had pulled the dinghy in close to *French Mustard* and dropped a blue sports bag into it. I kept waiting for him to call to Marcelle or even go to the cabin and get her. Instead he climbed down into the dinghy, fitted the oars in place and cast off. When he began to row towards the bit of beach on the right of the marina, I nearly called, 'Hey, wait for Marcelle.' I didn't though because in the very next moment I knew she wasn't even on *French Mustard*; that she'd gone, had left us the way Angel did. And all the time Jim Donally was rowing to the shingly little beach and pulling the boat up onto it, I was hating her more than I'd ever hated anyone. I could *feel* the hate inside me – felt it spread into my limbs and neck, almost choking me. I thought of the stupid grin she'd had on her face when she told me the story about the afterbirth, and when Donally grabbed his bag and went towards the back of the apartment block, I turned and ran down into the cabin of *Destry* as clumsily as she might have done.

J-Max had the lamp alight and was still drawing. As I blundered down the steps, he looked up and I shouted at him, 'She's gone. She wasn't on the boat. She's pissed off like Angel. She didn't even *care* about us,' and I remember that when I stopped speaking I left my mouth open the way a kid does when it's lost control.

J-Max went on looking at me, then slowly he began to shake his head. Without taking his eyes from me, he pointed in the direction of Bobby Deerfield who'd curved himself around the table support and was playing with a ball of crumpled paper.

'She didn't care about him either,' I shouted.

J-Max's answer was to get up and go into the forward cabin where he lifted the corner of Marcelle's mattress. The next moment he was back plonking a little bundle of five dollar notes and some coins on the table.

'She doesn't *need* that,' I told him. 'That man's taken her to some place on the coast – his house probably, and he's given her all the money she wants. She'll be able . . . '

My brother wasn't listening to me. He'd flipped to the next page in the scribbler and was writing the word *Never*. At the end he put about six exclamation marks. Then he put the pen down and folded his arms across his chest.

So we stared at each other and in a little while I dropped my eyes because I was remembering the way Marcelle had cleaned up after me when I was sick. I remembered too how worried she'd been at the thought of Allie in hospital without a visitor. After that it didn't take me long to work out that Marcelle wouldn't have left us, not for *anything* and when I had, I groped my way into the table seat and whispered, 'Something's happened to her, hasn't it?'

While J-Max was nodding his head at me, I began to think of the stuff she and Allie told me about gangs of men kidnapping boys. *Perhaps Donally's one of them,* I thought. *Perhaps they kidnap girls as well. Why* WOULDN'T *they?* I could see that Marcelle would appeal to such men. She was pretty and all that stuff, and if they talked to her for ten seconds they'd know that after one drink she'd do anything they wanted just so long as they promised to get her photograph in *Follow Me* or somewhere.

Suddenly the sides of the yacht were closing in on me like coffin walls and I pushed away from the table and ran for the steps. At the top I stood taking in long gasps of air. I was still doing that when I realized J-Max had followed me.

Swinging around to him, I said, 'You stay here. I'll only be a minute. I'm going to take a look at that other boat,' and without waiting to see what he made of that, I left *Destry* and went towards the hole in the cyclone fence. All I wanted was to get away from the yacht and the spooky closed-in feeling it gave me but once I was through the wire I realized I'd be stupid *not* to take a closer look at *French Mustard* because Marcelle could still be on it – drugged or something.

It was growing dark and the picture theatre beams were no longer coming through the clouds. Instead there was a weak band of light around the horizon. At that stage the big blue spotlights of the marina hadn't been turned on but the clubhouse was lit up and as I nicked past I saw a man with red hair opening a book beside the cash register. There was a man in one of the apartments too – not Donally, someone else. He was by the window, holding a ping-pong bat in one hand and what must have been a ball in the other because I saw him turn suddenly and slather something back into the room. Then I was past and moments later I was standing on the unfenced jetty at the edge of the marina.

French Mustard was about fifteen metres away from me, riding on water that was almost still. Till then I'd had some dumb idea about getting out to it and looking for signs of Marcelle but I knew I couldn't do it because the water, which had seemed so shallow from the window of the hospital, was suddenly deep and cold and scary. You could *tell* just by looking at it that silent things like sharks and sting-rays were sliding round beneath the surface. And anyway, even if I could have nerved myself to plunge in and swim out to the boat, there was no way I could have hauled myself aboard when I got there.

I was wondering if between us J-Max and I could handle the *dinghy* when suddenly the spotlights went on. I turned, blinking into all that prison-yard light to see Jim Donally coming towards me across the lawn.

I had this moment then of spin-out when I really did think of throwing myself into the scary water and thrashing my way to the beach. But I didn't do that either because already Donally was calling out to me, 'What are you doing here? Do you want something?'

He'd put a rugby sweater on over his little denim shorts and was exactly as Marcelle had described him, with a not-bad face and legs and everything. He was fairly close to me by then, looking at me with this really easy look on his face and God, did I hate him! Not in the turned-in way I'd hated Marcelle for a while but in the terrible way I'd hated the girl who stole my bag in Sydney. I wanted to crack *his* face against something too and because of that I sort of shouted at him, 'I'm looking for my friend Marcelle.'

He didn't answer until he'd reached me. Then he stopped, put his head a little on one side and said, 'I don't know any Marcelle. Why are you looking here?'

'You *do* know her. You took her out with you in that boat over there.' I jerked my thumb towards the cabin cruiser.

Still easy in his manner, he said, 'You've made some kind of mistake. Perhaps you're in the wrong marina. I don't know your friend Marcelle.'

'That's a lie. You took her out in *French Mustard*. My brother and I saw you.'

'There is a mistake,' he smiled at me showing the teeth Marcelle had mentioned. 'I took my daughter Kirsty out with me this morning. If you saw anyone, that's who it was.'

His way of speaking was so open and friendly, I swear I practically believed him. The thing that stopped me was that from the corner of my eye I could see one of his hands opening and closing all the time as if he wasn't really open and friendly at all. That hand frightened me into thinking I should stop shouting at him and get away as quickly as possible. I managed to do it by saying to myself, *Think of* ALLIE. *Think of her stooging checkout girls at the Big W, then try to do the same,* and after that I found it was easy enough to

say, 'I thought it was Marce. When she didn't come back
. . .' As I spoke I was edging my way around him. He
turned in time with me, and when I guessed the exit was at
my back, I said, 'I'll hop back to the flat then. She's
probably there by now.'

I don't know how I came up with the bit about the flat.
Perhaps that was part of being Allie too but anyway it went
down with Donally because he said, 'That seems a good
idea. Come along, I'll see you off the place.'

We walked side by side across the lawn and I don't know
how I managed it because although I was still trying to be
Allie, all I wanted to do was run. It was almost impossible
not to but I knew if I did, his big-looking white joggers
would catch me in no time, so I marched along with him
while my *heart* tried to do my running for me.

When we were level with the clubhouse, I'd had enough
and in this breathy voice, I said, 'I'll see you.' I even tried to
smile at him. Then I did run.

Night had come down the way it does up here but I
thought I could see the top half of J-Max's head watching
me from the cockpit of the *Destry*. I didn't think he'd be
thick enough to rush into full view but just in case, I made
this little batting movement at him with my hand.

By then I'd reached the road which led to the carpark.
Knowing Donally would still be watching, I kept going. I
went all the way to the highway and then, in case he was
sneaky enough to keep watching, I turned to the left and
with cars zooming past, walked until I reached the cover of
the local shops.

Looking back now it's easy to see I was off my face with
shock because what I did was rush to the public phone box
and use change from the bus fare Marcelle gave me that
morning to ring Allie. You see, I had to talk to someone. I
didn't go through with it though because just before the
man on the Hattan switchboard answered me, I heard
Marcelle's voice say, 'You dickbrain. Allie's got enough on

her plate,' and instead of asking for her, I blurted out this stuff about needing to get in touch with Ingrid Frew.

Instead of being aggro as people in those jobs usually are, the man was really nice, asking me who was calling, then saying, 'Hang on a mo. I think I've got Ingrid's number here.' There was a silence, then he told me to try 3914004 and waited for me to repeat it.

I had no way of knowing if I'd been given a home number or a work one but I rang it anyway. A woman answered and that was when luck piked on me because she told me Ingrid Frew was on leave and not due back for another week.

I stood without speaking then and she said, 'Can I help instead?'

'Yes,' I said. 'Yes, maybe you can. It's about someone Ingrid knows. A friend of mine who's disappeared.'

'Who's calling please?'

When she said that I remembered the man at the Manhattan Maternity Home asking me the same question, and the worst part was I remembered as well my lamebrained voice blurting out Victoria Ferguson instead of Morgan *Christie*.

I went right off then, clattering the phone down in the woman's ear and rushing out of the phone box. And after that bomb there was nothing for me to do but leave the shopping centre and go back to the marina.

Chapter Eighteen

O N T H E W A Y back I went so fast that when I reached the cockpit of the *Destry* I had to stop to get my breath. (I ran like that because blokes in cars kept calling out these dumb things at me. One even stopped but took off again when I kept going.)

While I was still there in the cockpit Jim Donally's voice floated up to me from the cabin. I wasn't sure it was Donally's but I thought it was and my heart shot up like a lift because I thought he'd brought Marcelle back. I thought they'd been playing a trick and that when I got down into the cabin I'd find them sitting at the table with J-Max like a little family or something.

But Marcelle wasn't there at all – just Donally and my brother. They were both standing. Donally had hold of J-Max's shoulder and was saying, 'You little bastard – answer me.'

Rushing to him, I said, 'He *can't* answer. He can't speak.' (J-Max says then I punched him but I don't remember doing that.)

Donally let go of my brother and sort of held me off. 'I knew you were here,' he said. 'All I had to do was look.'

'Where's Marcelle,' I shouted. 'Tell me that. Where is she?'

Instead of answering me, he said, 'You're trespassing. You know that, don't you? Either you leave this yacht in fifteen minutes or I call the police.'

'Go on – call them. If you do they'll ask you where Marcelle is.'

Donally took a step away from me but before he could speak again, I said, 'They know she's missing because I rang them and told them.' Where the lie came from, I don't know but it was there waiting for me and I used it.

'You shouldn't have done that.' Donally spoke so quietly he frightened me. *Christ, he'll kill us*, I thought. But all he did was turn away and go to the bench where Marcelle and I had left bottles of booze and things. I watched him as he poured some Bacardi into a dirty glass then tossed it down neat. After that he stayed there leaning his weight on his hands. He was still there when he said, 'Your friend can't come back. She's dead.'

I heard the water lapping against the boat, heard the clicking sound of something up in the rigging and in a voice as light and dry as that clicking, I said, 'She can't be.'

Donally turned to face me then. He had this drained look on his face which made him look about *fifty*. 'She tripped and went overboard. We were well out and coming home – east of Stradbroke. One minute she was there on deck, the next she'd gone.' He lifted his hands. 'Just like that. I turned the boat and searched for hours but there was no sign of her. She must've hit her head on the way down because she didn't ever come up.'

While he was telling me, I *saw* it happen. I saw it in slow-motion. Saw Marcelle in the T-shirt with the flower on it, trip and disappear beneath the oily rolling surface of the sea. I was still seeing the spot where she vanished, when Donally said, 'No one's going to believe me. Not a soul.'

Still in that high clicking voice, I said, 'I believe you. Marcelle tripped all the time. She couldn't see properly because she threw her glasses away when she left home. She threw them out of the bus.'

I don't think Donally heard me because he said, 'I'm finished, you know. I'll lose everything that matters – my kids, even my future.' Then focussing on me again, he said, 'Did you really ring the police?'

He waited, watching me and while my mind stopped-and-started as it tried to work out which answer would be the least dangerous to J-Max and me, I noticed with some other part of my mind that the cabin still smelt faintly of my brother's diarrhoea mixed up with the chemical stuff in the loo.

In the end I came out with a sort of *section* of the truth. 'Not exactly. I rang this youth worker I know and told her.'

'So the police may not know yet?'

'Maybe not.'

I saw a little of the strain leave Donally's face. 'Did you give her name – Marcelle's I mean?'

This time I lied and said I had.

Donally took his time thinking about that. Then he turned, went back to the bench and poured himself another Bacardi. He didn't drink it though. Instead he turned back to me with the glass in his hand.

'I liked Marcelle,' he said and his voice was friendly the way it was then I first met him. 'She was a great kid. But nothing's going to bring her back, you know that, don't you?' He lifted the glass then and took a drink, watching me over the top of it.

When I didn't answer he lowered the glass and went on, 'Neither the welfare people nor the police can do anything y'know, and when it comes down to it, they won't care much. To them she'll be no more than a statistic.'

'*Someone's* got to know.'

'*We* know, love. Who else will care? You're old enough

and bright enough too, I'm sure, to realize that no one's going to thank us for reporting what was, after all, nothing but an accident.'

I said again, 'Someone's got to know.'

'But there'd be other things they'd have to know as well. Like your being on this yacht – the mess you've made and the food and stuff you've had. That's called stealing, y'know, and once we've put the law in motion, it'll take its course, with you and your mate here ending up in detention centres. Different ones – you won't even be together.'

I took a quick look at J-Max. He was standing by the table, his face small and pinched and his foot on one of his drawings. (I don't think he'd moved his eyes one centimetre from my face since Donally let go of him.)

'Don't forget,' said Donally turning to put his glass on the bench, 'that if I choose to lie a little, there's no one to substantiate your story.' He stayed where he was, making patterns on the bench with the bottom of the glass. 'You say this boy here can't speak, so that leaves your word against mine, and believe me when I say I wouldn't have a lot of trouble getting the barman or someone to swear it *was* my daughter I took out today.'

What he said made me feel a nothing and a nobody the way I'd felt I was a nothing and a nobody that night my father came into my room. It frightened me as well because I could see that most of it was true. I was standing not knowing what to say or even *think* when Donally swung around and said, 'Wouldn't it be better if we played it another way?'

'I don't know what you mean.'

His voice went back to being friendly. 'Well, let's put it this way – I could let you stay here, say, tonight. In the morning you could move on and that'd be more or less the end of it. If you like I could give you a few bob to help out with fares and so on.' He paused, watching me again. 'What do you say?'

'But what about Marcelle? What about *her*? She might still be alive – *floating* or something. Perhaps the police . . .'

He didn't let me finish. 'You mustn't think that. Marcelle's dead. She didn't even surface. I looked properly, I promise you that. I did it for my own sake as well as hers and I can tell you I've been around boats long enough to know how to do it.'

I believed him. I believed him in spite of the fact that he'd just told me he was prepared to lie to the police and everyone. I don't know why I did. I think it was because he was no longer trying to stooge me with his pitsy charm when he said it.

In the same straightforward way he said, 'If you leave here, do you have somewhere to go?'

Thinking of the house in Leopard Tree Lane, I said, 'Yes, we do.'

'Then wouldn't that be best?'

I couldn't bear to let Marcelle go as easily as that but while I stood with the weight of it all on me, J-Max, moving so I could see him clearly, began to nod his head.

'You see,' said Donally. 'Your mate agrees with me,' and after a while I nodded my head too.

Donally clasped his hands together then and kept them that way with the elbows held high. 'Right,' he said, 'that's settled. You two try to get some sleep. I'll come over about eight and help you tidy up here. Then if you like, I'll drive you to the bus or wherever you want.'

I nodded again and let my breath go. (I hadn't even known I was holding it.)

With his hands still clasped in that funny way, Donally went towards the steps. At the bottom of them he stopped and turned in almost the same spot Marcelle was in when she made the speech about the man eating the afterbirth. Donally made a speech too. He dropped his hands and said all this stuff about his wife moving to the Gold Coast after their divorce and how he'd followed her. He said she'd married again but it wasn't a success. I don't know why he told me all that stuff, and anyway I didn't listen to him. I was seeing Marcelle standing there all lit-up and laughing. I had this crazy moment then of thinking I could get the spear-gun and shoot Donally dead. But Marcelle had hidden it and I didn't know where it was.

By the time I'd worked that out, Donally was saying, 'See you at eight then,' and he turned, and on his big new-looking Adidas, ran up the stairs and out of sight.

Chapter Nineteen

A LONG TIME after all this stuff happened, I found out that in spite of being so smart at maths and things, J-Max had this really dumb idea of death. He thought dead people popped up again the way they do on television. I suppose he'd seen so many people die only to bob up again in another series that he thought everyone did it. So when Jim Donally told us Marcelle had drowned, my brother expected to meet her again in a few months time. He thought she'd probably have a new name and so on but as we'd already changed *ours* that seemed reasonable enough to him.

I didn't know all this at the time and expected him to put on a spaz act the minute Donally left the yacht. Instead he let me wash his face and feet and was soon asleep on his bunk with his head close to Bobby Deerfield's.

I lay on *my* bunk and with my breath panting in and out the way it did earlier when I ran back from the telephone, I watched this picture of Marcelle's body turning over and over in the bottomless green water while her hair floated above her face like seaweed. Even when I jammed my face into the pillow to stop it, Marcelle went on turning with her hair floating like weeds.

The wind had stopped at last and the boat was still. That stillness seemed more horrible to me than all the creaking and clicking because it made it easier to see Marcelle in the water. In the end I sat up, hitting my head the way I'd done on the first day. Then I got up and began to pack our things.

I'd made up my mind earlier to be gone long before eight o'clock. I wasn't letting *Donally* drive us anywhere. In fact I didn't mean to let him see us again because I'd watched enough television drama and stuff to know that for him we were a pair of two-legged time bombs.

While I packed I worked out that Donally had gone back to his apartment to sit in a chair and wipe himself out with his favourite drink the way my father did when he thought things were out of his control. But I guessed he'd wake still pissed some time during the night and that's when he'd come looking for us. Because of that I packed like fury. I packed everything. I even packed Marcelle's stuff. She had a lot and although I'd meant to take it with me, when I saw it sitting in a bunch I knew I couldn't. It would have taken us half the night to get it through the fence and as far as the carpark, so in the end I put the things she liked best in her case and stood it with ours. Till then I think I'd had some dopey idea myself that she might come back but when I'd jammed the leftover gear back into her plastic bags and put them in a pile beside her bunk, I knew she wasn't going to. The sight of those bags with their stupid brand names on them made me think of her the way she was that morning as she scrabbled through them to find things to wear. I can tell you that of all the time J-Max and I were on the run, that moment was the worst. I think perhaps when I get to the end of my life and look back, it'll stand out as the worst of *anything*. The funny part about it is that I didn't think of going home. I didn't think of it once.

That last thing I did before waking my brother was write a note with the word 'Safehouse' on it. Then I put it, together with half Marcelle's money, under the corner of the mattress where J-Max had found it. I knew there wasn't any point in doing it but I did it just the same. And if you're wondering why I kept the rest of the money, I kept it so I'd be able to feed Bobby Deerfield and J-Max until I got a job.

I called a taxi from the phone at the shopping centre while J-Max waited with the cases and everything under one of the trees that bordered the marina carpark.

By the time the taxi turned up we'd moved our stuff out to the road. That was a mistake because finding us there made the driver suspicious. He was only young with this long chin and one of those fake Greek fishermen's caps and although I still can't see it had to matter to him he asked us why we were waiting there alone.

I gave him my old story about going to our nanna's while our mother was in hospital.

'Where's your Dad?'

'He's taken Mum up to Brisbane.'

The taxi driver was still undecided, looking from me to J-Max and back again. In the end I think it was the sight of Bobby Deerfield sitting cheerfully in my brother's arms that convinced him it was okay to take us.

When we were all settled in the cab, he said, 'Don't let that mog pee.'

'He *never* pees.'

That made him laugh and we began to move. I looked back at the marina, ghostly again with its masts and everything, and seeing it, I felt this blockage in my chest as if a clot of blood or something had settled there.

The driver let us out at the corner of Leopard Tree Lane. He was still fussing over us and fussing too about a storm he said was coming. 'It's going to be bad,' he said. 'The worst of the season.'

We were outside this little timber place with lights on and I told him it was our grandmother's. By then he was too busy talking about the *ozone* layer to listen. In fact I only stopped him talking all night by taking a case from him and marching in through the gateway. He got back in the cab and sturged off up the hill then and we were free to start moving our gear to the safehouse.

This place Marcelle had chosen was a small double-decker Queensland house with lattice work all around the bottom storey. It had no fences, but a row of mango trees shielded it from the mauve-y lights in the street. *Behind* the house was this four-storey office block painted white and with each level stepped back so that the whole thing looked like a P. & O. liner sitting there on top of the hill.

J-Max and I went between the mango trees and found the bathroom window. We knew it was the right one because of the pipes and things coming out of the wall below it, and anyway, it was open a fraction. (Queensland people often leave a window open in a shut-up house because if they don't the hu*midity* makes the place smell of things like mouldy gym shoes and rotting grass and stuff.

The window was out of reach. To get to it, I stood on my case and Marcelle's as well while J-Max, who'd give the Rialto in Collins Street a try if you asked him, grabbed a water pipe and climbed onto my shoulders. He stood there a moment pulling at the window then put his foot briefly on my head and launched himself up into the house. When he'd vanished, I went around to the steps leading up to the front door and waited, I knew J-Max would find it hard to see inside. Just the same I'd expected him to reach the front door in two or three minutes. It was more like two or three *hours*. I think the little dickbrain took the time to check the place out while he was there. In the meantime, spinning-out with fright, I'd backed under the nearest mango tree where I stood imagining all these gruesome things happening inside.

When he did appear, J-Max popped his head out, spotted me, stuck his thumb up and nicked down the steps to scoop up Bobby Deerfield. He turned then and belted back to the door while I followed him, hissing, 'Is it empty? Is it *empty*?'

It was, and although the shut-up smell was hard to take, it was a really dinky little place – a true seaside shack I'd call it, made up of one big room with a kitchen tacked on at the end and a bedroom and bathroom at the back. Right along the east side were these windows which looked over the roof of the house in front to a park and the Broadwater. (All the windows in the house were push-out ones with panes of frosted green glass at the top.) A street light a few metres downhill was beaming enough of its spooky intergalactic light inside for us to be able to look around the living room. It was furnished with lots of bits of cane and some fat old floral armchairs. In the corner by the kitchen was the start of the staircase which led downstairs.

Using a fading torch he'd found, J-Max took me on a tour of inspection. We even went downstairs to find the loo and an oldfashioned washtub standing on a dirt floor almost covered with these dead or dying potplants. (They were orchids. I knew that because my *real* nanna used to grow them.) We also found a door in the lattice and after getting the rusty bolt undone went out to bring our luggage inside.

That house was the perfect squat for kids like us. The mango trees hid it from the one across the lane and on the other side of it, there was only the empty space of church tennis courts. That meant that as long as we stayed away from the windows at the back and didn't press our faces against the ones at the front, no one was going to know we were there.

I wandered around the living room trying to work out what kind of people lived there and where they'd gone. On the way I trod on a cockroach, squashing it, so its creamy insides came out. As I scraped bits of it off my foot, I heard Marcelle's voice say, 'Get some baits tomorrow.'

At first I was so spooked I felt my hair go cold. Then J-Max bumped something behind me and when he did I told myself, *Don't be a dipstick. You know what she'd say if you asked her – that's all.* What that did though was make me

miss Marcelle desperately and with the blood-clot feeling
back in my chest, I went to join J-Max who'd moved again
and was peering out one of the front windows.

Beyond the park, the Broadwater was a dark mass with
one red light winking in it. For once there were hardly any
lights on the highway either. (Usually headlights made
yellow rivers going north and south. That night there was
almost nothing.)

The house below us was screened by a verandah covered
with creeper but the place opposite it had a glass door at the
back so that we could see into the kitchen. A man was
kneeling there beside this big red motorbike. Bits of it lay
on the floor around him and every so often he'd take
another piece from the bike and put it with them.

While we were watching this other man, wearing
a sarong with splashy colours on it, came into view. He had
a camera hanging on his chest and he used it to take some
shots of the motorbike mechanic. That reminded me of
Marcelle too and I saw her kneeling in the cabin of *French
Mustard* with half her clothes off while Jim Donally took
photos of her. Then I began to see her body again turning
over and over in the water. I could still see it later when
I was lying on the double bed with J-Max asleep beside me.
I tried to stop it by starting this film in my head about two
kids, girls, I mean, who meet at Central Station in Sydney
and decide to go to Queensland together. The picture of
Marcelle drowning kept getting in the way though. Even
when I *slept* the picture was still there.

Anyway the storm woke me. It woke J-Max too as it
tried to smash the house down on top of us. Outside there
was a sort of half-light but when we got up the nerve to
look, we found the entire world had disappeared behind this
*hori*zontal rain. The only way I can describe that rain is by
saying it was as if hundreds of millions of little arrows were
hitting the house and straightaway turning into water. For
me the wind was the worst part though. It'd sort of hold its

breath for a minute then with this awful howl attack the doors and windows like something live trying to get in.

I think it was some sort of miracle that we were in the safehouse because the storm lasted three days, making this gully in the middle of Leopard Tree Lane and tearing up half the trees down in the park. The house stood beneath it all like a rock. Water came in around the windows and under the door but that was all and by the end of the first day I'd realized the place was built to hold out against such storms and could still be standing – paintless and defiant – in a hundred years. After that I stopped being frightened when the walls shuddered each time the wind hit them.

That first day J-Max found the meter-box and turned on the electricity so at least we had the use of the stove and the dinky hot water canister above the sink. We also had this little black and white television set. The power went off now and then and even when it was on, reception was rotten with all the action taking place in heavy snowstorms, but at least it was *something*. The other thing we had was a Monopoly set. My brother loves Monopoly because he loves money and we played it until I could have hurled the poxy little houses and things out into the rain.

There was a lull in the storm on the afternoon of day two and although fairly heavy rain was still falling we put on these woman-size hats and raincoats and made a dash for the shops. My hat had 'Southport Croquet Club' embroidered on the band. (I think I've forgotten to tell you that till then we'd been living on the tinned soup and stale Salada crackers we found in the house.)

Outside we had to creep along the gravelly edge of the *ravine* in Leopard Tree Lane, and down in Scarborough Street there was water everywhere. Lots of places had lost their roofs. (We saw gangs of men tying tarps over the damage.) In the shopping area some of the neon signs beneath shop verandahs had broken free at one end and were hanging down like *bombs* or something.

Coles New World was open with just a few of its checkouts operating and none of the lights. In the gloom there I bought a heap of food and because one of the girls warned me the storm was only taking a breather and would soon be lashing us again, I stocked up on pens and scribblers for my brother.

When we'd waded home again and were getting out of our storm gear, J-Max took all these Mars bars and things from his pockets and plonked them on the table. That shocked me, and sweeping the stuff off onto the floor, I said, 'We only take stuff when we're broke. If we have money, we pay.' Then stooging a bit, 'That's Allie's rule.'

Watching me with this know-it-all grin on his face, J-Max touched the change I'd put on the table.

'I know it's Marcelle's,' I said, 'but she'd want us to have it,' and remembering for no reason at all the lonely-looking pile of plastic bags we'd left behind us on the *Destry*, I began to cry.

My brother watched me for a while, then came around the table and reached up and pulled off my sodden hat. After that he handed me the shirt we'd been using as a towel. I took it from him and went into the bathroom where I knelt beside the bath and cried until I dry-retched.

For the first time I understood J-Max's teacher, Mrs Golding. You know – the one who cut her hair off with a knife when her son Garth died. I wanted to do something crazy to myself too, even *hurt* myself because of this hole in my heart where my friend Marcelle should have been.

In bed that night, so I wouldn't see another bunch of rotten pictures of her, I made myself work on my film about the two runaway girls. I won't go into detail because I used a lot of the stuff I've told you here. (Later, when I got to The Rose Club I decided to include J-Max because by then I'd worked out that the best way to do it was to write it first in story form and put down things just the way they happened.)

Day three of the storm was pretty hard to take. The wind had started again and on top of that everything inside as well as out was damp. It's true we'd found a rusty one-bar radiator in the bedroom and although we'd been able to dry our hair and stuff with it, it wasn't much use when it came to drying out the *at*mosphere.

J-Max was bored enough to be a nuisance. He kept letting me know he wanted to go out and I kept letting him know he couldn't. At lunchtime after hearing on telly that the storm was almost over, I told him that unless he co-operated, he wouldn't be seeing Allie the next day. That made him pull all these monkey faces at me but at least he quit wanting to go outside and began to draw instead. An interesting thing I have to tell you is that he didn't ever go back to drawing Mr Mecho-Muscleman. He'd found this big bird book in the house and began drawing things from that. And even later, when we'd moved again, he still didn't go back to Mr Mecho-Muscleman.

About seven-thirty the wind dropped and the rain became a drizzle which made giant sparklers out of the lights down in the park. Every so often there'd be a play of lightning out over the ocean but this was only the storm's dying effort.

When the junk we were watching on telly ended I told J-Max to wash himself and go to bed. After a bit of hassling, he went to the bathroom but almost straightaway was back in the doorway beckoning me. Then he shot into the bathroom again. I found him at the window staring across the garden at the P.&O. liner. One room of it was directly opposite us – an office of a company called Futures Pacific or something. There, in semi-darkness, these two men were working. One was sitting at a computer tapping the keyboard now and then. The other had a torch and was using it to peer into this filing cabinet. There wasn't time to see more because suddenly a flash of lightning lit us all up

like crazy. The man at the cabinet looked up and for a
second he stared at us while we stared at him. Then it was
dark again and almost immediately the glow from the
computer disappeared and the torch light as well.

The next thing this funny little *Japanese* voice beside me
said, "ee thaw uth.' And J-Max pushed me and said, 'Lun,
lun.'

That's how my brother started speaking – by telling me
to run. I didn't do it though. What I did was grab him and
haul him to the bath where I sat on the side of it, holding
him and saying, 'We don't have to run. They will. They
were doing something dodgy and they'll piss off.'

'Bud they *thaw* uth.'

'Yes, but they don't know we aren't meant to be here.'

After that we sat and listened and minutes later heard this
car come out from underneath the P.&O. and take off up
the hill like the first rocket for Mars.

Because of all that stuff about the two men and everything I didn't get around to asking J-Max why he'd never
spoken before and by the next day I'd decided it was just as
well because if I had, he might have clammed up again for
good. As it was, that night before taking our Quik into bed
we had this conversation with J-Max using his awful Japa-
nese-English and me trying to help him get it out. We
talked about Allie and her baby, and tried to work out what
had happened to Joss. I didn't bring up the subject of Marcelle. To tell you the truth I didn't think I could handle it.

I thought about her in bed though. I thought about her
when I tried to work out why the worst possible thing and
the best had both happened to me within days. That stuff
led me to thinking about God. Is there one or not, I mean.
I even tried to work out what it'd look like and when I did
the only thing I could picture was this bunch of pale gas-y
stuff floating somewhere out in space with all these sort of
rubbery *arms* coming out of it. I guess I was hysterical

because I laughed at the thought of people praying to a bunch of gas. If you want to know I laughed about God for a long time.

Chapter Twenty

I WAS SO pleased to see Allie. You wouldn't believe how
pleased. Wearing thongs and a hospital dressing gown,
she'd been watching for us from the fifth floor of the
Hattan.

J-Max and I were late again. We'd spent the morning
cleaning up underneath the house. Storm-water rushing
through the downstairs part had piled the potplants against
the lattice and we had to clear a path to get to the loo. Once
we'd started we decided to rescue the pots that hadn't lost
their contents. In a way it was good fun sloshing barefoot in
the mud and leaves and stuff. J-Max spoke every so often,
sounding like someone with no roof to his mouth. When I
told him so, he shied an orchid plant at me. That led to a
mud fight, and it was washing our hair and everything
afterwards that made us late.

The Broadwater that day was swollen and a funny copper
colour and when J-Max and I finally set off for the hospital
we saw people everywhere hauling carpets out of buildings
and putting them to dry on fences and tennis courts and
places.

As we passed the post office J-Max pointed out a piece of
graffiti which said *Flo Blows Joh*. I don't know if he knew

what it meant but I think he did because he laughed. (Little kids know *every*thing these days.)

At the hospital as we stepped from the lift, Allie rushed forward. Grabbing my wrist, she said, 'Jesus. I didn't think I'd see you again. I thought the yacht'd be smashed to bits.'

'I reckon it was,' I said, 'But we'd moved. We moved to Leopard Tree Lane just before the storm.'

'Shit! How lucky can you be?' Allie let go of me then and stepped back so she could see both of us. She was even grinning a bit and she said, 'Listen. I've got something to tell you. I've got a job – one I can go to when I leave here. I'll have money and that to help me get my kid back.'

'That's *great*,' I said. 'But how did you get it?'

Instead of telling me, she said, 'Hang on a minute. Where's Marcelle?'

I couldn't do it. Tell her, I mean. I'd meant to. I'd made up my mind to get it out as soon as we got to the hospital but seeing her so thin and everything in the towelling dressing gown with a rust stain on the lapel, I found I couldn't. What I did was put on this fake voice and say, 'She got a job too. Over on Stradbroke Island.'

'Stradbroke *Island*? How the hell did she get over there?'

'This man at the marina took her. He knew about the job – that's how she found out.'

'What sort of job is it?'

From somewhere along the hall I heard the rattle of teacups and said, 'Waitressing and stuff. She said if she didn't come back we'd know she'd got it.'

Allie was using those Resistance-hero eyes of hers to stare first at me, then at J-Max. *He* was staring at me and I strained myself to will him not to speak. (That's a laugh. I'd spent eight years waiting for him to say something and five minutes after he did I was wanting him to stop.)

Allie's eyes were back on me so I said, 'Marce promised to send a postcard. She said she'd sent it to the Southport post office. I guess the storm's held it up.'

She accepted that and because the nursing sister who'd put us out the day before was at the door of her office watching us, she said, 'Come on, let's go to the ward so we can talk.'

The ward wasn't like any hospital room I'd seen. The curtains had a zebra-skin pattern on them and the furniture was made from shiny white plastic and glass. Four of the five beds were occupied and everyone but Allie had flowers on their bed-tray. I can tell you I felt a real dickbrain for not bringing some. *Tomorrow*, I thought, *if I can find one undamaged, I'll bring an orchid plant.*

The woman in the bed next to Allie's was only young with streaked hair and these big slightly-bulging eyes. One of her visitors had brought her an icecream. We arrived just as she was finishing it. Grabbing a tissue from the box in front of her, she wiped her mouth and fingers. 'Boy,' she said, 'I needed that. The food here's the pits. Clear soup and salad!' She pulled a face. 'If someone doesn't bring me takeaways tonight, I'm moving out.'

Allie gave me the deadest of her deadpan looks and went into the corridor to grab a chair. As soon as she'd gone I whispered to J-Max that he wasn't to mention Marcelle.

'Why not?' he mouthed at me.

I could hear Allie coming back, so I told him I'd tell him later and went to help with the chair.

We settled ourselves and from my perch on the bed, I said, 'We've got news too. You won't believe it but Max is talking. He started last night and he's been saying bits and pieces ever since.'

Allie spent a moment making bug-eyes at J-Max, then she jabbed him with her finger. 'Is this true?'

He wriggled away from her finger and nodded.

Allie jabbed him again. 'Your sister's right – I *don't* believe it.' Another jab. 'Say something. Say, G'day Allie.'

My brother looked at the floor.

'Go on J-Max,' I said.

There was a silence while he went on looking at the floor. Then, still looking at it, he said, 'My mame's *Math*, nod J-Math.'

That made Allie squeal and hug him while I launched into the story of the two men we'd seen in the P. & O. liner. I told about the lightning flash, and ended saying, 'It was shock, I s'pose, that made him speak but he's going to need some sort of help because his tongue keeps getting in the way.'

'Give him a chance,' said Allie, hugging J-Max again. 'He'll do all right, won't you mate?' She let go of him and leaned back in her chair to look up at me. 'But first things first, as my grandad used to say. If those blokes saw you they might make enquiries and work out you're just squatting in the house. Once they know that they could come back.'

'I don't reckon. If you'd heard the way they took off . . . If you want to know, I think they were shitting.'

Allie shrugged. 'Maybe, but that can make someone dangerous.'

Thinking of Jim Donally who really was dangerous, I said, 'Those men don't bother me. Only one saw us and that was only for a second. He'd know we couldn't identify him or anything. My guess is they'll just keep away.'

'Why take the risk?'

I got down off the bed then and said, 'Listen Allie, I've got to stay in that house for a bit. I've got to stay while I find a job. I *need* a job. Max's turning into a real little scav. The other day he took this stuff we didn't even need. That bothers me I can tell you.'

Allie turned her head to give *J-Max* a deadpan look. Instead of meeting it, he slid his eyes to a wheelchair over by the windows. In the end, Allie said, 'You don't need a job, Mrs Lau. I've got one. I told you when you first came in.'

'You didn't say where it was.'

'I haven't had the bloody chance.'

'Do you think there'd be one for me?'

'Not just now but later on there might be.'

'So where is it?'

'Down at Byron Bay. It's with this women's theatre group . . .'

She was going to say more but I stopped her by wailing, '*Byron Bay!* That means you'll be leaving here.'

'We all will – Marcelle too, because I can't see her lasting as a waitress. She'll try to put the coffee on the table and put it in someone's lap instead.'

While I was trying to force a smile at that, Allie said, 'The other day when you were here, did you see the girl in that bed?' She nodded at the empty bed opposite hers.

'I didn't even look.'

'Well this girl from Byron Bay was there. Ro, her name is, and we got friendly. She's a member of the theatre group but came up here to have her baby.'

'Is she married or something?'

'No, but she's got this boyfriend who works in Southport. That's why she had the baby here. Anyway she got me a job too and what I'm trying to tell you is that you don't need one because I'll have enough for all of us.'

I wanted to ask what her job was going to be but couldn't because I thought that if I spoke, I'd start bawling the way I did the day J–Max and I took our groceries back to the house in Leopard Tree Lane. The thing that made me want to bawl was realizing that Allie whom I'd never even liked was accepting us as her friends, her *family* almost.

Being her it's a wonder she didn't get onto the fact that I'd come undone. Perhaps she did, because suddenly she began to talk about her job. 'The troupe at Byron Bay call themselves the Nin Theatre Group after this European writer who was about the first to say that women have to make up their own myths and things instead of letting men hang theirs on us. Anyway they've got this government grant which will let them expand a bit and they've bought a secondhand bus so they can take their show to other towns along the coast. The thing is that they needed someone who could sew.' Allie grinned at me. 'I used to sew for Mum in the holidays. I even learnt to put in zips and things. So here I am.'

By then I'd got myself together enough to say, 'It's incredible. I mean it couldn't *happen* that way.'

'It did.'

'Is it certain? I mean is it *fixed*?'

Allie made the okay sign with her thumb and forefinger. 'On Monday this bunch of girls came up from Byron Bay to visit Ro. She told them about me being into films and stuff as well as sewing and they came over to my bed and spoke to me. Then they took a vote right here in front of me and told me I was in.'

Again I said, 'It's incredible.'

'I know,' said Allie, 'And the best part is they care about my baby. I mean *really* care. They're going to help me. Peter, Ro's boyfriend, has already arranged for me to see someone at Legal Aid.'

'So when will you be going? To Byron Bay I mean.'

'As soon as I leave here and that reminds me. I'll need my clothes and things. Can you bring them?'

Allie's clothes – Jesus, where are they? rushed through my head. For the life of me I couldn't remember what happened to them the night we left the river bank. I remembered Marcelle shoving a lot of things back into the place she called the colonial cabinet but I had no idea if Allie's things went in too. If they did, they'd have been well and truly mashed by the storm and if they didn't – if they'd been among the stuff in Marcelle's plastic bags, they were probably out at sea and drifting towards the Ant*arctic*.

Allie was waiting for me to answer so what I did was tell her half the truth. 'We had to leave the marina in a big hurry,' I said, 'and we left some of our gear behind. But we took a lot too so I'll bring you something even if it's Marcelle's.'

'It's only to tide me over.' Allie gave this rough little laugh. 'When I think about it, I didn't have much of my own anyway.' I hardly heard her. I was thinking that if I had to look at Allie walking around in Marcelle's things without knowing the truth, I'd *die*.

Will I tell her now? I thought and looked at her. In the past I'd thought of her as being plain, even ugly but I found out there in the hospital that wasn't true. In a way she was plain but only because her face was sort of perfect. I know that doesn't make sense but what I'm trying to·say is that with her face and neck and everything suddenly thinner, you noticed her cheekbones as well as her excellent eyes. Her plain little freckled nose was close to perfect too and beneath it was the mouth with the television-ad teeth I told you about before. With the short little haircut and everything, this all added up to something so good I had the spooky feeling that her face would end up one day in glossy magazines in the place of Marcelle's. I don't mean I thought she'd be a fashion model. I just thought she'd be in there for *something*.

I wanted to tell Allie about this but didn't know how to do it without her telling *me* I was seriously retarded. Anyway, I didn't get the chance because one of the people visiting the woman who liked takeaways came over to us to hand around this packet of scorched almonds. He was an old bloke with a pair of glasses as thick as the bottom of bottles. (J-Max got onto those glasses straightaway and practically climbed up on Allie's bed for a better look.)

The man with the scorched almonds stayed for a few minutes asking J-Max if he played football and stuff like that and when he'd gone, Allie said, 'Joss was here a while ago. You missed him by about two minutes.'

It was the last thing I'd expected to hear and while I was

still grinning at her, she said, 'He wasn't put in the lock-up here. He was taken to some place up in Albion then brought back to front the court on Monday.'

'So he's been here all along?'

'No he hasn't, because after the case, they took him back to Albion and when he finally got out the storm had hit and there weren't any buses coming down the coast.'

'So what did he do?'

'Stayed with Master Ho. You know – that teacher of his – the one the kids call Father Christmas.'

'And what about the court? What happened there?'

'This youth worker, Tony Driscoll, got him off on a bond on condition he goes down to Melbourne to see his old man. He's going tonight. They've given him his bus ticket and everything.'

I heard my voice burst out, 'It's not fair! *Everyone's* going away.'

'You can't blame Joss,' said Allie. 'Tony Driscoll found out his father's out of Pentridge. He's been out about a year.'

'How did he swing that?'

'He didn't have to. The cops pulled in one of the guys who set him up. They pulled him in for something else but while they had him he talked. The next thing the papers took the story up. Then the Chinese community got behind Joss's father and made enough waves to get him released.'

In this slow voice, I said, 'P'raps he won't come back?'

'Joss? Don't be lame. Of course he will. He was off his face when he heard I hadn't seen you kids, and he only rushed away because he had this appointment with Tony. After that he was going home to pack his gear. Then he was going round to see Gerry and find out which marina he took you to.' Shooting out her hand to grab my wrist the way she'd done when J-Max and I got out of the lift, Allie said, 'Hey, his room's not that far from here. If you burn up there now you might just catch him.'

I stared at her and she said, 'Go on, go now – straight up Delaware Street.' She jerked her thumb in that direction. 'Past the little bunch of shops and take the second street on the left, then the first on the right. Daniel Street it is and Joss's place is the last one. You'll know it because it's on the top of the hill by itself – a daggy old joint everyone calls Tibet because all the winds hit it.'

While I hesitated she said, 'Joss's room is on the ground floor at the back. You can't miss it. Number four.'

I shot a look at J-Max. 'Leave him,' said Allie. 'We'll get into the speech therapy. Just *go*.'

Without saying anything else I went, not stopping for the lift but rushing down the stairs two at a time. On the third flight I realized that, left alone with J-Max, Allie would probably start asking questions about Marcelle. That only held me up for a few seconds because I could see that by going back *I'd* be telling Allie something dodgy was going on.

In the main doorway of the Hattan I was held up by a man manoeuvering through it in a wheelchair. He was wearing a football beanie and I think he was spastic because his arms waved all over the place as he tried to press the control buttons on his chair with this long pencil thing attached to his forehead.

I wanted desperately to help him but thought he might be humiliated if I did, so in the end I left him still poking at his buttons and began to run.

Chapter Twenty-One

I N SPITE OF all the sunshine, the air was still pretty
damp. This seemed to bring out the smell of things and
when I slowed down just past the shops, I caught the
Queensland smell of strong grasses and jungle-sized vines.
In Victoria the smells are different. Sometimes in spring you
get a whiff of jasmine growing on someone's fence or the
castor-oil scent of old red roses. Up here the big bright
flowers hardly smell at all. But when I reached the gate of
the place people call *Tibet* I smelt these two frangipannis
growing by the front steps and stood taking the strong
perfume in in gulps while I looked at the house.

It was an old two-storeyed place high above the others.
The walls were painted grey and had a lot of dark little
windows in them. In a corner of the top verandah there
were a few straggly potplants and sitting among them on a
cane lounge was an old man. He had on one of those
fisherman sort of sweaters and a pair of shorts and when he
saw me at the gate, he put his newspaper down and swung
this pair of thin old bare brown legs around so that he was
facing me. (He had slippers on his feet.)

I went in the gate and around the side of the house. The
path was a tunnel between ferns on one side and traveller's
palms and paw paw trees on the other. As I dodged my way

along it, the old man on the verandah got up and leaned over the rail to watch. I know because I looked back and saw him.

Joss opened his door wearing nothing but a pair of those black Japanese trousers that tie in the front like pyjamas. He had a T-shirt in his hand and a big bruise on the left side of his chest. His wiggy hair had been cut and his ears stuck out and when he saw me and said, 'Shit – Morgan,' instead of me saying hallo or anything, I blurted, 'Marcelle's dead,' then I rushed at him and butted my face into his shoulder.

He put an arm around me and we stayed there with me bawling while he held me away a bit and said, 'Come on inside, Mrs Werther's watching from the garden.'

Not letting go of me he took me into his room. When he had I blurted again, 'Marcelle's dead.'

Joss let go of me then and turned to grab a tissue out of a box on a chair. As he gave it to me I saw his skin had gone a sort of yellow grey. (I didn't know that Asians do that – lose their colour I mean, the way we do.)

I took the tissue but instead of mopping at my face, I said, 'She drowned. The day before the storm. She went out on this boat with a man called Donally and she tripped and went overboard.'

'Jesus Christ!' Joss turned away from me – right away this time and in a little while he said, 'Does Allie know?'

'No. I tried to tell her. I tried to tell her today but I couldn't.'

He stayed with his back to me and in the end, guessing that he was crying too, I whispered, 'I'm sorry.'

He came back to me then and not wanting to stare at his face, I fastened my eyes on the bruise on his chest. As he'd done before he put his arm around me and led me to the bed where we sat side by side while I dried my eyes and blew my nose.

I looked around for somewhere to put the soggy tissue. Everything in the room was so tidy I ended up shoving it in my sleeve. As I did, Joss said. 'Tell me what happened.'

'She went out on this boat called *French Mustard*. She went
. . .'

Joss interrupted. 'Start at the beginning. Start from where
the cops took Allie and me away.'

I told him. I told him everything – from the way Angel
climbed out of Gerry's ute to the way Donally said, 'See
you at eight,' and turned and ran up the steps on the yacht.
Sometimes I mixed the story up and had to go back and
correct myself but in the end I got it all out.

When I'd finished, Joss said, 'Maybe Donally was bullshitting. Maybe Marcelle isn't dead at all.'

'Yes she is,' I said grabbing his elbow. 'It was sort of
printed on him. If you'd been there you'd have seen it too.'

We looked at each other and as I let go of his elbow he
said, 'Does Donally know where you and Max are now?'

'No. That's why we nicked off in the middle of the
night.'

'And does anyone else know about Marcelle? The cops or
anyone?'

'Nobody knows – only Max and me,' I said and went on
to tell him how I'd tried to get in touch with Ingrid Frew
but stuffed things up by giving my real name to the man on
the hospital switchboard.

As I talked I watched Joss's eyes. They were like black
glass that day but as I went on I saw this kind of softness
come into them and at the end he said, '*Victoria*. So that's
who you are.' Then he drew his finger slowly down my
cheek, letting his hand fall onto my shoulder and stay there.
The way he did it was so sweet it made my chest all squeeze
up and I said, 'Why did she die? Tell me that.'

He had no answer and I went on, 'We only knew each
other a few days but she was just ace. She made the whole
world different and now she's gone.'

Joss looked away from me, stared over at the window
and in a little while he said, 'My mother used to say that

people come into your life for a purpose and when the purpose is done, they go.'

I thought that over and said, 'But what purpose could Marcelle have in my life and if it comes to that, what purpose did I have in hers?'

'Mum said it sometimes takes us years to work out things like that and sometimes we don't work it out at all. Maybe we aren't meant to.'

I told him then about the Tarot lady who'd refused to read the cards for Marcelle. 'Do you believe that stuff?' I asked.

'No, but my Mum did. She was baptized and everything in a Christian Church but I reckon underneath it all she was some sort of Buddhist.'

After thinking that over too I said I wasn't altogether sure what a Buddhist was.

Joss looked back at me then and said, 'It's someone who believes in reincarnation. You know – getting paid off in your next life for what you did in this one.'

'Do you believe in that?'

'I don't believe in anything much.'

I kept on at him, 'But do you believe in reincarnation?

Before answering, Joss tucked the side of my hair back behind my ear. 'I believe in the present. Being *here*. That's about it.'

The words were tough enough but the way he said them was so sad it made me go stupid the way I'd done a couple of times already since coming to the Gold Coast and I turned my head and plonked this crazy kiss at the side of Joss's mouth. It surprised him, I could see that and he stared at me. Understanding in the end I think why I'd done it, he let himself fall back on the bed pulling me with him. We stayed there just being together, sometimes talking about Marce, sometimes kissing each other. But one kiss, longer than the others gave me this funny shock wave – a kind of cramp that came and went down below my stomach and after that the kisses changed so that when Joss lifted up the front of my shirt and touched me, I slid my hand down and pulled the string on his trousers.

We had sex after that which is a pretty terrible thing to have to say with our friend just dead but the truth is that what I did with Joss that first day at Tibet was about the best thing that happened in my life.

I don't remember taking off my clothes but I must have because I had nothing on and Joss, naked too was lying on me. There was a time of hurting at the entrance to my vagina but Joss said, 'Ease down – ease down,' the way the Emperor would say it to his favourite Arab pony with jewels and things on its bridle. After that I opened myself to him, my arms, legs, everything and I began to feel this sort of *con*centrated pleasure which took me right across the sky until in the end I had this whole series of shock waves somewhere behind my pelvic bone. They spread through me, even my *neck* seemed to feel them. Then they slowed, stopped, and with my bones gone limp I fell all the way back to earth and it was over.

Thinking about it now it's hard to understand why I didn't connect what I did with Joss with the thing that happened between my father and me but I didn't. I didn't even think of my father. In fact in a way it was as if I really *did* become a new person in that little room with hardly any furniture in it and a Cooktown orchid in a milk bottle on the window sill. And when it was over, I felt so *right*, so much Morgan Christie that I took my time in exploring Joss's body, taking in the difference between his skin and everything and mine. He had hardly any body hair (neither did I if it comes to that) and the shadings on his penis were black like those on his lips.

I know people compare the bits and pieces blokes have for doing sex with all sorts of things because Amanda Reece showed me in a book at her place where some old Russian bloke likened the markings on a man's penis to a geranium.

I tell you that day with Joss I couldn't see any damned geranium. Not unless he was talking about a bud or something. Thinking of the stuff I saw at Amanda's though made me say, *There's a flower called Golden Rod. That's what I'll call Joss.* But I didn't say it out loud.

Joss was taking in all this exploration of mine, and thinking what a nerd he'd call me if he read my mind, I lay down again with my head close to his and asked him how he got the bruise on his chest.

'I got it in the bloody pit they put me in up at Albion.'

'From the cops?'

'No.'

'You mean you had to fight and stuff?'

'I didn't get the chance. These two Skips jumped me in the bog and held me while their mate kept punching me in the same place.'

'Was it *terrible*?'

'Pretty crook but just when I was ready to chuck this cleaner came in and they let me go.'

'From then on I suppose they really had it in for you.'

'No thank Christ, they didn't . The finals of their head banging competition were on and they concentrated on that. I had another bit of luck because this psychologist up there asked me where I could get a reference to be used in court. I told him to get in touch with Master Ho because I knew he'd give me one. Some of the blokes found out and after that they left me alone. They hung shit on me and stuff but they kept their distance.' Joss laughed. 'They probably thought I was the new Bruce Lee.'

'*Are* you?'

'Master Ho doesn't think so.'

I asked him then what the head banging competition was. 'Did they all line up and butt their heads together like rams?'

That made Joss laugh again. 'Not exactly,' he said. 'Two of them would sit side by side at the table – they did it at night when the little kids were locked on the tube. And when the starter whistled they'd bring their faces down as hard and fast as they could go and bash their foreheads on the table. They kept doing it while everyone counted and the one with the highest score won.'

'Didn't they hurt themselves?'

'Of course they did. They whacked themselves stupid and thought that was half the fun. Even the ones hurt worst thought it was funny. I reckon at least six blokes at that place were walking round punchy.'

'What would Master Ho think of you being somewhere like that?'

'The old dag would probably see it as a test for me or something.'

'What about the head bangers? What would he say about them?'

'That they were shit, I s'pose.' Joss paused to rub a hand over his hair, 'No, that's not true. He wouldn't judge them that way but he wouldn't bother about them either. I reckon he'd just think they were a long way down the ladder and had to spend a few lifetimes working their way up.'

'Is he a Buddhist too?'

'I don't know what he is. I think old Father Christmas has some little religion of his own.'

'What does that mean?'

'Well he's a vego and all that stuff but I know he likes to smoke dope and there's always some chick at his place with downcast eyes pouring out the tea and fixing the rice paper blinds.'

'What would he think of us being here like this?'

'He wouldn't think it was his business and anyway he says you should start sex early, specially girls. He says if they don't, they get self-conscious and never learn to enjoy it.'

I said something then that I'd been wanting to say for about an hour. I said, 'Marcelle told me you had sex with her. Did you?'

I didn't think he was going to answer but after a while he said, 'A couple of times, I did.'

'She told me she didn't think bonking was any big deal. Is that what you think too, Joss?'

This time I was *sure* he wasn't going to answer but I guess he was just thinking because finally he said, 'If you want to know the truth, no I don't. I crap on to my mates that I do but you've got to remember my parents were real old-fashioned Chinese and they spent a lot of time hanging their ideas on me. In a way I guess I'm stuck with some of them. I mean my olds thought you didn't even take a chick to the pictures unless you meant to marry her.

Grinning at him I said, 'Does that mean you have to marry me?'

'Not until I take you to the pictures.'

That made me laugh and I got up and went to the window and looked out into this piece of garden with long shadows in it and trailing vines and rain-rotted deck chairs. Beyond it the hill fell away sharply with this row of stilted houses clinging to it. At the bottom there was a big clay-coloured area where graders and things were working and behind that some bushland with the 'Magnum P.I.' mountain range showing blue at the back.

From somewhere down the hill a kid let go with a Tarzan call. It rose and fell across the hill, a lonely sound but a sort of defiant one too. I don't think I'd heard anyone do it outside a television set but it seemed so familiar to me it made me sad about a lot of things without even knowing what they were. I was still looking out, still hearing it inside my head when Joss asked me how old I was.

I wanted to lie. Nearly did lie, but because I guessed I wouldn't get away with it, not with my two-centimetre-wide backside was facing him, I mumbled, 'I'll be fourteen in June.'

'Christ!' I heard Joss jump off the bed. 'Don't stand there like that. Get something on.'

'Why should I?'

'Because if someone sees you here, I'll be put away for ninety years.'

'I thought Master Ho said girls should start young.'

'Jesus, not that young.'

I behaved like an absolute nerd then. Pushing the window open and leaning out, I shouted, 'I don't care who sees me. I'm going to be *myself* from now on and never be ashamed of anything I do.' In a way I wanted to stop when I'd got that far but couldn't make myself. What I did was twist back into the room and say to Joss who was pulling on his trousers, 'Allie says you're going home. Well, *I'm* not. I never will because I wasn't allowed to be myself. I wasn't even allowed to *laugh*. No one was unless my father made a joke and his idea of a good time was picking up some poor old newsreader who scrambled his grammar on the ABC.'

Suddenly I had nothing left to say and feeling small and silly I walked over and picked up my T-shirt. I was starting to put it on when Joss said, 'Okay that's your side of it, but what about mine?' (His eyes were like black glass again.) 'I'm on a bond, remember? That's why I'm going home.' He paused and touched the bruise on his chest. 'But I want to see my old man anyway. He's been ill they tell me and I'm sorry now I pissed off and left him. I reckon I won't feel right till I've told him so.'

Looking at the floor I said something about being sorry I'd chucked a wobbly.

'That's okay,' said Joss. 'But listen mate, we've got to sort a few things out.'

Certain he was going to say we wouldn't be seeing each other anymore I tried to nerve myself for it but all he said was, 'We've got to work out what you're going to do while I'm away.'

'Then I'm *not* too young?'

Joss frowned. 'What do y'mean?'

I shrugged and looked away from him.

'For me, you mean?'

Still not looking at him I nodded.

'Your age doesn't bother me. Well not that much. We've got to wait, that's all. No fucking till the bond runs out.'

'How long will that be?'

'Twelve months. But don't worry I can make it. The Chinese are very patient people. My old man says it's our great talent.'

Remembering the super-nova buzz I got when Joss went into me, I said, 'I don't think its mine.'

Joss was watching me and when I said that suddenly banged on this cracker of a smile. 'Don't put yourself down, Morgan. I reckon you could do anything.'

I felt great when he said that and looking back I can see why. It was about the first time anyone had praised me without it turning out to be a trick to con me into doing something like having my teeth checked out by Mum's rotten old tobacco-smelling dentist.

While I was still soaking up the compliment, Joss said, 'You haven't told me what you're going to do while I'm away.'

'Stay in Leopard Tree Lane of course. It's smashing there.'

'If you stay in Southport, odds are you'll run into Donally.'

'No we won't'

'You will. For all it's hype and stuff the Gold Coast's like a little country town. You bump into the same people all the time.'

'So we'll be careful and anyway its only for a couple of weeks. Then we'll go down to Allie at Byron Bay. She's asked us to. She even said she'll keep us and I think she meant it but she's got no money – not even any *gear* so I want to get a job for a while so I can pay my whack.'

'You've got Buckley's hope of getting one.'

'If Allie can just because she sews . . .'

'Because she what?'

'Because she sews. She got the job at Byron Bay because she did all this sewing for her mother.'

'Allie got the job, dilberry, because she's been in plays and things.'

'*Allie* has?'

'Yeah. She told me she was always doing stuff like that at school and she must've been pretty good at it because one of her teachers got her into some actors' outfit in the suburb where she lived. *That's* what got her the job, though the sewing probably clinched it.'

Starting at him. I said, 'I can't believe it. She didn't say anything.'

'Well Allie wouldn't.' Joss stopped and snapped his fingers. 'But wait a minute. There just *might* be a job for you.'

'How do you mean?'

'Earlier on today I saw Gerry and he told me he'd been down to the marina looking for you because he had this job lined up for Marcelle.'

'At the restaurant'

'No, something he'd heard about. A job at some hotel down at Mermaid Beach.'

'What sort of job?'

'I think he said in the laundry. I didn't listen all that much. I was shitting because he said there was no sign of you and half the yachts were matchwood.'

'Maybe he'll help *me* get it.'

'That's what I thought.'

'It'd be creepy though wouldn't it, scabbing one meant for Marcelle?'

'Don't be dumb. She didn't have it. Gerry was going to tell her about it, that's all. Besides, Marce'd be the first to say, go for it.'

After a moment I said, 'I guess she would. Specially if it'd help Allie out.'

Joss let go with another of his smiles. 'That's settled then. I'll ring Gerry right now. I'll ring on Mrs Werther's phone.' Already on his way to the door he paused to say, 'You get the rest of your gear on while I'm gone.'

I did what he said, using the end of his towel and the water from the orchid's milk bottle to wash myself a bit first. Joss was away longer than I'd expected and I used the time to look around his room. Not that there was much to see. The walls were made of the same VJ boards as the ones in the house in Leopard Tree Lane. They were painted a blue that had faded almost to white and one of them had a water stain on it like an elephant's head with a trunk and everything. On another Joss had Blu-Tacked this smashing photograph of two men fighting. The shot was taken so that they appeared to be about three metres in the air and you could almost feel their fury. They were facing each other with their backs curved and their arms and legs forming a pattern so that instead of looking like *people* they looked like some ancient symbol for the verb to fight.

Below the photo Joss had made a sort of chest of drawers from nine pineapple cartons – three across and three down. For the rest of it there was a card-table with a packed Puma bag sitting on it, a yellow kitchen chair and the bed along with a striped cotton rug on the floor which looked as if it had started out as someone's bedcover.

I'd picked up this library book and was reading the blurb about some master spy when Joss came back into the room. 'There is a job,' he said. 'It hasn't been advertised yet and Gerry says he can't see why you wouldn't get it.'

'Does he know about Marcelle?'

'Yes I told him. I had to, didn't I?'

'How did he take it?'

'Pretty hard. Surprised me a bit. In fact after I told him he was quiet so long I thought we'd been cut off.'

Remembering the way Marcelle had said, 'One more bastard,' as Gerry drove off the night he took us to Blue

Waters, I kept quiet too. Joss didn't notice because he was already saying, 'Gerry said you should dob Donally. And he said you should try for the job because it's at this hotel down at Mermaid Beach. That would get you out of Southport.'

'What's it called?'

'The hotel? The Rose Club and the job *is* in the laundry. Gerry said as far as he knows it's only light work and the best part is there's this mini-flat downstairs that you might get.'

'I bet I don't.'

'If you say that you won't.' Joss wagged a finger at me in a way that made me giggle. 'And don't giggle either when you get there. Now listen . . . the pub's in Tallulah Court.' He went on then to tell me how to get to Mermaid Beach and how to find the right street when I did. 'You're to see a Mrs McLeod. She's the housekeeper.'

'Don't worry. I'll be there by seven.'

'No need. Gerry said they aren't early starters. Ten would probably do. He must know this Mrs McLeod because he said he'll give her a ring and tell her to expect you.'

'I just hope she takes me on.'

'I reckon she will.'

'She might change her mind when she sees my little brother.' I stopped to thump my forehead. 'Shit! I left him with Allie. She'll kill me.' Then beginning to laugh, I said, 'Y'know what? He's started talking. I forgot that too.'

At seven-thirty that evening J-Max and I went down to the bus stop in Scarborough Street with Joss. The air was full of petrol fumes and overhead the stars were so big and *washed* looking they made me feel sad again the way I'd felt when I heard the Tarzan call floating past Tibet.

The driver who was standing by the bus checked Joss's

ticket then stowed his bag in the compartment down by the wheels. Ater that Joss hugged J-Max, then me. 'Take care,' he said. 'Both of you.'

With my face pushed against his shoulder, I said, 'I don't want you to go.'

His arms tightened. 'I'll be back before you know it,' he said and let go of me and turned and hopped onto the bus.

A minute later a window near us shot open. Then Joss's head came out and something clinked onto the footpath beside me. 'It's the key to my room. You might need it. The rent's paid to the end of the month and the landlady's name's Mrs Werther.'

The bus began to move. With Joss hanging out of it, it went down Scarborough Street past the post office. When it was level with Coles New World, Joss's head disappeared and after that we watched the tail-lights until the bus turned left at Short Street and went towards the highway.

It's a terrible feeling, I can tell you, seeing someone you care about go away from you like that on a bus at night.

Part Three

THE ROSE
CLUB

———————————————

Chapter Twenty-Two

X AM SAYS THAT that part of Mermaid Beach where Tullulah Court is, used to be mangrove swamp and not so long ago at that. He swears this is true but I'm not so sure because the house right next door to The Rose Club, with just a path down to the canal separating the two of them, looked as if it had been there *forever*. It was the presbytery belonging to a Catholic church further up the coast and had tall dark trees shading the side and front of it and a tennis court at the back. In front there was an old-fashioned porch and showing through a glass panel beside the door was this spooky red light in the shape of a heart. It was kept on even in daylight and caused some first-time callers to The Rose Club to pull up at the presbytery and go in there and ring the bell. When that happened one of the priests would come to the door and start in with this really bitter stuff about the evils of visiting women who'd abandoned God.

The same priest always answered the door, a tall man with a shiny white face and 'Reilly Ace of Spies' hair. Sometimes he'd follow the caller as far as the footpath, telling him to go home and recite a whole lot of Hail Marys. Mrs McLeod told me that the owner of The Rose was always trying to get the light removed. She said that one such attempt had caused the priest to have a mild stroke which left the side of his mouth twisted. (Mrs McLeod always laughed when she told me. She didn't want to, I could see that, but she did just the same.)

The Rose Club itself was a modern building of white brick with brown and white striped canopies over the door and windows. There was no name on it anywhere and if it hadn't been for a big brass nine on the front wall I might have ended up at the presbytery door too.

Even the number wasn't that easy to see. You had to look for it because this carport consisting of a series of arches and columns ran right across the front of the building, filling the space between it and the street. Three cars were parked there, although it would have held a dozen easily. One of them was like the van Angel disappeared in but without the sunset scene on the side.

The morning I went there for the job I had J-Max with me because I wasn't game to leave him alone at the safe house, so, before I went across the hectare of brick paving to the front door I made him sit with his back against the end of the carport and promise not to move. (To make sure he'd stay there I said all this stuff about how we'd have to go home to Ivanhoe if I missed out on the job.)

When I rang the bell, at first nothing happened then the cover on a grill thing slid back and a Filipino-looking woman peered out. She frowned at me but didn't speak so I told her I'd come about the job. Still frowning she looked me over all the way down to my thongs and because I knew my clothes weren't exactly jobified, I rushed out with, 'I was told to ask for Mrs McLeod.'

'Oh,' said the girl, 'Downstairs, was it?' And when I said I didn't know told me to go around the side of the building until I came to a door, then knock on that.

I did as she said, turning the corner to find the block of land fell so sharply towards the canal that the hotel had been built on three levels. They were connected by this path broken now and then by flights of steps. A dinky timber decking extended out from the second level and when I was halfway along it I found the door.

Mrs McLeod opened it before I could knock. Later I was to work out that the Filipino woman had buzzed her from the master phone upstairs but at the time I was really spooked when she appeared and said, 'You must be Morgan. Come on in.' (I knew no one had seen me coming because the windows along that side were those jazzy modern ones that angle back into the roof.)

I went past Mrs McLeod straight into this smashing kitchen with tomato red walls and tiles of dark slate on the floor. Along one wall were these three posters advertising concert performances of the singer Desli Martins who lives in America now and only comes out here for guest appearances and things. One of the posters was from Chicago and showed a line of black musicians standing at the back. I wanted to go over and look at it but Mrs McLeod had pulled a chair out at the table and was inviting me to sit.

A man was already seated there with the crossword page of the paper lying in front of him. He wore a T-shirt with the sleeves cut out and had burnt-brick skin and bleached hair. We both sat and Mrs McLeod said, 'This is Curtis, my son.'

He said 'G'day,' without looking up but the dog beside him, a bitser with a lot of blue heeler in him got up stiffly and came over to sniff at my leg.

'And that's Clancy who's not supposed to be inside,' said Mrs McLeod, then while I stroked the dog's head she began to talk about the storm and stuff. She spoke quickly, so fast in fact you only caught one word in three and had to guess the rest. Not that it mattered – I wasn't listening anyway because while she talked I was using the time to check her out.

She had this smooth brown face and hair of that baby blond some women choose when they begin to go grey. It was shortish and cut so that one side of it stayed back and the other fell in a curve down the side of her face, finishing in a point near her chin. Her eyes, which were checking *me* out as she talked, were small and almost navy blue, with loads of mascara and stuff on the lashes.

Mrs McLeod finally stopped talking long enough to locate a cigarette and get it going. When she had, she said to me, 'Gerry says you're free to start here straightaway.'

'Yes, yes I am.' I'd rushed the words out as if I was prepared to give her my *life* and because of that probably Curtis raised his head and gave me this long hard stare. Then he looked across at his mother. 'Aren't you going to ask about work experience?' he said. 'She looks about twelve.' He had this slow deep voice which seemed to make the words keep hanging in the air after they'd been spoken.

'Gerry says she's a good kid who deserves a break.'

'Huh – that's not likely to satisfy Merna,' Curtis told her and returned to his crossword.

Mrs McLeod tapped her cigarette over the ashtray in an agitated sort of way. 'She leaves downstairs to me. You know that.'

Curtis's answer was to read out a crossword clue. 'The end of the face goes gently towards foreign people.'

Without even thinking about it I said, 'Chinese.' I've no idea where the word came from. It was just *there* and that's really weird because I've never been into crosswords specially not cryptic ones. Anyway, the next moment Curtis shouted, 'Jesus! It fits.' And he looked across at me and grinned showing two rows of enormous teeth which were extremely white in his bricky face. (His eyes were like his mother's but with these pale lines spoking out from the corners.) Still grinning he told her to give me the job before I got away.

I said, 'It was only a fluke. I wouldn't do it again in a million years.'

'They're all flukes,' Curtis said. Then he gave a squinty look up through the window. After that he threw down his pen, scraped his chair back and stood. 'The breeze's up. I'm going to the beach.'

He was as tall and tough as a surfboard and as soon as I'd thought that I realized he was a surfboard *rider* and I knew then without being told that he didn't care about anything really except the times when he got to be part of a big wild wave which carried him like a god or something towards the beach.

On his way to the door – an inside one – he stopped to say to the dog who was hobbling after him, 'Move it you old bastard or I'll leave you behind.'

When they'd gone, Mrs McLeod said, 'Clancy should have been put down ages ago but Curtis won't hear of it.'

'He looks okay to me.'

'Curt keeps him full of cortisone, that's why.' She'd moved, was over at the bench near the posters, reaching her arm behind a potplant. The next moment she came back to the table carrying a glass of white wine. After taking a gulp from it, she said, 'You *can* start straightaway, can't you?'

'Tomorrow, I could.'

She put the glass on the table and sat, leaning over to stub out her cigarette as she did. Then she gave me the kind of squinty look Curtis had given the weather.

'Just how old are you?' she said.

I made myself meet the look the way Allie would have done. 'I'll be fifteen in June.'

Still giving me the squinty look she said, 'I'll believe you – thousands wouldn't,' and picking up her glass of wine, went on, 'Mrs Swann does leave downstairs to me. She's the owner by the way and she's fussy about the laundry. You can see why, but the work's easy enough. More a matter of being here than anything else. If you get going by nine each day you'll find you'll be finished by one.' She paused to take a drink. 'The money's good – no tax of course – and if you help me in here a bit, I'll see you get your meals.'

I waited with my breath slowed down while she said, 'A hundred and eighty a week. You work the same schedule as the girls. Twenty-eight days straight and then a week off. You won't get paid for that week and there's no sick pay or holiday pay.' Another look from her. 'Is that okay with you?'

I nodded but didn't speak because I was busy thinking, *If I can stick it for the full four weeks I'll have over seven hundred dollars. J-Max and I can live on that* FOREVER.

Realizing Mrs McLeod was waiting for more than just a nod, I said, 'It's fine. In fact it's *great*.'

She stood then, went to the fridge and topped her glass up from one of those wine cask things. With her back to me she took another drink before turning and saying, 'I'll show you around, then we'll have a cup of coffee while you tell me a bit about yourself. We don't expect life histories from laundry staff but I'll need to know something.'

I watched while she went over and put her drink behind the potplant again, took some keys from a row of hooks on the wall and grabbed her cigarettes and lighter. Then the pair of us went outside.

The first thing I did was look up at the carport to see if my brother was still in place. I could see the spot where he should've been sitting but he wasn't there. In a panic I swung my head around and saw him lying on this little orange painted jetty at the bottom of the path between The Rose Club and the presbytery. He was lying on his stomach looking through the slats the way he used to do on the jetty at the place where we stayed by the Nerang River.

Mrs McLeod hadn't spotted him. She was too busy pointing out the priests' strip of vegetable garden which had been well and truly mashed by the storm. (Another thing I learned later was that Mrs McLeod was obsessed with that garden. She couldn't *wait* for it to be productive again. Apparently she'd had this habit of making little night-time raids on it to grab a couple of tomatoes and a handful of silverbeet. Those raids must have been a big thing in her life because she talked about them a lot, especially at breakfast time when she'd groan because there was no nicked tomato to slice onto her toast. I don't know why she did it. Stole things I mean. She didn't need to. The food at The Rose was smashing and anyway Mrs McLeod did the ordering so she could get anything she wanted.)

Talking all the time about the priests and their garden she led me past the decking and down a flight of steps to another level of the building where she stopped to unlock a door.

After taking a quick look inside she turned to me and said, 'Bloody Curtis! He hasn't done the wash.'

'Was he supposed to?'

'Yes, until we found someone. He does it anyway on the laundry girl's week off – cursing like a trooper while he's at it, I might add.'

'Did the last girl leave?"

'She got sick of working weekends. They all do.'

I saw then that Mrs McLeod's face wasn't smooth after all. It *looked* it because she'd put some sort of shine on it but with the Queensland sun lighting it up I could see about a million little cracks in it and knew then she was quite old. Fifty perhaps or maybe more.

She was watching me and in case she'd read my thoughts I ducked my head and went past her into this room set up like a little laundromat with four washing machines against one wall and two dryers, big ones, against another. There was a handbasin too and on the floor a row of bulging garbage bags.

Going over to a bench and pulling out one of the cartons underneath it, Mrs McLeod reached inside then held up a pair of rubber gloves. 'You wear these all the time you're in here,' she said. 'Never do even one load without them and each time when you finish you take them off, roll them up and put them in the bin in the corner. Then you wash your hands in the basin before leaving the room.'

'You mean I'm to use a new pair every time I come in here?'

'Exactly, and you take them off and dispose of them when you leave even if you only pop out to the loo.'

'Isn't that sort of wasteful?'

'Better than getting AIDS, you goose.' Mrs McLeod flipped the gloves back into the carton. 'The machines bring the water to the boil and we use a germicide as well but I don't believe in taking chances. Merna's line . . . Mrs Swann's line is that *our* clients don't have AIDS and I'd say she's convinced herself it's true but how can anyone be sure of a thing like that? And if someone here did catch it, we'd be out of business in a week.'

By then anyone with even an eighth of a brain would have begun to wonder if The Rose Club was a hotel at *all*. Not me though. I thought Mrs McLeod was talking about the risks attached to sheets and things stained by honeymooners and when she went on to say the girls upstairs were happy to go along with Mrs Swann's claim that the clients were AIDS-free, I thought she was referring to the people who made the beds and did the dusting, and instead of asking what the girls *did* do upstairs I asked her to show me how to operate the washing machines and dryers.

In the end, satisfied that if I wanted to I'd be able to do the job standing on my head, I asked Mrs McLeod about the flat Gerry had mentioned.

'You know about that, do you?' she said and getting out a cigarette went to stand where she could look across at the flattened garden next door. (The gardens at The Rose consisted of white pebbles and palm trees and any damage suffered during the storm had already been cleaned up.)

Mrs McLeod stayed where she was. She was thinking, I suppose, because finally she said, 'I was hoping you wouldn't know the flat existed. Come on. I'll show it to you.'

She took me to an outside door near the end of the building and after unlocking it, waved me in. I went into this tiny room with two bunks in it, one above the other.

There was no bedding on them, instead each one was loaded with above a dozen of these extremely healthy looking potplants.

While I stood looking, Mrs McLeod said, 'It's where Curtis grows his dope. He hides it here because Merna's paranoid about drugs. Another of her boasts is that The Rose is drug-free. Of course half the girls do coke and some do worse but Merna manages not to know.' She went to the plants and poked at the soil of one. 'They grow like weeds in here because of the window in the roof. Mind you, Curt's forever rotating them and feeding them and so on.'

'Doesn't Mrs Swann come in here?'

'No, the flat's been empty for six or seven months so there's no reason.'

'Well I don't mind the plants, and I need *some*where, so if you've got a mattress I'd be happy sleeping on the floor.'

'If you had the flat Merna would look inside. She couldn't help herself. She's that sort of . . .' Mrs McLeod stopped, turned her head towards the door and said, 'and who are you?'

I turned too. My little brother was standing in the doorway, hands on hips as if he owned the place and this beamer of a grin on his face.

He didn't answer and because there was nothing else to do, I said, 'It's Max – my brother.'

'Why isn't he at school?'

'We've been moving around and I haven't had the chance to get him in somewhere.'

'So he's part of the deal is he?'

I had a few seconds then of thinking I could send J-Max down to Byron Bay with Allie but when I did a funny thing happened. Right in the middle of wishing him away my eyes homed on the old tennis-club scar on his chin and I felt exactly the way I'd felt the day he sailed off the roof there to land face first among the spectator benches. All I wanted to do then was rush to him and bearhug him because I knew that if I had to do without the mad little nong for even a week, I'd *die*.

Having worked that out I could see *both* of us going to Byron Bay so I told Mrs McLeod the truth, saying, 'He lives with me if that's what you mean, because there're just the two of us and we've been squatting in this house up at Southport but it's got so that we need to move and when I heard about the job and the flat and everything I thought it'd be just right for us.'

Mrs McLeod blew cigarette smoke out like a sigh. 'Merna wouldn't want a kid here.'

'I realize that now,' I said, 'But thank you anyway.' I was ready to go to J-Max and hurry him through the door but Mrs McLeod said, 'Don't rush off.' She was staring at J-Max. (He'd stopped grinning and, with his head bent, was examining one of his thongs.)

Mrs McLeod went on looking at J-Max for so long that I began to think she was seeing *Curtis* soar off a tennis club roof or something. Then, in her rapid-fire way she said, 'I think we can work something out. There's another room here – look . . .' and opening a door I hadn't noticed, 'We could shove the plants in here for a few days while we find something else for you.'

I went to stand beside her and leaning forward a bit looked into a miniature kitchen with a sink, a stove and a little fridge. Piled on the floor was the bedding from the bunks.

'It's perfect.'

'Don't get carried away.' Mrs McLeod edged her way in

past the bedding to stub her cigarette out in the sink. 'It's only temporary and won't be all that convenient. You realize you won't be able to turn the lights on at night because they'd be seen from upstairs?'

'We don't mind. We're used to that.'

'The shower and loo are outside round the corner but at your age I guess you won't mind that either.' She stepped back past the stuff on the floor. 'One other thing – when you come in here at night you lock the door and don't open it to anyone. Right?'

'Right,' I said and because I was *rapt*, I giggled.

'As for Tiger here,' she levelled a finger at J-Max who'd joined me at the door. 'He'll have to keep out of Mrs Swann's way but that shouldn't be too difficult because at nine on Monday I intend trotting him around to the local primary school. I think I can get him in. I've got a contact there.'

'Sending him to school's not that simple,' I said. 'He's bright enough but he's only just learned to talk, so his speech is pretty daggy.'

Mrs McLeod looked at J-Max again for a while, then she said, 'I'll tell them that. They'll have someone to handle it. And now let's go back to *my* kitchen and find him a piece of sultana cake.'

Chapter Twenty-Three

J-MAX AND I spent the rest of the day ferrying a load of our stuff up to Joss's room then a load of Marcelle's to Allie.

At Tibet the old man wasn't watching from the verandah and in a way I missed him because I wanted things to be exactly the way they were the first time I went there.

When we got to the back of the house a woman kneeling in the garden bobbed her head up the way a bird does in the bush when it's feeding on the ground. She was about sixty with wild hair and she asked us what we wanted.

'Are you Mrs Werther?' I said.

She nodded but didn't speak and I noticed one of her eyes had a funny fixed look as if it was made of glass or something.

'I'm just popping this case in Joss's room,' I told her. 'He gave me the key.' Then before she could tell me not to, I hurried across the verandah to Joss's door, unlocked it and slung the case inside.

The woman had stood up. In a man's cardigan with these two wads of hessian tied to her knees she looked like the Drover's Wife – or maybe his mother.

She'd seen me looking because she said, 'I get rheumatics,' and knowing I'd been rude I went a few steps towards her and said, 'I'm Morgan Christie. The storm made a mess, didn't it?'

'Too much bloody mess.' She said, then asked why I was leaving the case there.

'My brother and I are going down to Mermaid Beach. I'm starting a job there. We won't need the things till we're settled. It's okay isn't it?'

'If it's all right with Joss, I suppose it's all right with me.' Turning her normal-looking eye on me she said, 'Are you his girl friend?'

I felt my face begin to redden. 'Sort of,' I said and going to J-Max I gave him a shove in the direction of the gate. At the corner I looked back. Mrs Werther was already kneeling in the garden again on her hessian kneecaps.

The visit to Allie wasn't as easy. To start with I can't tell you how rotten it was carrying Marcelle's clothes up the hill to the hospital. It was as if I was carrying bits of *her* and in a way I was. I mean for the first time I was admitting, proving really, that she wasn't coming back. Till then, in spite of the things I'd said to Joss about believing Jim Donally's story, there'd been this quinchy little corner of my heart that thought she might.

On top of that I knew Allie would ask me if I'd heard from Marcelle. (J-Max had already told me that when I left him at the hospital the day before she'd asked *him* what he knew about Marcelle going to Stradbroke Island. Then he spat on his hand and held it up and swore blind he didn't tell her the truth.)

Allie met us at the lift again. She'd been watching for us because she'd been told she could leave the hospital. She said Ro's boyfriend was picking her up at four-thirty to take her to Byron Bay. After that she looked at the case and said, 'You found my things.'

I put the case on the floor and keeping my eyes down said, 'No, they're Marcelle's.'

There was a silence so I went on, 'I couldn't find any underpants so I bought a pair on the way here.' Another silence which I filled by saying, 'I meant to bring an orchid plant but I guess I forgot.'

Then I heard Allie say, 'Aren't you going to tell me what happened to her?'

I lifted my head to shoot a look at J-Max.

Allie said, 'He didn't say anything. If you want to know, he buttoned up. That's what told me really. That and the sort of *shock* I saw on your face yesterday.'

I told her then, standing in the corridor with the suitcase between us. I didn't make a big drama of it the way I'd done with Joss. I just told her quietly in these blunt little sentences. When I got to the end Allie was white and her breath was going in and out in *puffs*. I thought then that she'd keel over or something but what she did was stand there and say this extremely unselfish thing. She said, 'I'm sorry you had to go through all that alone Morgan.'

'I'm sorry I had to tell you. I didn't want to.'

'I know that.' Allie reached out and brushed her knuckles against the side of my face and tried to say something else but stopped I think because she knew she wouldn't get it out without howling. Then she bent and picked up the suitcase. I slipped my hand under hers and together we carried it into the ward.

We talked for a while in there about Marce and how much we'd liked her and what a nut she was and everything. In the end Allie said, 'Life's *perilous* for girls, isn't it?'

Looking at my brother with his tender little neck and grasshopper legs, I said, 'It is for boys too.'

'Yeah – little ones.'

'Big ones too. They get sent to war.'

'Yes but a girl's whole life is war. She can't even walk around after dark in her home town. And if she does and gets bashed and raped or tortured to death or something, some sodding old judge will say she asked for it.'

I agreed and after a moment J-Max piped up, 'Then you've got to grow big and lift weights and things so you can *fight*.'

Hearing him say that in his spooky Japanese – English made Allie and me laugh and while we were, the thought, *Or learn to do it Master Ho's way*, went through my head. I didn't get to say it aloud though because as soon as Allie had stopped laughing she told me that instead of hanging around the Gold Coast looking for a job I should go to Byron Bay that afternoon with her.

I said I already *had* a job, that I was going to stick it for four weeks and then arrive in Byron Bay in style.

Allie did everything she could to put me off, saying they'd work me like a slave at The Rose Club. 'I know about those chaddy little fleapits,' she said. 'They'll work a kid like you fourteen hours a day and dock your pay every time you do something wrong. And they'll get away with it because you've got no one to help you stick up for your rights.'

'It isn't like that at all,' I said. 'In the first place, it's not a chaddy little fleapit. It's really something. You should've seen the kitchen, it was like . . .'

Allie stopped me there by saying. 'So much the worse – all paid for out of the wages of kids like you.'

That made me laugh again. Allie didn't laugh though. Instead she made me take down Ro's telephone number at Byron Bay and said I had to ring her at the first sign of what she called *standover tactics*.

After that we talked about Marcelle again. Allie asked a heap of questions about Jim Donally and at the close of visiting time as she walked us to the lift she brought up the subject of The Rose Club again. 'When I come up for my interview with Legal Aid,' she said, 'I'll check it out myself.' Then she stopped and facing me added, 'Morgan, take care. The way I see it is you're all I've got left.'

With my voice gone funny I said, 'I'll ring you. I'll ring

you tomorrow,' and I lunged at her and hugged her till I probably hurt. J-Max hugged her too then we got in the lift. As the doors closed I saw her face, big-eyed and anxious as hell, still watching us.

Sometimes now I think of our Sunday morning trip to Mermaid Beach and laugh. At the time though I didn't do any laughing. The bus was almost empty. Three women who looked as if they were on their way to church sat near the front and these four teenage boys in beach gear were in the slightly raised bit at the back. One of them had a baseball bat on his knee.

J-Max and I went to the back too, with our suitcase and Bobby Deerfield in a butter carton. When we'd left Main Beach and were bowling along beside the ocean, Bobby let out a wail. That made the beach boys pull faces and give each other these dumb looks. At the Cavill Avenue traffic lights in Surfers, when Bobby poked his head out of the carton, they began miaowing.

At first the driver took no notice, but as the miaowing went on he started glancing up at his inside mirror and when we'd pulled into Pacific Fair he climbed out of his seat and came back to where we were sitting. Seeing the carton and everything, he told J-Max to get off the bus.

Half-standing, I said, 'We're only going as far as Markeri Avenue.'

The boy with the baseball bat was in the seat in front of me and he lifted it and used it to tap the window beside him. 'Do the world a favour, Grandad,' he said, 'and let them stay.'

The driver's face went red. He had these goitry sort of eyes and I thought they'd pop there and then but all he did was glare a bit then turn, stomp back to his seat again and take off with us still aboard. He stopped to let us out at

Markeri Avenue and J-Max and I got off the bus to a chorus of miaows and shouts of 'Moggy-Moggy'.

When we'd crossed the highway J-Max, giggling uncon-*troll*ably, let Moggy-Moggy out of the carton and he walked with us all the way to Tallulah Court.

We found Mrs McLeod in the garden of The Rose Club. She had on this white leisure suit with strands of coral around her neck and was over by the priests' garden finishing a cigarette.

Catching sight of Bobby skittering down the steps behind us, she said, 'Oh God! I might have tipped it.' But when she heard his name she put her head back and laughed, then picked him up and with us following carried him down to our flat.

Inside it the marihuana plants had been moved to the kitchen and the bunks made up. Someone, Mrs McLeod I guess had put a fresh hibiscus bloom on the tiny strip of dressing table. I thought that an extremely *welcoming* thing to do.

When I told her so, she thanked me and said I could please myself what time I started work, adding, 'It'll be a long shift though. The laundry's been piling up.'

'Will Max be okay?'

'Sure. He can hang round outside most of the day. Mrs Swann never gets here before five on Sundays.'

'Doesn't she live here?'

'No, she owns the penthouse suite at Electra in Surfers and comes down every day. Usually she arrives at one-thirty but on Sundays we get a break from it.'

'Will she mind about the cat?'

'Merna minds about most things so if she sees him we'll say he belongs over at the presbytery. She'll probably swallow that.'

I guess I looked unconvinced because Mrs McLeod said, 'Forget the cat. Just put your case down and decide what you're going to do.'

I said I'd start work straight away so she unlocked the laundry for me then went back upstairs after saying to me, 'Rubber gloves – remember?'

The washing certainly had piled up. There seemed to be twice as many bags as the day before. With big yellow gloves flopping on my hands I lifted one and tipped the contents into a machine. Out came a bunch of towels in shades of pink and as they did the smell of semen came up and filled my nose and throat.

Yuk, I thought, looking in at the towels, *the honeymooners go at it in a big way*, and grabbing the bottle of germicide I sloshed in twice the amount I'd been told to. There was a bad moment for me then because suddenly I was back in the bathroom at home sponging myself with Dettol to get my father's semen off me.

Sort of crouching against the machine, I looked in at the towels. They were in three shades of pink – baby-pale, a buffy pink and deep rose. All I wanted then was to be away from there and remembering myself as I was at school, gossiping under the trees with my friends, in shirts and ties and shoes and things, I found I couldn't bear what had happened to me. The next moment though I saw myself back in Barbie's house in Canterbury while she pretended to believe I was telling lies about my father. Knowing then there was no way I could go back. I whispered Marcelle's name and asked her to tell me what to do.

There was no answer from her. In fact at that moment the world was so empty of her it was as if she'd never been. But as I crouched against the washing machine I did hear something. I heard J-Max give this squeally little laugh and say something about a funny name to give a boat.

I don't remember going to the door but the next thing I was there looking down towards the canal. J-Max was by the jetty watching a man sanding this little dinghy on the bit of beach behind the presbytery. Catching sight of me, he grinned and gave a wave.

I grinned too. If you want to know it was an *ace* moment for me because it made old Barb and even the semeny towels seem like nothing and as I turned back into the laundry I said to myself, *And if being without Marcelle is hard at least I've got . . . I've got . . .* I was trying to tell myself that her *essence* was still with me but I couldn't find a way. (I didn't ever find the right word. It was Xam who supplied it later on.) That day I knew what I meant though, and Marcelle-style I made myself say, *Dirty towels are no big deal. Go back and bang in the soap powder and get the bloody things on the go.* And I did just that then filled the other machines as well.

With the four of them chonking away I sat on the step and thought about Marcelle, asking myself where she was and why she died the way she did when J-Max and Allie and I were all still alive. I thought about it until my brain practically *melted*. I didn't come up with any answers but at least I sorted one thing out because by the time the third lot of towels was ready to come out of the dryer I'd made up my mind to get on with the story I'd started writing in my head. I mean the one about the two girls who meet and team up after nicking off from home. *Only this time*, I thought, *I'll write things just the way they happened. I'll pinch some of J-Max's paper and I'll start from the moment we got on the train at Spencer Street.* Then I thought, *No, I won't I'll start at the beginning. I'll start with my father coming into my room because if I'm writing it as a sort of monument to my friendship with Marcelle I should try to tell the truth – even if telling it cuts me in two.*

At the bench folding towels, I realized that knowing where to start and how to start are different things. *How could any writer*, I asked myself, *be expected to launch into a chaddy sex scene involving their own father?*

Not me, I said turning back to the dryers. As I did the figure of a woman appeared in the doorway and because my mind was somewhere else I gave this little shriek.

'Your nerves are not good dulling,' said the woman and stepped into the room. She had this faint but extremely attractive accent and the way she said the last word was neither darling nor dolling but an absolute *balance* between the two.

When I didn't answer she came closer. 'Why do you scream at me?'

Mumbling, I said I wasn't expecting to see anyone.

'Of course not, dulling. I am not usually here on Sundays.' She gave me a look which had something in it I couldn't read. 'I am Mrs Swann. I own The Rose.' When she said that she turned towards the light and lifted her chin like someone getting ready to have their photograph taken.

Her face was a thinnish one with these big slatey eyes in it. There was a lot of life in it too because it altered all the time as she quirked her mouth and widened her eyes then narrowed them again. Although easily as old as Mrs McLeod she wore her hair – light brown and crinkly – pulled back into a silver ornament then falling in a thick stream down to her waist.

She was dressed like a peasant girl in an *opera* or something. Her blouse had big puff sleeves and her skirt had these little pieces of mirror let into the embroidery around the hem. It was her jewellery though that made me stare. She wore loads of it, all silver – earrings, necklaces and about forty bracelets on each arm.

She'd seen me looking at the jewellery because she flicked the bracelets on her left wrist and set them spinning. 'Mrs Lumley who reads the Tarot cards so successfully tells me these are a symbol of sexual potency. Do you agree, dulling?'

Still mumbling I said I didn't know.

Mrs Swann sighed then pulled a comic face. 'Hattie McLeod told you about me?'

'Yes.'

'And you're going to be happy here?' (She said *heppy*.)

'Yes I think so.'

Suddenly she lifted the lid of one of the machines and peered inside. While she was doing it I saw that she had on the kind of Kung Fu shoes Joss wore. The ones you buy at the market for six dollars a pair.

'Hattie told me about *you*,' she said turning back. 'But she didn't tell me how pretty you were.' Coming close enough to put her hands lightly on my shoulders she went on, 'A ripening little Dolly Haze, eh dulling? And who knows – if we put our cards down very carefully we may turn you into a rich little Dolly Haze.' Her eyes opened to the full as she dropped her hands and stepped back. Then without another word she turned and swept out.

I walked slowly over to the door to stand and watch her go up towards the decking. She was no longer sweeping along but putting her feet down carefully so that she swayed a little as she went. And it was while I was watching her that I worked out the Rose Club wasn't a hotel at all. It was a massage parlour. A brothel.

I think dodgy little clues about the place had been floating in my head all along but it took the sight of Mrs Swann's long hair and mirrored skirt swaying up the steps to make them pop into place. Her last remarks helped too because although I had no idea what a little Dolly Haze was I knew Mrs Swann was making some connection between me *physically* and money.

Anyway, what I'd just worked out was so revolting it made me slide back into the laundry to press my back against the wall beside the door and stay there.

Chapter Twenty-Four

I DON'T KNOW how long I hid by the wall but I was still there in my silly gloves when Mrs McLeod came in. She was clutching her cigarettes and lighter and began talking before she was even in the door. This time her speech was so fast I missed whole slices of it.

'On Sunday . . . *has* to see . . . wouldn't read about . . . know everything . . . my domain . . . nothing on its mind'. Then, focussing on me, she said more slowly, 'You all right, Morgan? You're very pale'.

Shoving myself away from the wall I blurted, 'This place is a brothel, isn't it?'

She leaned towards me a little and shifted her grip on her cigarettes. 'Didn't you know, dove?'

'No.'

'Didn't Gerry tell you?'

'Did *he* know?'

'Of course he did.'

'He said it was a private hotel.'

Mrs McLeod gave this sigh and I saw that her eyes were puffy that morning. (I can't be sure but I think one corner of her mouth was puffy too.)

'I expect he thought you'd understand,' she said. 'Lots of

men call parlours that. Especially ones from overseas.' Still watching me, Mrs McLeod tilted her head to one side. 'Merna upset you, didn't she? What did she say?'

'She called me a little Dolly Haze. Mrs McLeod, 'What does that mean? Does it mean I'm a prostitute?'

She gave a gasp of laughter. I don't think she meant to because after it she said quickly, 'Of course it doesn't, dove.'

'Then what does it mean?'

'I haven't got a clue, but Merna's Polish and comes out with some queer things. I must say I've never heard that one though.'

'She said she'd make me a rich little Dolly Haze.'

In this dry voice Mrs McLeod said, 'That's typical. But don't let it get to you. She didn't mean it. She was crapping on. She does it all the time. Merna *has* to impress, *has* to be someone, even to the kid in the laundry.'

'She *sounded* as if she meant it.'

'Well she didn't. You can put your mind at rest on that score. One thing I'll say for her, she doesn't have any kinky business here.' Mrs McLeod paused to give me a different kind of look. 'She told you about The Rose though did she?'

'No, I worked it out. I worked it out by looking at her.'

She gave another laugh, a shouted one this time. 'God, I hope you didn't tell her. She kids herself she looks like a diplomat's wife.'

'I didn't say *anything*.'

Still amused she said, 'Just as well.'

We were both silent and while we were the last of the dryers stopped. When it did I heard something that sounded like Allie's old friend the Red Baron droning overhead. I took this deep breath then and said, 'Mrs McLeod, I can't stay here.'

'Why not, dove?'

'I just can't, that's all.' I said, then burst out, 'It's not the place to have my little brother, is it?'

'He looks okay to me. Have you checked on him lately?'

She'd turned to look out the door and I did the same. J-Max's friend had disappeared but he was still there, sitting on the side of the jetty with his head up watching the Baron's little plane as it dived down on Surfers. On the edge of the jetty peering at the water was Bobby Deerfield.

'A man was there a while ago,' I said. 'The one who owns the boat.'

'That'd be Brother Pat. He's a nice bloke.' Mrs McLeod gave a bit of a grin. 'Curtis says he calls that boat the *Holey Ghost* because the first time he took it out, it sank.'

Ignoring the joke, I said. 'My friend Allie says that these gangs of men on the Gold Coast kidnap young boys. She said they keep them prisoner and use them for sex then kill them or something.'

In the dry voice she's used before, she said, 'Well I doubt that Brother Pat's one of them.' Frowning a little she went on, 'I've heard that sort of thing happens and not only on the Coast either. Certainly it's something kids need to be warned about but I think you've got to achieve a balance between making them frightened of their own shadows and letting them lead normal lives.'

'It isn't normal though is it, . . . I mean it can't be safe to have James living in a place like this.' I was so rattled I used my brother's real name but Mrs McLeod didn't notice or if she did she didn't let on.

'Morgan, if you but knew it, he's safer here, *both* of you are, than anywhere else in Queensland. The top cops, the very top ones come here, and cabinet ministers, even the odd ambassador. The Rose is, well more of a club than anything else. You don't get in without the right introduction and Merna's tough on introductions. And she won't be putting you up for auction if that's what's bothering you. Apart from any other consideration she values the reputation of this place. She thinks it gives her clout and she loves that.' Mrs McLeod stopped there to get out a cigarette. Her lighter was playing up and it took her a while to get it going. When she did she said, 'We can't afford even a breath of scandal because at the first whiff of one, the clients would vanish. You could say discretion was our hallmark. For instance, your friend Gerry comes here to play cards but only in the kitchen. He wouldn't be welcome upstairs.'

'That doesn't make it right for my brother to be here.'

'I can't see that it matters. I expect to get him into school tomorrow so he won't *be* here that much. And by the way, I've persuaded Curtis to take him to the beach this afternoon.'

'He *couldn't* take him. Max is an absolute maniac in the water.'

'He won't be a maniac while he's with Curt. If he is he'll get a thump, that's for sure.' Mrs McLeod was watching me through a stream of smoke. 'Listen dove, why don't you take it day by day. You'll be properly fed here. I'll see to that. And you've got your little flat to sleep in. Why not stay till Saturday – that's pay day – then see how you feel with a bundle of twenty dollar bills in your hand.'

I shook my head. 'I don't think it's right to stay.'

'Well look at it this way – if you were in the laundry of a big hotel up along the Strip, the same thing would be going on upstairs but you could pretend you didn't know. Does that make it any different?'

'I don't know. I don't suppose so.'

'And in the place where Gerry works – half the well-dressed women eating there are working girls. That's what tarts call themselves these days by the way. Does that mean all the staff should quit?'

Thinking then of how Joss had turned up at the river each night with food he'd probably nicked from the same restaurant, I said again, 'I don't suppose so.'

'Morgan, as far as I can see there are two ways of looking at the world. You can see everything as evil and then it is. Or you can be a fool and see it all as sweetness and light.

The trick is to strike the balance I was speaking of before and you do that by keeping yourself decent the way I do. Then what the rest of the world does, needn't bother you.'

While I was thinking over what Mrs McLeod had said, she started off again. 'In any case, don't make a decision while you're still upset. Sleep on it tonight and see how it looks in the morning.' She went to the washbasin and stubbed her cigarette out in it. 'Now come along – take off your gloves and I'll feed you. Things will look different you'll find with some braised steak inside you.'

Following Mrs McLeod up to the kitchen I told myself her suggestion of sleeping on my problem was a reasonable one but later at the lunch table when I saw J-Max shovelling her tomato pie into his mouth, I knew I didn't need to because if humanly possible I'd be staying at The Rose until I had the money to feed both of us while I looked for a job at Byron Bay.

I could say that lunch altered my ideas about a lot of things because for the first time I understood why girls sell themselves for food during wars and things. And I could see that no one had the right to judge them or even say a *word*.

I'd meant to ask Mrs McLeod who owned the Desli Martins posters but as things turned out I didn't get around to doing it. In fact, although it was extremely pleasant in the kitchen with the sun coming through the roof I was actually looking forward to getting back to the laundry so I could take out all the things I'd seen and heard and *look* at them.

At the end of the meal, Curtis left the room saying he was off to fire up his bong. Mrs McLeod then told J-Max that if he wanted to go to the beach he must go outside and sit somewhere quietly for half an hour. He pulled a face but went and as soon as he had Mrs McLeod began to talk about Merna Swann.

She was standing at the fridge refilling the wine carafe and she said, 'I was gobstuck when she turned up this morning. You know why she came, don't you?'

(I wanted to laugh at the way she'd used the word gobstuck but didn't let myself.)

'She came because I put you on. She told me to find someone. "I'll leave it to you", she said but as soon as I did she had to come sticking her finger in like a . . .' Without finishing the sentence Mrs McLeod slammed the fridge door shut and came back to the table.

'Is Mrs Swann still here?' I asked.

Pouring wine Mrs McLeod said, 'No. On Sunday mornings she visits her husband down at Burleigh then goes somewhere for lunch. As a rule she doesn't show till three, sometimes later.'

'Doesn't she live with her husband?'

'Gerald's in a nursing home. He drank his liver to extinction, his brain too if you ask me and lives in a semi-vegetable state. Merna won't have him here but sees he has the best of everything and visits him nearly every day.'

'Is he terribly old or something?'

'Not really – sixty at the most.'

I thought to myself that was old but instead of saying so, I asked if The Rose was originally his.

'No, he was in real estate and sold her the place. That's how they met.' Hattie was staring at one of the Desli Martins posters. I don't think she was seeing it though because in a little while she went on, 'In those days he wasn't bad looking, a bit beefy in the face but tall and fair and sporting the regimental tie. I think Merna was impressed by what she called the British-look because after he'd squired her around for a few months, they married. As soon as that happened Gerald sold his business and bought a yacht. From then on he spent his time playing on it.'

'*Playing* on it?'

'Yes, like a little boy. He moored it in the canal and went out to it after breakfast each day to polish the brass, look at the charts and try to use the sextant but not once did he sail even as far as the Broadwater. In bad weather he'd put on oilskins and practice storm drill, still in the canal of course. And the worst part of it was he called the damned thing *Captain's Courageous*.' Mrs McLeod gave one of her bitten-off laughs. 'After he became ill he gave up canal yachting and took to wandering around The Rose in a pair of white shoes and pyjamas. Some days he walked around crying. He wasn't exactly an advertisement for the place and finally Merna put him in the nursing home.'

Mrs McLeod was quiet again, thinking I'm sure about the past so I said to her, 'Have you known Mrs Swann a long time?'

'Practically forever. We go back . . .' She broke off because the inside door opened and Mrs Swann herself came into the room. When she reached the table, she stopped and her eyes swept the remains of our lunch. You could *see* them counting the number of places.

'You've just missed Dandy,' said Mrs McLeod, who'd got to her feet. 'He called in on his way to Currumbin.'

'Ah, Dandy.' Mrs Swann put her hand on the back of my chair. 'And this little dulling has had lunch too?'

'We've just finished and now she's going to load the dishwasher for me.'

Without pushing my chair back I squeezed away from the table and took some plates to the dishwasher. Behind me I heard Mrs Swann say, 'I should have lunched here too. As it was I had a little piece of dried-up barramundi with the Grimblatts, who could speak of nothing but the insurance claim on their Melbourne warehouse.'

'The fur people?' said Mrs McLeod.

'Yes and they made my poor head ache. I'm going now upstairs where I'll have a brandy in a pretty glass and I'd like some of my friend Hattie's beautiful coffee sent up to me too.'

I'd turned to watch by then and as Merna Swann went towards the door, I said, 'Mrs Swann?'

She turned too. 'What is it, dulling?'

'I'd like to know what a Dolly Haze is.'

'Ah – you remembered.'

I waited while she tilted her head back and looked at me through her eyelashes. 'If you ask me when I'm less fatigued I'll tell you,' she said and turned again and made another of her cool exits.

Mrs McLeod and I looked at each other. 'She saw the four plates,' I said.

'It's okay. I covered that.'

'She'll find out we're in the flat for sure.'

'Don't worry till it happens.' To my surprise Mrs McLeod grinned and I had this feeling then that for some reason she'd *welcome* it if Mrs Swann did find out. I tried to think of a way to ask her about that but I couldn't and anyway she'd already dropped her eyes and was busily sweeping crumbs into her hand.

Later, when I'd stacked the dishwasher, I said to her, 'Mrs McLeod, why do men come to places like this?'

She'd just switched off the coffee grinder and she looked around at me to say, 'To get their rocks off. You know that.'

'That's not the real reason. Men can get all the sex they want just by going to a disco or something. So why do they come here?'

'Men in the public eye can't go to discos.'

'I'm not just talking about the men who come to The Rose. I mean why does *any* man go to a brothel?'

Mrs McLeod came to the table and took her time in refilling her glass. When she had, she used this half-jokey voice to say, 'Curtis thinks they go to get away from women.'

'That doesn't make sense.'

'It does to Curt. He says men are manipulated by them – cornered, is the word he uses. According to him, a parlour is the one place where there's none of that because everyone concerned knows exactly what the other side's getting.'

'Is that what you think?'

'It's part of it.' Her voice had changed, become more serious. 'Jean Rhys, the writer, said the thing that attracts a man to a woman is other men. I go along with that because when it comes to sex, I know they like to get where other men have been.'

Thinking of Joss I blurted, 'I don't believe that.'

'At your age, of course you don't and anyway there are exceptions. Some men have evolved past pack behaviour. The trouble is there aren't many of them about.'

We looked at each other. Then for no reason we both smiled. I don't know why that smile made me feel good but it did and later when I went back to the laundry I could see that the bags of soiled towels and things had nothing to do with me *personally*. After that I was able to shy them into the machines without thinking about it.

J-Max had a smashing time at the beach with Curtis but it wrecked him. That night his I'm-not-ready-for-bed performance was what I'd call a pikey one. We'd eaten again in the kitchen along with one of the upstairs domestics, a sixty year old Tasmanian called Elsie. She and her twin sister worked alternate shifts at The Rose and Curtis called them the White Mice. It was a good name because they both had pink skin and straight white hair and they sat at the table with downcast eyes eating their food with these dainty mousey movements.

Mrs Swann didn't appear but Hattie's boyfriend, Dandy Palmer, turned up towards the end of the meal. I don't know where his nickname came from. It certainly wasn't because of his appearance. He had a pale baby face with limp hair falling onto the forehead and his clothes were daggy to the last degree – no shirt, a stained sweater and trousers so insecurely held up the crack in his bottom was on permanent display.

Because he talked about himself all the time I soon found

out that Dandy was a poet who worked part-time at the mortuary. (The People's Poet he called himself but Curtis, who loathed him, said the Pisspots' Poet was closer to the mark.) Anyway, someone up in Brisbane had published a collection of his stuff and he'd become a sort of celebrity on the Gold Coast, always being interviewed on the local radio station and being asked to spout his poems at smoke nights.

I disliked him too. Not just because of his insecure trousers but because he was so rotten to Hattie. I think he was quite a bit younger than she was and he kept calling her Mother Goose and banging his fist on the table and saying, 'Chop-chop,' when he wanted another beer. And the most amazing thing was that while all of this was going on, Hattie kept quiet. Even her laugh became a silent one. (Dandy told this story about a man who put a light bulb into his anus and couldn't get it out. Curtis who'd taken his can of Fourex over to the bench, asked if he'd tried connecting it to the electricity supply. Hattie laughed like mad then, putting her head back and opening her mouth. But not a squeak of sound came out.)

J-Max, I might add, shrieked with laughter so before he could hear about someone putting a standard *lamp* up their backside I told him to say goodnight to everyone and marched him off to bed.

When he finally flaked, instead of going back to the kitchen I walked to the phone box on the corner and tried to ring Allie but although I dialled the number three times no one answered.

After that I went back to The Rose and still not wanting to be with the people in the kitchen walked slowly down through the garden to the fence overlooking the canal. I'd stopped underneath a palm tree and for a while there was frantic rustling among the fronds as if I'd disturbed a flock of birds. When that quietened I heard a water-lapping sound which whipped me back to the yacht *Destry*. Marcelle seemed so close to me that I could almost *feel* her.

Closing my eyes I whispered, 'If you're there, say something to me now,' but instead of Marcelle's voice what I heard was a man singing. He was singing a song I knew because my Aunt Penelope sometimes sang it when she'd been drinking. It was about going to San Francisco with flowers in your hair.

At first I was too frightened to open my eyes but I *made* myself and when I did I looked up into the tree expecting to see someone hiding there.

That night there was only a slicey bit of moon but it was enough to show me no one was perched above my head. I looked around me then. The beach on our side of the canal was in shadow but against the glow from the houses opposite I could see these two people dancing on the jetty. The man was singing and they were turning slowly in time to it with their arms around each other in the way people used to do.

As they got closer to me I saw that both the dancers were men. One had on dark trousers and a pale sweater, the other this long black robe thing.

When the song ended they stood with their arms still around each other. I knew that if I went on watching I'd see their faces move together in a kiss so I turned away. I didn't do that because I was shocked. I wasn't. I sort of liked seeing them there together in that sweet way and I went to the unlit flat and floundered around getting ready for bed with the song about San Francisco still singing itself in my head.

Chapter Twenty-Five

M Y LITTLE BROTHER'S full of surprises. After I'd
wrecked myself thinking up threats to hang on
him when he refused to go to school with Hattie,
they weren't needed. He went off beaming. He even let her
take his hand. (It's only now I realize he'd probably been
dying to be with other kids ever since he found he could
talk.) I should stop here for a moment and say that when J-
Max began speaking, he seemed to lose his ability to do
maths and stuff in his head. He's still okay at maths but he's
not brilliant. (Xam says he probably used that ability as a
sort of language and once he found the one other people use,
he put it away and didn't bother with it again. Ingrid *Frew*
says as this is the only explanation we're likely to get, we
might as well accept it.)

I don't know what lies Hattie told to get my brother into
school. I didn't ask in case she'd said his mother was a
prostitute or something. But she came back to say she'd
managed it and that J-Max would see a speech therapist
there every Thursday afternoon. Hattie thought he needed
more than that though so she devised her own lessons for
him. Each day when he got home from school, she'd take
him into her sitting room, put some mad old song on the

tape deck and then the pair of them would sing along with it. I can tell you that if I live to be two *million*, I'll remember them rolling their eyes and making exaggerated lip movements as they sang daggy numbers like, 'I Want to be Seduced'. Hattie chose that one because of all the *esses* in it and I must say her system helped J-Max a lot. In fact I'm surprised *schools* don't use it.

As I think I told you earlier, my brother's extremely musical and he loved those singing sessions with Hattie. He loved the old songs too and sometimes now when he's drawing or doing his homework I hear him humming one of them to himself. By three-thirty in the afternoon Hattie was ready to sing anyway because she was already a bit whacked by then. She'd start drinking at ten-thirty on the dot. She'd start with a can of beer then go onto cask wine. At one-thirty each week day Merna Swann visited her in the kitchen and the pair of them would spend the next two hours over coffee and brandies. Mrs Swann drank her brandy neat. Hattie added lime and soda.

I don't know how to explain this but although Hattie said she hated Merna she acted as if she lived for those early afternoon sessions when they discussed the daily running of The Rose together. (Once Hattie told me she sometimes felt like a partner which is pretty sad because she didn't even have a *share*.) On certain days Merna brought some ledgers with her and wearing glasses halfway down her nose, would copy figures from cheque butts into them while she drank her brandy and chatted. (I know all this because later Hattie would tell me about Merna's visit down to the last detail.)

At three-thirty Merna went back upstairs to rest till six and she stayed there in her office, which Hattie said was done-out like a Regency drawing room, until she went home about one in the morning.

My early afternoons were spent on the step of the laundry, working on my writing and listening to the two or three prostitutes who'd be sunning themselves on the decking above me. They sat there every day and I listened every day because I thought it was good for me as a *writer* to find out what made them tick. I mean it's not a chance everyone gets. Of course I learned a lot of practical things too. For instance I found out that they earned between thirteen and eighteen hundred dollars a week. Almost twice as much as girls in other parlours. And that they were able to work four weeks straight because when they had what they called *the wimp* they stuffed themselves up with sponges. (When they got *dry* inside they used Lubafax, the stuff I'd seen on the *Destry*.)

I also learned that they were pretty dumb. In fact if you ask me I'd say that's the main difference between them and other people because all the time they were sitting there talking about snogging coke and trying to work out why the Fijian Throttle – whatever *that* is – gives sex such a buzz, they believed that all they had to do was wait and sooner or later one of the clients would slide an emerald the size of an acorn onto their finger and whip them off to millionaires' row in Hong Kong. They even went on about the silk undies they'd have and the servants when they got there.

The average age of the girls at The Rose was twenty-five and although you always hear that prostitutes look the same as anyone you see in the supermarket, it wasn't true of them. Merna Swann chose them partly for their looks so they weren't bad, with lots of glossy hair and good tans and stuff. Their clothes were okay too but their names were the pits – things like Jade and Sherry. There was even a negro girl called Coco but I didn't get to see *her*.

Something else that made them different from other people was that while they sat they did nothing. I mean most women sunbaking day after day would be writing a letter or reading or maybe knitting. These just sat and smoked and talked.

They called abortions, parlour babies, and the clients,

creepers, though Mrs Swann tried to put a stop to that. Their idol was Susan Renouf. She was practically their patron *saint* and they talked about her clothes, her houses and her husbands exhaustively. They also talked about the creepers. It was from them I learned the Chinese are big brothel users. (So much for Joss's claim about them being patient.)

I heard stories of men who called their mother's name as they 'climaxed' and of a man who crowed like a rooster. That bit caused a lot of laughter. I laughed too, only when the others stopped, I found I couldn't. I went on until my eyes gushed. Even then it took me a long time to stop and I still don't know why I laughed like that.

It was from the prostitutes I learned that Desli Martins was Hattie's daughter. I learned too that she kept marrying men who bashed her. According to the decking girls she'd made that mistake three times. They said that wearing big dark glasses, she lobbed in from America every so often to hide at The Rose until her bruises faded. I don't know if any of that was true because I didn't ever ask Hattie about it. A funny thing is that although I found out so much about everyone else at The Rose I found out very little about the McLeods. As far as Hattie and Curtis were concerned it was as if they'd always been there, always been the age they were when I met them and I must say that for all Hattie's friendliness and all her gossip there was something about her that stopped you asking questions of the personal kind.

Dandy, the People's Poet, turned up to play cards with Curtis on our second night at The Rose. It was Gerry's night off and he was there too along with this anorexic bloke called Desmond who had birch-broom hair and the biggest Adam's apple in the world.

When they arrived I was down in the flat trying to get

J-Max to bed. I was still there when Curtis knocked on the door to tell me someone wanted me on the phone.

Hearing Allie's voice at the other end of the line made me want to blurt out everything that'd happened since we parted. I didn't let myself though because the poker game had started and I was standing ten *centimetres* away from Curtis and his big bamboo bong.

The first thing Allie did was ask me about the job.

'It's great – just great.'

'No standover stuff.'

That made me laugh. 'No, the opposite.'

There was this silence from Allie, then she said, 'How long will you stay?'

'I'll have to let you know.'

'You sound funny.'

That made me silent but after a while I said, 'The phone's in the kitchen.'

'I get it – you're not alone'. A pause. 'Listen is the job really okay?'

'I swear it is. Now tell me about yours.'

'It's ace. I'm rapt and can't wait for you to see the set-up down here. Of course I'm not doing much but I'm learning all the time. The troupe's starting work on a new show and I'll be helping write the songs and things.'

'That's fabulous!' I said. 'And hey, when's your appointment with Legal Aid?'

'Thursday at two. I have to go to Southport so when I get through there I'll come down and see you.'

The thought of Allie running her Johannesen eyes over nine Tallulah Court made me rush to say, 'No, I'll meet you in Southport. I'll be there by two and we'll have a chance to *talk*.'

I laid a lot of emphasis on that last word and after another silence, Allie said, 'Okay. Where will we meet?'

'I'll be on the seat outside the post office.'

'Bring Max, won't you?'

'I can't. He'll be at school.'

'He'll be *where*?'

'At school,' I said, then speaking at rocket pace, I added, 'look – I'll tell you everything on Thursday. See you,' and before she could get another word out, I'd hung up.

When I turned around the men at the table all stared at me the way people do when you finish a phone conversation, so picking out the moony face of Gerry because it was the one I knew, I said, 'That was my friend, Allie, ringing from Byron Bay.'

'Allie?' said Gerry. 'How's she going?'

'Great,' I told him. 'She's got this job with a bunch of girls who do theatre and stuff.'

Still staring, he said, 'Time that kid got a break.'

Desmond of the birchy hair was staring too and I wanted to get out of the room but didn't know how. I think Curtis guessed that because he said, 'Mum's fastened on the tube, if you want to go in there.'

'I guess it's pretty late,' I said, 'I think I'll just nick off to bed.'

I don't know what it was about our little flat at The Rose – perhaps the marihuana plants gave off a gas or something – but while we were there, J-Max and I slept like crazy. On the night I spoke to Allie, I went into this *total* sleep but some time in the night a noise woke me out of it. It was a kind of scratching and at first I thought it was a palm frond brushing the roof, but while I listened it changed to a light tapping sound which frightened me because I realized it was coming from the door. Suddenly it stopped and I thought whoever it was had gone away but after a silence almost as bad as the tapping, it started again.

There was no moon that night and in the awful dark, without touching them, I could feel the tender nipples on my chest, and other parts of me, all as easy to damage as baby snails.

Then the tapping stopped again and this voice, whispering and quick, said, 'Morgan, wake up. It's me – Gerry.'

Almost dying with relief I got my blanket around me and groped my way over to the door. After a bit of fumbling I popped out the bolt and opened it a little but while I was still saying, 'What is it?' Gerry had shoved it back against me and pushed his way into the room.

Not letting go of the door, I said, 'What do you want?' (I could smell these fumes on him. Cigarette and sweat and rum or something, with a kind of jasminey perfume mixed in too.)

His hand came onto my shoulder and *stayed* there like a big fruit bat. I shrugged away from it and said, 'I don't want you here. My brother's asleep.'

He put his face close to mine. 'Don't you want to thank me for getting you the job?'

'You didn't get it for me. You told Joss about it and I got it myself.'

'Same thing. Don't I even get a kiss?'

I thought then of dodging outside but as I did I heard J-Max stir in his bunk so what I did was let go of the door and push at Gerry's chest with my two hands. 'Go and kiss your*self*,' I said, grabbing at my blanket.

I saw his white shirt lurch back against the wall. He stayed there for a moment. I could hear him breathing. Then he straightened up and said, 'You owe me, Morgan.'

'I don't and you know it. Joss said . . .'

He interrupted. 'Forget Joss. This's between you and me.'

'Nothing's between you and me. Joss'll be back and he'll . . .'

Again he interrupted, 'Joss won't be back. Get that into your head. He's gone home to his family and he'll stay there.'

'He won't. He promised.'

'Jesus Christ! Wake up. If he *did* come back he wouldn't piss on a girl working in a parlour.'

'I'm not working in a parlour. I'm working in a laundry.'

He gave a laugh then and I got a blast of his breath and because I couldn't bear to have him in my little room with his chaddy man smells, I took a step towards him and said, 'Get out of here because if you don't, I'll ring your wife and tell her that you like little kids. I'll even tell her about Marcelle and the night you drove us to the marina.'

When I'd said it, I started blinking because I thought he'd take a step sideways, then call me a bitch and hit me. Well he did take a step sideways and he called me a bitch too but the amazing thing was that his voice wasn't angry when he did. In fact it was . . . well, not *pleased*, but at least as if he liked me. And still with the same thing in his voice, he said, 'You don't mean that.'

'Try me.'

He gave the tail-end of another laugh and edged around me to the door, stopping on the step long enough to say, 'I meant it, Morgan, about Joss. He won't be back but I'll still be here. You might find you need me. Marcelle did.' He had the arse to add, 'Goodnight Sweetie,' then he turned and his big sweaty shirt went off up the path.

I had the door shut and bolted in one second. The next thing I did was ask J-Max if he was awake. He gave a muffled, 'Yeth', from somewhere close to me and the next moment I bumped into him as he bent over something on the floor.

'What are you doing?' I said.

'Rooking for m'knife.'

I got laughy myself then. Told him he didn't need it, and after a bit of carry-on got him back to bed. I guess I was on some sort of high because still wearing the blanket I curled up at the end of his bunk and talked to him until he went to sleep again. One of the things I said was, 'I never knew before but boy, it feels good to piss off a nerd like that.'

I said a lot of other stuff too and I was still thinking about it later when I got into my own bunk. In fact I thought for half the *night*. I even worked out how to do the first chapter of my book. The one I felt was too bad to tell. I was going to write it as if I had everyone I knew sitting in a circle listening while I told it to them. *I'll put in everything*, I thought. *So they start to understand what it's like being a girl at war, as Allie says, practically every* MINUTE of your life.

Chapter Twenty-Six

AFTER LUNCH ON Wednesday I settled myself on the laundry step to work on the final and *true* version of my story. I was slow in getting started because at first I had one ear on the prostitutes on the decking. They were talking about a dwarf who'd been arrested the day before at Surfers after running along the beach with nothing on. (For some reason the prostitutes found this *hilarious*.) In the end I stopped listening to them and got stuck into my writing. To my surprise it turned out to be almost easy because I found I could make myself stand back and look at everything as if it no longer had any connection with me. In fact, when I got going the stuff came out of me so fast I had a job to get it down.

I'd done about four pages in one of J-Max's exercise books when I heard Hattie's voice sing out, 'Hey Morgan, come and see. There's going to be some filming down by the canal.'

I lifted my head. She was over by the garden fence along with two of the prostitutes. They were all staring down at the beach. I stood on the step then and looking towards the beach saw this group of people milling around on the sand. There were eight or nine of them. One had this two-tonne camera on his shoulder and someone else had one of those clapper-board things. The men in the group wore joggers and tight jeans; the women, the kind of clothes arty people in Melbourne wear – black tank tops and gunfighter belts with khaki skirts. I mean they *looked* like film people but that's as far as it went because although I watched for about an hour, no filming was done. Instead there was this big argument with a lot of swear words being flung around while the cameraman shuffled here and there looking at the others through the viewfinder.

In the end I went back to my writing and before long Hattie walked over to me to say, 'Well, that's the end of that. They've decided to go round to the surf beach. A pity because I was about to give Desmond a call.'

'Desmond?'

'Desmond Roper. I think you met him the other night. He's on the local paper and likes to know what's going on.'

I was gobstuck, but before I had time to take in the fact that a journalist had seen me, had *stared* at me, Merna Swann appeared from somewhere at the back of the building and came swaying up the path towards us. She had a bunch of keys in her hand and when she reached us, she stopped to look down at me and say, 'Are you heppy, dulling, in my flat? Are you heppy with the little boy you and Hattie hide from me all the time?' Having got that off, she lifted her chin, beamed first at me, then at Hattie and started up the path again.

Boggling at her back, I whispered, 'She knew. She knew all along.'

Hattie's answer was to put her head back and give the kind of soundless laugh she used in front of Dandy Palmer.

'What will she do?'

Still bobbing her head backwards and forwards, Hattie said, 'Not a thing. She's just told you you can stay.'

She left too after that and as she did, I said inside my head, *Okay, so one problem's solved but what about scrawny Desmond?*

What if he comes back to stare some more then write this piece for his paper or something about runaway kids who go to work in brothels?

I put my writing away then and after dodging back inside the laundry tried to work out if Desmond Roper was a big enough threat to make me pack and leave The Rose that afternoon. But by the time Hattie called to ask if I intended picking J-Max up from school, I'd decided that as long as I took care not to bump into him again, Desmond I mean, it was okay for us to stay. In a day or two we'd be gone anyway and he'd have no way of knowing in which direction.

We'd moved into this weird weather pattern of rain-storms which blew in from the ocean late in the morning to pound on the roofs and gardens for a few minutes and then stop. (One brought with it a cloud of mosquitos which came into the laundry turning the air dark.) These sudden showers left the palms and things sparkling and that's how Southport looked to me the day I went up there to meet Allie. I know I'd only been away a few days but a funny thing is that when the Surfside bus turned into Scarborough Street I had this feeling of coming home.

Outside the post office I found a seat between a Maori woman and a man in an old army jacket with his neck all bandaged. He was drinking something from a thermos flask and muttering a bit to himself. I pretended not to notice and sat thinking of the smashing times I'd had with Allie and Angel and everybody. I thought about Joss too and each time the traffic lights changed I expected to see him come across the road with the wave of people.

I was still thinking about him when the Maori woman left to join someone on the corner. Moments later Allie slid into the space beside me. She was still wearing Marcelle's clothes and instead of saying hello or anything, she put her hand down on mine and held it there hard enough to hurt. While she did that she stared out into the traffic with her face sort of shrunken.

'What's wrong?' I said to her. 'What's *happened*?'

She didn't answer straightaway but finally she loosened her grip on my hand a bit and said, 'At Legal Aid I got landed with this callous bitch all laired up with these big shoulder pads and earrings like baby crocodiles. She hated me on sight. She said I didn't have a hope in hell of getting the baby back. She said, apart from anything *else*, I didn't have what could be classified as an acceptable lifestyle.'

'But you didn't sign the *adoption* papers or anything.'

'I told her that and she looked at her fingernails and said that would be very hard to prove.'

'Then you'll have to go past her. Get to someone else, I mean.'

'That'll be hard too.'

At that moment the bandaged man beside me leaned out and said to Allie, 'Wanna go for a drink love?'

I don't think she even heard him because she said, 'In the hospital Ro told me about an anthropologist or something in Africa who did all this work on chimpanzees, and *she* said that when there's a new-born baby in the tribe the other females take it away from its mother and pass it around. They even *throw* it around. The mother goes frantic of course and sometimes the baby dies from shock and everything.'

'But why? I mean why do they do it?'

'Because they're jealous and Ro says women are the same.'

I took that in then I said, 'Hattie McLeod at The Rose believes we go in for a lot of animal behaviour.'

'Well the creep at Legal Aid certainly did.'

The bandaged man who'd been leaning out listening said, 'Stick to pigeons is what I say,' and he got up and lurched across the road towards the hotel. As he did Allie and I looked at each other and gave these sort of *desperate* laughs. Then Allie said, 'I was going to stay up here with you and Max tonight but if it's okay with you I'll go back to Byron Bay. I want to talk to Ro. She's clue-ier than me.'

'How will you get there though?'

'This bloke Barry Sturges, who lives near us, works three days a week in a furniture factory way down Ferry Road. I know I can get a lift with him if I'm there by three-thirty.'

Sorry she was going but relieved as hell I didn't have to tell a lot of lies about why she couldn't come to The Rose, I said I'd walk to Ferry Road with her.

As we went past the hotel I turned to Allie to ask if she'd heard anything of Joss but I didn't ever get it out because coming across the road towards us was my mother. She was wearing her short-sleeved black jumper and her face was lit up like mad because she'd seen me. I had time to wonder why she was carrying a Cabbage Patch doll by one of its arms then she'd reached the footpath and stopped to kiss this woman waiting there. After that she bent over a kid in a pusher and made a lot of stupid noises at it, because you see the woman wasn't my mother at all. She wasn't even *like* her and I stood with my chest all tight and my dumb eyes messed up with tears.

I guess I looked pretty wrecked because Allie who'd walked on, came back to touch my arm and say, 'Morgan are you all right?'

'I thought I saw my mother,' I said, 'I thought she'd come to get me. I thought . . .' I stopped there and didn't go on.

Cupping her hand over my shoulder Allie said, 'I know what *that* feels like. After Mike died I saw him all the time. I'd see him get off his bike and take off his helmet and it'd turn out to be some bloke with bright red hair or something. I even saw Marcelle the other day. I was in the main street of Byron Bay and I saw her as plain as day going into this little cafe.'

We'd started walking again but in a little while Allie said,

'Would you feel better if you went back to the post office and gave your mum a call. You wouldn't need to say where you were.'

I thought of the way my mother looked at me the last time I saw her. 'She wouldn't want to hear from me,' I said and after that we were halfway to Ferry Road before either of us spoke again.

That evening when J-Max and I went up to the kitchen to get our tea the only person there was Curtis. He was making this big ham sandwich and said, 'You kids will have to fend for yourselves tonight. Mum's *hors de combat*.'

I asked him what he meant and he said, 'She's wiped herself out with whisky.'

I had one of those times of not knowing what to say and after a moment Curtis went on, 'That poofter, the People's Poet, turned up this arvo with a belated birthday present for the old girl. He was grinning like a Cheshire cat and when Mum got the wrapping off there was this miniature coffin, all french polished and everything. It even had satin lining in it. Christ knows where the bastard got it but he told her it was to keep her jewellery in.'

J-Max gave a squeal of laughter and I said, 'What did Hattie say?'

'Nothing at first. I think she'd gone into shock because she went to the fridge, put the coffin in, paper and all, and slammed the door. After that she and Dandy had this blue. She accused him of wanting to see her dead, and he told her that from the shoulders up she already was. It went on until Dandy shot around the table and tried to deck her. At that stage I ran him out and Mum started on the Black Label.'

J-Max, who'd gone to the fridge and opened it, asked where the coffin was.

'I took it out and stashed it where Mum won't see it,' Curtis told him.

'Maybe it's a good thing,' I said. 'Maybe Dandy won't come back.'

'You kidding? That bastard is the biggest freeloader in the business. See him giving up a marshmallow like my old lady? Not a chance.'

I watched while Curt slapped the top on his sandwich, then knowing that every night at six forty-five, Hattie sent this really gorgeous tray of food up to Merna Swann, I asked Curtis what we'd do about it.

'Forget it,' he said. 'I've rung the Gourmet Goose. They're sending crab and stuff.' Picking up his sandwich he headed for the door, stopping on the way to shoot a look back at me and say, 'It's not the first time it happened, you know.'

Curtis was right about Dandy. He rolled up the next night as if nothing had happened, and Hattie greeted him the same way. I've jumped ahead a bit because I have to tell you that at teatime that night I got my pay. I didn't get the full hundred and eighty dollars. I got six-sevenths of it but I was so rapt at having earned it myself I took it down to the flat and put it on the floor. Then J-Max and I danced in it.

Later on I went back to the kitchen. That's when I saw Dandy. He'd arrived with some of his mates and a carton of beer. (Desmond Roper wasn't there and when I asked Hattie about him in a round-about kind of way she said he was off somewhere working on this big story.)

Before long Dandy stood on one of the chairs to recite his latest poems. We all had an extremely good view of the crack in his creepy white bottom, and his poems were about God and gully traps and things. He sort of sang them in an imitation of that Welsh poet Dylan Thomas. (My Aunt Penelope's a great fan of his and plays his tapes when she's in one of her depressions.)

Dandy's second poem had a lot of little-kid swear words

in it like bum and poop, and every time he said one of them the audience screamed. Even Curtis did and ever since that night I've thought a lot about the way those words gave them such a buzz. I've asked myself if maybe that's why grown up people are so hung-up about sex. I mean if they can't come to terms with things like bottoms and stuff how can they be cool about the *pleasure* which comes from those places too.

The kitchen of The Rose was growing crowded. You couldn't *see* for cigarette smoke, then two young coppers came in. (They'd left their hats outside but were wearing these gross guns.) While the gunmen were at the table getting drinks, I edged my way round to the door and without anyone noticing, nicked out.

It was quiet in the kitchen of The Rose the next night. Hattie said they tried to keep things that way on Saturdays because they were never sure what would happen upstairs. If, for instance, there'd been races on at Southport a group of politicians might take over the place for the night. That meant the kitchen too because about 1 a.m. a few of them would troop down and ask Hattie to make things like brandy pancakes.

That evening J-Max, who'd been at the beach again with Curtis, flaked early so I went back up to watch television with Hattie. We saw this mad old film about a car race. It was pretty good but before the end of it the kitchen phone rang. 'Bugger,' said Hattie and hoisting herself out of her chair went to answer it. She came back and gave me this funny look. The kind you give someone when you haven't seen them for about fifteen *years*. 'Merna wants to see you upstairs.' She bunched her lips up briefly, then said, 'You don't have to go. I told her I'd sent you round to the shop for chocolates.'

But I was already on my feet. I'd been *desperate* to see the upstairs part since the first day.

'I don't mind,' I said, 'But how will I find Mrs Swann?'

'She'll be in her office. Once you get up the stairs, turn left into the hall and follow it all the way along. The office is the last room on the right.'

At the door, though, I hesitated. 'What do you think she wants me for?'

Hattie bunched her lips up again. 'You'll soon find out. And don't worry. If you're not back in fifteen minutes I'll be up to see what's going on.'

I went then. Out into the passage where I hadn't been before and up the stairs. When I reached the hall above, I stopped and looked along it. The floor was covered with carpet of champagney colour and there were two of those phoney blossom trees in big pots. There was also a polished table with spindly legs and an arrangement of posh-looking flowers on it. (People came from Surfers three times a week, I knew, to do the flowers, while someone else came to do the vacuuming and stuff.) Beyond the spindly table the hall crossed another one and at the very end I could see the slightly open door of Merna's office.

With the carpet thick and sort of spooky underneath my feet I began to walk towards it. I passed a closed door with voices behind it, another where I heard Richard Clayderman flinging out daggy stuff from the piano keys. Then I crossed the other hall and looking to the right, saw the front door with its grill and everything. From somewhere in that second hall a man laughed then stopped. I went on past a gold birdcage on a stand. There was a bird in it with pale blue feathers (I still don't know if it was real or not).

When I was almost to the door of Merna's office I stopped to smooth my hair and stuff. From where I was I could see a piece of the room. A man was standing in it with his back to me. He was wearing a dark jacket, then I had this mini spin-out because I realized I was looking at Desmond Roper and his birch-broom hair.

Too shocked to move I heard Merna Swann say, 'Tell me, Mr. Roper, what is your interest in this little matter?'

I think even my *skin* listened with me as Desmond answered, 'I want the story, Mrs Swann. It's a hot one. It'll headline in every paper in the country.'

'And what of the two dullings? Do you think at all of them?'

'They'll be taken into custody . . .'

That's all I heard because I'd moved without even deciding to and was flying back along the hall. At the corner I turned left, went past another tree and this big desk with an open door behind it. A bell rang somewhere in the building and I was at the front door. The dumb thing had a deadlock on it and while I was twisting at the knob a voice behind me said, 'What are *you* doing here?'

A woman was standing behind the desk. She had masses of red hair and was wearing something black and floaty.

'I'm on a message for Mrs Swann.' The words came out quick and cheeky. Fright made me do that but the woman didn't realize it.

'Then use the stairs,' she said and turned away.

I went back, wheeled into the other hall and with my heart about two steps in front of me, tore to the top of the stairs. I stopped there long enough to try to swallow before rushing to the bottom. I made myself slow down then, slid without a sound past Hattie's door (end-of-film music was crashing from the telly) then across the kitchen and outside.

When I shook J-Max awake and told him we were leaving, it sort of *hurt* me to see the way the poor little bugger got up without a word and began to dress as if moving house in the middle of the night was the normal thing to do.

It took us about three minutes to grab and pack the few things lying around. One last on-the-run check of the room and then I herded my brother and the cat out into the cloud-covered night.

Instead of going up through the grounds of The Rose we battled our way over two fences into the garden of the

257

presbytery. The case was pretty hard to handle but anything seemed better to me than having to cross the lit-up area of brick paving in front of Merna Swann's poxy place. Bobby Deerfield followed us over both fences and up through the battered plants in the priests' garden. As we went I was trying to work out how Desmond Roper got onto us. *Perhaps he's been down south,* I thought. *Perhaps there* WAS *a little piece in the papers down there and perhaps he saw it.*

At the top of the garden I told J-Max to stay in the shadow of the cypress trees while I sussed out the street. Everything was quiet but as I stepped back to get the suitcase a taxi came sailing around the corner. We watched while it dropped a u-ee then pulled up at The Rose to let a creeper out. He had on one of those teatowel things Arabs wear on their heads and the first thing he did when he got out of the taxi was take it off and stow it inside his jacket. Then he spoke briefly to the driver and headed for the brothel.

'Whistle!' I said, belting J-Max on the back. 'We want that taxi,' and not caring if the creeper saw me or not I rushed into the street and began to wave my arms. My brother let go with a screamer and when he did the taxi came skittling back towards us.

I swear that driver with his thick lips and big bully neck wouldn't have spoken if God and *Jesus* and everybody had come out of the shadows because all he did when J-Max emerged from the presbytery grounds dragging the suitcase was get out and open the boot so I could take it and heave it in. He didn't even speak when I said we had a cat as well.

So we set off in silence for Joss's room at Tibet with Bobby riding on the ledge up by the rear window and me leaning against the chaddy-smelling leather of the seat pleased as hell that I'd got my pay when I did, and making up this daggy little jingle about going to Byron Bay in the morning.

Part Four

TIBET

Chapter Twenty-Seven

XAM AND I have these crazy arguments about things. Mostly he wins because even when I can see his arguments are *tricks* I can't see a way around them. For instance the day I asked him why he'd never married he said that at the age of thirty he'd realized how corrupt the human race was and decided to secede. He said from then on he regarded himself as a two-legged fruit or vegetable but as he'd been unable to find a female of the species, marriage was out of the question.

I said if he couldn't bear being human why didn't he just commit suicide.

His answer was, 'Why should I? No one expects a watermelon to suicide because it's realized it's not a man.'

Allie told me that Xam comes out with this sort of nonsense because in the bottom of his heart – and in spite of everything he says – he'd like me to become a barrister and what he's doing is trying to teach my mind to dart around and light on the unexpected.

Allie has these really cool insights into the way Xam thinks and because of that I've more or less let her take over the fights I used to have with him on the subject of things like male/female relationships. Before she did, Xam and

I had some *zingers*. The first one was on the morning after J-Max and I arrived at Tibet and the funny thing is that it was really because of that fight we stayed on. Not that I'd have got my brother to leave anyway. He took to Tibet like a duck to the river. As a matter of fact he likes it so much he's become practically *normal*. About the only time he's acted the full retard was on the day he arrived home from school to find the Moke of that youth worker Ingrid Frew parked outside.

He did play up a bit the night we arrived and I'm going to get onto that in a minute but first I want to tell about the argument Allie and Xam had the day *she* first visited us.

Xam had been listening to a talkback program on ABC radio about this book with a sex-oriented name like *Men into Women* or something. Anyway he heard all these women ringing in with their views on men and according to him each one said the same thing. They each said what they most wanted out of life was for their husband or boyfriend to *help with the dishes*. That caused Xam great amusement and he said it made him realize the kitchen sink is the altar of a woman's existence – the place where she celebrates mass. And he said that women don't really want their husband to clean the dishes at all. What they want is for him to get elbow deep into the suds and celebrate the mass with her. Then he backed his argument up with this dumb story about how he'd once seen some landlady of his practically rugbytackle a female visitor away from the sink after she'd offered to help with the dishes.

Furious, Allie said, 'What's wrong with giving importance to the kind of work women do? Washing dishes and floors and stuff?'

'Not a thing,' said Xam, 'but don't expect men to see it as important because their way of celebrating mass is to be swearing and sweaty and dodging napalm with a mate in a foreign field where some woman can't materialize to ask if he's remembered to put his underclothes in the wash that morning.'

He paused then to offer Allie the shortbread biscuits and when she ignored them, went on. 'To point out the obvious, men use football and cricket as substitutes for the religious ceremony of battle.'

I don't think Allie heard that bit because she seized on his remark about underclothes and said, 'What's wrong with keeping things clean? Being clean helps keep disease away.'

'Dust causes asthma,' I chimed in.

Giving me a sideways look, Xam said, 'Men see cleanliness and safety as piddling objectives in life because since the first humanoid legged-it out of a tree, masculine culture has been embedded in battle. A man's unconscious is full of it and the archetypal heroes lurking there are all warriors.'

While Allie was taking that in, Xam went on, 'The archetypal figures in a woman's unconscious, on the other hand, are people like Ruth in the Old Testament and Martha in the New. Women who've earned their place in history by being the keepers of the hearth, keepers of the family.'

'If that's the case it's time we found new ones,' said Allie. 'And men should too.'

'Perhaps one day we will,' Xam told her, 'but I doubt it'll happen at the kitchen sink.'

Allie was quiet after that and I knew she was putting Xam's remarks away in her head so that when she got back to Byron Bay she could take them out again and lay them on the table to be examined by her friends. And that's what happened because that discussion of hers with Xam inspired The Nin Theatre Group to write the dance-drama they put on later in the year.

I'm dying to go on now and tell you about that drama. It was called *Careful What You Call Your Daughters*. But I know that unless I start talking *right now* about the night J-Max and I arrived at Tibet, I never will.

After the taxi driver with the bully neck had let us out at the gate he zoomed off without a backward glance. We were left to grope our way to Joss's door in the dark. I remember as we went smelling the garden smells of wet earth and leaves and frangipanni and telling myself that's probably how Paradise smelt to Adam and Eve and everybody. Those thoughts didn't last long because another sudden rainstorm swept in on us as we stood on the verandah looking for the key. I'd had it in my bag. It had been there since the night Joss gave it to me but although J-Max and I each went through the contents about a dozen times we couldn't find it. We'd already tried knocking on the door (on the one further along as well) and with our feet and legs being soaked by the rain I was too wrecked to bother arguing when J-Max said, 'I'll get a blick from the garden and ss-mash the nindow.'

He actually dived out into the rain and appeared a few minutes later, wet as a tadpole, with a lump of rock in his hand. I was rushing to stop him hurling it when a beam of light pinned the pair of us. It came from the direction of the second door I mentioned and was strong enough of make us turn our heads away. Then this quivery old-man voice said, 'What in damnation's going on?'

With my face still turned away, I said, 'We've lost the key.'

'What are you talking about?' The voice stopped to make a gasping sound. 'What key?'

'To Joss's room.'

Still gasping the voice said, 'What right have you to that?'

'He gave it to us. He said we could use the room.'

There was silence while the beam moved down to our wet feet then up again.

'My name's Morgan Christie,' I tried to make my voice sound confident. 'Mrs Werther knows me. I think I'd better speak to her.'

'You'll have a job. She's gone to her daughter's at Beau Desert.'

I started scrabbling in the bag again and while I was doing it the torch moved, then went out as the verandah light came on. For a few seconds my eyes followed a pale little flight of insects as they left the vicinity of the torch to hover in the air and then flutter towards the overhead light. After that I stared at the person who'd turned it on.

It was the million-year old man I'd seen on the verandah the day I visited Joss. He had this plastic raincoat on over funny old flannel pyjamas. The rain had wet the bottoms of the pants plastering them to a pair of skeleton-skinny legs. He was bent a bit the way old people are but I'd say he'd once been extremely tall because he *towered* over us. His face, which was thin and a bit eagle-ish, had a surprisingly neat little moustache on it. I was still concentrating on that moustache when my fingers found the key underneath the lining in my bag. At the same moment the rain stopped and Bobby Deerfield, who'd been sheltering in the garden, shot onto the verandah and rubbed himself against J-Max's legs.

My brother squatted to put his arms around him, then looking up at the man, he gave his lost-angel smile and told him what the cat's name was.

'Is it indeed?' said the old bloke, but I thought his face softened about a millimetre. Perhaps it did because the gasping seemed to ease a little and when I finally hauled out the key and flourished it, he said, 'You'd better try it, hadn't you?'

I did and as soon as the door swung open I picked up our suitcase and used it to herd my brother and Bobby inside. Then before the man had a chance to speak again, I said, 'Thanks for the help.' The words came out sarcastic as hell. I hadn't meant them that way and in my embarrassment I rushed inside too and shut the door, leaving the old dag alone on the wet verandah.

It was then that the business of being got out of bed in the middle of the night and whizzed off in a taxi caught up with J-Max. He became extremely hyper, putting on a milder version of the act he pulled the night we boarded the *Destry* with Marcelle. I forcibly stopped him dismantling the chest of drawers made from cartons and when I did he flew to an inside door I hadn't noticed and after unlocking it rushed out. The door led into a hall with the most ancient gas stove in history standing by the wall.

At the end of the hall my brother found this crazy old bathroom with a window of green frosted glass and one of those loos you flush by pulling a chain. I followed J-Max into the bathroom and while he was laughing this high laugh and standing on the seat to pull the chain I opened the window and looked out at a big tree beside the verandah. It had ivy growing up its rough old trunk and the leaves, wet and reflecting the light, made it look like an advertisement for pricey French soap or something. (Later we learned that hardly anyone at Tibet bothers to lock their windows. They don't need to because the locals think the place is haunted. Xam says the story of a ghost has been around for years and started when some visitor saw the tombstone which leans against the traveller's palm in the garden. The inscription on the tombstone is in Indonesian and Xam told us that Mrs Werther's husband stole it from a cemetery up near Cairns just before he joined the army in 1939. He went on to say it's Tibet's air of impoverishment that keep thieves away, not the tombstone in the garden.)

It took ages that night to calm J-Max so that he'd sleep. Finally I did and was able to curl up myself at the other end of Joss's bed. I'd been missing Joss desperately ever since we reached his room but being there on his bed where I thought I could smell his *hair* made me ache for him. I tried not to think about the way we'd had sex together there. I did think about it though and when I did the thought rushed into my mind: THAT'S *what they do in the rooms at the Rose Club – the girls and the old men and everyone. It's what the man who crows like a rooster does.* IT'S WHAT MY FATHER AND I DID! I sat bolt upright then, staring into the dark and trying to tell myself that with Joss and me it was different. In a little while I lay down again determined to stay awake until I'd worked out what the difference was but almost straight-away it seemed the sun was making green coins out of the leaves beside the verandah and J-Max with his face a few centimetres from mine was asking where his breakfast was.

While I'd slept my brother had been somewhere and learned it was after ten o'clock. That piece of news made me think we'd miss the bus to Byron Bay and I rolled out of bed.

After a milk-bar breakfast I settled J-Max with his draw-ing things and went to find a telephone. First I made a circuit of the ground floor level but in that place of shadows and silences the only *remotely* human things I saw were the turtle doves feeding in the garden. In the end, not knowing what else to do I climbed the front steps in search of the old man we'd met the night before.

Although I could hear this whining Indian music playing in one of the front rooms upstairs no one came when I knocked. After waiting and trying again I dodged around the corner to knock again at a door close to the bunch of cane furniture where I'd seen the old bloke sitting. This time I thought I heard a faint call inside so I really *bopped* the door.

The sound came again. It was like a far off gasp with the word help swallowed somewhere inside it. I went to the nearest window then and peered into a room so dimly lit I had to cup my hands around my face before I could see anything. The old man, still in pyjamas, was lying on a bed on the opposite side of the room. He looked terrible. His face was turned towards me and he was fighting to drag a breath inside himself. He'd seen me and his hand moved, turned towards me too and without stopping to think I shot the window up and climbed into the room. (The tobacco smell in there was thick enough to touch.)

On my way to the bed my foot touched something in the mess of newspapers and overflowing ashtrays on the floor. It was one of those puffers asthmatics use. I bent and grabbed it and still without thinking shoved it into the man's hand. Then using my hand on his, got it to his mouth. Between us we managed to work the thing and gradually the awful eye-rolling breaths quietened. I took the puffer then from his dry old hand which in its *detail* was sort of perfect, like one of those cicada shells you sometimes find in the garden.

I was still staring at his hand when he spoke. 'Damned back – done it in. Couldn't reach the spinhaler.'

'Can't you move?' I said.

A tiny shake of his head. 'Good as paralysed.'

'Then I'd better get someone.'

The man started to say something but I was already on my way, leaving dumbly by the window instead of the door.

I went back to the front verandah where the music had changed from flutey sounds to drums and gongs. This time I kept knocking until finally the door opened about fifteen centimetres and this woman looked out. She was about my mother's age and had hair as light and uncombed as J-Max's.

I don't know why but I acted then as if I thought she was deaf and dumb, flicking my hands around as I said, 'The old man next door is sort of paralysed. Can you come and help?'

She frowned at me, frowned *more* actually, because her pinchy white face was frowning even before she saw me. 'Ring his doctor,' was what she said. 'He always comes.' Then she shut the door.

I went back to the old man's window, leaned into Tobacco-land and told him what had happened.

He tried to raise himself up but swore under his breath and fell back. 'Would *you* come in and ring the vet for me?'

'Don't you mean the doctor?'

When I said that he gave this spooky smile and as I rushed to try the front door I thought, *Hell, that's his idea of a* JOKE.

The door was locked so I rushed back to the window and began to climb in.

'The place isn't alight, you know,' the old man said and although I pretended not to hear, the words stirred me a bit because after all I didn't *have* to stay and help.

His phone was in what he called the den, a dark little room with two big leather chairs in it and about sixty thousand books. I found the Teledex buried under another pile of newspapers and was halfway through ringing the doctor's number when I realized I didn't know a thing about the old man. After going back to the bedroom to learn his name and everything I told the woman who answered the phone I was ringing for Mr Arnold, Mr Max Arnold. When she heard that she said the doctor was out on a call but would be at Tibet as soon as possible.

While I waited I made a cup of tea. Mr Arnold hadn't had breakfast but I didn't realize that and made the tea because I couldn't think of any other way to pass the time.

There were ashtrays in the kitchen too, and things were lined up in a funny way with the sherry bottle standing next to the can of insect spray but at least it looked as if someone shot a broom around the floor now and then. (The other rooms were full of dust. I'd seen *balls* of it under the furniture.) When I opened the fridge though to get out the milk I was gobstuck. It was a big nearly-new one all gleaming inside but the only things in view were a small carton of milk, a mouse-sized piece of cheese and a packet of Arnott's shortbread biscuits. After sizing up that lot I opened the freezer compartment. It was jammed with packets of apple Danish and I thought, *God, that's what he lives on!*

I was sorry for the old nong then but the feeling didn't last because when I took his cup of tea in to him, he peered at it and said it wasn't strong enough.

I went back to the kitchen and tried again. This time he said 'Too much milk,' and when I arrived in the bedroom with my third effort he swivelled his eyes around at me and said, 'You women can't get anything right, can you?'

Something happened to me then because this cyclone thing seemed to gather up inside me and burst out. I went so mad I couldn't even see anymore and while I was like that I hurled the cup and saucer at the place where I thought the old man was.

'My father came into my room,' I shouted. 'He did terrible things to me. So J-Max and I left and came up here. Then my friend Marcelle drowned and I had to go to work into this rotten brothel washing towels and things for disgusting old creepers. And now I'm . . .'

By the time I'd got that far my eyes were focussing again. Mr Arnold, drenched with tea, was staring at me. His eyes were huge and the top of his ear was bleeding from a cut made by the saucer which lay in two pieces, one on the bed, one on the floor. When I saw all of that I slid down to my knees and jammed my face against the side of the bed.

After a while something as light as a moth landed on my head. It stayed there then began to pat me. 'When we were boys,' said Mr Arnold's voice, 'my brother Lyn and I each had a cat. Mine was called Harold after the gardener and Lyn's was Toodle-oo. I don't know where he got that name from. I don't remember.'

I began to cry then, blubbering like mad with my face still buried. Mr Arnold went on patting my head and talking about himself and his brother until I'd almost stopped, then he said, 'Will you help me out of this wet pyjama top and when that's done perhaps we can concoct a tea recipe which suits both of us.'

I got up then and too ashamed to look at him properly

began to clean up the mess I'd made. First I got things from the bathroom and after mopping him up a bit, cleaned the cut on his ear. Then I sat him up to get off his pyjama jacket. It must have hurt him but he didn't make a sound and when the top of him was naked, I was un*done*. His chest was sort of *parched* looking with the ribcage sticking out like those burnt-up carcases of sheep and things you see in paintings of the outback by Sidney Nolan and people. The skin on his arms was loose and patterned everywhere with little creases like wet sand when the tide's gone out. Seeing all of that I began to cry again.

He weighed about as much as one of those cicada shells I mentioned earlier so I had very little trouble changing his pillow and sheet and everything. Later, when I took the wet things to the bathroom to shove them out of sight I stayed there still bawling a bit and watching this big butterfly with lacy black and white wings tiptoe its way along the top of the window. Seeing it there in the dark little bathroom made me remember the day Mrs Van Buuren came to our place in Ivanhoe for afternoon tea. My mother served it in the garden under the camphor laurel and did it in style with herb scones and meringues. She was still potting profession- ally then and Mrs Van Buuren owned a posh gallery in South Yarra. I didn't like her, Mrs Van Buuren I mean. She was supposed to have this marvellous personality but she didn't ever put it on for me because although she *seemed* to make a fuss of me I could tell she was always waiting for me to go away so she could get into the confidential stuff with Mum.

Anyway that day when we were sitting on the white wicker chairs this tiny butterfly landed on my mother's hair and stayed there. It was only about two centimetres across and its wings seemed to have been powdered all over with this pale greeny-blue stuff so that it looked like an orna- mental pin or something Mum had put in her hair.

Because I was sitting on the left of my mother and a little

to the back I was the only one who could see the butterfly. I was pleased about that because I wanted it to stay there. I thought that in choosing my mother's hair to land in it would probably bring her good luck and things. But she moved her head and Mrs Van Buuren saw it too and shrieked, 'There's a moth in your hair,' and leaning across the table brushed at it, getting a bit of it's blue powder on her fingers. It flew away of course and when Mum asked me to pass the scones to Mrs Van Buuren I said she probably wouldn't want one because she'd had three already. Then I went inside.

Later that day I got into a tremendous row from Mum for being rude to Mrs Van Buuren and she wouldn't even listen to me when I tried to tell her how beautiful she looked with the butterfly sitting in her dark hair.

When the one in Mr Arnold's bathroom reached the end of the window frame I balanced myself on the side of the bath and after opening the window shoo'd it out with my hand. It flew up under the verandah roof, stayed there for a while then came down and went out into the garden. As it did I saw these two patches of poppy-red on the back of the wings. I kept watching it until it disappeared among the trees, then I sloshed my face with water and went back to Mr Arnold to say, 'Okay, tea mark IV coming up and this time we both drink it.' (He gave another of his spooky smiles when I said that.)

We had the tea with me sitting on the floor, my back against the bookcase and my feet among the newspapers, while Mr Arnold asked me all these questions about Marcelle's death.

I told him almost everything that happened on the *Destry* and in the telling I found out why catholics and people go to confession because I could feel the horror of that time sort of sliding away from me so that I could see Marcelle again as she was when she was laughing and acting the fool and stuff. I'm not saying that I thought I'd be able to forget the way she died and everything. I knew I wouldn't. But I could see that in time I'd be able to *cope* with it.

When I'd finished talking, Mr Arnold said that without a body and without any witnesses to the accident there probably wasn't much we could do legally. Then he said, 'But I've been a member of the Liberal party for donkeys' years and we can certainly put paid to Donally's political aspirations. No one would endorse a candidate with a scandal like that in the closet and as soon as I'm up again I'll be ringing people in high places. You'll find not only will Donally resign from the Liberal party, he'll also fold his tent and quietly creep out of Queensland.'

Straight after that – to cheer me up I suppose – he began to tell me stories about himself and his brother, saying that they were twins who'd grown up in the south of England and gone to Cambridge and everything before joining their uncle's law firm in London.

'My brother's name was Evelyn, so we called him Lyn. I was known as Xam because at the age of seven when told I could decorate our birthday cake, I carefully wrote Max backwards on it in green angelica.'

That story sent me down to check on *my* brother. He'd disappeared and when I raced back upstairs to tell Mr Arnold, he said, 'Don't fly into a panic. He'll have found a mate, that's all. Boys grow like mushrooms on this hill. Just go to the verandah, face north and like a monk invoking the gods who play hide and seek in the Himalaya, bellow your brother's name.'

I did what Mr Arnold said and on the second call J–Max's head rose up from the hedge two doors down. Then his shoulder emerged and an arm which waved wildly. I waved back and watched as he disappeared again into the hedge like someone sliding into the sea.

I was still on the verandah when Dr Linfors pulled up outside and a moment later came racing up the steps in a plum-coloured track suit. He was dark and young-looking with all these silver streaks in his hair. Not that I got much of a look at him because after reaching the top of the steps and nodding at me, he whipped around the corner and disappeared into Mr Arnold's flat.

When that happened I perched myself on the verandah rail and took my first good look at the view. Most of Southport and all of Labrador was spread below me. The main body of the Broadwater was hidden by a fold of the town. Sailing in the sky above it like a giant tulip was the coloured parachute I'd seen when we lived by the river. To the north was the blue bulge of South Stradbroke Island and beyond it all, the glassy green of the ocean with this minute ship creeping along out by the horizon.

I don't know how long I stayed there goggling at that smashing view but suddenly Dr Linfors was beside me saying, 'You're Morgan, I understand.'

'Yes.'

'And you're staying here?'

I nodded.

'Well, Morgan, I've given Mr Arnold a subcutaneous injection. Do you know what that means?' He'd raised one eyebrow and was studying me. I studied him too and wondered if the streaks in his hair were natural or not.

In the end he must have guessed I had no idea what a subcutaneous injection was because he told me he'd given Mr Arnold an injection under the skin. (He had this sort of detached voice like the ones people use in 'Oxford Blues' which is my mother's favourite television programme. When it's on she always watches it and if I moan enough lets me watch it too. One actress she's *nuts* about is Patricia Hodges but she doesn't let my father know because when he thinks you like a person or something on television he watches too and makes jokes about them until you get embarrassed and switch the programme off.)

'The injection will help his asthma,' Dr Linfors said, 'but by rights he should be in hospital. He won't go of course but at least this time he's agreed to have the Blue Nurses in each morning and a physiotherapist as well. In the meantime I'd better have a word with Mrs Werther.'

'You can't. She's gone to Beau Desert.'

'When will she be back?'

'After the weekend, I expect.'

Dr Linfors had tilted his head and was studying me again but suddenly he turned away, filled his lungs with air and said, 'What a view!' Then, looking out over the town, he said, 'Mr Arnold says you did a good job this morning. Probably saved his life.'

I gave this silly little gasps of laughter. 'He wasn't that bad.'

The doctor had turned to me again. 'Do you think you can look after him till Mrs Werther gets back?' He paused there but before I could answer, went on, 'His *back* isn't the problem. I'll give you a script for that. Most of it's tension anyway. The thing is, he shouldn't be here alone and he knows it.'

'Why is he then?'

'Because he's eighty, as proud as sin, and knows that when he does leave here he won't be coming back.'

I thought of Mr Arnold's old skeleton chest and didn't know what to say.

'A few months ago,' said Dr Linfors, 'we managed to get him a place at the Baptist retirement home up by the college. At the interview when they told him he'd have to give up his fags and sherry he stalked out. But not before he'd told the superintendent he was a dedicated atheist and that at his age a little loose living was in order.' The doctor gave a laugh which ended with a sigh. 'All the other places are chockablock and the waiting lists stretch from here to Burleigh. I think that suits Mr Arnold. I think he's made up his mind to stick it out here. At the same time of course he has all the normal human fears that go with such a decision.'

'He's not eating properly. Did you know?'

'I can see he's not. That's why I wanted to speak to Mrs Werther. You'll cope though, won't you? Mr Arnold says you will.' Dr Linfors had squatted to open his bag, which was just as well because I felt my eyes pop as he went on to say, 'You're his great-grandniece he tells me. Down from Cairns. He's never let on before that he had relatives in Australia.'

I didn't say anything, just waited while he put a pad on his knee and wrote out a prescription. After giving it to me and shutting his bag and everything he stood up and said, 'Take the script to the twenty-four hour chemist and if you have any problems call me. I'll come immediately – anytime – night or day.'

'You didn't this morning.'

He screwed up his face in a way which was suddenly funny and friendly. 'I didn't get the message. That's why I'm giving you this,' and he handed me a card with a number on it. 'You can get me on that even in my car. Okay?' He gave me this sort of *shining* smile and when I smiled back, picked up his bag and headed down the steps. At the bottom he looked back up at me. 'A spot of vacuuming might be in order. The dust, y'know.' A wave of his hand and he got in his car and shot down the hill.

I went in to Mr Arnold and teased him a bit about my being his great-grandniece. Joining his hands in a prayer position he said, 'Forgive an old fool. If I hadn't told him that he'd have clapped me into a home along with four hundred senile tabbies singing hymns and wetting the bed.' He looked at me then with eyes that were suddenly round and – well, *trusting*. 'We'll manage, won't we?'

'Yes, we'll manage,' I said though I wasn't sure we would.

I didn't even start the vacuuming that day because when everything else had been done it was time to haul J-Max

276

back inside and get him clean enough for bed. (One of the Blue Nurses had called after lunch when Xam was asleep. Her name was Jeannie and she had big hands and arms and a bottom which Xam later described as monumental. He hated having her there and nicknamed her the Beefeater but her visit was a great relief to me because after waking him she took charge in a really no-shit way. For instance when he refused to use the stainless steel teapot thing she brought for him to pee in, she said, 'That's fine. It's better for you to get up anyway.' And she called me and showed me how to help him out of bed and along the hall to the loo.)

That first day ended with a supper of biscuits and milk in Xam's room while he told us a story about a monkey and a grasshopper. (I guess it was a parable or something because the grasshopper turned out to be smarter than the monkey.) At the end of it we tossed to see who'd sleep downstairs and who'd have the bed and skinny mattress in Xam's spare room. J-Max won the right to Joss's room but during the day his mates had told him all this spooky stuff about the ghost in the garden and at the top of the steps he turned back saying he'd decided it was his job to keep Xam company.

At that stage I didn't know about the ghost and when I finally got downstairs I showered with the window open a bit so I could see the ivy-covered tree. About a hundred thoughts were tossing in my head like birds in the wind but they seemed to settle when I got into bed. I lay thinking about Xam then and wondering what would happen to him. I was remembering the way his mothy old hand had come onto my head when suddenly this *other* thought flooded my brain. It was the answer to my question about the difference between the sex Joss and I had and the kind the creepers at the Rose Club get into. Joss and I had wanted each other because it was *us* – I mean I wanted him because I'd already seen he was the other half of me. And even if he didn't feel that way at least he wanted me because I was Morgan, the girl he'd brought food to at the river, the girl who'd been allowed to see his tears. As for the *creepers*, they were just scavving on the human race.

Working that stuff out made me feel great and after going over it all again I stretched out and with every one of my muscles relaxed, slid into the best sleep of my life.

Chapter Twenty-Eight

I WAS WRONG about Mrs Werther. She didn't come back after the weekend. In fact she didn't come back until the next one but with the help of the Beefeater and the physiotherapist we did manage. (Anna the physio was either Dutch or Swedish and on her first visit greeted me with, 'A lovely day – aren't I?' She wore her hair in a single plait the way Mrs Golding, J-Max's teacher at Durbridge did, and her method of dealing with Xam was to smother his complaints with a laugh I could hear out in the kitchen. At first he loathed her, saying she'd done her training with the *Wehrmacht* whatever that is, but in the end her good humour got to him and he admitted he'd rather have her taking liberties with his back than the Blue Beefeater who had what he called a morbid interest in his bowel.)

The doctor called every day so I had to fit the cooking and shopping and stuff around all these visits. (When I went shopping Xam made me bring the cash register slips back to him and on the Wednesday, when he was able to get up unaided, he paid me back in notes from his handkerchief drawer, then gave me an extra hundred dollars. 'That's carry-on finance,' he said. 'I'm not short of a bob, you know, so when you need more, just tell me and I'll tonk off to the bank in a taxi.' This was a relief to me too because I'd found that when you get into the supermarket, money's as hard to hold onto as *smoke*.)

By the time Xam was allowed up I'd found his vacuum cleaner. It was a brand new one still in its box in the bottom of the hall cupboard. After that I embarked on The Great Clean-up, vacuuming and scrubbing until Xam said I'd become as obsessed as the Beefeater. Later on Allie's friend Ro said I'd been cleaning my *past* away. All I know is that I enjoyed doing it. I even cleaned our part of the verandah, throwing buckets of water on it and getting this buzz as it rushed across the rough old boards then broke into fat diamonds which cascaded onto the leafy branches and things below.

I've just realized I haven't given a proper description of either Xam or his flat yet. As far as the flat goes there isn't much to say. The floors are covered with fairly plain lino and the furniture is old and dark and heavy. The walls, painted timber like the ones downstairs, have hardly any decorations on them. A couple of faded photographs of Xam's property out west and a print of a ballet dancer doing up her shoe – that's about it. In one corner of his bedroom there's a pyramid of leather suitcases. For some reason they are his pride and joy and he likes to keep them polished. When we arrived they looked as if they hadn't been done for *years* so I bought some GY and spent Tuesday morning 'dressing' the five of them. When I'd finished Xam stuttered with pleasure and sent me round to the milkbar to buy Iced Vo-Vo's for afternoon tea.

I know you can't call someone as old as Xam handsome or anything because he's wrinkled to the *limit* but one night, watching him read to J-Max, I decided that if you stopped thinking of him as human and saw him as a rock carving or a weathered old eagle or something, he'd be – well, sort of beautiful in a weird way. Allie says he's like one of those dried old men you see in films about India during the time of the British rule. He certainly sounds like one with his much-imitated-by-J-Max, super-posh vowel sounds.

His eyes are bluer than anybody's, including my grand-mother Barbie's, and he makes them even bluer by wearing these old blue shirts and sweaters. Both his little moustache and his hair are white, but stained yellow by the never-ending cloud of cigarette smoke which goes past them. (I should have pointed out earlier that the tobacco smell is the main furnishing feature of the flat and when I first came here I was constantly swishing windows up and opening the doors at each end of the hall so that the wind could go through the place at three hundred kilometres an hour. In the end Xam took to smoking only on the verandah. The tobacco smell will never leave the place though. I think it's imbedded in the walls. It's certainly imbedded in Xam.

The section of the verandah that belongs to Xam is my favourite part of Tibet. Up there you feel you're living in the tree tops. The rail – its paint burnt off by sun and wind – is silky beneath your hand, the floor boards dark and grooved. In one corner the boards've buckled a bit and don't look safe but all this weathering gives the place an extremely comfortable feel. Each evening a family of pos-sums does a march-past along the rail and in the mornings when I lean out into the paradise-smelling air to pick our breakfast paw-paw, I get this ace feeling that the trees and things in the garden are pleased to see me. I guess that sounds ridiculous but if you want to know, I seem to feel this through my *skin*.

On the Wednesday evening of our first week at Tibet I tackled our mountain of washing, doing it in the machine on the downstairs verandah. This machine is set up so that the used water runs off into Mrs Werther's vegetable patch, irrigating it.

Ellen Petherick, the woman in the front flat had a vegetable plot too. I'd seen her down there working sometimes in
a big straw hat. Xam said she lived on welfare but had spent
several years in Arnhem Land working with a team of
anthropologists. She'd lost her job there when she tried to
adopt a nine year old aboriginal girl in order to bring her up
as a sort of black Joan of Arc who'd lead her people to
freedom. Xam also said she had about fourteen locks on
each of her doors and windows because she thought someone from ASIO was watching her.

When I got to know Mrs Werther she told me Ellen
Petherick's parents called on her one Christmas but she
wouldn't open the door to them. In the end, after stacking
all these presents beside the door, they went away. Ellen
didn't touch the presents, just walked past them each day
and they stayed where they were with the ribbons and
wrapping fading in the sun. Finally the paper started to tear
and when that happened Mrs Werther went up and
removed the lot.

I was *dying* to get to know Ellen Petherick so I could ask
her about the black saviour, but each time we met on the
steps or in the garden, she'd duck her head, beam at the
ground and sidle past me.

The only other person living at Tibet was a young bloke
who worked for the electricity board and had two rooms at
the front downstairs. He used to go off in the mornings in
his SEQEB safety helmet and again in the evening in a
velvet jacket and carrying a guitar case. Apart from that we
hardly saw him. I used to hear him though because when he
showered he shouted some kind of mantra while he was
doing it. When I asked Xam about him he said he'd been in
an ashram at one stage but left when the swami ordered him
to give up his music. He's a classical guitarist who practised
at weekends and sometimes late at night as well so that I'd
go off to sleep with this sort of *distilled* music falling all
around me. (According to Xam, John's not likely to know

I exist. Just the same after I'd heard the shouted mantras I started locking the bathroom window as well as the door when *I* showered.)

By the time Allie visited us on Friday I'd worked out it was going to take Sylvester Stallone to move my brother out of Tibet. (Before I go any further I should explain that he'd introduced himself to his mates in the street as *Matt*. I don't know why. He'd learned to pronounce Max in the normal way except for a bit of a hiss at the end. Perhaps he was scared the other kids would copy the hiss or perhaps he thought *his* Max would end up as Xam. Whatever the reason he was stuck on Matt and ready to fight me when I failed to use it, so from time to time I'll be referring to him by that name but in my story, for the sake of convenience, I think I'll stay with J-Max.)

As I said earlier he took to Tibet like a duck to water. There *were* boys growing like mushrooms in our street – fourteen of them, five in the house two doors away from us. The family there was Basque but with the un-Basque name of McIntyre, a fact which always made Xam give a grin beneath his moustache when they were mentioned. Mr McIntyre who was tall and thin and very Spanish-looking was a piano tuner. Because of this the latticed-in space under their house had about six pianos standing among the dust and shadows. This place became J-Max's passion. He loved the pianos, not just to play but as *objects*. (Mr McIntyre who occasionally called on Xam in the evenings to talk about politics and stuff said my brother even borrowed a towel from Mrs McIntyre and dusted them.) He told Xam too that J-Max played a sort of music down there though he wasn't sure it *was* music because there seemed to be as much emphasis on the pauses as on the notes themselves. He said that late one afternoon he heard him playing this really spooky piece and when asked about it J-Max said it was the song of someone drowning. Mr McIntyre said the song sounded the way you'd expect dolphins to sound when they were crying. Of course J-Max didn't spend all his time with the pianos. He spent a lot of it zooming around in the bush with a reed tied around his head and a spear or something in his hand.

The day Xam was well enough to sit out on the verandah was the day J-Max disappeared altogether. At the end of an afternoon spent searching the entire suburb we learned he'd taken himself off to school with his mate Carlos McIntyre. Apparently the teacher let him stay and when he insisted on going back the next morning Xam rang some chap he knew in the education department and had it made more or less official.

Apart from the friends he'd found, the thing my brother liked about Tibet was Xam's library. It had everything in it – a set of encyclopedia as well as Robin Hill's bird book and things like first edition copies of Rudyard Kipling's jungle stories. At bedtime I'd sit on the side of J-Max's bed, while Xam, in the armchair, read to us in his quivery old voice. He'd read slowly, stopping now and then to give a detailed description of the life cycle of an *armadillo* or something. Sometimes instead of reading he'd tell stories of his life out west. (At one time he'd had this thin ginger cat called Gandhi who used to accompany him to the place where he caught the rail motor for an occasional trip into town. Each time just before he got aboard, Gandhi would brand him as spoken-for by peeing on his shoes and long white socks.)

One evening the name of his brother, Lyn, came up and when it did J-Max asked if he was still in England.

'No, he died. He died two days after our twenty-fourth birthday.' Xam looked towards the window and gave this big feathery sort of sigh.

J-Max who has the tact of a *bee* asked how he'd died.

Xam was silent for ages then he said, 'He died of tetanus after a fall from his bicycle.' Very slowly Xam took off his glasses, folded them and put them in the pocket of his shirt. 'He was in Germany. Had gone there on a cycling tour with friends. I was in Wales. Climbing.' Xam turned his head to look across at me. 'It was the first birthday we'd spent apart and perhaps because of that I had my first and only psychic experience.'

I waited for a moment, then said softly, 'What happened?'

'I didn't know Lyn was ill let alone in hospital, but the night he died I was woken by something battering at the roof of my tent. It was a drumming sound, a tattoo almost, and at first I thought it was the wind. Then, realizing there was no wind, I got up and went outside to investigate. Instead of stepping from my tent into a piece of the Welsh countryside I found myself in a place completely unfamiliar to me – a place of dark fields and brooding pine trees. I was standing on the bank of a river and my brother, in a suit I hadn't seen before, stood on the other side. I was about to call to him but he'd already seen me and lifted his hand. Then he waded into the river. I sang out that he'd ruin his new suit but he smiled at me and kept going through water that reached his armpits.

'He'd started off at his normal height but when he walked out of the river on my side he was the size of a child but still dressed in a tiny tailored suit. I bent to pick him up but he shook his head, still smiling, and going to a bank of hyacinths I hadn't noticed before lay down beside them. Then he closed his eyes and turned his head away. The vision ended there. I was back in Wales with the dawn beginning to show in the east and I knew my brother was dead.'

I said, 'What did you do?'

'What could I do? I went down to the village and was there when the news of his death came through. After that I crossed to Germany and took his body home.' Xam stopped again and stared into the empty corner of the room, then he said, 'I didn't return to my uncle's law firm. I found I couldn't. Instead I sold up my bits and pieces, everything in fact but my clothes and books and I came to Australia to jackaroo on a cousin's property. In time I got my own place and stayed there alone until I retired here to the coast.' Xam cleared his throat and after a moment added, 'When I came here, this stretch of coast *was* Paradise, you know.'

After that I told him about our visit to the Tarot lady and asked him if he believed people really could see into the future.

He said, 'I think they occasionally see into our *unconscious*.'

'What's that got to do with it?'

'Well, that old philosopher Carl Jung said the unconscious plots our life-story for us, I see no reason to disagree. After all, it's where we hide such things as hopes and fears and dreams.'

'So if someone sees inside, they know everything about us.'

Xam smiled. 'Not quite, but they might know enough to make one or two fairly accurate predictions.'

'And that's all they need to do, isn't it?'

'Exactly. Mind you, the people we call clairvoyants may merely be dab hands at reading body language. Who knows – in the case of your friend Marcelle, the woman may have thought her impetuosity had an element of self-destruction in it.'

I thought that over and said, 'She told me I'd end up with everything I wanted.'

'If Jung was right, that'll be up to you, won't it?' Xam sat sort of boring his eyes into me for a while, then thinking, I suppose, that so much talk of death and stuff would give J-Max nightmares, he turned back to him to begin another story about Gandhi the cat.

Xam was almost always gentle with my brother. Not with me though. We didn't ever reach the stage again of what he called the Tetley Tea Debacle but he found fault with most things I did. He didn't say much. He didn't need to. I'd know he was cross by the way he'd clear his throat at the table when he saw I'd bought cavandish bananas instead

of lady fingers, or wholemeal bread instead of his favourite
white loaf. When he was really *flicked* he'd give these little
asthmatic gasps. He'd do that when I used words like shit or
sat on the verandah rail with my underpants showing. Allie
said this was because he loved me to pieces and didn't want
to admit it to himself let alone to me.

I replied to that with one of Xam's favourite words –
frogwash.

Allie met Xam the Friday after we'd arrived at Tibet. She'd
been furious with me for not ringing her as soon as we got
there. I guess she had reason to be because she'd rung The
Rose Club the day after we left and been told we'd disappeared. When I did get in touch with her I copped a serve
and I'm sure she was planning to give me another the day of
her visit. The thing that saved me was the *weather* because
she arrived too frazzled by the unexpected heat to think of
other things. Xam and I were waiting for her on the
verandah. Xam had put on his hand-knitted tie for the
occasion and when she came around the corner to see us and
say, 'Jesus, I'm wrecked. It was boiling on the bus and I was
jammed in beside this old sod who smelt like mushroom
fertilizer,' he stood up. I stayed in my chair and died.
I needn't have bothered though because Xam already had
his hand out and was beaming. Perhaps he looked into *her*
unconscious or something because from that moment on he
thought everything she said and did was wonderful. In fact
if she'd sat down and suggested we play strip-poker there
on the verandah he'd have probably given his wheezy
chuckle and told her what a character she was.

Needless to say I'd asked Allie not to mention the baby.
(Xam believed that unmarried mothers were practically the
sole reason for what he called the shaky state of the economy.) She did mention it though because later when I saw

her getting the worst of the kitchen-sink argument I decided to change the subject by saying that Xam had once been a solicitor.

That made Allie swivel in her chair to face him. 'Then you know a lot about the law?'

'A little,' said Xam which was the understatement of the eighties because he'd been studying it off and on all the years he lived alone out in west Queensland.

Allie immediately launched into the story of her lost baby but I needn't have worried about that either. Xam's horror at the hospital's disregard for everything British law stands for blinded him to the fact that Allie had no wedding ring.

'You'll get the child back of course,' he said. 'Nothing can stop that. The thing is that we have to work out how to achieve it with a minimum of delay.'

Allie told him then that she'd had a meeting with a Legal Aid officer down at Ballina. 'He was really helpful. He said almost the same words you did but went on to say it might take a couple of years and he warned me that if a baby *racket* was in operation there might be cops and people involved who'd be prepared to perjure themselves in court.'

'I doubt it,' said Xam. 'It's more likely some do-gooding social worker has elected to parcel out the babies according to his or her idea of what's fitting.'

'The bloke at Ballina said anything can happen up here,' said Allie. 'He reckons the Queensland police force could teach the Los Angeles Mafia some tricks.'

Xam said 'No one would argue with that, so the thing will be to get the case heard in New South Wales. And that may be difficult.'

Allie made a groaning noise and Xam warned her that whatever she did she must remain within the law. 'That's your only chance of winning,' he said. 'You mustn't throw it away.' He was still lecturing her on that point when I stood to clear away the afternoon tea things.

Allie left Tibet that afternoon happier than I'd seen her.

She'd have died for Xam I can tell you that. And because she was in such a good mood I confessed on the way to the bus stop about The Rose Club turning out to be a brothel. She *did* rip into me then, saying, 'You crazy bastard. You're lucky you didn't end up like Marcelle.'

I'd been ready to argue but didn't because her words sent a shiver through me and I stopped walking and stood remembering the way Hattie McLeod had looked at me on my last night at The Rose when she told me Merna wanted to see me upstairs. At the time the look had puzzled me but seeing it again in my mind I know exactly what it meant. Hattie's eyes had become envious eyes – cat's eyes because she thought I was being invited upstairs to a better world than hers.

Allie who'd turned around and was walking backwards sang out, 'What's wrong?'

Hurrying to her I said, 'Allie are women *always* jealous of each other?'

'Ro says they are. She says they have to be because their survival depends on whether or not they please men.'

By then we'd both stopped walking and Allie said, 'Delia says . . .'

'*Delia*?'

'Yeah she writes our music for us. Most of the songs too.'

'Has she got sort of wine-coloured hair and granny boots?'

'No, blonde hair and famine sandals.'

'On our way up here I saw a girl called Delia leave the train at Byron Bay. She had this pink hair and her gear was hanging out of a big basket.'

'Must be two Delias in Byron Bay. Anyway *ours* says that being jealous of each other was our first mistake and the one that really mattered because it keeps us permanently divided and that makes it dead easy for men to colonize us.'

'What do you mean – colonize us?'

Laughing Allie said, 'Men con us by telling us they love

us and then put us to work for the rest of our lives. They say we can't think and then because we can and do, they pinch our ideas. Delia believes women do a lot of the creative thinking and then stand around like salt cellars while men take the credit.'

Walking again I said, 'If that's true – I mean if all this stuff's been going on since the *ice*-age how's anyone going to change it now?'

'By being a wake-up. That's how.'

'I'd like to see it.'

'When you get to Byron Bay you will. The gang there's terrific. They support each other in *everything*. If one has a fight with her boyfriend the rest pile into him too. And that's a real eye-opener because believe it or not the bloke immediately heads for his mousehole.'

'There must be times though when they disagree. Among themselves I mean.'

'Of course there are but when that happens they sit down together and thrash things out.'

'Sure,' I said in this sarcastic voice. 'I know all about that. My Aunt Penelope used to belong to a heap of those women's groups. *They'd* sit down and thrash things out – I've heard her telling Mum – but they always ended up with everyone hating each other.'

'P'raps they didn't want it to work. The girls in our group do and if the system does bomb they write a little drama about the problem and act it out so the people involved can take a gander at themselves.'

We'd reached the bus stop where Allie went to the kerb and turned to say, '*That* works. I know because I've seen it.'

Watching Allie as she climbed up into the bus I saw how thin she'd become. (Her legs looked like J-Max's.) I realized then that although she didn't say much about the baby she probably thought about him all the time. *Unless someone does something mighty soon*, I thought, *she'll end up fretting herself to death*. The next minute though a bit of the old Allie appeared because she shot one of the windows open the way Joss did the night he left. Grinning at me she stuck her head out to say, 'I was bulldusting about Delia. It was her. She changes the colour of her hair every week.' Then she thumbed me as the bus began to move.

Chapter Twenty-Nine

I MET MRS Werther in the side garden when I carried down a load of washing the next morning. I'd already seen Ellen Petherick digging in *her* patch. She was on hands and knees hacking away at the earth with a chisel. (In her big coolie hat she looked like someone out of *A Town Like Alice*.) She saw me too and her greeting was to hunch up her shoulders and smile down at her chisel hand.

Around the other side, Mrs Werther, carrying a bunch of mint, stepped in front of me on the path. 'What are you doing here?' she said.

I don't think she'd been home long because she had on a shiny straw hat and a floral dress. Around her throat was a double row of fake pearls with some of the pearly stuff worn off so that the glass underneath showed through.

I said, 'I'm Morgan – Joss's friend. We met before.'

'I know that.'

'I've been looking after Mr Arnold.'

She'd known all along what I was doing there because fixing me with her funny eye she said, 'He told me. I spoke to him on the phone last night.'

'He didn't say.'

'No need to.'

There was this silence, then I said, 'I stayed on because he wasn't well enough to leave.'

Mrs Werther made a sort of 'huh' noise in her throat. 'Silly old goat should have been in care years ago.' (While she said that she was really *examining* me.)

'But he's much better,' I said. 'The doctor's not calling any more and the physio's only coming twice next week.'

With the mint still in her hand Mrs Werther reached out and took some of the washing from me. 'I'll take these before you trip and break your neck.'

Together we stepped up onto the verandah. 'It's not only the asthma,' she said. 'There's emphysema there as well, you know.'

We were at the washing machine by then and she fixed me again with her weird eye. 'I shouldn't be bothering you. No doubt you're ready for off.'

'Well I meant to be in Byron Bay a week ago.'

'Then you pop along and don't fret over old Max. I'll tell him I won't renew his lease unless he gets in home-help and Meals on Wheels into the bargain.'

I was imagining Xam's reaction to that when Mrs Werther dumped her load of washing onto the machine and said, 'I've got a letter for you inside.'

'For me?' I said. 'Why would anyone write here?' but my heart was already side-drumming because I knew the letter had to be from Joss.

'God knows, but put the clothes down and come and get it.'

I followed her along the verandah and into her kitchen where practically *everything* had a kookaburra motif on it. Mrs Werther reached up to take the letter from the mantel-piece and as she did all these dumb questions were piling into my head about why Joss had written instead of just turning up.

The writing on the envelope was small and squashed up into this neat oblong.

'It's from Joss, isn't it? Aren't you going to open it?' Mrs Werther was standing *practically* on my *toes* so I said, 'I'll take it into the garden,' and without stopping to say thanks I left the kitchen.

I took the letter over to the traveller's palm and sat down alongside the tombstone. Before opening it I wanted to spend some time sorting out the questions inside my head but I didn't get the chance because my hands were already tearing the envelope. Just before I started to read I saw this picture of Hattie McLeod bundling up the coffin-birthday present and slamming it into the refrigerator. Then I was reading.

I suppose I thought about Hattie and the coffin because I was sitting practically on top of a tombstone but perhaps it was a premonition or something because that letter from Joss was about the biggest disappointment of my life. It was three quarters of a page in the neat squashed-up writing, starting off, Dear Morgan, and going on to say that his father was much sicker than he'd expected when he went down on the bus. He said at first he hadn't recognized him because his hair had gone white and he'd lost nearly twenty kilograms. He'd had two operations for a detached retina and was waiting to go back to hospital to be operated on for a stomach ulcer.

That's really all the letter said except for the last paragraph in which Joss added that his father was looking for a tutor for him because he wanted him to finish his education. He didn't say anything about coming back to Southport and although I read it through about eighty times in case I'd missed something, I couldn't find one word about *us*.

In the end I put the letter back in its envelope and got up and went to stand at the door of Joss's room. Looking in at the picture of the two men fighting I wished I could be just a shadow on the wall like them, not feeling anything, because if you want to know, at that moment, I felt so unwanted I wouldn't have minded being right *under* the Indonesian's

abandonment

tombstone. The worst part of it was that at odd times upstairs when I'd been vacuuming and polishing things I'd made up this whole life scenario about Joss and me living with the Nin Theatre Group at Byron Bay. I'd be ashamed to tell you of the sloshy stuff I'd dreamt up. I'd be ashamed to even think about it. And suddenly there was just this Chinese kid in Melbourne being educated and a girl in Southport who'd been lame enough to expect an ace love poem or something in the mail.

I was still in the doorway doing my life-ends-here bit when Mrs Werther's voice sang out, 'Morgan! Joss said to ask you to return his library book. He said he forgot to tell you.'

I spun around. She was at the end of the verandah with the crazy bunch of mint still in her hand.

'Did he *ring*?'

'No, I got a letter too. He sent his father's cheque for three month's rent on the room so if you want to use it, that's okay by me.'

'Then he might be coming back.'

'Either that or he's got money to burn,' said Mrs Werther and after taking off her hat and shaking out her wild hair she turned and walked away.

For a while I stayed where I was, trying to work out why Joss hadn't mentioned his room or anything to me. Not being able to, I went upstairs to flop into the cane chair opposite Xam on the verandah. He'd been reading the paper, and flopping my letter on top of it, I said, 'What do you make of that?'

After studying the envelope for about two hours he took the letter out and read it, then, holding the side of his glasses as if that would make him see better, he said, 'What do *you* make of it?'

'I think he's telling me he's not coming back but Mrs Werther said he's just paid another three months rent on the room.'

'You realize, don't you Morgan, that it's probably better if he doesn't come back?'

'You say that because you're prejudiced. You don't like anyone who's not blond and blue-eyed.'

Giving one of his spooky smiles, he said, 'I like *you*.'

'That's frogwash.'

'It's not, y'know.'

'Well it's beside the point. All I wanted was your opinion on the letter. I didn't want a lecture on race relations.'

There was much clearing of the throat, then Xam said, 'Oh, the letter, I see.' He picked it up again and skimmed through it. 'It seems okay to me.'

'But it doesn't say anything *personal*.'

'So that's the problem – no hearts and flowers.' Folding the letter Xam said, 'My dear, what do you want? Lies from a Don Juan or news of a friend?'

'What does that mean?'

'It means, child, that a boy like Joss Lau would have no idea how to express his emotions on paper. How could he? Instead he's written telling you he's not coming back immediately and he's paid rent on his room because he hopes in time he will. For the moment you'll have to be satisfied with that.'

'Well I'm not,' I said and after snatching the letter I got up and rushed back to Joss's room where I wrote this insane one to *him*. In it I said that as he hadn't mentioned coming back to Southport I guessed he'd stay in Melbourne and end up marrying some horn from PLC. After that I went right off, saying that if he did I'd come down there too and get a job in his garden digging with a chisel or something so I could see him every day, but not to worry about it because I'd take care not to bother him. I didn't say a word about his father and I signed it at the bottom, Morgan l.F. Christie.

Thinking about that letter makes my face fry even now because what I did next was go out and *post* it. If I'd waited ten seconds of course I wouldn't have but as it was I tore down to the milkbar, bought a stamp and shot the letter through the slot of the mailbox on the corner.

I was back at Tibet sorting the washing I'd abandoned earlier when Xam, who hadn't been downstairs since his asthma attack, appeared beside me.

'I bring consolation,' he said handing me a book. (It had a hard black cover and looked as old as Christmas.) '*The Hundred Names* – a collection of ancient Chinese poetry. If you dip into it you'll find that separation plays a great part in the love literature of the Chinese people.'

He was watching me sort of sideways like an old *crane* so I opened the book and started to read this poem by a bloke who lived during the time of the Han dynasty. (Actually he was the Emperor but I didn't know that then.) What I read was, 'Alas! In vain I listen for the rustle of your silks O my lady!'

The rest of the poem was about the Emperor looking at the fallen leaves piled against the door of this woman who was dead and stuff like that. When I'd finished I couldn't look up at Xam because I'd begun to giggle. I realize now I was giggling because I didn't know what else to do but anyway I stayed there staring at the page and hoping Xam wouldn't see me shaking until finally he said, 'You might find something in it you like,' and turned and shuffled off around the path.

I guess it was pretty smart of old Xam to give me that book because with nothing to do while the washing woo-shed around I sat on the edge of the verandah and read some of the poems. As Xam said they were nearly all about separation and stuff like that but there was one by this woman called Tsang Wan Sheng about the death of her little son. I don't know how to tell you about that poem. It was so simple. Just three little verses in this plain language but it made you *see* the dead baby being dressed for his grave. And it made you *feel* the mother's grief. After reading it through a few times I was so ashamed of the shit I'd written Joss all

I wanted to do was get my letter back from the mailbox and after shredding it, flush the pieces down the loo.

As soon as I'd finished the washing I went upstairs to Xam and said, 'If I wait down at the mailbox in the morning, do you think the man will give me back my letter when he comes to collect it?'

Instead of answering Xam asked why I wanted it.

'Because it was silly?'

'How silly.'

'Well, you know . . .' I stopped and shrugged but Xam sat waiting for me to go on and in the end I said, 'I wrote this dumb stuff about how if Joss didn't want me for his wife or anything I'd go and work in his garden instead.'

Xam gave his old–man's tee–hee laugh. 'Is that all? He'll probably be flattered.'

'But I forgot to mention his father being sick.'

'Not to worry. When you're working in the garden you can grow Chinese gooseberries for the old boy and make it up him.'

I stomped downstairs after that where I wrote a *second* letter to Joss telling him how sorry I was about his father and that I hoped he'd soon be better. Then I nicked out and posted that one too.

At dinner that night after I'd served out our Big Sister self-saucing pudding I told Xam that later on I'd ring and find out what time the bus left for Byron Bay on Sundays.

He looked up from his pudding to say, 'You're going then?'

'Of course. We'd meant to be in Byron Bay a week ago – remember?'

'I thought you might have changed your mind.'

'But Allie's expecting us.'

'Then I shan't say, "Don't go".' Xam looked down at the

table again. 'And I shan't complain. It's been wonderful having you here at all.' His voice was firm, just the same it told me that for him, life had suddenly become one big pile of *ash*.

Telling myself there was nothing I could do about it, I filled in the silence by saying, 'Allie says there's a speech therapist at the school down there.'

'They exist in Southport too.' Xam raised his eyes again. 'If it comes to that I doubt young Matt needs one, in the last week his speech has improved out of sight. In three months I'll wager he'll be as fluent as a politician.'

I filled the next silence by saying I was hoping to get a job at Byron Bay.

'You've got a job here.'

'Doing *housework*? That's not enough.'

'Of course it isn't.' Xam cleared his throat. 'I see your job as putting your head down and getting ready to go back to school, though if you wished to take time first to finish the story you've begun I don't think that would hurt you. Indeed it may be what you need.'

Because he was making things hard for me I shouted, 'You *know* we can't stay.'

At that stage J-Max, whose face had been turning from Xam to me and back again like someone at the tennis, pushed his untouched pudding away. 'Scuse me, Zam,' he said and got off his chair and headed for the door.

I knew then there'd be some kind of performance from him before I got him onto the bus. He'd never passed up Big Sister pudding before and he'd only remembered to excuse himself from the table once that I could think of since we'd been at Tibet.

Next to go was Xam who said, 'I'm in need of nicotine,' and *not* excusing himself got up and disappeared in the direction of the verandah.

I left the table too and as I stood at the sink scraping the three serves of pudding onto a piece of newspaper I could feel about a tonne of cement inside my chest. I shoved the wrapped-up pudding into the kitchen tidy then ran water for the dishes telling myself Xam wasn't *related* to us; that we'd landed in his life by accident and that Mrs Werther and Dr Linfors would see he was okay. I was still finding arguments for leaving when Xam loomed up beside me with a tea towel in his hand. I didn't exactly *look* at him but I could tell he was more stooped than ever. (The reason I didn't look at him was that I thought that if I did, he'd catch my eye and say, 'Don't go'. And I knew if that happened the next moment would be the pits for both of us.) By that time I was practically holding my breath in embarrassment but I needn't have worried. Xam didn't mention Byron Bay. Instead he launched into this story about his cousin Gwynneth being trapped in Cannes for the whole of World War II. The story went on and on. If it had a point Xam didn't get to it but anyway it lasted through the dish-washing exercise and when we'd finished, Xam hung his towel carefully on its rack, then he said 'I've one or two letters to write,' and after giving me this death's head smile went off to his study.

I spent some time making the kitchen *immaculate* and when that was done went downstairs to pack our things. At five to nine J-Max was still absent and guessing he'd be down at McIntyres' I went to get him. It was an ace Queensland night, big-sky'd and starry, and as I went down the hill I began to smell this creeper which was slowly pushing over a timber dove-cote thing in McIntyres' front garden. The creeper had clusters of creamy-white flowers all over it and that night they were bombing out this spicy perfume as if they meant it to reach *Hawaii*.

At McIntyres' gate, seeing a dim light in the underneath part of the house I shoved my way through bushes and stuff to get close enough to peer in through the lattice. The pianos were there, dark and quiet and I saw Mrs McIntyre's big bra and underpants hanging on a line with a heap of boys' T-shirts but there was no sign of my brother. I saw him though as I turned to push my way out again. He wasn't far from me, standing at the end of one of the pianos, his face pressed against it and his hand holding onto the edge of it. He was so small against the piano, and the way he was grabbing it made me think of this baby elephant I saw once on television holding onto its mother's tail for comfort.

It was a giggly thought but the next moment the words, *The piano isn't his mother, it's his* FRIEND, went through my head followed by, *and I'll bet he sees Xam as his* FATHER. I had this picture then of old Xam searching for the book of Chinese poetry. I saw him climbing painfully up onto his two-step ladder and reaching out and up for the book then bringing it all the way downstairs to give to me.

He's MY *father too*, I thought and fitting my lips to one of the gaps in the lattice I sang out, 'Hey Matt, come over here.' It was a dumb thing to do. The words came out distorted, frightening J-Max. I saw his back go stiff then he turned slowly, found himself alone and began to bawl. The next moment I was shoving my way to the door to rush inside and grab my brother. Squashing him to me I said over and over, 'We're staying at Tibet. We're staying here forever.'

The day ended with this big philosophical discussion about God and things over cocoa in the study. Xam started it by saying, 'If I had some of Ellen Petherick's incense sticks I'd light them tonight and give thanks.'

'Who to?' I said, then corrected myself, 'to whom? You don't believe in anything. Dr Linfors says you're an atheist.'

'What I tell my doctor and what I believe are two different things.'

'What *do* you believe?'

I expected Xam to put me off with some trick answer but after reaching out to stash his mug on the coffee table, he said, 'I'll admit that at Cambridge, Lyn and I were dedicated atheists. We thought we knew everything, as young men do, and when he died at twenty four, the senselessness of it served to reinforce that assumption in me.'

'But what about *seeing* him that night and everything?'

'It was easy to write that off as thought transference, which I'm sure it was.'

'So?'

'So years later living alone in west Queensland I'd sit outside in the immensity of the Australian night and be aware of a vibration, a kind of humming, communicating with me. When that happened I'd have a few seconds of being in touch with some force I felt was monitoring the land – monitoring me if it comes to that.' Xam surprised me again by stopping to laugh. 'I was crass enough in those days to try to bargain with whatever it was, saying, "Give me a sign – just one – and I'll believe in you." The fact that I offered such a bargain showed of course that I already believed in it.'

J-Max who was sitting on the floor had swivelled a bit to give me a puzzled look.

'Xam's just admitted he believes in God,' I told him.

My brother swivelled back. 'Do you, Zam?'

'Dear one, I believe in something, I'm not sure what.'

I said, 'Allie's friend, Ro, told her God's a female because only females create life *successfully*.'

'That's an argument I'm not getting into,' said Xam, 'except to point out that even the Virgin Mary had some help from an angel and I understand *he* was a male.'

I persisted, 'But do you believe in God?'

Before answering Xam fumbled in his dressing gown pocket and brought out his asthma puffer. For a while he looked at it as if he'd never seen it before then he put that on the coffee table too.

'If you push me into definition then I'd say my God is a force both male and female which sits somewhere breathing in time with the universe. I see it as detached, unshockable and generous beyond our dreaming. It's as close as one's own hand and as hard to know as the wind that moves the grass in spring.'

During the silence that followed Xam's speech this *enormous* cockroach came whirring in through the open window. It homed in on the puffer on the table and landed on it, feelers waving, wings not quite closed.

Spontaneously, the three of us laughed then J-Max shouted, 'Skelch it, skelch it.'

Leaning over, Xam tipped the cockroach into his hand then put the other over it making a cage. 'I think not,' he said. 'If a Blue Triangle had fluttered in to land there or even a common Wanderer no doubt we'd have viewed it as a sign from our hermaphroditic God but because a lowly cockroach turned up we say, squelch it.'

'But we always do.'

'Not this time,' said Xam and he got up and took the cockroach outside to let it go, pausing on the way to say, 'To bed both of you or I'll have two crosspatches to deal with in the morning.'

When my brother was in bed I went to Xam who was on the verandah smoking, 'Xam,' I said, 'why do men commit incest?'

I was standing at the edge of the light coming from the window and when I spoke Xam turned to peer at my face. 'Such a question to put to an old bachelor and it would take this old bachelor a lifetime to find a satisfactory answer.'

'But what do you *think*?'

There was a prolonged throat clearing. 'The things that come to mind, Morgan, are selfishness and immaturity but because this has been almost certainly the happiest evening of my life I'd add that there may be another dimension to the act, another dimension to the need.'

'What does *that* mean?'

'It means the perpetrators may be so aware of their grossness they seek for a moment to be joined to some form of perfection, and cruelly they choose a child as that form.'

'That doesn't make sense.'

Xam sighed. 'I don't suppose it does.'

'And what about the child? What about that? What about *me*?'

He reached out and touched my cheek with his dry old hand. 'Seeing you now, Morgan, I cannot think that you've been harmed.'

'How can you say that?'

'I say it because I see every part of you as shining. At the moment some of it's indignation, I'll admit, but you shine at the best and worst of times. Tell me then, how have you been harmed?'

'Because I lost everything in the world.'

'But you brought with you the person you love most.'

'Xam, I lost my *home*!'

'Only to learn you are at home everywhere.'

'That's just bullshit.'

'Dearheart, it's not even a *fib* and as you think about it, and grow a little wiser, you'll see that for yourself.' He stepped back and clapped his hands together making a surprisingly loud *klok*.

'Now go to bed so I can too.'

I left him then, skittling down the steps with this smile on my face because Xam's wobbly old voice had just told me he loved me the way Allie said he did.

Chapter Thirty

ELLEN PETHERICK FINALLY *spoke* to me. Looking at me and smiling she said, 'Hi Morgan.'

I got such a shock at her knowing my name and everything I didn't answer, so I missed the one opportunity fate gave me to have a conversation with her and steer it in the direction of the black saviour. We met in the downstairs hall with the gas stove in it. Ellen was clutching this embroidered orange kimono around herself and when she'd spoken she ducked her head and hurried towards the outside door. Her feet were bare and as she went I saw they were big ones like my mother's. It was only when she'd gone that I realized she'd come from the flat of John Anstis the guitarist.

I didn't tell anyone about Ellen being downstairs. I don't know why except that in a funny way I liked her. I think I liked her because of the unopened Christmas presents and the chisel and everything. I also had this crazy feeling that although we didn't really know each other she'd trust me somehow not to dob her in. Anyway the whole thing went out of my mind when I got upstairs because Xam met me on the verandah to say Allie was on the phone wanting to talk to me.

As soon as I heard Allie's voice, I blurted out that J-Max and I were staying at Tibet.

'I saw that coming,' she said.

'You *did*?'

'Don't be dumb – blind Freddie would've seen it.'

'Don't you mind?'

'Of course I don't.'

'But what about our plans?'

'Give it time, they'll come good. You'll get an education where you are. Old Blue Eyes will see to that and when you do join the Nin Group, you'll be a right little asset. But listen, I didn't call to talk about you. I called to pass on this news I've had from Mr Egan down at Ballina.'

'Who's Mr Egan?'

'The bloke at Legal Aid, of course, and he's been in touch with the hospital. Would you believe the management there is leaning over backwards to help? They've given him the name of the people who've got little Michael. They're Americans for God's sake – Glenn and Elsa Greenly. He's a bigwig in real estate and she runs one of those crappy charm schools where they teach you all about deodorants and stuff.'

'At least you've found out where he is.'

'I know but listen, there's more. The hospital has agreed to provide photocopies of all the documents and things which means I'll be able to prove any signatures supposed to be mine are forgeries.' Allie then said that what the hospital *hadn't* told Mr Egan was that at the weekend they'd suspended a sister, a probationary nurse and a social worker because of a suspected attempt to hand another baby over to the wrong people. (A friend of Mr Egan's sister had supplied this information. She worked in the office of the Hattan Maternity Home and said that in this case as well, the baby's mother was an un-married teenager.)

When I passed Allie's news on to Xam he was *gobstuck* making me wonder if he'd believed all of Allie's story in the first place. Anyway after taking it all in he went off to his study to ring some retired QC mate of his in Brisbane. Later he came back to the verandah to say, 'Monty thinks as I do that if the child was handed over illegally, these Yanks have no claim to it at all and that holds good of course whether or not they themselves are innocent parties.' He went on to say that his friend Monty who'd been nursing a grudge against Americans since *1942* was prepared to throw his resources behind Allie.

I said, 'Won't that offend Mr Egan?'

'I doubt it. Monty's no fool. He'll tread carefully and I think you'll find Allie's man will be delighted to have this sort of help from inside Queensland.' Xam finished off as he always did when speaking of Allie and the baby by saying how important it was for her to act strictly within the law.

Allie didn't stay within the law though or rather her friends at Byron Bay didn't but before I get onto that I must detour a moment to tell you that our domestic arrangements at Tibet had changed a little. With Dr Linfor's approval Xam had dispensed with the services of the Beef-eater. When she went he'd planned to hire what he called a daily but deciding he didn't want a *fixture* in the place he interviewed about five hundred cleaners and finally arranged for this young bloke Daniel to do out the flat for us each Thursday.

Daniel who came to work in just a pair of bib and brace overalls, turned out to be a member of this church called the Assemblies of God. Each Thursday when he'd finished, he'd join Xam on the verandah to tell him what scavs Roman Catholics are and stuff about the Vatican having its own stock exchange. Xam wasn't exactly rapt in these lectures but he kept Daniel on because when it came to cleaning he was ace. I suppose you'd call him a compulsive cleaner. For instance in the middle of a speech about what a peanut the Pope looked in his jewels and little cocktail hat, he'd leap across the room to polish up the door handle then leap back again. (J-Max found this habit of Daniel's hilarious and even now when he wants to let you know the conversation's bogging down he'll dart at a door knob and give it an imaginary going over.)

With no cleaning to do myself I'd started work again on my story. As I said earlier, I wrote in Joss's room, sitting at a little table J-Max and I carried down from upstairs. I was there on Friday reading over what I'd written when Xam appeared in the doorway. He was puffing like a dragon and he said, 'Allie's got her baby back.'

I heard him, I even took in the meaning of the words but what I said was, 'Do you need your spinhaler?'

'No I don't.' His voice was cross and while I swung around to watch him he went to the bed and sat on the end of it. I saw him struggling to make his breath normal then he said, 'The child's with her at Byron Bay.'

'You mean those Greenly people gave it *back*?'

Xam shook his head. 'Allie's friends took it.'

'What do you mean, *took* it?'

'Just that. One of them drove up to the Gold Coast and took it.'

'Who told you this?'

'Allie. She rang. She wants you to ring her back.'

After that Xam and I stared at each other while somewhere in the building Mrs Werther sang a line about wanting a white Christmas. Finally I said, 'What will happen?'

Before answering Xam surprised me by doing one of his little tee-hee laughs. 'D'y'know I believe Allie's in a strong position. *She's* done nothing illegal. Someone took her child and now someone else has given it back.' He giggled again. 'The fact that the child is now out of the state will make it jolly hard for the Greenlys to get even temporary custody.'

'Do you think they'll try?'

'Undoubtedly.'

Again I asked what would happen.

'After much ado I should think nothing. Allie may have

to get a court order preventing the removal of the child from her care and that'll probably be the end of it.'

'How can it?'

'Dearheart, if someone down at Ballina knows about the scandal at the hospital you can be sure half the people on the coast do too. In the light of that, any halfway decent counsel will advise the Greenlys against lodging a legal claim for the child. Mind you people will be buried under the paperwork for years but that won't be Allie's worry.'

'But who'll pay for it all?'

'The hospital I'd say, or their insurers. But again that won't be Allie's concern.'

Later when I rang Byron Bay to ask about the kidnapping and everything Allie was still too far above the moon to give what you'd call a *lu*cid account of it. What she did instead was keep telling me how amazing, fabulous, *divine* little Michael was. Since that day though I've heard the story so many times I can practically run it through my head like a video.

It starts after Allie's long phone conversation with Mr Egan of Legal Aid. That night when she'd gone to bed the other members of the theatre group had a meeting. During it they smoked joints made from dope grown in this blue plastic igloo in their vegetable garden. Allie says that probably influenced their thinking but anyway after deciding that if they waited for what they called the bullshitting male bureaucracy to move itself Allie's kid could be at high school before she even *saw* him, their next decision was to send someone up to the Gold Coast to watch the Greenlys in the hope of getting hold of some dirt or something which could be used against them.

The one they sent to do it was Luann Matthews. They sent her because this ex-boyfriend of hers who was always trying to get her back, lived on Washington Drive at Surfers just along the block from Greenlys. As far as I can see that's all Luann had going for her because she's certainly not the kind of person you'd normally choose as an undercover agent. (She's twenty-five, part-Aboriginal and very tall, with almost Indian features. In her teens she was a professional runner and has these smashing long dark sprinter's legs.)

Luann's proud of having Aboriginal blood. In fact you could say she's used it to make a tourist attraction of herself at Byron Bay. Wearing a T-shirt with a slogan on it like *I'm a Lesbian Archbishop and Mother*, she'll go into a shop and say, 'Is this the place that bars sexually active Kooris like me?'

Some of the shopkeepers enjoy it and play up to her. Others climb out of their tree. One even called the police but all the cops did was come around grinning and drive Luann home. (They told her all these dumb dirty jokes on the way.)

On the morning after the meeting, Luann – with a wad of the group's grant money stuffed in her bag – moved back in with her ex-boyfriend at Surfers. (Allie was told she'd gone to visit relatives.) By mid-afternoon Luann had conned the woman in the local milk bar into telling her that Elsa Greenly worked each day from 2 p.m. till seven at her poxy charm school at Pacific Fair. She also learned the baby spent those hours at home with the Filipino maid.

The next day Luann spent a whack of her expense money on this dinky little white suitcase which she fitted out with skin lotions and things in gold-topped bottles. At three o'clock, wearing big white earrings and a white mini-skirted dress she rang the bell of Greenlys' apartment, telling the sad-looking seventeen year old who answered that she represented the Ever-Eve Cosmetic Company. Minutes later she was in the Greenlys' sitting room with its moss green carpet and four couches covered in squashy pale grey leather.

After saying all this stuff about how her company was giving free facials and things she set about tarting up the

girl's face. She'd meant as she worked to get all this information out of her about her employers but she didn't
because all she could think of was the pram she could see on
the patio just outside the windows. It was one of those
collapsable ones and had nylon netting stuff draped over it
as if a baby was inside.

Luann says anyone with three per cent of the normal load
of brains would have *smelt* her interest in the baby but the
girl, Serena, was so rapt in the cosmetic routine she probably wouldn't have noticed mortars being wheeled up to the
windows.

When her face was done Serena was *ecstatic*, making these
bird noises and asking Luann to stay for coffee.

'Real coffee,' she said from the doorway. 'And cheese
cake. I've just got to decorate it.'

As soon as she'd gone Luann shot to the windows, slid
one back and stepped out. She says that when she looked
inside the pram and saw Allie's baby, her heart practically
dis*solved*.

The next thing she did was check out the property next
door. In the garden a man was cleaning the swimming pool.
His back was turned towards her but behind him about two
hundred of those smoky one-way windows were staring at
her.

'Up all troglodytes,' Luann said to the windows then,
bending, she threw back the nylon netting and scooped the
baby out of the pram. He made a little noise and she put one
hand quietly over his face while she replaced the netting.
Then she went back through the window, closed it and
slipped out of the apartment.

I love the picture I see of the long-legged black girl and
the pale little baby going proudly down the block together
while hoons in cars whistled at them and shouted obscene
things.

Safely inside her ex-boyfriend's flat Luann plonked
Michael in the middle of the bed and changed into a shirt

and jeans. (At that stage she was saying to herself, 'Come on girl. Just pretend you're Bobbi Sykes.')

After shoving her gear into the boot of her bomby old Toyota she put Michael in a beer carton, draped a tea towel over it and like someone taking a cat and kittens to the vet put it on the front seat of the Toyota and took off.

At Coolangatta she did this really gutsy thing. She drove into the airport, parked, and carrying Michael again, went inside and telephoned the police station back at Broadbeach.

When someone answered she said she was speaking on behalf of the Mothers' Liberation Front, and into the silence that followed said she was about to board a plane with a baby which had been stolen but was now being returned to its mother.

The man on the other end of the line said, 'Just a minute, will ya . . .'

'I haven't *got* a minute,' said Luann. 'But have a word with the Hattan Maternity Home. They'll fill you in on the details,' and beginning to shake she hung up and raced back to her car.

An hour and a half later Luann reached Byron Bay with a baby bawling its head off for food. Then, while someone went out to buy a pack of infant formula, Ro unbuttoned her shirt and, with Allie holding her son's feet and bawling too, coaxed him into having some of her milk.

There's all this other boring stuff I could tell you about the Greenlys' attempts to locate the baby but you wouldn't want to know and anyway after all this time he's still with Allie at Byron Bay and according to Xam and his friend Monty, likely to stay there.

Chapter Thirty-One

AFTER GIVING MRS Werther two days notice Ellen Petherick left Tibet. She left in the driver's seat of this hired stretch limo. She was wearing a man's panama hat with a ribbon on it the colour of Keen's mustard.

John Anstis from the downstairs flat was in the passenger seat with his guitar case sitting up in the middle like another person. In the back were all these cartons and suitcases. I saw a pair of kitchen chairs there as well.

We'd all collected on the verandah to watch them go, even Xam, and just before Ellen got in the car she looked up at us and *giggled*. I knew then they'd been married or something and were going away together to set up house with their two red chairs in some smashing place like the Tweed Valley.

I don't know why, but seeing Ellen go like that made me feel as if I was losing something that really mattered to me and instead of staying with the others to talk about it I went down to the garden and sitting by the tombstone, had all these really pitsy thoughts. I won't go into them except to say that I even got around to remembering how my mother called me Carmen Jones and stuff like that.

I suppose I should explain that even though I knew it wouldn't come, I'd been watching for a letter from Joss. I'd go about fifty times a day to this place on the verandah where you could lean out into the wind and by looking down through the branches of the bauhinia tree see if there was anything lying in the letter box. Of course nothing came for me and by the time Ellen went off in the limo with John Anstis I knew it never would.

Even Allie wasn't visiting us those days. She said she wasn't game to bring the baby over the border in case the Greenlys snatched it back, and thinking of the way she'd drool over it if she did, I wasn't all that fussed about seeing her. At least that's what I told myself but the next night when I answered the phone and heard her voice, the truth is that my spirits came up out of their depression like a SAM missile.

Allie said she wanted J-Max and me to come to Byron Bay on Saturday for a try-out of the dance-drama *Careful What You Call Your Daughters*. (They were inviting about twenty people because they'd set up these special effects and wanted to see how they'd go.) She said Ro's boyfriend, Peter, was travelling down with a mate who was prepared to take us too.

Just before she rang off, Allie said, 'Tell Xam to come,' but when I told him he said, 'Thank you, no. The trip down there would pulverize my old bones.'

As things turned out it's just as well Xam didn't go because we went to Byron Bay in the back of this bloke Nigel's panel van which had no back seat so my brother and I sat behind the others in two big Tongan-looking cane chairs. We couldn't see much but I can tell you it was a fabulous way to go – sort of scary but million*air*ish too.

I think Peter wanted us to enjoy the trip because when we'd crossed the Tweed he kept telling us to bob our heads and look at what he called the Martian flowers blooming in the terraced banana plantations. These 'flowers' were the blue plastic bags covering the bunches of ripening fruit, and to see them hanging among the ragged leaves really did make you feel you were whizzing through an extraterrestrial landscape.

Murwillumbah with the river and trees and blues and greens and dusk coming down was beautiful enough to make you want to devote your life to poetry or something. So was the view from the hill above Brunswick Heads where we stopped for a moment to look across this sort of patterned plain towards Byron Bay and the darkening sea.

When we got going again I couldn't stop thinking of myself coming the other way in the bus with J-Max a few weeks earlier. God, what a lamo I was! What a *sponge* cake, as Xam would say. I thought too about my home. The real one, I mean, back in Ivanhoe. In fact I made myself picture it – the house and the blossom tree and everything. I even went inside but the place seemed as foreign to me as one you'd see in *Norway* on some television show. Then wham! There was my mother coming out of her bedroom. She was tying the sash of her winter dressing gown and her hair was as messed about as Ellen Petherick's. I wanted so much then to grab her and hold on that I made a noise like someone being punched in the stomach and put my head down on my knees.

The others must have thought I was sick because J-Max touched my arm and Peter's voice said, 'Hang in there, mate. The road straightens in a minute and you'll feel better.'

He was right about part of it. The road did straighten and soon we were zooming across the plain towards the source of the lighthouse beam which was sweeping the mangrove-smelling air. By then Nigel was telling Peter about the little country school he'd taught at back in the Nimbin district. He said that on the first day of school each year, all these children would file down from the hills with bare feet and lunches of soy bread and sprouts. They were the children, and even grandchildren, of the hippies who dropped out in the sixties. From year to year, Nigel said, he wouldn't know whether to expect nine or thirty-nine.

I listened to him for a while, then I went back to thinking about my mother and by the time we'd reached Byron Bay and its lighthouse I'd told myself that someone who's too rapt in their pottery class to even know their kids have nicked off can't be classified as a mother at all.

I'd hoped we'd go first to the farm where the Nin Group lived. (Allie had told me all this stuff about the houses there and I wanted to see the bathroom in her place because I knew that on one of the walls someone has painted a field of purple irises with angel-fish swimming among them.) But instead of going to the farm we went to the place where *Careful What You Call Your Daughters* was to be performed.

It turned out to be an old timber church with a tarpaulin covering part of the roof at the back. Inside, instead of the usual churchy smell of old flowers and Brasso there was this mixture of sweat and marihuana. And hanging from the ceiling halfway between the door and the back wall was this row of black theatre lights. The rest of the place was normal – I mean there were pews and everything with people sitting in the two front rows. Up by the altar in the area which was supposed to be the stage, others were doing last minute things to the set. Allie was there and when she saw us she shrieked and waved but didn't come to meet us, so what we did was follow Peter who was striding towards a pair of carrycots sitting on the floor in front of the stage. When he got there, he made a joke about baby Jesus and his under-study. Then he picked up one of the cots and edging past us took it to the back row of pews where he sat with it on the seat beside him.

As I stood lamely by the other carrycot, Allie called, 'You'll look after ours, won't you, Mrs Lau?'

Ours! That's what she said, as if the baby was mine and maybe J-Max's too. I looked inside the cot then and when I did, although I hadn't expected to be impressed by the contents, I just *died*. There was this breathing doll, smaller than I remember my brother ever being. It had an *abundance* of straight dark hair made of silk and tiny hands with nails and everything as complete as those trick photographs you see of flowers unfolding.

Allie was waiting to see what I'd do, so after giving her a kind of salute I picked the cot up the way Peter did and took it to the nearest empty pew. Sitting beside it I waited till no one was watching then I put my hand, palm-up, in the cot beside the baby's feet and left it there.

Before long my brother came to sit with me but I guess the activity in the church had got to him because about eight seconds later he shot away again to pull faces at me one minute from the choir stalls and the next to rush at the stage and kick at these parallel rows of crumpled plastic lying there. When he reached the synthesiser beside the altar a woman in orange overalls grabbed him and frog-marched him back to his seat.

'One move, cock,' she said as she plonked him down, 'and you're dead.'

She stayed to eyeball him for a while then turned away. As she did she winked at me. I recognized her then. It was Delia, the person I'd seen in the Clifton Hill underpass the day we left home. Half-standing I went to speak to her but she was already hurrying back towards the stage.

Except for jiggling his feet and stuff J-Max stayed put from then on which was just as well because soon the lights dimmed and after a lot of rushing in and out of the side door the show began.

I can't remember if I told you before but *Careful What You Call Your Daughters* is a myth about the creation of the world. Parts of it are done in mime and when I start describing it, you'll see why.

Act I began in near darkness with the goddess Nuke sitting crooning on a patch of sand at the front of the stage. (Nuke was played by this Persian girl Lal, who had long hair and long dark eyes. In this scene she had nothing on, not even a string around her *waist*.) As she crooned, Nuke drew the ocean from the sand, and behind her the rows of crumpled plastic began to glow with gently rocking lights of bluey-green so that they looked like waves.

At the end of Nuke's song three dark figures lying in foetal positions among the waves uncurled themselves to come forward and sit with her. They were her daughters and she named them Honor, Grace and Sacrifice.

Nuke then created a son called Thatcher. (The black girl Luann, playing the part of Thatcher, was as tall and proud as hell in a rugby jumper and a pair of those tight almost knee-length black pants professional cyclists wear. Allie told me later she had padding in the groin of her pants and that her boobs were fastened down with crepe bandages.)

After checking out her children and being pleased with what she saw, Nuke left but before she did she anointed her daughters with her menstrual blood so they'd have the spark of creativity.

Honor, Grace and Sacrifice then went into the sea and began to dance while Thatcher sprawled on the sand to watch. As they danced they created the mountains and rivers and forests and everything. Then, worn out, they rested and Thatcher did his dance which was so full of beauty and virility the girls were enslaved by it. When he'd finished and was lying on the sand again they made offerings to him of things like chocolate mousse and a Man from Snowy River raincoat.

At the beginning of Act II Thatcher is still seen enjoying the enslavement of his sisters but in time he becomes bored with it and leaves to build a church in his own honour.

With the building finished he finds he is lonely and goes inside and does a version of the dance of creativity. By doing this he hopes to make a son who will share his pleasure in hunting and things. All he manages to do though is trip on the altar rail and wound his thigh. Mad with pain and frustration Thatcher goes on the rampage, firing rockets and laying waste to continents.

At the end of Act I the tarpaulin on the roof had been pulled back so that Thatcher's rampage could be symbolized by four skyrockets being sent up through the gap. One after another they wooshed off with fiery tails, leaving the smell of gunpowder in the church.

In Act III Honor, Grace and Sacrifice, appalled by their brother's rotten behaviour, cut off their hair and weave it into ropes which they hide. When Thatcher returns from his warfare they dance for him again and give him pipes of dope until he pikes-out. Then, after tying him with their ropes of goddess hair, they hold a kind of court to pass judgement on him. Honor thinks he should be killed. Sacrifice says his manhood should be taken from him and Grace, who can't make up her mind, sends for Nuke. She arrives wearing goggles and these overalls with black-ringed holes in them as if she'd been *welding* something.

After listening to her daughters, Nuke gives each of them a cocktail made from the juice of mushrooms and a rare white lily. This is to make them immune to Thatcher's power and beauty. She then changes their names to Self Reliance, Humour and Don't Look Back. That done she unties Thatcher but only after anointing him too with her menstrual blood. She refuses to change his name though because she wants the creatures of the earth to remember the things he's done.

Nuke adjusts her goggles and leaves and the drama ends with her four children dancing together in the sea. This time each one's dance, including Thatcher's, is a blend of beauty, power *and* creativity.

'Would you believe,' I said to Xam, 'the applause at the end woke both the babies though they'd managed to sleep through the music and rockets and everything?'

'It was probably their supper time.'

'It was, because Allie appeared from nowhere and with me in tow took Michael out to the bus where she produced his bottle from this dinky little heated container.'

Sitting over a late breakfast I'd been giving Xam what I hoped was an *acceptable* version of *Careful What You Call Your Daughters*. J-Max was downstairs with Mrs Werther helping organize her weekly bonfire. Earlier, after about two hours sleep, he'd gone to the beach at Surfers where he and the McIntyre kids had scavved the sand for treasure. For weeks he'd been telling me that if you got there early enough you could get anything you wanted – money, a new watch, board shorts, even a camera. What he'd ended up with was sixty-three cents which Xam said he could keep and the bottom half of someone's false teeth which Xam said had to be handed in at the surf lifesaving club.

At the table, after telling Xam about the applause and everything I sat remembering how I'd knelt on the seat of the Nin bus and watched while Allie fed the baby. His head was about the size of an *apple* but he pigged-out on the bottle with a ferocity that made me laugh.

'Don't you shit,' I said to Allie, 'at the thought of keeping him *alive*?'

Her answer was, 'If I let myself, I would, so I just put my head down and barrel on.'

I was still thinking about Allie and the baby with his silky apple head when Xam said, 'And afterwards, I suppose you met all of Allie's friends.'

'I met some of them because we went back into the church where wine and biscuits were being served but by the time we got there this big discussion was going on and really, people were too rapt in it to notice me.'

Xam put his hand up to the side of his glasses and waited for me to go on.

'It seems all these bigtime developers have discovered Byron Bay, and the Nin girls and their friends say they'll ruin it. They say that if they get their way the developers will make the place as pitsy as the Gold Coast.'

'And *I'd* say they were right.' A looking-back expression came over Xam's face. 'In my palmy days I used to come to this part of the coast each year for my vacation. While here I'd motor down to Byron Bay for picnics and so on. With its poetic mountains and siren beaches it always seemed to me the pick of the coastline – the jewel.'

Xam went on to talk about the damage that developers do to places but instead of listening to him I sat trying to imagine him when he was young enough to drive a car and go to picnics and stuff. I succeeded to the stage of seeing this picture of him in creamy clothes and a straw hat. He was reclining on a rug spread on coarse, *coastal* sort of grass. Standing to the side were these two swan-ish women in high-necked dresses made of tucks and flounces and broderie anglaise. The funny part was that I saw all of this in the faded brown tonings of old snapshots I'd seen at Barbie's place. (Even the canvas-hooded car in my picture was a faded brown.)

I was thinking, *But it would have been in colour, dillberry, and so would Xam*, when I realized that the Xam sitting opposite me had said *twice*, 'Your mates down there are conservationists, I take it.'

'Of course they are and the worst part is that they think in the end they'll have to leave.'

'Why should they?'

'Because there's all this rotten stuff going on. People who are anti-development are having their houses firebombed and their dogs and things poisoned. Allie said the Nin Group's turn can't be far away.'

'One can't give in to that sort of thing. They'll have to stand and fight.'

'Some of them want to. Luann does. That's what the big discussion was about.'

While Xam was shaking his head over what he'd just heard, I wriggled around on my chair then moved to the edge of it and said, 'Last night the conversation finally got off the fire-bombing and stuff and onto violence towards women. Everyone there seemed to think it's increasing.' I paused. 'Xam, do you think it is?'

He didn't answer me for ages. In fact I thought he wasn't going to when he said, 'I believe it *has* and I believe it *will*.'

'But why?'

'Don't you know?'

'How could I?'

'Then I'll tell you.' He leaned back, took his cigarettes from his pocket and put them on the table. 'Once, men had the power to decide which women would be impregnated – given a child. I suppose you could say that power was accepted as the yardstick of masculinity. Then the contraceptive pill came along.' Xam stopped to give an embarrassed cough. 'Suddenly the power belonged to women. And men will never forgive them for it. Why would they? It's an awesome one.'

I gave myself time to absorb all that, then I said, 'But that's crazy. A man *invented* the pill, didn't he?'

'I doubt that lessens the pain.'

'So what will happen?'

'I've no idea.'

'Make a guess then.'

Before answering Xam took a cigarette from the packet and laid it on top. 'I'd say that if the human race isn't blown to smithers in the next few years it will adapt. But because men still make the rules it may adapt in a way that women won't like.'

I was getting ready to ask what *that* meant when Xam

said, 'Morgan, while we're on this particular subject, I feel I must tender you an apology.' He gave this immense rattle in his throat before continuing. 'The night you asked me about incest I told you you hadn't been harmed by it.'

'I remember.'

'I had no right to say such a thing. Of course you'd been harmed. Your trust had been betrayed and I compounded the betrayal by speaking as an ignorant old fool.'

'No you didn't, Xam.'

'Indeed I did but since then I've read several articles on the subject. Young Linfors supplied them for me and I know now how arrogant I was when I spoke before.'

I sat gobstuck while he went on, 'I haven't mentioned it because I thought my motives might be . . . well, misinterpreted.'

I didn't know what he meant by that. How *could* his motives be misinterpreted? I didn't know either why his face had begun to go the colour of sunburn. The only reason I could think of was that being so old he was embarrassed off his face by the whole subject. Just the same the thought of him reading all that rotten stuff because of me made me want to grab his old see-through hands in mine and tell him in some un-corny way, if I could, what an ace he was.

I didn't do it though because at that minute the wind which was whiffling the grass-smoke smell of Mrs Werther's fire through the flat, carried up this shriek of laughter from J-Max, followed by the word, 'Whacko!'

It was the first time either of us had heard him get the letter *double-u* out and we sat grinning at each other as if we'd just won the Nobel Prize or something. And when that sort of *cele*brating moment was over I decided to let the incest stuff drop and I began telling Xam about our trip home the night before when Nigel drove gangbusters up the coast road while our chairs slid around in the back and Peter whistled bits of songs from the show we'd just seen.

Chapter Thirty-Two

THE WEDNESDAY WE later spoke of as *Crunch Day* started out with Allie ringing to say the Greenlys had abandoned their claim to Michael and were returning to America.

'When they've gone,' she said, 'You'll see a lot of us.'

Rapt with that news I went downstairs beaming to help Mrs Werther do an out-of-season spring-clean of her kitchen. I was kneeling on her sink, washing the window and humming to myself when she asked if I thought Xam would be interested in engaging her to cook for us four or five nights a week.

I told her I thought he'd rush at the chance. 'He thinks you're an ace cook,' I said. 'He raves about your chocolate tart. "The Duke of Edinburgh wouldn't scoff at it", is how he puts it.'

Mrs Werther, who was standing in a sea of old-fashioned egg beaters and things said, 'The family's asked me not to let the two empty flats again. They want to use them as holiday homes. That's fair enough but in the meantime my income has gone down with a wallop and although I can manage, a little extra would be handy.' Bending down to pull an old cockroach bait out of the cupboard, she went on,

324

'My sister's boy, Tris, who makes a shaky living by doing up what I call junk and he calls antiques, wants to store some bits and pieces in John's old flat. He's offered me a fair rental. I'm not likely to *get* it but he's a strong lad who can mend pretty well anything and I think it'd be worth all our whiles to have him coming and going from the place.'

Mrs Werther went on talking for a while about her nephew's ability to repair clocks and unblock stuffed drains and things and when she finally stopped I re-introduced the subject of the cooking job by saying, 'Why don't you ask Xam about it? Why don't you ask him now?'

'I'll ask him when we've finished the kitchen.'

'Shall *I* ask him at lunchtime?'

'You can put out a feeler if you like.'

When I *did*, Xam made me laugh by repeating the bit about the Duke of Edinburgh and the chocolate tart.

Still laughing I said, 'Then you think it's a good idea?'

'Good? I'd say the gods have smiled at last.'

At two-thirty, with the kitchen what Mrs Werther called shipshape, I went back upstairs. At three she followed. She'd put on her floral dress and chipped pearls and when she reached Xam's study and *sat*, he held out the chair for her. He'd already surprised me by putting sherry glasses on the table and when *I* went to sit surprised me again by asking me to take his Telecom account down to the post office and pay it.

Because I tried to avoid the main shopping centre in case I ran into someone like Desmond Roper, I started to ask Xam why he didn't pay the account by cheque. The look on his face stopped me. He'd obviously decided he didn't want me there when the bargaining began so after giving this tubercular sort of sigh, I did as he said.

I reached the corner of Nerang and Scarborough Streets

without meeting anyone I knew but being back in that part of town must have bent my brain a bit because inside the post office when the girl in front of me asked the counter clerk if there was a letter there for her, I had this overwhelming feeling that when my turn came all I had to do was ask too and moments later I'd be handed this breezy little postcard from Marcelle.

I didn't do it of course but later as I left the post office, even though I knew no card was there, I was still sorry I hadn't asked. (I know that's stupid, I'm just telling you how I *felt*.)

Leaving the bus and going back up the hill towards Tibet I was still thinking about Marcelle. I was thinking about the crazy film she and Allie worked on down by the river. Because of that, even though I saw the purple Moke parked outside our gate, I didn't realize straightaway what it meant. Then I did and dodging into someone's driveway, I flattened myself against the gate in the way I flattened myself against the laundry wall the day I worked out that The Rose Club was a brothel. This time though instead of my brain turning to *custard* it was already working out that I must get to the school and grab my brother and hide somewhere with him until dark. Then I thought, *But it must be nearly four. He'll be home by now. He'll have gone there to dump his bag and find the biscuits. Which means that Ingrid Frew already has him by the collar.*

I came out of the gateway and started slowly up the hill again. For me things had become the way they are in dreams when there's nothing at the edges of your vision. I mean that everything had disappeared except the footpath and me. And when I reached the house and was going up the steps, instead of trees and sky and Tibetan wind there was only my feet on the worn old steps. It was the same at the top, but at the corner, there was suddenly too much of everything because on our stretch of verandah there was this *crowd* – all of it in the brightest undreamlike colour.

I think now shock did that to me because there wasn't a crowd at all – just four people, one of them my brother. I didn't look at the others until my eyes had sought and found him. He was opposite our front door, squatting with his back against one of the verandah posts. His hands were clamped over his knees and his face was pale and sort of tight the way it used to be when we lived in Melbourne. Next I looked at Xam who was by the door. His head was lowered and thrust forward so that he looked like some old waterbird resting after a flight against terrible headwinds or something.

Opposite him, a fattish young woman with a Tina Turner hairdo was leaning against the verandah rail.

Closer than that, wearing yellow and already turning to look at me, was my Aunt Penelope.

The next moment she was coming towards me. 'Victoria. Victoria,' said her top-tomato voice, then something I'd never heard it say before, 'Vicky!'

I waited until she'd nearly reached me then I stepped aside and ignoring her, went to Xam.

'When did they get here?' I said.

He lifted his shoulders. 'Half an hour ago.'

'Did you know they were coming?'

'I did not.'

My voice rising, I said, 'Why didn't you send them away?'

'How could I?'

'You *should* have. You should have thought of *something*.'

Before answering, he lifted his head a bit and cleared his throat. 'Once they were here, it was too late.'

'You could have lied. You could have given us some *time*.'

'And lost you altogether? They would . . .' Xam stopped there, out of breath.

I grabbed his arm. 'Do you need your spinhaler?'

He shook his head and seemed all right, so not letting go

of him, I turned to face the person I guessed was Ingrid Frew. 'We're not going back,' I told her. 'You can send us but we'll nick off again. We'll nick off a thousand times. We'll make it our *life's* work. Even if you put us in a home or something we'll get out and come back here.'

In this Canadian voice as slow as honey she said, 'Hold it, babe. I don't wanna send you anywhere.' She was smiling at me and behind her shoulder the end of the violet scarf she wore lifted in the wind. I found I couldn't take my eyes from it as it swayed there, as eerie and hypnotizing as a cobra. Finally it dropped from sight again and when it did, I looked at Ingrid herself.

I'd imagined that if I ever met her she'd turn out to be a sort of sensible version of Olivia Newton-John. Instead she was fat with this marvellous skin and her hair dyed about three different colours. In loose dark clothes and that dancing scarf she was the absolute opposite of skinny-rib Gold Coast fashion. The easiest way to describe her, I suppose, is to say you could tell just by the way she stood that nothing, not even my Aunt Penelope, would *throw* her.

I'd let go of Xam's arm by then and moved a little closer to her. 'What will happen?' I said.

She didn't get to answer because Penelope, her yellow earrings swinging, marched between us. 'You'll come home of course. Your mother . . .'

'I haven't got a mother.'

'*Victoria!*'

'I haven't. The one I had didn't care about what happened to me. She didn't care at all and when we left she didn't even try to find us.'

Penelope's eyes *bulged*. 'Didn't care? Didn't *care*? For Christ's sake, girl, don't you read the papers?'

Shifting my feet a little, I said, 'I saw a few. There was nothing in them.'

'Then let me be the one to tell you that your mother has

crossed and *re*-crossed this continent looking for you. She's lived out of a *shoe* bag. She's been up as far as Alice Springs and right this minute she's over at Kalgoorlie because someone in a hot bread shop there said they'd served a little boy who couldn't speak.'

I was too surprised to answer and after brushing her hand across the top of her head, she said, 'Victoria . . .'

'My name's Morgan.'

'*Victoria*, the last time you saw your mother she was in a state of shock.' Penelope shot this quick look at Ingrid Frew. 'Who wouldn't be? But she came out of it damned quickly and rushed off to find you. She went to the school, then around various members of the family. For the entire day she was about half an hour behind you. The one place no one looked was Spencer Street.'

With my voice small and quiet, I said, 'I didn't know any of that.'

'No, and you didn't wait to find out.'

'How could I?'

'Well, that's not all. When your father took the overdose . . .'

'*Overdose?*'

My aunt raised her hand and flapped it down. 'Oh yes, he did the full *mea culpa*. Your mother had moved out by then. Was living with me. Tony swallowed a heap of tablets washed down by whisky. He took care of course to let everyone know in plenty of time and I mean everyone. The night he was rushed to hospital your mother had to choose between staying to see if he'd survive and leaving for Adelaide where the police thought they had a lead on you.' Penelope's eyes were scanning my face. 'She went to Adelaide.'

'I didn't know . . . I didn't want . . .'

My aunt waited.

'I mean, my father . . .'

She surprised me by giving a puffy little laugh. 'Don't fasten on that and start feeling guilty. It was just a social action and I suppose, a necessary one.'

'Is he okay?'

'Of course he is. I told you – it was just a gesture.'

'Where is he now?'

'Living with his mother.'

'And the house?'

'Still there. Your mother's expecting you to come back and live in it.'

'And my father?'

'There's no way he'll be included in the package. Sue and I have talked that through, and believe me when I tell you her decision to become a single parent wasn't made solely because of what happened to you. Your mother's determined to have a life of her own because it seems that all these years she's been quietly bleeding away with the need to get back to pottery at a professional level.'

There was a silence on the verandah and during it Ingrid Frew's scarf rose up again to look over her shoulder. Finally I said, 'I'm sorry about my mother. I really am. I suppose I'm sorry about Dad too. Just the same we won't be coming back. This is our home now and like I said earlier, even if you force us to go with you, we won't stay.'

'That's childish talk. How can you stay here? Who is there to care for you?'

'Mr *Arn*old does. And we care for him.'

'That's nonsense,' said Penelope.

Xam spoke then. 'It's not, you know. We manage surprisingly well. A contract cleaner comes in once a week, and today Mrs Werther agreed to be our cook.'

'Who, might I ask, is Mrs Werther?'

'Our landlady.'

'If you're referring to the Meg Merrilies type who was here when we arrived, I can only assume you're joking.'

'The Duke of Edinburgh wouldn't scoff at her chocolate tart.'

Xam told me later that when J-Max said that he felt a flutter of something like happiness go across his heart and he said he thought it probably showed on his face. If it did, I didn't see it. I was watching Penelope. It seems no one had told her my brother could speak and when he did she was absolutely *gobbered*. While she was, I rushed to say, 'Now you know why we're not coming back. We're happy here. Matt goes to school and talks and everything. People like him. He's got a cat and even plays the piano.'

And while Penelope was grabbing her head to let us all know how surprised she was, I looked across at Ingrid Frew and said, 'He *is* happy.'

Ingrid shifted her weight onto both feet then and said, 'I know. They told me at the school.'

'Is that how you found us? Through the school?'

'In a way it was, hon, but we'd already sussed that you were in the district. You'd been traced as far as Murwillumbah and for a while some of us thought you'd gone Nimbin way. Then a kid who said her name was Victoria Ferguson called the Hattan Maternity Home. She rang off before the guy on duty could talk to her but the next thing, one of the drivers on the Surfside line reported taking a pair of kids your age down to Mermaid Beach.' She grinned. 'That was the first mention of the cat.'

'How did you lob on Tibet? Was it through Desmond Roper?'

'No, hon. By the time he got to us, we knew as much as he did.'

'Who was it then?'

She turned to look at J-Max who was now *sitting* on the verandah. 'I guess young Matt's the culprit there. In Show and Tell at school he demonstrated all too graphically how his sister fought some girl in the toilet after her bag had been looted at Central Station in Sydney. His teacher, Louise Kerr, was so amused she told her fiance. He's a police officer stationed at Broadbeach and the person who finally stitched the scenario together. When he did, because he's not exactly rapt in the methods of his superiors, he brought it round to us.' Ingrid spread her hands. 'So there you have it.'

By the time she'd finished speaking we were all looking at J-Max, who scrambled to his feet, marched across the verandah and in through the open door. I guessed he'd stay there somewhere out of sight but still able to hear what was being said.

'Morgan,' said Ingrid, pleasing me with the easy way she brought it out, 'you asked earlier what would happen. Well that decision isn't mine to make. As I see it, it'll be your mother's because from where I stand, she's holding all the cards.'

I wasn't sure what she meant and she must have seen that because she said, 'I'll put it to you this way – your mother didn't tell the police why you left home. As far as they know, you went because of a quarrel over some dress. And by the way, she did that to protect you, not your father. It was pretty cluey of her just the same because it left her in the position of being able to bargain with him. By that I mean she was able to use the threat of publicly airing the rape issue to get him to vacate the house. No doubt his suicide attempt was a counter threat. But that's not the point. What is, is that it's given *you* bargaining power too.'

While I was still taking all that in, Xam said, 'Are you saying, Miss Frew, that Morgan should use the rape issue as some sort of lever in her fight to stay in Southport?'

'Mr Arnold, you've got it.'

'And you're prepared to support her in that?'

'Why not? You see I believe that women and *only* women are going to put a stop to the epidemic of father-daughter rape. Let's face it, it's not in the interests of men to do so.'

In his driest voice, Xam said, 'From what I've read, Miss

Frew, not only *men* condone such behaviour. There are women who do as well.'

'That red herring's so tired, it smells,' said Ingrid. 'You and I both know, Mr Arnold, that because of social and economic pressure certain women have been forced to look the other way, but I can tell you such women are not to be found in my department.'

Xam stood nodding his head. He went on nodding it while we waited, then he said, 'If the police don't know why Morgan left home, how did you know?'

'I guessed. I guessed because I find the same thing every-where I look.'

'And you haven't reported it either?'

'No, I haven't.'

'I've always understood it was mandatory for officers of your department to report such cases.'

'In Queensland that applies only to medicos and the police.'

'Then I agree with you – Morgan certainly has bargaining power.'

'So we're halfway there, aren't we? Because if the parents can be . . . shall we say, *persuaded* to give permission for her to stay here with her brother, that's more or less the end of it. From there in, my department's involvement will be restricted to a supervisory capacity. Mind you,' she gave another sudden grin, 'we'll be doing some digging into *your* past but we've already done a little and liked what we found. If we hadn't, we'd have swooped in here last night and removed the kids.' Her voice changed. 'Hey, you shouldn't be standing all this time. Let's sit.' And she moved to one of the wicker chairs and plonked down in it.

Xam waited for Penelope to sit too. 'Don't mind her,' Ingrid told him. 'She's about to have a little talk with her niece.' She'd turned to look up at Penelope and seemed to be issuing some sort of *challenge*.

For a while Penelope met the look but in the end she

dropped her eyes and with all the bounce gone from her voice, said to me, 'Is there somewhere we can go?'

I didn't want to be alone with my aunt and was about to say so but Ingrid stopped me by saying, 'It'll only take a moment, hon, and then I think we should call your mother. Do y'think you could handle it?'

I stood then thinking about my mother. I thought of her sitting by the phone in some unfriendly little motel room, or perhaps a *police* station and in the end I said, 'I'm not sure, but I'll give it a try.'

With a bit of her bounce back, Penelope said, 'Shall we go inside then?'

'Matt's in there. Let's go round the front,' I said and led her around the corner. There, at the top of the steps with the smashing view in front of us and the wind trying to snatch our hair, we faced each other.

Not meeting my eyes, Penelope said, 'It's about the day you came to see me.'

When I didn't answer, she said, 'I lied to you. When I told you I'd slept with your father, I was lying. I don't know what that makes me, but it's what I did.'

After a while I said, 'No one would tell a lie like that. No one *could*.'

'I did.'

I was looking at her and thinking, *She's hardly any taller than I am. I used to think she was about as tall as Curtis* MCLEOD *and here she is – just a little nothing. Shit, in no time I'll be as tall as she is.* Then, realizing Penelope was waiting for me to say something, I shrugged and said, 'It doesn't matter anyway.'

'But it does. Don't you see? I can't live with myself until we talk about it, work it *through*.'

I found I didn't even want to discuss the time of day with her so I said, 'You were pissed, that's all.'

'Victoria, I need you to say more than that.'

'Okay then, tell me why you did it.'

It's really amazing because she sort of cheered up then and after taking a breath, rattled off, 'Beth, my shrink, says I spoke the way I did because of an unconscious fear of death. She says that's the cause of almost all our neuroses, and that by bringing me face to face with the fact that my time as a sexually potent woman was ending, you'd made me aware of my mortality. Because of that I lashed out at you on an *instinctual* level.'

She had this really *animated* look on her face which made me think, *She's a dickbrain*, but what I said was, 'If you're asking me to forgive you or something, okay I do. I just don't want to see you again, that's all.' Then I turned and walked back along the verandah.

Her cry of 'Victoria!' came after me. When it did I turned again and said, 'My name's Morgan now. It really is.' This time I stayed looking at her and in a little while she went off down the steps and towards the gate. Just before she reached it she had to stand aside and wait while this bloke with long bare legs and *string* in his boots instead of laces, manoeuvred the table he was carrying, in past the frangipanni trees. (He was holding it above his head and on his way up the hill must have stopped to grab a couple of hibiscus blooms over someone's fence. I could see them lying in the upside-down table as it went along the path and around the corner of the house. By then Penelope, who hadn't responded to his muffled, 'G'day', was outside sitting in Ingrid Frew's Moke.)

The crappy scene with Penelope seemed to use up all courage, all my *spunk*, as Xam would put it, because later in the study, when Ingrid spoke to my mother then handed the phone to me, I was suddenly back in the bathroom at Ivanhoe with the stained dress between us and my mother hating me. What I did then was stand as dumb as death while her voice said, 'Darling, can you hear me? Are you there?' She said some more but I didn't answer and suddenly Ingrid's springy hair was squashed against my face as she spoke into the phone. 'She's listening to you, Sue. If there's something you want to tell her, she'll hear it. And by the way, she likes to be called Morgan.'

Ingrid moved away again and I hear my mother say, 'Dearest girl, if you're there and feel you don't want to speak, don't worry about it. The day might come when you'll want to talk to me and if it does, I'll be here. I'll be waiting. I'll wait as long as you need me to.' There was a pause then she said, 'Do you understand?'

I stood nodding my head and in a little while Ingrid took the phone from me and I went towards the door. When I left Ingrid was telling my mother that I'd *heard* her and everything.

Xam was out on the verandah smoking and as I went past him we grabbed hands for a moment and squeezed. After that I went down to the garden and sat with my back against my old friend the tombstone while branches of the traveller's palm made little surf-noises above my head. I was still there when Ingrid came across the grass and kneeling in front of me on one knee, said, 'Honey, I've had such a talk with your mother. She laughed a bit and cried too and in the end could see that at least until we sort things out, it's commonsense for you and Matt to stay here. Of course she doesn't want to do that. She wants to see you, wants to *hug* you – and wants to do it all today. I told her you may not be ready for that.' Still kneeling, Ingrid adjusted her scarf. 'What I'm trying to do is buy you a little time.' She stopped there to give me this searching look and when I didn't say anything, went on, 'You might change your mind, you know. You might decide you want to go home.'

Putting my head back against the tombstone, I looked up at shabby old Tibet and said, 'We'd never leave here. We'd never leave Xam either, and when he *dies*, I'm going to find a way to buy the place.'

That made her smile. 'I guessed you'd feel that way.' She shifted then, brought the other knee down and rolled onto one hip. 'As I see it, Morgan, your mother will have the deciding vote on whether you stay or go. Your father might demand a vote too but his won't be worth a mustard seed because a lot of people, including me, will be leaning on him and leaning heavily. So what I want you to do is write to your Mum. It doesn't matter what you say, just establish contact because in the end it'll help.' She studied my face again. 'Will you give it a shot?'

'I suppose so.'

'If you get stuck, I'll help. I'll be calling in each day anyway.' With a smothered, 'Shit!' Ingrid heaved herself to her feet.

Looking up at her, I said, 'You knew my friend Marcelle, didn't you?'

'Sure I did, and when we've sorted this lot, I'd like to talk about her.'

Ingrid left soon after that and when she did I lay down with my feet crossed and my head touching the tombstone. I was planning to do all this *thinking* but before I'd even started, Xam's voice called, 'Morgan, this came for you. I'm sorry – I forgot.'

I sat up and turned to see him waving a letter from the top verandah. 'Send it down,' I said, scrambling to my feet.

He hesitated, then extended his arm and posted the letter into the air. Cream-coloured against the leaves and things, it sailed down, stopping on the way to rest for a moment on a feathery branch of the jacaranda.

When I'd picked the letter up, I went back to the tombstone. I didn't open it straightaway. I didn't need to. I knew it was from Joss and I knew what it would say. It'd be about his father's health and stuff; probably about some *soccer* game as well. I even knew there'd be nothing really personal in it, that he probably wouldn't even mention the poxy stuff I wrote to him. The funny part is that I didn't mind because I had this feeling that not just me, but all the world around me, had relaxed a little and I knew that in a day or two I'd write Joss a really sensible letter telling him all the things that'd happened since he left. I felt that instead of being pissed-off with my revelations, he'd be . . . well, *comforted* because I'd shared them with him. I suppose what I'm really saying is I could see at last that Xam had been right all along when he said it was enough that Joss had *written*.

Crunch Day didn't end with Joss's letter. It ended just before dark when my brother broke into Mrs Werther's toolshed, found her hatchet, then used it to attack one of the downstairs verandah posts.

Mrs Werther was having her dinner at the time. Hearing the noise of chopping, she rushed out and in a pretty gutsy way grabbed J-Max's wrist and squeezed it until he dropped the hatchet. I guess she knows a lot about kids because what she did next was pull him back against her body and hold him while she called him all these silly little love names like *Mingle McDuck* and her *Little Platypus*. She went on doing that until finally he turned his face into her soft old grandmother dress and began to bawl.

Chapter Thirty-Three

WHEN I SAT down to write to my mother, I didn't have a clue what to say. I didn't even know how to *start*. Then suddenly this picture floated into my mind of Luann Matthews carrying Allie's baby along Washington Drive at Surfers. And that's what I wrote about. I wrote about Allie and the Greenlys and the Filipino maid and everything. After that I got onto the subject of *Careful What You Call Your Daughters*. I even put in a bit about the angel-fish wall in Allie's bathroom.

I knew it wasn't the sort of stuff I was *expected* to write, and when I showed it to Ingrid Frew, I said, 'I'll start again if you think I should.'

She was sitting on Joss's bed – *my* bed – at the time and after taking about *eight* hours to read it, she said, 'It's fine. Just send it off the way it is.'

So I posted the letter and when I did, this amazing thing happened. My mother answered straightaway saying that I'd *inspired* her.

It seems she'd been planning to do a series of bowls in this special dark blue glaze but had been having trouble lobbing on what she called a *satisfactory motif*.

All this time, she wrote, *I've been overlooking the one staring me in the face – the more or less universal one of a mother's search for her lost child. So I'm using that and seem to have unlocked a flood of creativity, or more correctly, you have, because I'm now planning a second series to represent mythic figures from the female psyche.*

None of this sounded at *all* like my mother but at least it was interesting. I suppose I should explain here that we've been writing that sort of stuff to each other ever since. About drama and poetry and everything, I mean. We don't write about the past, although according to Ingrid, we are. She says that we're using it as raw material for our creativity and that we're *burying* it at the same time.

I should also explain that after about three hundred and eighty phone calls between Ingrid and my mother, it was agreed that we'd stay on at Tibet. Ingrid says the argument turned into a non-event when my mother learned of the changes in Matt. But the thing that clinched it as far as Mum was concerned was hearing that when my brother thought he'd have to leave his version of paradise, he tried to chop it down. After that she wrote to Xam giving what she called her formal permission for us to stay.

The next argument was about who'd support us. My father wanted to – was *desperate* to – but Xam said as far as he was concerned Dad had already surrendered that privilege. (None of this was *openly* discussed in front of Matt and me but I've worked out that for the time being Mum is sharing the 'privilege' with Xam.) (Apparently my father pays money into a trust or something for us in case we need it later on and as Ingrid is always pointing out, no one can stop him doing that.)

As part of Mum's bargain with Xam I went back to school late last year. Before I did, Xam gave me all this coaching in maths and stuff so I more or less took up where I left off. I can't say I'm exactly rapt in the lessons but I guess in some ways it's okay being there.

Back in June when the Greenlys left Australia, Allie began

visiting us again. I think she comes partly to see Xam, because the minute she gets in the door, she hangs some provocative statement on him. Last weekend she told him she'd decided that all men long like mad to be women. While Xam was still gobstruck she said she'd worked this out because in some film she saw she noticed that ninety per cent of the blokes who marched in Sydney's gay Mardi Gras were dressed as women and wore these enormous boobs which they kept grabbing and shaking at the crowd. Then she said this proved that what they really want to wear is a womb, but can't because they've nowhere to *put* it.

Holding the side of his glasses and glaring, Xam told her the militants of Byron Bay had filled her mind with frog-wash. But even Bobby Deerfield could have seen what a buzz he was getting from it all.

Using the word *gobstruck* has reminded me that when Matt and I no longer had any reason to hide, I wanted to get in touch with Hattie McLeod to let her know we were safe and everything.

When I mentioned it to Xam he got right out of his tree, saying that an inquiry into police corruption was finally going to be held and he was sure the *last* thing my mother wanted was to see me called as the star teenage witness.

I kept thinking though of the flower Hattie put on the dressing-table to welcome me and how old Curtis took Matt to the beach and everything, so in the end I asked Ingrid to telephone Hattie for me and she did. I don't know what she said but she told me afterwards that Hattie, who sounded what she called *crocked*, thanked her about eight hundred times for calling.

I meant to start this chapter by saying it's now February and my parents are coming up to see us at Easter. (Mum was coming at Christmas but her mother had a heart attack and she had to put it off. She sent me this groovy little typewriter though which I'm using now instead of one of Matt's biros.)

Mum and Dad are travelling up together but staying at different places. I think they expect to see Matt and me every day. Ingrid says that when the time comes Dad will probably pike. I wouldn't be surprised and to tell you the truth, I don't mind if he does. In some ways though I guess it would be better to see him and get it over. One thing I've worked out since I started writing all this stuff is that I used to be in love with him in this really dumb way. It's just that he wasn't bright enough to understand there was no sex in the way I loved him because I didn't even know what sex *was*. And that's what *he* should have known. Anyway, if he gets stupid this time, I've got a surprise for him. For eight months now Matt and I have been going up to Brisbane on the bus after lunch on Saturdays to study Aikido with old Father Christmas.

I've heard people say that girls end up being sexually assaulted because they display the wrong body language. I don't think that's true. I think men *read* it wrongly. And they do this because they want to but I doubt there's anyone on earth dumb enough to misread the *Kamae*, which is the correct name for the fighting stance in case you hadn't heard it before.

The funny part is that when we started our lessons with Master Ho, it was me, not Matt, who turned out to be the one with natural ability. My brother has plenty of *aggression*, but that's not the idea behind Aikido at all. In fact he has so much aggression his balance is wrecked and he's pretty easy to beat.

One of the reasons why *I* did well is that Master Ho started out with all this antagonism towards me. He'd call me 'Girl', swallowing the 'l' so the word came out 'Gurr'. He was always trying to undo my composure and I was always trying to keep it. He'd hit me harder than the others and throw me further, and although I sometimes had a howl on the bus going home, I was determined not to let him make me chuck the lessons. I'd practise harder, that's all.

Finally I worked out that Master Ho's dislike of me was just the same as Xam's was when we first met him. I stopped worrying after that because I could see that's something men put *on* as a protection against what girls can do to them.

The first time I entered a competition and won all my fights, Master Ho came to me and called me his son.

Forgetting the rule of courtesy, I told him I wasn't *anybody's* son. He stepped back then and bowed to me – not one of Joss's little bows, but the full thing.

Sorry then that I'd been so *grace*less, I bowed too and said, 'Why don't you try daughter?'

After that we grinned at each other like a pair of clowns and we've been pretty friendly ever since.

I'm fighting again next Sunday. If I win and Master Ho says I might, I'll get a trip to Perth. (Joss doesn't know any of this. He knows I've been having lessons from Father Christmas but he's no idea how much I've put into them.)

I've forgotten to tell you that from Joss's letters I've learned all this stuff about how his uncle came from Taiwan to keep the family business going while Mr Lau was in Pentridge. He did it so well, they expanded into several new lines, including computer hardware. Now the company is considering expanding up *here* and in June, Joss and his father are coming to suss the place out.

Mr Lau's health is still dodgy and Xam keeps telling me not to make plans in case the proposed visit is cancelled at the last minute. I *do* make plans though. I plan to take Joss to the beach at night and challenge him to fight. I suppose when faced with his wiggy hair and Asian eyes *my* balance will be wrecked but I don't mind much if it is. (If you want to know, I think some of the *formal* aspects of the martial arts are extremely sexy.)

It's great down at the beach in the evenings. Matt and I go there a lot with out dog, Clancy Deerfield, who followed Tris Dubedat to Tibet one day and stayed on. (We've still got Bobby of course but he stays at home.) Sometimes the moon comes up big and red and glowing. Then the ocean and the wet sand turn red too. With the skyscrapers and everything making a *contrast*, it's pitsy but stunning at the same time. And I guess I won't be leaving here. Not *permanently* anyway.

s.p. (As Marcelle would say.)

I thought you'd like to know that since I wrote all that stuff, I've seen my mother. We met at this waterfront coffee shop called the Viennese Mermaid while outside, big grey waves ate away the beach and the wind sent seaspray right across the road.

At the coffee shop they specialize in little cakes shaped like mermaids with pink icing for skin and green for hair. (Sometimes when your mermaid arrives its tail has broken off.)

I got there first and sat with my back to the beach. About five minutes later the door opened, letting in the wind. Then my mother's voice said, 'Hi, Morgan.' (I thought that was pretty classy of her.) The next moment she slipped into the chair opposite me.

I looked at her quickly and away again. She had on this smashing cherry-coloured shirt and I guess she was pretty cold because her face was practically *chalk*.

I could feel her looking at me. It seemed to go on for ages, then she said, 'You've become so . . .' a long pause, 'so strong . . . and beautiful,' and her hand came out and clasped my arm just below the elbow, staying there, so that I could feel this sort of current running from the inside of her wrist into my arm. It felt okay.

'You've passed the stage, I'm sure,' she said, 'when you like fizzy fruit drinks. I suppose you'd like coffee.'

Looking at her again, I said I would.

The coffee was a long time coming and when it did, Mum was still holding my arm in that special way.

#1 Tote cart
$29.95   19½" H
         15" W   P
         12" L